BURIED ALIVE

Buried Series Book 1

VELLA DAY

Erotic Reads Publishing

ABOUT THE BOOK

Criminal Minds meets Bones
Four skeletons in a mass grave—who will be next?

Loner homicide detective, Hunter Markum, tries to remain detached when he sees the pile of bones, but something inside him snaps. His missing sister could be one of them. His only hope of learning their identities is to team up with Dr. Kerry Herlihy, a forensic anthropologist. As much as he works to keep his distance, something about her compassion strikes a chord with him.

As the attraction ignites between them, their quest to find the killer soon reveals the identities of the victims. But that puts Kerry right in the path of the killer. In a race against the clock, Hunter must apprehend the murderer if he hopes to save the woman he loves once she's BURIED ALIVE.

PROLOGUE

Tampa, Florida

Longingly, we bare our bones
To champions imbued with heart and mind
To track the killers who crushed
Our kin with pain and tears.
Beware cold danger
That masquerades among us
We beg you
Take away our fears.

-anon

PRESENT DAY

Ugly. Scarred. Abused.

Tameka Dorsey dragged her palms down her faded jeans to dry them, hoping the doctor couldn't smell her sweat as he unwrapped her facial bandages.

He'd promised she'd look normal again. Now, after three weeks of waiting, she'd finally see her new face. No man would hit her again just because she was what her first husband called *butt ugly*. Too bad she didn't have the courage to face the man who only married her to be his punching bag. She'd wanted to stand up to him. Wanted to show him she was a survivor and that he hadn't ruined her as he'd hoped.

"All finished." The doctor from the free clinic smiled down at her.

She shook her shoulders. "Can I see?"

"In a moment. I want to take a look first." He lifted the lid to the red biohazard pail and tossed the slightly stained gauze inside. He returned and touched her cheek. His jaw muscle twitched. "What's this?"

Oh, shit. His voice had dipped a few notches, just like her fiancé Jamal's had when he became angry.

"What's what?"

"You have a contusion, a bruise, the size of a quarter on your cheek."

"I, ah, fell."

"Jamal hit you again, didn't he?" A vein pulsed in his forehead.

She flinched. Tameka cast her eyes downward for a moment. "I'm fine. Really." She glanced up at him, hoping to see the tight lines around his mouth soften.

Wrong.

His eyes narrowed even more. "Didn't I tell you to leave that bastard?"

He leaned closer. So close in fact, his stale breath raked down her cheek and forced her to shrink back in the reclining chair.

Why was he yelling at her? Doctors weren't supposed to yell. "Yes, you did, but—"

"How many times have I told you men who abuse others are worthless pieces of shit?"

Spit flew into her face, but she didn't dare wipe it away without permission. Her first husband had taught her that lesson. "I'm sorry."

"Sorry isn't good enough."

"Wh-why do you care?"

"Because I can't stand to see a woman hurt." His clenched fists made it seem like *he* was trying not to hurt her.

Mama always encouraged her to tell the truth. "It was my fault." Fear sharpened every nerve. "Jamal didn't mean to hit me. He was real sorry when he learned he was going to be a daddy."

"You're pregnant?" His jaw tightened. "Are you sure? The blood tests didn't show anything. I wouldn't have operated if I'd known."

"I just found out."

The doctor stepped back. "Ta-me-ka."

What was his problem? "Jamal promised he wouldn't hit me again now that I'm carrying his baby."

"Men make a lot of promises they won't keep. Jamal will never stop abusing you."

She'd heard all this before from her well-meaning friends, but they didn't understand how much she loved him and how sorry he was he'd hurt her.

The doctor strode over to a wall cabinet and unlocked the door. His back was toward her and his shoulders were bunched.

Where the hell was the nurse who'd shown her into the room? And why had she left right as the doctor began to remove the bandages? Wasn't she supposed to stay?

The doctor spun back to her, took three steps, and stabbed her upper arm with a needle. The liquid burned as it raced through her veins. Then a numbing sensation slid down her spine, stealing her breath. "What was that?"

"It's a paralytic. Don't worry, it'll wear off in twenty minutes or so."

"Para-what-ic?"

"It means you won't be able to move for a while."

She choked. "Why?"

"I won't give Jamal another chance to ruin *my* masterpiece. And I won't let you bring a baby into this world just to have Jamal abuse the child too. You should have left that animal when I told you."

Without warning, her head lolled to the side. She tried to yell an obscenity, tried to tell him he wouldn't get away with this, but nothing moved—not her lips, not her tongue, not her vocal chords. She struggled to stand, but her legs had turned useless and her hands were like blocks of cement. Her heart beat so fast she feared it would explode.

"No one's going to hurt you ever again. Or your baby. Don't worry."

Don't worry? Was he fucking kidding?

Her brain fogged. *Move something.* Anything—a finger, her tongue, a toe. Nothing even twitched. *Focus.* Her throat turned dry.

He slid his hands under her legs and picked her up. The doctor then staggered toward the back door. What was he doing? She needed to stop him. Her eyes darted right, then left, hoping someone would see them as he slipped into the alley. Hadn't one of the nurses heard him yelling? Or was she too busy with other needy people from the clinic to bother checking in on them?

Cars filled half the lot. Surely, a patient would come out and see her. The clinic didn't close for another hour.

Tameka strained to hear voices coming her way—any voice—but silence surrounded her. *Someone save me!*

The doctor's knees buckled. She slipped out of his arms and crashed to the ground, landing on her back. Her head tipped to the left, and her cheek rested on the pebbled pavement. Tameka sensed nothing other than sheer panic splintering her mind into a million pieces.

A key clicked and the trunk creaked open. Her breathing took more effort. Air—she needed air. The liquid pooling in the back of her throat nearly drowned her. She couldn't swallow. Oh, God.

The soft tones of him punching numbers on a cell phone reverberated in her head, her ability to hear fading with each breath.

"I have another one."

She tried to concentrate on his words.

"Yes, same place," he said.

Feet first, the doctor dragged her to the back of a car, grunting like a boar in heat. After several attempts, he managed to lift her into the trunk. He slammed the lid and darkness enveloped her. *Please, please, don't let him do this.*

Tears leaked from her eyes as she tried to focus on her mom's smiling face—anything to keep her mind off the dank blackness of the dusty trunk and whatever horror awaited her. She wanted to blink away the tears, but her lids wouldn't move. Her chest felt as though she was pinned under a two-ton weight. She gasped.

Tameka needed to live. For her baby. For Mama, for Jamal.

Poor Mama. She'd have a heart attack when she learned her only child would never come home. And Jamal would go ballistic.

She concentrated on taking slow, even breaths, but all she could manage were small puffs. She choked on the gas fumes filling the trunk's sour air as she went in and out of consciousness.

Some time later, the car halted and the lid popped opened. A pink dusk had settled outside. How long had they been driving? The doctor ripped her from the trunk and half carried, half pulled her to an...ambulance? What was he doing? Taking her to a hospital? Was he trying to protect her from Jamal, after all? She thought he wanted to kill her. Her mind refused to work right.

Once the doctor placed her on the gurney, he shoved a horrible tube down her throat. She gagged. Couldn't breathe. Oh, God. She fought to move her arms to stop him, but nothing budged. The ambulance door closed, enclosing her in a cold cocoon. The engine started. Mercifully, air came down the tube and invaded her lungs.

Tameka lost track of time as she stared at the vehicle's ceiling, her thoughts racing to understand why she was here.

Then the ambulance jerked to a stop.

Now what? Was he really taking her to the emergency room, or had he kept her alive to abuse her? Would he beat her? Rape her? Would she feel anything before he killed her? Nothing made any sense.

Voices filtered in from outside before drifting away. When no one came to rescue her, an overwhelming depression crushed her.

A slow tingle pricked her hand, causing hope to surge. Concentrating, she moved her fingers. At least she thought something moved. Before she had enough time to test the rest of her body for movement, the back door whipped opened and a flashlight shone in her eyes, and blinded her.

"You want me to git her?" a stranger asked.

"Yes."

* * *

THRILL SHIMMERED in the doctor's voice. Bastard.

"The paralytic should have worn off by now. You can breathe on your own."

The doctor ripped out the tube, and Tameka sucked in a rasping breath. Her raw throat screamed as pulses of blood snaked up her body. She wanted to feel, wanted to move, wanted to escape.

"Here, let me help you out of those clothes. We don't need any evidence left behind," the stranger said.

He ripped out her earrings, tugged off her shoes, and stripped her bare. Tamika was helpless to stop him. He tossed the clothes into the back of the ambulance, and when he stepped back, the cool air rippled over her skin.

"Carry her up to the site." The doctor's voice dripped with anger.

Oh, please don't rape me.

She couldn't make out the face of the man who dragged her off the gurney, but he reeked of body odor and alcohol. He slung her over his shoulder and carried her up a long, dark path.

She couldn't lift her head to see where he was taking her, but the pounding of another set of footsteps told her the doctor was right behind.

When the man flung her off his shoulder, she waited for the pain to rip up her spine when she landed, but instead, soft wet dirt slapped her back and head. Air whooshed out of her lungs. Dirt walls rimmed her body.

A grave? Noooo. *Please, no.*

She sucked in wisps of air. Her heart pounded full blast.

Tameka squeezed her eyes shut a split second before a shovel of dirt landed on her face. A scream of terror bubbled in her throat as another heap of earth landed on her chest. Her right arm twitched, but not enough to stop the soil from raining down on her.

Bless me Father, for I have sinned. Oh, how I have sinned.

Tameka tried to curl into a fetal position, to hide, but her muscles wouldn't obey. Dirt splattered across her chest, but her numb mouth wouldn't move to tell him to stop. *Dear God, have mercy on me.*

A shadow blocked the last rays of dusk.

"At least your child will never feel the back of a hand or the sting of a whip. Look how pathetic you are. Bruises. After all my work, you made yourself ugly again."

He was wrong. She wasn't ugly anymore. He'd made her beautiful. Her unborn child was beautiful.

He tossed another heap of dirt over her body, over her face, and over her legs. "You should thank me for putting you out of your misery."

She couldn't move, couldn't breathe. Needed air. More air.

Oh, God, forgive me. I don't want to die.

CHAPTER ONE

T AMPA, *Florida*

Fifteen months later

"The guy from the Environmental Protection Agency nearly tripped over the damned thing," Homicide Detective Hunter Markum said as he slid from the sheriff's cruiser he'd parked under a clump of pine trees.

His partner, Phil Tedesco, huffed. "That would take anyone's breath away. Is he sure the head's human?"

"We're about to find out."

His body still thrummed from the jerky ride to this woodsy patch of land, his back jarring with every bump. Hunter shaded his eyes against the bright Florida sun, rolled down his sleeves and searched for the man who'd called in his gruesome discovery.

Phil pointed to a portly, older gentleman picking his way down the dirt road two hundred feet away. "That him?"

The old man waved. "Hey." A handkerchief over his mouth muffled his voice.

Hunter's stomach roiled, the same as it did every time he had to face the dead. After all these years, he should be immune, but he wasn't. "Must be." He took a deep breath. "Here goes."

As he and Phil strode toward the guy from the EPA, a white speed-boat zoomed down the murky Hillsborough River, playing hide and seek with the dense foliage. The whirring and whining of the engine grated on his taut nerves.

Hunter returned his gaze to the elderly gentleman, who stumbled a few steps before he caught his balance. "Whoa. Watch yourself," Hunter called out. Poor guy. Finding a skull out here would be enough to shake anyone up.

The moment the man reached them, he flashed an official-looking badge with shaky fingers. "Bill. Bill Ebsary."

Hunter introduced himself and his partner. "Are you up to showing us what you found?"

"Sure." Ebsary nodded. "I've been studying the land for over thirty years, and this is a first for coming across a body. Gave me the creeps."

"I hear ya," Hunter said. "Bill, you didn't touch anything, did you?"

"Just brushed away the leaves, that's all. Once I realized what I was looking at, I backed off and called you guys."

Hunter glanced at the cloudless sky, thanking the gods for small favors. He waved a hand for Mr. Ebsary to lead the way. "What were you doing here anyway?"

The drug deal Hunter had investigated on this land last year filtered through his mind—along with the three dead teenage girls who'd died from overdosing.

"My job. The Altwood Company purchased this property a few weeks back. They plan to build a business complex here, but we have to make sure the land doesn't need any more clean-up before we issue a permit."

"And is it? Clean, that is?"

"Yes, sir. I was ready to sign off on this parcel and go home to grab a cold beer when I noticed this odd looking rock. Right over there." He pointed to a nearby scrubby patch of weeds. "Let me show you." He continued through the underbrush to the area.

A palmetto's saber-sharp tip pricked Hunter's arm and penetrated his long sleeves. Blood pooled up through his blue shirt. Damn.

"What led you over here?" Hunter said, pushing ahead.

Phil cursed as he tripped on a long brambly vine.

"The holes caught my eye," Mr. Ebsary said. "After I moved the leaves, I had a near heart attack."

Hunter knelt, careful not to touch anything as he studied the empty sockets of a human skull gaping back at him. His gut soured as he stared at the remains of what once was a living, breathing, human being. *Who are you?* Someone's sister? Mom? Dad? A child's parent? Someone's spouse?

Don't do this to yourself, Hunter. Stay detached, stay focused. These aren't Denise's bones.

Hunter took a deep breath but couldn't smell a damn thing other than the damp soil and the scent of mild algae bloom coming off the river. He prayed he wasn't growing desensitized to the smell of death after ten years on the force, but then again the body was skeletonized.

Hunter was almost positive the skull was human, but he still needed confirmation. Department rules.

Hunter studied Bill Ebsary. Poor guy looked pretty green around the gills. "Hey, Mr. Ebsary. Mind stepping back a bit?"

Hunter didn't need him puking on the grave. Not a chance in hell the investigative gurus would find much evidence after all this time, but he owed it to this person to be thorough. Someone had to look out for the dead.

When Hunter stood, prickly plants stuck to his pants legs, but there was no use pulling them off. They were everywhere.

A rustling in the brushes caught his attention. He whipped around and reached for his gun, but he didn't draw. A second later, a squirrel dashed through the leaves and stilled, no doubt as jittery as he was. Christ. He'd thought the sound might have come from another drug dealer. *Get a grip.*

Hunter stood. "We'll need to call in our crime scene unit."

Ebsary nodded.

Once they arrived, Hunter and Phil worked with the CSU for a good two hours doing a complete grid search of the area. The prickly vines tore holes in five pairs of his gloves, and the knees of his jeans were stained brownish red from the clay soil. They'd found nothing except beer bottles, cigarette butts, a couple of needles, condoms, and

Styrofoam cups. Good thing someone bought this parcel. It might cut down on future crime.

His cell rang. It was John Ahern, the deputy Medical Examiner. Hunter spoke to him for a moment, and then disconnected before finding Phil. "M.E.'s finally on his way."

"Better late than never."

Hunter clasped Phil on the shoulder. "Make sure the CSU team doesn't muck anything up. I'm going to meet the M.E. by the cruiser."

"You got it."

Ten minutes later, Hunter pushed off from the hot hood of his Ford Taurus. A white van bumped down the winding, pot-holed dirt road. He'd worked with Dr. John Ahern many times before. He was a good man and an even better forensic pathologist. Too bad promptness wasn't on his list of credentials.

John pulled to a stop behind Hunter's car, his tires kicking up enough dust to nearly choke him. The deputy M.E. stepped out.

"Hey, John." Hunter extended his hand.

John winced and straightened slowly. "Hunter. Sorry for the delay. It's been a long day. I was tied up handling a real stickler of a case."

"Figured."

"Heard you got something interesting out here."

"You could say that."

The passenger side door opened and a tall, long-legged brunette eased out, and Hunter couldn't help but stare at the enticing vision in chocolate brown.

"I thought you always worked alone."

The pathologist chuckled. "Dr. Herlihy's a forensic anthropologist who'll be teaching at Brahman University in the fall, but she'll be working with me this summer on a case-by-case basis." He wagged his index finger. "Now before you start griping about how I get help when the sheriff's department is on a hiring freeze, I say you talk to the mayor, not me."

"Got it." Wasn't Ahern's fault he was lucky.

"Kerry Herlihy." She extended her hand.

The doctor had a strong, firm grasp, and her hands were cool to the touch. No surprise. The M.E. always set the van's air conditioner high enough to keep a body chilled.

Dr. Herlihy looked him straight in the eye. He liked that in a person, not to mention she had to be close to six feet, a few inches shorter than him.

Hunter slid a look to her left ring finger. Bare. Then again, who would wear a diamond ring to a crime scene?

He cleared his throat. "Hunter. Hunter Markum." He inclined his head in the direction of the dirt road. "The body's this way—or rather the head. The CSU team arrived a couple of hours ago."

As both doctors spun in the direction of the scene, Dr. Herlihy's eyes widened.

"Don't worry, they know not to touch anything without your permission," Hunter said.

Her shoulders relaxed. "Thank you." Dr. Herlihy turned to John. "I need my bag from the back."

Ahern clicked a button on his remote and the back door popped open. She grabbed a brown leather carryall with a hand shovel and a red-handled brush poking out of the top. She nodded and stepped back onto the path.

"Here, let me carry that for you," Hunter offered.

"Sorry, no. I never let anyone else handle my tools."

Hunter held up his hands. "Suit yourself."

Ahern's temporary hire kept her gaze straight ahead as they walked the five hundred feet to the crime scene, her attention riveted on the path. Twigs cracked under their feet and birds warbled out their mating calls. Given Dr. Herlihy didn't ask a single question on the way, he guessed she didn't want any information to prejudice her investigation.

Once the three of them reached the site, Hunter hung back and watched the experts at work. A young, female CSU, with a camera dangling around her neck, spoke to the crime scene lead, while a middle-aged man he'd just met today, mapped the area and triangulated the region to the crossroads. Two others, identical twins, Maggie and Molly something, joined the medical examiner's team.

The forensic anthropologist knelt and pulled an everyday garden shovel from her bag. Her clean, unpainted nails were clipped short. She seemed to be a practical woman. Nice.

The good doctor tapped the ground with the bottom of the trowel, stabbed the earth with an orange flag and tapped again. Every so often, she'd plant another flag.

Hunter was fascinated. "What are you doing?"

She looked up and blinked. "I'm outlining the gravesite."

Okay. "Unless you have X-ray vision, how do you know exactly where the body is?" Especially since no bones were showing, other than the skull.

Her face lit up as she smiled. "I listen and feel. Once someone disturbs the ground, it remains soft for years. I tap the ground until I reach an area that's hard-packed. I then know the body is inside that perimeter."

She was good.

Kerry Herlihy moved around the perimeter of the site with the grace of a dancer. Her long brown, curly hair was tied back in a neat braid, a few loose strands lifting in the slight breeze. She pushed the wisps behind her ear with her left hand as she brushed away the dirt from around the body with her right.

After the technicians helped clear away some of the soil, she crooked a finger in a come here motion to the photographer. "Could you take a shot of this shovel mark?" She pointed to some striations about a foot deep along the inside of the grave.

Hunter stepped forward. "Hard to believe a shovel mark would be present after all this time."

"I worked a case in which the police were able to find the exact shovel used to dig the grave by markings such as these."

"Interesting."

"Grave's too shallow for this to be premeditated," Phil said.

Hunter looked over his shoulder. "Don't sneak up behind me like that."

"Since when did you become Mr. Jumpy? You always had nerves of steel."

He shouldn't have snapped at Phil, but he was enjoying his conversation with the new doc. "Maybe the guy didn't read the *How to Bury a Victim* manual."

Phil laughed.

Kerry Herlihy looked up, her lips nearly lifting in a smile.

Phil planted his hands on his hips and looked around. "I'm going to recheck the area to see if we missed anything."

"I can't imagine we missed much, but go for it," Hunter said. "Too bad there aren't any neighbors to interview. Standing around is not my thing either."

"Don't I know it."

Dr. Herlihy hadn't unearthed enough of the body to give Hunter any details of the victim, so he did what he dreaded most—continued to fill out the report. Hunter reread Bill's statement. He checked his watch and scribbled the departure time of the informant.

Half-hour later, Phil returned. He wiped his brow and peered down at the gravesite. Kerry Herlihy had exposed about half of a human body.

"Looks like whoever buried this person took his clothes."

"Yeah, naked of everything, including jewelry." Sweat trickled down Hunter's back, and he fanned himself with his notebook.

Dr. Herlihy had a healthy pink glow. No clinging fabric on the curve of her slim back.

Phil nodded toward Kerry, breaking Hunter's attention. "She figure anything out yet?"

"Just that we have a dead person."

Phil laughed.

"Wasn't meant to be funny," Hunter said, and Phil sobered.

Hunter crouched across from her and pointed to the skull. "I see the skeleton has a piece of metal in the cheek. I read in a journal it's possible to get an ID from it."

His stomach churned. His older sister's pretty face flashed before him, not the cracked bones of her skeleton, causing Hunter to suck in a long breath. If his sister had survived her mugging and possible rape, she might have had a plate in her face too.

Kerry tapped the metal with the handle of a brush. "The titanium in the cheek is a result of a bad break. We can get the serial number off the moldable plate and run it, but don't get your hopes up. That will only tell us where the plate was manufactured, not who received it or implanted the device."

"Damn. I was hoping it would tell us which doctor performed the surgery."

"Sorry. I know everyone believes that." Kerry lifted a spongy looking piece of transparent rubber and twisted it around in her fingers. "This is a PTFE implant used to augment the contour of the chin. We might get lucky with this." Her brows raised, and her pretty eyes sparkled.

"I hope you're right."

Twenty minutes later, she sat back and swiped her sleeve across her face, leaving a reddish brown path across her cheek. She leaned over again and brushed the dirt from the skull. Her tender administrations reminded him of a mother caring for a young child.

As Kerry continued to expose more bone, Hunter drummed his gnawed yellow pencil on the pad. After another few minutes, she exposed the victim's hips. He studied the structure. This body's hips had a wide pelvic inlet. "Looks female."

She glanced up, her brows raised. "You're right."

Guess she didn't expect him to be able to differentiate between sexes. She probably figured he was just another dumb cop. It was a good thing one of his forensic classes included remains identification.

When she ran a hand gently down the woman's hips, something unfamiliar tackled his gut, but the sensation disappeared the moment she looked away.

Hunter wrote *female* on his report, and then peered down at the doctor again. "What about her age?" He dragged a handkerchief across his brow to mop up the sweat.

"I'd say she was in her late twenties, early thirties. Look here." She pointed to where a shoulder should be. "The growth plate is located at the end of this bone." She tapped one of the knobby ends. "This is called the epiphysis, which fuses around the age of thirty. This female's is almost completely fused. That, and the pitting on her ribs, tells me my guess about her age is close."

Hunter stood to stretch his legs. She looked up at him as though she were seeing him for the first time and held his gaze. Her eyes were a soft, leafy green.

"Thanks, that helps."

She nodded, blinked, and dropped her gaze.

He ran the Missing Persons cases through his head for a young female who'd been missing for some time but came up empty. "Can you take a shot at her race?" Could Kerry Herlihy make it three for three?

She glanced at her temporary boss. "With so much racial mixing these days, race is a lot more complicated to figure out."

"If I may," Ahern said, pointing to the skull's cheekbones. "The square eye orbits would indicate Negroid, but the fact she has a narrow interorbital breadth might imply classic white European. But then again, her nasal width and prognathic alveolar region push me more toward Negroid and—"

She lightly touched her boss's arm. "So, what he's trying to say, Detective, is we don't know."

"I see."

"When I get her back to the lab, I'll do a bone density scan on her. Those numbers should give me a clearer indication of race."

"I'll also need to know her height once you dig out the rest of her body."

"I'll have to measure the femur, along with a few other bones, to determine that."

She knew her stuff all right. "That's pretty impressive."

"Thanks."

Hunter was finished with the crime scene. He planned to run the numbers through Missing Persons when he returned to the station. If luck was on his side, he'd find a match.

"Any idea how long she's been here?"

A frown creased her brow. "Not without more—"

"Tests?"

A small chuckle escaped. "Yes."

He nodded to the CSU team leader. "If you guys don't need me anymore, I'm going to head back to the station and get to work."

"No problem. I think we have everything covered."

"Call me if you unearth any personal effects," Hunter said.

"You can count on it."

A slight breeze provided temporary relief as he jogged down the uneven path to the cruiser. Phil sat perched on the cruiser's hood filling out his report.

"Let's get out of here." Hunter placed his hand on the door handle.

"Hey, Hunter," the CSU team leader called. "Hold up a sec." The man waved him back.

What the hell? How could they have found something in a minute flat?

"Be back in a sec," Hunter said.

He hurried up the path, his shirt so wet with sweat, the cotton stuck to his back. "What do you have?"

"She found another bone. And not one that belongs to the first skeleton."

CHAPTER TWO

MUSCLES KNOTTING HIS THIGHS, Hunter squatted opposite Dr. Herlihy, anxious to view her discovery. "Tell me."

Back rounded, she ran a hand over a large bone. Some of those green sand spurs that had previously attacked him had found their way into the doc's curly hair.

She dusted the remaining dirt from the bone's surface. Once she'd freed the object, she held up what looked like a femur. Angling the bone so that a shaft of sunlight speared her find, she rolled the bone between her fingers. The expression on her face transformed from one of intrigue to acceptance. He said nothing, taking in her intense expression.

She finally placed the bone on a brown paper bag beside her, and then locked her gaze with his. Her green eyes appeared saddened by her find.

"It's a third femur."

His gut clenched. Shit. "Female? Or male?" He grabbed a handful of dirt, squeezed the daylight out of it and tossed the sandy heap back on the ground.

"I can't tell yet."

The desperation in her voice tore at his protective instincts. The discovery seemed to sicken her as much as it did him. Had the anthropologist who'd found his sister's body died a little too that day?

Shrouded in hushed silence, she went back to work uncovering more bones. The CSU team, who had crowded around to watch the new find, wordlessly scattered to continue documenting the evidence.

Mud streaked his pants where he'd wiped his hands, and for once, he didn't care.

Fifteen minutes later, she unearthed a second pelvis and stopped brushing. "It's a female." She drew in a long breath, closed her eyes for a moment, and exhaled slowly.

"So we're looking at two bodies," he mumbled to himself. Christ. A sharp jab raced up his spine at the thought.

"Yes and we're not finished digging either."

An ugly, sludgy sensation grabbed his insides and yanked hard. *More digging.* Two horrible words he'd heard many times. "We could be looking at a mass grave then."

Dear Lord. His ribs tightened around his lungs, squeezing the air from them. His chest hurt as he recalled another tragedy.

She lowered her head. "It's possible."

Hunter stood and moved away from the mound of pine needle laden dirt and away from the bone doctor, not wanting to take his frustration out on her or any of the other workers. He wanted to strangle the jerk who'd dumped the bodies. Wanted to lock the killer up and make the bastard spend the rest of his goddamn pathetic life digging graves or making coffins to honor the dead. And he really wanted to find the man who'd killed his sister—but that would never happen.

Christ. Right now, he'd be content pummeling anything into a million pieces. He picked up a rock and chucked it a couple hundred feet away from the river. It smashed against a tree and thudded to the ground. Squirrels scurried away.

Phil was already making his way up the path.

"What's wrong?"

Hunter told him about the second body. "We need cadaver dogs."

"Good idea. Otherwise, we could be here for days."

Hunter scanned the large wooded area. Had to be a good thirty acres, but only about four or five of them were free enough of large trees and scrub for someone to bury a body. "Too bad there's no way to tell if the psycho spread the bodies out or piled more victims on top of each other. Call the captain and see if he can send over a team. Ask him to find Jimmy what's-his-name." Hunter snapped his fingers. "The captain will know him. He's the best technician for leveling the ground."

"I'm on it like maggots on shit." Ah, a new and better twist to Phil's usual spiel.

Once Phil walked away to make his call, Hunter stepped back to the gravesite. Dr. Herlihy carefully removed the bones of the other skeleton and set them aside.

He glanced at his watch. Oh, crap. He'd promised to take his daughter to Burger King, and it was already past five. He'd never make it in time.

Poor kid. He'd told Melissa he'd take her to Busch Gardens last weekend and then had to cancel when another case came up.

Hunter turned his back to the burial pit and dug out his phone to call his sister. A pack of love bugs flew in his face, and he swatted them away. He punched in the memorized number.

"Hi, Hunter." Gotta love caller I.D.

"Jen, I wondered if—"

"Let me guess. You want me to keep Melissa for dinner. You got tied up."

Even to him, his refrain was becoming tiresome. "Yeah. Something like that. You know I hate to trouble you—"

"Hunter. Don't worry about it. You know I love having Melissa around, and so do Emily and Jake. She's like a younger sister to them."

Melissa had probably spent more time with her cousins than she had at home. "Make me feel guiltier." He kicked a stick and watched it skitter along the ground.

Jen didn't answer for a second. "I'm sorry. I know you can't help it. It's your job to catch the bad guys and make us feel safe."

"Thanks for trying to boost my spirits." Hunter wasn't used to spewing sentimental stuff. He cleared his throat. "Tell Melissa I'll be by after I finish here. Okay?"

"Sure. I love you."

"Love you too," he mumbled, forcing the emotion from his voice. The sheriff's department had dubbed him Mr. Spock because of his inability to express his softer side. They'd mock him for sure if they'd heard him say those three little words.

He stashed his phone. He didn't deserve such a wonderful sister. Without Jen, he never would have survived his wife's death. It was his Melissa who had been his inspiration to keep going when he'd had serious thoughts about eating his gun.

Hunter turned back to the gravesite and caught Kerry looking at him with an odd expression. Before he could react, she looked away.

He rolled up his sleeves. Sunburn be damned.

***

KERRY PLACED a femur on the cold, stainless steel lab table, and smothered a yawn. She took another gulp of her coffee, hoping the drink would give her a jolt of energy.

It had taken all day to separate Jane Doe #1 bones from those of #3's. The other two bodies, found closer to the river, still had some soft tissue on them, and John Ahern was attempting to autopsy them in the hope of determining their cause of death.

All through the night and into the early morning hours, Kerry couldn't rid her mind from the four bodies they'd found in the field. Four women. Four lost souls. Each discovery had taken another small piece from her heart.

She wasn't the only one affected. Kerry was sure the pinched lines around Detective Markum's handsome mouth during the exhaustive search had mirrored her own.

When she'd drifted off to sleep last night, all she could see were the cadaver dogs sniffing the ground, finding the bodies. Kerry had worked with them before on other cases, but she'd never seen them race about so frenetically. She'd spent all night fighting the disturbing images that invaded her imagination, and now she was paying for it.

One of the detectives had found a belt loop several feet from the first gravesite. Even if the loop belonged to the killer, she doubted the police could trace such a small piece of evidence to anyone, especially months after the deaths.

She shook her head to clear her vision and a sharp, stabbing pain crossed her forehead, but she refused to allow a migraine to delay her. Grabbing her purse from across the room, she located her much-needed prescription bottle and swallowed two without water. Yuk.

Ignoring the rush of goose bumps that rippled up her arm from the air conditioner's cold blast, Kerry returned to the table and studied #3's skull. Her heart tore. She ran her hand tenderly over the dry, bony surface. "I hope you didn't suffer."

Squeezing her eyes shut, she tried to imagine the dead woman. She must have had a family who loved her. Had anyone reported her missing? Had some special man loved her? Was he grieving her loss? Or had he been the one who'd killed her?

Kerry opened her eyes and fought to push away her tangled emotions. Science would solve this crime, not her heart.

Her fingers touched the rather apparent sutures in the skull. What a shame. The woman was probably about thirty, not much younger than Kerry. She swallowed the biting ache that always came when she handled a victim's remains.

The only good news was all four females had intact dental work. Maybe when Detective Markum provided a list of possible victims, she might find a match.

A knock sounded on the lab door, and John Ahern sauntered in with a frown. "You okay? You've been closeted in here all day."

A large African American, John had kind eyes and a wide, gentle mouth.

"I'm fine. I've had a lot to keep me busy." Her smile faltered as fingers of fatigue crawled up her spine.

"I hear you."

"Don't tell me you're done with your autopsies already?" Kerry wanted to get her hands on the other skeletons, needing to find a connection that would provide names to the victims, and provide their families with closure.

"Hardly. I'm taking a break between autopsying Jane Doe #2 and

#4. It's slow going." He pointed to the display of bones on the table. "So what've you found?"

"The jaw on Jane Doe #3 had been broken at one time. From the size of the fissure, I'm speculating she'd been beaten about a year or so prior to her death."

"Anything else?"

"The back of the woman's cranium showed blunt force trauma strong enough to break her skull."

"Good."

"And #1?"

"Not much. I catalogued and photographed each bone and took dental molds of my two bodies, but I won't know much more until after X-raying them."

"Were you able to get any DNA?"

"I have a small sample from an extracted tooth from #1 and a little more from her femur. I asked Darla to take the DNA to the FDLE lab for analysis."

"Good."

A squeaky gurney rolled down the hallway, past her door. Another death. Kerry blew out a breath.

"Did that detective call with any names of missing persons?" she asked.

She crossed her fingers on both hands, hoping for the best. Stupid superstition, but her mom had been afraid of black cats, cracks in the sidewalk, and full moons, and had passed on that superstition.

If Hunter had a possible name for any of the victims, he might also find a photo of the victim. Then, she could superimpose the photograph over the skull's X-ray to see if the two matched.

"Not yet."

Too bad. It was agonizing to have a loved one missing and never know what happened to them—like her brother. Long ago she lost hope of ever finding him, and a band constricted around her heart. *Don't go down that dark tunnel again or this time I might not emerge.*

Pushing back her nightmare, Kerry took a long sip of her now cooled coffee and stared at the next set of bones.

John picked up a femur from #3's body, twirled it around in his fingers, and nodded to #1. "Looks like the time of death is roughly the same for these two. You agree?"

She retrieved the femur John was manhandling and replaced it on the stainless tabletop with care. "I need to do a few more tests, but from my preliminary observation, I believe they died within a few months of each other."

"When I complete work on my two victims, I'll send the results over," John said. "Hopefully, I can figure out their cause of death."

Kerry ran a hand along the smooth cold metal. "I did notice one thing. Jane Doe #1's facial bones had only begun to heal from reconstructive surgery. Could her cause of death be an infection resulting from that operation?"

His brows rose. "If so, why not bury her in a coffin?"

"Good point. I'm so frustrated, I'm not thinking straight. I guess I'm desperate for some clues."

Dr. Ahern chuckled softly and shook his head. "Not all deaths we investigate are the result of foul play."

"They are when all four bodies are near each other in shallow graves."

"True." He tapped the end of the table with his finger. "I won't keep you any longer." He'd walked halfway to the door before he spun around. "Good job at the site yesterday. You handled yourself very professionally."

He left before she could even say thank you, or before she could ask why he sounded so surprised. The depressing sadness of her find blocked out the expected rush of pride from his compliment.

By five, she couldn't concentrate anymore. It was time to head home. She cleaned up, tossed her paper gown in the disposal unit, and headed out the front door. Pedestrians scurried down the street as cars whipped by in front of the building.

Gas fumes mixed with the sweltering heat sucked her breath away. Maybe taking a job in Florida in the summer wasn't such a good idea after all.

Just as she crossed the street to the parking lot, her cell rang. It must be Grandpa wondering why his dinner wasn't on the table yet.

Her gaze shot to the phone display. It wasn't her grandfather, nor did she recognize the number. Her thumb hovered over the button to turn off the ringer, certain it had to be a wrong number since she hadn't been in town long enough to know anyone.

Oh, what the hell. "Hello?"

"Dr. Herlihy?"

The voice on the phone sounded familiar. "Yes?" Kerry tried to put a name to the deep, rich tone.

"This is Detective Markum. Do you have a moment?"

She was surprised she hadn't recognized his smooth timbre. "Sure."

"I know it's the end of the day, but is it possible for you to stop by the station? I have a theory I want to pass by you.

CHAPTER THREE

As Kerry entered the sheriff's station, a somber young man sitting behind a worn desk glanced up. "May I help you?"

"I'm here to see Detective Markum."

As the officer typed something into his computer, Kerry studied the place. Officers sat at desks, phones pressed against their head while computers clicked away. Busy place, even at six p.m. The office didn't look anything like the snazzy FBI offices on television. Those were classy. This place needed a coat of new paint and some air freshener. The old building had some serious mold issues.

"Dr. Herlihy."

Kerry spun around. Red veins were visible in Markum's intense blue eyes, but an inner strength radiated around him. "Hello."

Her pulse sped up. *Don't do this. No doubt he's married.* Her gaze shot to his ring finger. While it was bare, she detected a faint line where a ring had been. Was he divorced, or had he forgotten to slip the band on today. It made no sense to wear it to a crime scene. "Thank you for coming."

He came across as proper and professional. Good. If he'd flirted, she wouldn't have known how to respond.

Fortunately, she didn't have to worry about that since his gaze didn't even linger. He turned and strode down the hallway.

Was she just supposed to follow like a puppy? His footsteps echoed further down the hall. Guess so. Even at five foot eleven, she had to take long strides to keep up with him. He stopped in front of a door, held it open, and swept an arm for her to go in. At least he had manners.

The stark white room smelled of fresh paint. Hmm. It contained a rectangular table covered in a brown laminate, four straight back chairs, a television with a VCR, and a much-used dry erase board. On the table were photos of the human skeletons she'd helped unearth.

"Please have a seat."

As Kerry sat, she couldn't take her eyes off the pictures lined up in a neat row on the table. While she'd dug up the women, she'd been on automatic pilot and hadn't considered the rather obvious pattern.

She waited for him to say something. When he pressed his lips together, she shifted her focus to the photos and studied them. "I can't believe I didn't notice how spread apart their legs were."

"I didn't either until I viewed them side by side." Pain rippled through his voice. "Is there any way, forensically, you can tell if these woman were raped?"

Raped?

Dear God. What had these women endured before their deaths? No one deserved to die this way.

"Not for the first two women. Hipbones won't show signs of sexual trauma and the semen would be long gone. While #2 had some soft tissue on the lower part of her body, there wasn't enough to determine any molestation. Our only hope is this one." She pointed to the last body found. "I'll pass your concern to Dr. Ahern. Perhaps the autopsy will reveal something."

Detective Markum nodded, and then opened another folder containing snapshots of women alive at the time. "I pulled all of the Missing Person's files from the last eighteen months that meet the description of the victims. Didn't you say you could superimpose an X-ray of the skull on top of the photo to see if there's a match?"

"Yes, but this assumes the angle of the two faces is the same. I can scan the photo and resize it to match the X-ray, but if the head is angled differently, the comparison will be difficult. I should be able to tell you which of the women *couldn't* be one of our victims."

He dragged a hand down over his jaw. "Where does that leave us?"

"With not much. I can do a dental comparison if you can obtain dental records, but that assumes you know their identity. If they do match, and you want absolute proof, then perhaps a relative has an old hairbrush belonging to the victim we can match against the person's DNA."

He drummed his fingers on the table. His gaze shot down to the left, as if he were planning his next move. "What about the metal plates you found in the bodies?" He flipped open his notebook.

She couldn't recall what she'd told him. "I thought I mentioned they can't be traced to a specific person?"

"Then they're no help at all."

"That's not entirely true." She leaned forward, happy to be discussing academics, rather than the women themselves. "Suppose we believe the body is say, a Linda Richards, from Newport, Florida. We find proof she underwent facial surgery in Newport Hospital. If that hospital never bought any plates from our distributor, we'd know we have the wrong woman."

He leaned back in his chair. Deep lines etched his forehead. "Then we need to find the right woman."

"Eventually we will."

He huffed. "How can you be so sure? We have almost nothing to go on but a bunch of old bones."

"Hey. Those *old bones* can tell a powerful story."

He held her gaze, studying her. "Tell me, how did you ended up in this line of business?"

His change of subject took her by surprise, but he truly sounded interested in the answer. "It's not a business to me. I want to help people, help the families who lost someone they loved."

He waved a hand. "Bad word choice. Why forensic anthropology?" The detective leaned forward, his eyes wide.

His attention made her uncomfortable, but if they were to work together, she wanted him to understand how much her job meant to her.

"I had an older brother who ran with the wrong crowd. He did drugs, gambled, raced fast cars, you name it, he did it. When he was twenty-three, he disappeared."

Hunter Markum's brow furrowed. "He never surfaced?" His eyes turned a darker blue, as if he'd lost someone he loved.

"No."

"I'm sorry. How old were you when he disappeared?"

Normally, personal questions unnerved her, but his question didn't seem invasive. "Eight."

"That must have been tough. Did the police have any leads?"

"No. Nothing."

His jaw clenched. "How did your parents take his disappearance?"

Kerry looked deep into his eyes. Many men had asked her questions but only as a vehicle for her to accept an invitation for a date. Hunter could be like the others, but her intuition told her otherwise.

She hesitated. Kerry had never spoken about Keith to anyone outside the family.

"Mom never accepted Keith's death. Every holiday, she keeps a place at the table for him in the hopes he'll return. She blamed Keith's bad behavior on my father's divorcing her two years earlier."

"How did your dad handle Keith's disappearance?"

"We never discussed it. To this day, my sister and I haven't talked about what might have happened. It's as if Keith never existed."

"That's a shame. One should never forget a family member." He swallowed hard.

Before she had a chance to question him back, Hunter pulled the photos of the woman toward him and placed them in a folder. "Did you decide to help other victims locate their relatives so they wouldn't have to suffer like you did?"

Kerry nearly lost her breath as her stomach did a little somersault. "Yes."

Hunter reached out and squeezed her hand. Even though heat rushed up her arm, she shuttered her emotions. "Then we will find out the names of these women. You have my word."

* * *

ANSWER THE DAMN PHONE. He paced outside Kerry's lab, debating if he should do something with the bones—like steal them.

"Yeah?" Loud mall-like voices sounded in the background.

Leaning against the cold, cement wall, he checked to make sure no one was within close range. "They found the bodies," he whispered.

"What bodies?"

"What do you mean what bodies?" With Kerry gone for the day, he punched in the code to enter.

"Tell me exactly what happened." A young child screamed in the background.

"Apparently, the dirt washed away one of the bodies and the cops got wind of it. Our office was called in, along with some new forensic anthropologist who unearthed all four bodies."

"Shit. Did he learn anything?"

"It's a she. After seven months I'm not sure what she'll find. Two of the women are in autopsy. Kerry, the anthropologist, sent DNA from one of the women to FDLE today. It's only a matter of time before they come up with something." His grip tightened on the phone. "You said you were careful."

"I can assure you I didn't leave any evidence if that's what you're implying."

He strode around the lab and checked the two bodies Kerry had stored in the cooler. Would the bones talk to her? "What do you want me to do?"

"Watch the anthropologist. If she gets too close, kill her."

CHAPTER FOUR

KERRY KNEADED her lower back after she eased out of her car. She stood on the street, hands on her hips and studied the three extra cars blocking her grandfather's driveway.

Duh. How could she have forgotten? Thursday night was poker night. Oh, joy. That meant she wouldn't get any more sleep tonight than she had last week. Grandpa's old cop friends didn't know when to stop.

She searched through the hidden treasures in her purse until she located her house key. If she entered through the back door, she might be able to sneak in unnoticed. That wasn't very nice of her, but she wasn't in the mood to socialize with Grandpa's friends after trying to piece together the bones of dead females all day. Tonight's newscast had reported the discovery of the bodies, but thankfully, the details had been sparse. If these nosy men learned what she'd been working on, they'd ask a gazillion questions, conveniently forgetting an ongoing investigation meant her lips needed to remain sealed.

She rotated the kinks out of her aching shoulders before heading around back. The sweet smell of night blooming jasmine rode on the humid air. After all the formaldehyde and dead flesh she'd sniffed, it was good to realize she could smell something this aromatic.

She prayed John could come up with a clue to help identify the four women lying on the morgue tables. If the stars lined up, Detective Markum would have a list of missing people for her by tomorrow and someone would have closure.

Kerry peeked though the kitchen window. No Grandpa. Good. She slipped inside. As she pulled the door closed, the dog's nails scratched against the wood floor. He was coming her way. Crap. Buster barked.

"Shh." As if telling her grandfather's Jack Russell Terrier to keep quiet would do any good. Buster was a born yapper. Kerry dropped to her haunches and scratched the rambunctious dog behind his ears, and he quieted. "That's a good boy." She could only hope her grandfather had been so engrossed in his card game he hadn't heard the frenetic alert.

"Hi, Kerry," her grandfather said.

Guess not.

"Hi, Grandpa." She stood and the stiffness in her back warned her she needed to find a Pilates studio soon. Nothing better than strong abs to help a weak back.

"You're late. I was worried about you."

"You of all people should understand how hard it is to work on a case and keep regular hours."

God only knows he'd put Nana through intense misery every time he didn't show up for dinner on time. It was no wonder she died of a heart condition. Nana had made her promise not to marry a cop, unless she wanted to be a young widow. Life was tough enough, she preached, without the agony of wondering when she'd hear the bad news her husband was dead.

"I do, I do." Grandpa stepped back and ran his gaze up and down the length of her. "You don't look so good," he said before sniffing the air in exaggeration. "You don't smell so good either. Tough day at the lab?"

"I'm fine, Grandpa."

He snapped his fingers. "I almost forgot. Your sister called for you tonight." Grandpa averted eye contact. "Twice."

The muscles in her neck locked. "What did she want?"

"You know what. You can't avoid Susan forever, you know."

Wanna bet?

* * *

HUNTER GRIMACED as the new intern, Gina Andries, joined him and Phil at the conference table. Too bad her uncle, aka, Hunter's boss, hadn't briefed her on the dress code. The woman looked like she was interviewing for Vice rather than Homicide.

Her straight black leather skirt came to mid thigh, and her too tight top showed more skin than was good for her in an office made up of eighty-five percent men. Fortunately, she had the body to carry off the sexy, slutty look. Her straightened black hair and large hoop earnings reminded him of Lara Croft on a mission to meet, or maybe kill, a man. On the upside, Hunter welcomed more African American women to the force.

At least Kerry Herlihy had dressed appropriately at the crime scene. Now there was a class act.

Out of the corner of his eye, Hunter watched his partner's jaw slacken and his eyes widen at Gina's slim body. Christ, Phil didn't need to lose focus this early in the case. Hunter could only hope his partner wasn't thinking of doing something stupid, like getting involved with the boss's niece.

She leaned over the table and stuck out her hand. "My bad. Where are my manners? I'm Gina Andries, Jack Andries' niece. But I'm sure you already know that."

Hunter and Phil exchanged greetings with her. Yes, they knew. Her uncle had given them a rundown. Gina was a big health nut, a stickler for details and hard headed.

They'd also been given strict orders to make sure Gina understand how tough it was to be a cop. Their mission? Convince her to return to teaching high school history. In Jack Andries' opinion, his brother's little girl didn't have what it took to be a cop.

Jack went so far as to suggest one way to dissuade her was to make her understand how rough things could get—with one caveat. She was only allowed to go on ride alongs where she couldn't be hurt.

As if he and Phil could control every situation. Thugs pulled guns on them all the time. If nothing bad happened, how would that dissuade her from joining the force?

God this was a bad idea. If something went wrong and Gina got injured, or God forbid killed, the legal ramifications boggled Hunter's mind. Hunter had failed to convince his boss this whole interning stuff was not only *not* department sanctioned, but it was way too dangerous. Too bad Jack wouldn't budge. He wanted to teach her a lesson, and that was all there was to it.

Gina leaned forward. "I want to thank both of you for helping me get my start in the department."

The woman had no idea how much help she'd get—only it wouldn't be in the direction she'd planned.

What he wanted to know was what the hell had Phil and he done to deserve this babysitting job? She might be enrolled at Hillsborough Community College and had taken some classes in law enforcement, but she was still a civilian; and civilians shouldn't investigate homicides. But an order was an order.

Gina had a file folder, a pad, a pencil and a bottle of Evian water. Hunter appreciated her enthusiasm, but he'd bet his finest bottle of scotch she'd be guzzling coffee before she left her six-week internship. To top it off, her health food regime would be kissed goodbye, and that alone might make her quit.

Phil stuffed a gooey, chocolate donut in his mouth and pointed to Gina's folder. "What you got there?"

As she watched Phil eat the sugary mess, her face scrunched up. "I was thinking about what kind of person would bury naked bodies in a remote site."

"A sicko?" his smart-ass partner tossed back.

"Well yeah, but that's not what I meant."

"Do you think if they'd been clothed they'd be any less dead?"

Hunter nudged Phil under the table. If his partner made it obvious they were trying to be jerks, Gina would catch on and run to Uncle Jack. And that would be bad. Hunter didn't want to fail at this assignment.

"Are you mocking me, mister policeman?" she said with a glint in her eye.

Phil placed a hand over his heart. "No. I wouldn't think of it." Then he smiled.

Gina batted her eyes. "I was thinking."

Hunter cleared his throat.

"What about?" Phil said, his tone back to being bad cop hard.

"I imagine as homicide detectives, you think these deaths were murder."

Phil chugged the rest of his Coke.

Hunter's partner swiped a napkin over his mouth "Yeah, well, you can't blame us. All four were abused, or so said Doc Herlihy. Kind of makes us think along sinister lines."

"I see where you're coming from," she said, "but hear me out." Her eyes widened. "I'm sorry. If I'm overstepping my boundary here, let me know, okay?" She straightened the pile of papers on the table. "Uncle Jack said I should pretend like I'm one of the team members." Gina's southern drawl turned even more pronounced.

"By all means continue," Hunter said, impressed she'd worry about police protocol.

Gina rifled through her folder. "Okay. I did a little research. I found out about a case a few months ago near Fort Myers where an undertaker didn't want to spend the money to bury some of the people who didn't have the funds to pay for a funeral. So...he dug this big old hole and dumped in the bodies. Can you believe that?"

Hunter scribbled some notes on his yellow pad. "I heard about that case, but I don't think it applies to these people—gut instinct only. Different MO. For starters, the undertaker hadn't stripped the subjects."

Gina tilted one shoulder forward. "Or they were all prostitutes and no one wanted to claim them. They'd likely be abused, given their profession, and the death rate for such women is rather high, you know."

"Point taken."

"Do you have any persons of interest?" Phil asked.

"As a matter of fact I do." She held up a police report and tapped the cover with a fancy red nail. "Samson DeMarco used to be a funeral director in Seminole. Emphasis on *used to*. He apparently made a deal with the county to bury any dead prisoners. He was paid by the state."

Hunter's patience was wearing thin. "I'm guessing Mr. DeMarco forgot to mention the burial fee didn't come with a wooden casket?" He guzzled down another cup of black coffee. Sugar gave him a headache, but oh how he loved sweet coffee.

"At least for one of them he didn't."

Phil grabbed another donut. "So how was he caught?" The man took acting indifferent to an art form.

"The report says some kids were playing near some preserve. Fishing, I think. Anyway, when they saw a finger sticking up from the ground, they told their folks, who then reported the discovery to the police."

"Don't tell me the body was in the North Tampa site," Hunter said, suddenly interested.

"No. West of here, near some wetlands. Closer to Westchase. The undertaker was caught about two months ago. I'm surprised you didn't hear about it."

Was the rookie actually challenging him? "Can't know everything." Hunter kept his gaze lasered on her face. He thought she blushed, though he was hard pressed to tell given her dark complexion.

"I like the idea," Phil said. "We could subpoena his records and see if any of the former morgue inhabitants match our bodies." Phil ping-ponged his gaze between Hunter and Gina.

Hunter decided to play along. "I bet he's not the only undertaker who's thought about dumping bodies if the families don't pay. I know the M.E.'s office spends a shit load of money burying or cremating their unclaimed bodies."

Gina leaned forward and her boobs practically spilled out of her top. Hunter didn't think her theory would pan out, but hey, he'd heard of crazier ideas. "I say, subpoena away if you can get a judge to go for it." He was rewarded with a smile from both of them.

"Great," Phil said.

His partner looked like a love-sick puppy. Stupid guy. But hell, who was he to criticize? Gina was single, close to Phil's age, and intelligent.

"Why don't you two follow up on that lead? I want to compare the missing persons' list against Dr. Herlihy's stats."

"Sounds like a plan." Phil stood. "Don't have too much fun." He turned to Gina. "Ready for your first ride along?"

"Absolutely." The excitement in her eyes spelled trouble.

CHAPTER FIVE

KERRY WIPED her forearm across her face to clear the cobwebs from her mind. She'd been lucky when she found an identifying mark on Jane Doe #2. The female had a tattoo of a sailboat.

During the autopsy John had called her in and showed her a faint discoloration on the ankle. Kerry had dabbed a bit of diluted household bleach on the skin, a trick she'd learned in New Orleans, and the image of a boat appeared. John seemed impressed—always a good thing for a person on contract.

Underneath the boat was the name *Bra_y_ne*. The skin had broken apart in the middle of the word, making identification difficult but not impossible. One good thing about the woman's choice of shapes was its uniqueness might help identify her.

Once John finished the autopsy, he handed the body over to Kerry. She photographed the details of the tattoo, and then began the painstaking job of cleaning the bones. She understood all too well the results from the autopsy would not be back for days.

It was evident from the fracture on the boat lady's body that her arm had been broken about three years ago. The spiral nature of the injury implied abuse. The broken jaw looked more recent.

Kerry had been working on the body for less than an hour when her lab door squeaked open and John popped his head in.

"Hey, Doc. I just received another call."

Her heart sank to her stomach. Another call. Another death.

"What do we have?" The usual heart thumping and belly souring blasted her.

"It's...bad. They think they found the bones of an infant. They're hoping you'll tell them the remains are animal." He scratched his beard and looked out the window.

"What aren't you telling me?" John was an easy read.

"A piece of a child's jacket was beside one of the bones."

Damn. "Let me gather my gear."

Forcing her emotions aside, Kerry grabbed her kit. She'd left the shovel and some of her digging tools in the M.E.'s van, ready to go at a moment's notice.

They drove in silence for a good ten miles, east past Brahman University, then headed north another five miles. The area was close to where they'd found yesterday's bodies.

For a brief moment she wondered if Detective Markum had been assigned to this case, but she refused to address the strange and unwanted flick of excitement that shot through her.

Crap. How could she forget? The man might be married. The last man Kerry had slept with had kept his wife hidden. Too bad he'd never told her until she joyfully informed him about their unborn child.

John pulled to a stop on the road behind a long line of sheriff cruisers parked along the rim of a wooden area. Some officers were leaning against the hood of their cars while other vehicles sat empty.

No doubt they were waiting for her and John.

As they traveled to where the crime scene unit was planting flags, Whit Jackson, the lead detective on the case, met them. From the ease with which they talked, John knew him quite well.

Kerry surveyed the area. Too many small flags stabbed the ground, each signifying a bone or a piece of evidence, and her gut churned.

God, she hated this job some days. Child deaths hit her the hardest. Kids shouldn't die, and parents shouldn't have to experience such loss. She never could erase her mother's wails when her older brother had vanished.

She gloved her hands, squatted, and picked up one of the bones. A wave of hurt assaulted her. "Human all right." Damn it.

From the chew marks, it looked as if the child had been dug up by an enthusiastic animal who'd deposited the remains everywhere.

A shadow loomed over her. Kerry looked up and squinted into the hot sun. Whit Jackson looked down at her.

His shoulders slumped. "Tell me what you need us to do."

"Find the head." The holy grail of body parts.

Without saying a word, he spun around and began directing his men and women in a militant manner to spread out—to search more.

Fifteen minutes later, a shout came from the far end of the field. "Over here. We found it!"

Kerry trudged to where several officers had gathered beneath a shaded tree. The front part of the cranium was intact but little else. Usually animals leave the skull alone because their teeth can't grasp the unwieldy bone, but a child's head was a different matter.

Kerry studied the skull. Once the CSU team triangulated its position, she bagged the head for further study.

"Can you tell the child's sex?" Whit asked.

"Not yet. I need more bones, but with a child this young, it'll be very difficult. The hipbones haven't developed yet." She noted the lack of teeth. "This is an infant." Kerry had a hard time swallowing. "I'd say between six months and a year old."

Her heart nearly broke when she thought about the pain the child's mother must have experienced not knowing if her baby was alive or dead.

"Thank you. That will help."

"Have any idea on the PMI?" John asked, sneaking up behind her.

The postmortem interval told her the time of death. "From the color of the bones, a year or more would be my guess. I'll have to do tests back at the lab to get a more precise estimate."

Kerry went from site to site, bagging the evidence as the CSU team drew careful diagrams and took photographs of the area.

"Hey, Doc," Whit called. He trudged up the path, wiping his brow with a handkerchief. From his red face, and overweight condition, she hoped he wouldn't suffer from heat exhaustion. It had to be close to ninety-five degrees with one hundred percent humidity. Even her limbs were growing weak with each passing hour.

When Whit reached her, his sagging cheeks told her they'd found something. "We located the grave, or least what's left of it. Um...part of the lower body is still there. It's a girl."

Oh God. Her insides turned to liquid. When Kerry had miscarried, she'd been carrying a girl. An intense pain squeezed her heart, almost causing her to miss a step.

Whit pointed up the path, and she followed him to the burial pit.

Flies had found the exposed flesh and were buzzing around the grave. The moment she neared the area, the smell of putrefaction assaulted her, which meant soft tissue, but soft tissue meant John could do an autopsy. This find might move them one step closer to finding out what had happened to this child. For a sliver of a moment, her heart stopped aching.

The lower half of the body was still in a body bag. Someone had cared enough to place the child in what he or she thought was a safe place. Little did the person realize the land sloped at such a pitch that when it rained, deep crevices formed, slowly washing away the soil, eventually exposing the bag.

For the next few hours, Kerry directed the team to gather bones. By four p.m., the sheriff's department decided to call it a day, having bagged and labeled all of the bones—or so they'd believed. No one had found any other evidence in the last hour. If any crucial bones were missing, they promised they'd come out tomorrow and search again.

Back in the SUV, John broke the news. "I think we need to concentrate on identifying the four women, Kerry. I'm sorry. I know you want to work on the child."

He was the boss and she'd do what he said, but she'd find a way to help Baby Doe. "Once you autopsy the infant, do you mind if I photograph and X-ray the body before investigating the others? I can do it after hours."

He nodded solemnly. "No *problema.*"

If she found some spare time—ha, ha—she wanted to try a facial reconstruction of the child. If that proved impossible, she'd try her hand with one of the skeletons she'd found yesterday. She'd read about a new technique to recreate faces with more accuracy and wanted to see if her skill could be improved. However, the chances of matching a face to her clay model would be slim given she wasn't a forensic artist by trade.

John eased into the morgue parking lot. "Was this your first time finding a child?"

"Yes."

"They're the toughest."

If only he knew. While she never knew her unborn little girl, she never stopped grieving.

John honked, signaling he needed help with the body bag. The autopsy technician grab one end of the bag and slip it onto the gurney.

"Kerry," John said. "This is Steven, my top autopsy technician."

The young man's gaze hugged the ground. "Thanks, Dr. A."

"He wants to be a pathologist. He's even going to school at night."

"Fantastic." She guessed the cheery conversation was an attempt to block the gruesome scene that swirled around them.

"Nice meeting you." Steven finally looked up.

"You too."

Kerry wiped a sweaty brow, collected her gear and trudged inside. She ignored the lingering odor of death surrounding her and enjoyed the cool morgue air.

John went one way down the hall, she the other. Since Kerry had to wait for the autopsy results on Baby Doe, she pulled her attention back to the Jane Doe cases. Something about these women had tickled the back of her brain all day. Snippets of a connection flitted in and out, but she couldn't connect the dots. Yet.

CHAPTER SIX

NORMALLY, Phil would be heading to the bar for a beer with some friends around now. Instead, he had to show the intern that cop hours sucked. Stupid idea, if you asked him, but Hunter insisted Jack Andries wanted him to work Gina hard.

Hard. He glanced over at the pretty woman. Big brown eyes that looked too ready to trust, and a killer body any man would want to run his hands down. Man, she was something.

Stop it. He needed to squash the image of them in bed. Talk about a career-ruining move. They'd already spent the day running around following leads regarding the undertaker. The last lead led them here to the Orient Road Jail off I-4.

"Here we are," he announced, careful to keep his eyes focused on the jail instead of Gina's legs.

"This is exciting."

She acted as if this was going to be some glamorous adventure. Boy, was she in for a surprise. Gina jumped out of the cruiser, ready for action.

Phil piled out. "Have you ever been in a jail before?"

"No."

"Then let's go." In a way he wished she'd step one foot in the place, turn tail, and run. Then this babysitting gig would be over and he could get back to finding the person responsible for killing those four women. On the other hand, he liked Gina, liked looking at her.

He hated being torn.

Phil led her through the main entrance, flashed his badge, and said he had an appointment with Samson DeMarco. After passing through a series of barred doors, the officer led them into a small room that contained a table and four scarred chairs.

As usual, the place stank of body odor and urine.

The first chair Gina pulled out had some gum or something on the seat. She pushed the chair back in and pulled out the second one. Then she inspected the third chair. Phil chewed on the inside of his mouth to keep from smirking.

Gina dragged the most sanitary of the four chairs around to the side by the entrance and sat on the edge. "This place could really use a good cleaning."

Phil swallowed a laugh. Guess the filth level wasn't so bad she'd wanted to run. A moment later, a man in orange strode in, with his guard right behind. The alleged criminal's appearance took Phil by surprise. Dapper was the first word that came to mind. A good six feet, the guy had neatly trimmed gray hair, was clean-shaven, and wore expensive looking wire-rimmed glasses.

In his mid to late fifties, Samson DeMarco held himself tall and walked as though he owned the place. Phil wondered how long that attitude would last if he were found guilty and sent to prison.

"Mr. DeMarco, have a seat," Phil pointed toward an empty chair.

DeMarco glanced at Gina, and then at Phil, his expression unreadable. "How can I help you?"

Educated, good. Phil liked smart prisoners. "Recently, we located some bodies buried in North Tampa—bodies that were not in caskets or in body bags."

DeMarco's lips pursed. "I had nothing to do with that. Actually, I had nothing to do with the body found at the Westchase site either, but these morons," he said, making a wide sweep with his arm, "don't believe me."

"Sure. Police always arrest people without evidence."

Gina leaned forward, her brow creased. "What evidence do they have against you?"

Oh, crap. They didn't need to be sidetracked with this guy's sad story, but he decided to let her have her fun.

DeMarco waved his shackled hands and the cuffs clinked together. "None. Absolutely none. I admitted the body came from my morgue. When I returned to the embalming area after I'd handled a particularly troublesome funeral, I found one of my corpses had been stolen. It upset the hell out of me." He tapped his chest. "I reported the disappearance to the police. They have no reason to hold me." His chin notched up.

Gina glanced at Phil, pleading with her eyes to help the man.

"Mr. DeMarco," Phil said, failing to keep the irritation from his tone. "The police had other evidence to detain you."

His jaw clenched. "They found a spare pair of my glasses at the gravesite. That was all the connection they needed to be convinced I was guilty of the unlawful burial. As if I'd drop a three hundred dollar pair of Gucci glasses. And besides, I'd never just dump a body in the ground. At the very least, I would have put him in a casket, albeit a pine one."

"If you didn't remove the body from the morgue and bury him on the other side of town, who did?"

DeMarco leaned forward. "A client who obviously wanted to get even for a small error this person believed I committed." Phil straightened at the snappy comeback.

"What kind of error?" Gina asked, jumping in ahead of Phil.

"There was a mistake made at the funeral home, or so my client claimed." DeMarco shook his head. "My now *unemployed* secretary told me his family requested the deceased be cremated. I honored their wishes."

"I don't see the problem."

"Unfortunately, they told her quite the opposite. Their accent was thick and my secretary misunderstood them. They were furious when I handed them the box with the remains. They yelled something about stealing the soul of their loved one. What could I do? I couldn't turn the ashes into a body again."

"You didn't double check? Cremation is a big step away from burial."

"It had been a long week. A mere slip on my part I shall regret the rest of my life." His jaw clenched, and he began to breathe hard through his nostrils, like a bull ready to charge. "I have the cremation orders they signed, but I doubt anyone in the family could read English."

What a cluster fuck. "So do you think this wronged family member was out for revenge?"

DeMarco sat up straighter, his eyes bright. "I wouldn't put it past him. The oldest son mumbled something about an eye for an eye. I'm guessing since I theoretically ruined their lives, or rather their after-lives, he would ruin mine."

"Do you have any proof this man was the thief?" His story seemed more than a little far-fetched.

DeMarco's shoulders sagged. "No. Just a gut feeling. But you know how those middle easterners can be. They're serious about the dead. From what the son said, they believe the body is a connection between this world and the next. Apparently, when I cremated the body, I stole this person's chance at salvation. How was I to know? It's not my fault." He wagged a finger. "Let this be a lesson to the son. He should have known what he signed."

It was DeMarco's job to make sure the client understood. "Anything else?"

"I'm convinced the son must have gone into my morgue and stolen one of the bodies. He buried the man to get me in trouble."

Phil doubted the whole crazy story, but he asked, "And the man's name would be?"

"Abdul Hakeem."

Phil made the note, though he couldn't prove Mr. DeMarco's innocence based on a hunch.

DeMarco slapped both hands on the table. "Or maybe Willie Wyble did it." DeMarco looked off to his left.

Phil had noted when the mortician recalled facts, he looked to his right. His left side was his imagination at work.

Christ. The man was a master storyteller. "And just who is this Willie person?"

DeMarco peered back up at Phil. "He works on and off at the cemetery. Willie is...what should I call him...mentally handicapped. He digs worms for a living, or anything else that requires a hole." DeMarco shrugged. "It's what he does."

"Now you think this Willie, and not Hakeem, stole the body just so he could have fun digging?" Phil had heard many a tale in his time, but this was for the books.

"My funeral home is only two blocks from the cemetery. It would have been easy for him to sneak in and take a body."

"So Willie works for the city then?"

"In a way. Jeff Lamont operates the cemetery. He uses Willie when his regular man isn't available. Jeff doesn't really want Willie around, even though he can handle a backhoe better than most. You see, Willie isn't the most hygienic person. He has this long, straggly hair that would make most people run. The thing is, Willie...ah... doesn't expect too much in the way of payment."

"Why else do you suspect Willie? It's a nice theory, but it had more holes than a sieve."

DeMarco's jaw clenched. "The glasses. When I was checking on the burial plot, I ran into Willie digging. Mr. Commens, my client at the time, insisted we bury his mother facing due west since she loved sunsets. I personally wanted to supervise the digging. Well, that evening Willie was working the backhoe. I had to come within a few feet of him before he recognized me. Apparently, he doesn't see well. I thought—" DeMarco touched his two index fingers to his lips.

"Thought what?" Phil was getting tired of the runaround, but Gina sat wide-eyed.

"I thought Willie might need glasses. He commented once on my how much he liked my wire rims, and how he bet if he had a pair just like mine, he'd be able to see a lot better. I figured Hakeem hired Willie to dig the grave of the stolen corpse. Willie must have taken my spare pair of glasses when he went into the morgue to get the body, then forgot my specs at the site."

Phil scribbled some notes. When he finished, he leaned back in his chair. If he had time, he might check out the Middle Easterner along with the worm man, but he wasn't convinced he'd learn anything. He would find out who the principal was on the case and talk to him. Reports didn't always tell the whole story.

It didn't matter if DeMarco's tale had any validity or not, he needed answers to his case. If Hunter believed there might be a connection to the four dead women, he had an obligation to investigate.

"Would you give us permission to check your records, to see if there's a connection to the bodies we found in North Tampa?" Phil asked. They might get lucky, but he doubted it.

"I'd like to help, but I, or rather the county, closed my business once I was arrested. Because of this...this... misunderstanding, I decided I was through dealing with irrational people. My brother has put the place up for sale. I have no idea if he's done anything with the records—or if he even kept them." The sadness in the man's eye made Phil wince. Hell, maybe he was telling the truth.

DeMarco dropped his head into his hands, and his shoulders shook. When he looked up, tears streaked his cheeks. "I have no idea where to turn. Can you help me?"

Phil couldn't take it when someone cried, be it man or woman. It didn't matter if he was acting or not. "I'll see what we can do."

Phil stood and Gina pushed back her chair. She probably wanted to stay and console the poor guy, but they had more pressing issues to attend to.

After they stepped outside, Gina ran her hand up and down his arm. "Are you going to help him?"

He was a sucker for a beautiful, aggressive woman, but she had something coming if she thought he'd ever change his principles when it came to police work. He refused to become interested in the boss's niece. He liked his job way too much.

"I'll try."

* * *

"YOU STILL HERE?" Jack Andries asked as he ducked into the conference room.

Hunter wanted to ask, "What does it look like?" Instead he admitted, "This case is eating me." Hunter moved the photos in front of him in a different position to give him a new perspective.

"Don't they all?" Jack sniffed the air. "You taken to wearing perfume?"

"Kerry Herlihy was here yesterday. Maybe that's what you smell. She'd been working with the dead all day. I think she splashed on a lot of cologne to mask the stench of death."

"That so?" Andries quirked a brow. "Why did she stop by?"

"I wanted her opinion on the Jane Doe cases." Hunter's tone came off defensive. Christ, he sounded as though she didn't belong here. Only she did. "She might be the key that unlocks this case."

"Ah." His tone lowered as if he didn't want to tear apart Hunter's ever-open wound. Jack tossed down another folder. "Did she call today by any chance and mention they'd found a female infant this afternoon?"

Hunter's heart turned heavy. "No." Losing a child had to hurt worse than death. If he ever lost Melissa, he wouldn't be able to go on. He still hadn't recovered from his sister's murder, and that was over ten years ago.

"She and Ahern handled the call. The M.E.'s office just sent over the photos. I had assigned Whit Jackson as principal, but his father suffered a heart attack this morning and isn't expected to make it. He flew out about an hour ago. I thought you could take over. You're working with Dr. Herlihy on the four Jane Does and thought it would be easier if you two also paired up on this case."

His logic was sound, Hunter guessed. "Fine." A strange excitement socked him at working another case with her, though he wasn't sure why. Yes, she was attractive, but he prided himself on his ability to focus. That trait sure disappeared the moment he met Kerry Herlihy.

As Jack turned to leave, Hunter decided to satisfy his curiosity. "What do you know about this new anthropologist?"

His boss turned and cocked a brow. "Nothing. Why?" A small smile lifted his lips. "You interested in her?"

He shouldn't be. "No. Just wondering how good she is at her job." Jack had tried to fix him up several times after Amy had died, but

Hunter couldn't bear losing anyone else he cared about, so he'd politely declined all invitations.

"Ask Ahern. He hired her."

"Good idea." Hunter saluted and turned back to the table.

When Hunter didn't hear the door close, he looked up. Jack was staring at him. "And Gina? How'd her internship go today?"

Damn. He thought Jack wouldn't ask. So much for his boss's promise not to interfere with his niece's temporary position.

Hunter sympathized with the man's need to know though. "I sent her and Phil to the Orient Road jail. I haven't heard back from them yet. If a trip there doesn't turn her off to pursuing a career in law, I don't know what will."

"You don't know Gina. She's as stubborn as they come. My brother is going to have my head if I can't persuade her to return to teaching. Just remember, safety first, when it comes to my niece."

"Yes, sir."

With that, Jack closed the door behind him.

Hunter leaned back in his chair and rested his eyes, blocking out the photos of the dead women, blocking out his sister's murder.

In its place, a tall, delicate woman with long, brown, wavy hair, the skin of alabaster and the eyes of an angel stared up at him. He missed his wife, yes, but Kerry awakened something in him he couldn't attach a label to and he had no idea why. Maybe it was her sad story about her brother that got to him.

He wanted to know more. That shouldn't be a problem. After all, he hadn't earned the rank of detective for nothing.

CHAPTER SEVEN

KERRY NEVER HAD the opportunity during the normal workday to start the facial recreation of Jane Doe #1. She figured it was better to create a likeness in a timely fashion than never begin the process, so she brought the skull home.

Guilt pricked her. Maybe she should have asked official permission to take evidence from the morgue, but John had been standing there when she'd boxed up the skull and had said nothing.

When Kerry had asked Dr. Ahern if the department was willing to bring in a high-level forensic artist to do the reconstruction, she received a definitive no. He'd said the citywide budget cuts had put a bite into many of their requests, and that they'd only bring in experts for high profile cases.

Had she not been new, or maybe if she were better with confrontation, she would have asked how many more women this person needed to kill to qualify for high profile.

That meant she'd just have to do it herself in her off-hours. The ends justified the means. Right?

In order to have room to work, Kerry cleared off one end of the kitchen table nearest the pantry. Grandpa had said they could eat in the formal dining room as long as need be. He understood her burning need to find the relatives of the Jane Does of the world. No doubt it was because he was a former cop.

Kerry leaned closer and ran a hand over the face. "I promise I'll find out who you are." Not only did this skull have the best teeth of the four women, the cranium was mostly intact, making her the best candidate for the clay reconstruction.

Kerry had already compared the Missing Person photos Hunter had given her to the X-ray of Jane's face. No matches—at least none that she could be sure about. Without a match, there'd be no dental records, which meant the clay model was her only hope.

"Need any help?"

Kerry jumped. Her grandfather pulled up a chair at the table and sat down.

"I wish you could. This is a long, tedious process."

"I can sort the stubby rubber thingies if that would help."

She smiled. "They're tissue depth markers. Thank you. That would help." Not really, but she wanted him to feel useful.

Grandpa went to work arranging the twenty-one numbered pieces, lining them up in a neat row. "You know where they go?"

This time she chuckled. "I hope so. I learned from one of the best in the country."

She'd spent the last hour measuring and cutting each marker. Given Jane Doe was Negroid, twenty-five to thirty-five, Kerry had used tables to determine the approximate tissue depth at each point around the face.

She picked up the first marker and glued the piece to the middle of the forehead.

After she double-checked the length, she glued three more markers. Next, she placed cotton pads behind the eyes, nose and mouth sockets so the clay would stay on the surface and not fall into the holes.

"You know, in all my years on the force, I've never seen anyone make one of these face things," Grandpa said. "That's not a real skull, is it?"

She smiled at her grandfather's transparent interest. "Yes. I didn't have time to make a mold."

The cheer in his eyes disappeared. "That skull is evidence. You shouldn't have taken it out of the morgue."

"I'll bring it back." She tried to keep her tone light, but her heart still raced.

He shot her a warning look, and then relaxed. "You normally would have made a mold, right? Like out of plaster of Paris?"

"Yes."

He smiled. "Why, I remember when you made a volcano for your eighth grade science fair project out of that stuff."

She'd forgotten that catastrophe. When she'd lit the powder for the volcano to spew lava, the whole thing exploded. "This plaster is a little different."

Grandpa fiddled with the neat row of markers. "Your sister called again today."

Her fingers stopped moving and her stomach soured. "Did she say what she wanted?" Kerry was pleased her tone lacked emotion.

"Same as last time. She wants to talk to you. To mend the fences, so to speak."

"I think we've said all we need to say to each other." She picked up the number four marker and placed it at the top of the nose. "What could Susan say to me now that would change how she treated me?"

"She had her reasons for doing what she did." He handed her the next marker.

Her sister had reasons all right. She wanted to be with her friends instead of with her seven-year old sister. Susan was the devil incarnate.

"Did she have a good reason for not going to Mom's funeral?"

"Yes."

Kerry turned toward Grandpa, and her heart skipped a beat. "What was it?" Her interest overcame her resentment.

"You'll have to let her tell you." He picked up a brown glass eye from the case and twirled it between his thumb and forefinger. "You sure this is the right size?"

His comment implied the conversation was over. "I measured the eye sockets back at the lab." She gently extracted the eyepiece from his gnarled fingers and placed it back where it belonged. "Don't you have to walk Buster or something?" She needed space as well as time to think, time to fight her demons—alone.

"All right. I get the hint."

As he scooted back his chair, sharp claws scratched their way into the kitchen. Buster slid around the corner and began barking in earnest.

"I swear," Grandpa said, "that dog can understand every word we say." He stood. "Come on, Buster. Let's go outside."

Kerry went back to placing the forensic markers on the skull. Number five went on top of the upper teeth to form the lip. She figured she should have the face done within a week's time if she hurried.

* * *

KERRY PACED the police conference room, waiting for the Channel 8 camera crew and Detective Markum to arrive.

She'd only taken six days to complete the reconstruction, which was a new record for her. The first few faces she'd created had taken her close to three weeks. This time she'd gone without much sleep most nights. She yawned, the effects of strain tightening every muscle in her neck and back.

Unearthing #1 might have given her a more personal connection to the victim, which created an urgency she hadn't felt with the other faces—or had she worked hour after tireless hour on this particular Jane Doe in order to push away the image of the infant they'd found, torn in half by an animal? The teddy bear they'd located the next day under some bush still made her sick.

Whatever it took, Kerry vowed to find the baby's identity and to bring closure to the grieving family.

You can't dwell on Baby Doe, or the horrors of your job will eat you alive.

Kerry mentally repeated the mantra her wonderful professor, Dr. Mary Strickland, had pounded into her head, but the usually calming refrain refused to fill the gaping hole in her heart. No doubt about it, she could handle adult skeletons a lot better than children's.

Kerry checked her watch for the fourth time in as many minutes and smoothed the wig on the skull. The few strands of the victim's hair she'd found underneath the skeleton had helped her estimate the hair texture and length.

She'd had to guess at the victim's lip thickness, the size of her ears and the eye contour, but despite the judgment call, she hoped someone might recognize this poor woman.

"Hello."

Kerry whipped around. Hunter Markum strolled into the conference room looking highly professional in his crisp, freshly pressed cop uniform that fit amazingly well over his muscled frame.

"Hi," she shot back.

He stepped close to her, examining the clay model she gripped. His musky scent made her inwardly groan.

Don't let him get to you, Kerry. Looks are superficial.

His hand lightly brushed Jane Doe's head. "This is quite remarkable. She looks so lifelike."

Some of her anxiety drained away after hearing his praise. "Thank you." When Hunter stepped back, she was able to breathe again.

"Ready?" He remained upbeat, yet solemn at the same time.

"As ready as I'll ever be. I just hope I don't make a fool of myself in front of the camera."

He smiled at her. "You'll do just fine. Have you ever been on TV?"

Oh God, he could tell she'd never made a plea to the public before. "No. Can't you see I'm a nervous wreck?"

"Don't worry. I'll do most of the talking. No one will notice you're out of your comfort zone."

Comfort zone? Hell, she was afraid her first real attempt at facial reconstruction wouldn't jog anyone's memory. Her hands were shaking, which was not a good sign.

Kerry took a deep breath and squared her shoulders. For the daughter of an actress, she should have been a natural in front of the camera. Unfortunately, she hadn't inherited her mom's dramatic flair.

A knock sounded at the conference room door and a cameraman and a reporter from News Channel 8 strode in. They introduced themselves. The reporter, Liz Culbertson, gave the two of them the spiel about relaxing and trying to ignore the camera. Right.

"If you two would stand by the wall," Josh Martin, the cameraman directed, "we won't have to worry about the reflection from the white board or the backlight from the sun coming through the blinds."

Kerry glanced at Hunter. He looked so at ease. Lucky guy. Hunter placed his hand on the small of her back to lead her to the other side, and the room seemed to shrink from his touch. God, she didn't need the added tension of being next to him, smelling his musky aftershave.

She needed to do what her mom always did when she performed— think of a mountain stream and forget the world was watching. Kerry had to stay calm for the relatives of this lost woman.

Kerry placed the reconstruction on the table and examined her creation one more time, looking for imperfections and uneven skin thickness. For the last time, Kerry smoothed the hair on the skull. The woman deserved to look her best.

The reporter held a white piece of paper in front of Kerry's face. She blinked and took a step back.

"It's for white balance," the reporter said. "You don't want to come out looking blue or green, do you?" Liz smiled. "Relax."

"I'll try."

The cameraman turned on a strong beam that shone into Kerry's eyes. She squinted for a moment, then tried to do as Liz instructed.

"Ready when you are, Liz," Josh directed.

The reporter walked back to Josh and stood next to him. Facing both Kerry and Hunter, she began the interview.

"Detective Markham, you've brought in Dr. Herlihy, a forensic anthropologist, to reconstruct the face of one of your Jane Doe victims. Why? Couldn't you have identified her some other way?"

"We're running some tests in the lab on evidence we found at the crime scene, but so far haven't much to go on."

"And Dr. Herlihy's model will help?"

"We hoped by creating a visual, such as the recreation, a relative or friend might identify this woman sooner than we could."

"Could you state the victim's age and nationality?"

Hunter nodded to Kerry. *Here goes.* "From her facial structure, we believe she's African American, though the bone density scan indicates a mix of white European."

"Were you able to determine how old she was?"

"She's most likely between twenty-five to thirty-five."

Liz's expression didn't change. "Can you tell how she died?"

Kerry spent about a minute discussing the woman's injuries. Because the interview was being taped, Kerry bet her boring explanation would land on the cutting room floor.

Liz Culbertson asked Hunter a few more questions, then had the cameraman shut off his equipment. "We'll have the detective's telephone number appear on the screen after the story airs."

The reporter and her cameraman disappeared as quick as they had arrived. Now that the drama was over, Kerry smiled at Hunter. "That wasn't as bad as I'd thought."

Hunter unbuttoned the top button of his uniform. "I can't wait to get out of this monkey suit." Only now did he look uncomfortable.

"I appreciate you setting up this interview. I think we'll reach a wider audience when the video appears on the evening news," she said.

"Let's hope."

Hunter said nothing more as he escorted her to her car. She could have found her way herself, but she was thankful he wanted to walk her out. They were a team, both focused on finding the identity of the victim.

"So now what?" she asked.

"We wait and we pray."

No way. The victims' families had waited long enough. She planned to begin work on the other women, and then she'd pray someone identified the poor soul.

* * *

"YOU LOOKED AS PRETTY as your mother," Grandpa said, as he clicked off the six o'clock news. He grabbed his beer off the coffee table and took a drink.

"I wouldn't go that far, but thank you."

Her mom. Now there was a unique woman. She would disappear for weeks to audition for the perfect movie role and leave seven-year old Kerry in the hands of her thirteen-year old sister. Too bad Susan often played hide and seek and left Kerry to fend for herself.

She'd loved her mom despite the fact the woman wasn't capable of keeping a husband around for long. Kerry definitely missed having supportive parents.

"You came off as very professional," he said.

A high compliment indeed. "You couldn't tell I was shaking?"

"You looked cool and calm to me."

Hunter Markum had been the cool one. "Thanks." Kerry stood. "I need to fix dinner before the poker boys come over."

As she made her way into the kitchen, the phone rang. "I'll get it," she yelled back to the living room. "Hello?"

"Is this Dr. Herlihy?"

"Yes." It wasn't Hunter.

"I saw the news tonight."

Her pulse shot up to over a hundred. Had someone recognized the woman? "Yes?"

"You didn't get the chin right, and her cheekbones were more refined than you made them."

"You know this woman?" Kerry gripped the phone. The man should be thanking her for finding his wife, or daughter, not chastising her for sculpting the face incorrectly. "Who was she? And what's your name?"

"Next time, pay more attention to the details."

Then he hung up.

CHAPTER EIGHT

"Stupid bitch." News Channel 8 shouldn't have aired that shit.

Who did Dr. Herlihy think she was trying to ape such a fine creation? She screwed up the shape of Tameka's ears and the fullness of her lips, not to mention the cheek line was all wrong. Tameka's face had been beaten so many times, her cheeks had sunken.

And I fixed her. Made her beautiful.

Then Tameka's stupid boyfriend had to mess with her face again. Christ. Why couldn't the woman listen to good advice and leave the prick?

And to think Tameka planned on bringing a baby into the world. Bitch deserved to die. *It's my duty to keep unborn children away from harm.*

If Tameka had realized how abuse destroyed self-confidence, ruined children's lives, and caused so much pain, she'd never have stayed with Jamal.

Like dad's abuse did to me.

Maybe worse than the actual abuse was the fact Mom knew what Dad was doing and refused to leave the SOB. Where would we go, she'd cry? Who would pay for food?

Fathers were supposed to discipline their children. Fine, but did it have to include punches, belts, and dark closets?

And Roger. As the older brother, he should have been the protector. Instead, he escaped. He'd never given a warning to stay hidden when Dad went on one of his rampages either. But Roger had gotten his due from his own son. Ha. Served him right. Fathers should know better than to treat their sons like dirt.

Just as sure as there were more abusive assholes like Dad, there would also be more women and children who needed to be saved. Unfortunately, now that the cops had found the gravesite, disposing of more bodies just got harder.

Thank God, he'd been careful and so far, and no one had been able to identify the victims or connect them to him.

If anyone did figure out who they were, that someone would have to die.

* * *

HER MIND REELING, Kerry dropped the phone onto the cradle. Her legs weakened and her hands shook. She couldn't process the conversation. She had to call him back.

Heart racing, she sat down at the kitchen table and punched *69 to redial his number. The call wouldn't go through. Dammit. Maybe that didn't work with cell phone. Shit. She had no idea.

Grandpa entered the kitchen. "Was that David?"

When she didn't answer, he shuffled over to the table and eased down onto the chair across from her. "You look like you've seen a ghost. Tell me what happened." He reached out and took her hand. His dry palm was warm and comforting.

Kerry detailed the strange conversation.

"And he didn't tell you the name of the victim?"

"No. He was angry I'd gotten some of the features wrong. That's all."

Grandpa scratched his chin. "If he recognized the victim enough to know what you'd done wrong, you must have had quite a bit about her correct."

That gave her some consolation. "True, but without a name, what good does it do?" Kerry slipped her fingers from his, closed her eyes, and ran her hands down her face. "Why wouldn't he tell me her name?"

"I have no idea. Maybe you should call your detective."

Hardly *her* detective. Her heart pounded. "You're right. Maybe he can trace the call."

"Plus, the man knew *our* number. The only one given out on television was the detective's I believe."

The ramification hit her. "Ohmigod. You're right. How did he get our number? Our last names are different. There's no way he could know I'm staying with you."

"That's why you need to find out. Call the detective."

How could Grandpa remain so composed when she was about to have a nervous breakdown? Kerry jumped up from the table and paced, needing to release her anxiety. Buster raced in and began barking.

"Stop that noise. Come here." Grandpa bent and picked up the dog who immediately licked his face.

Seeing the two act so normal together eased her fear a bit. Kerry stepped to the fridge and poured a glass of diet Coke from the near empty quart bottle. Her hand shook so much, she spilled some of the drink onto the floor. *Get a grip.* She grabbed a rag and cleaned up the mess.

"I thought you were going to call," Grandpa said. Now he sounded annoyed.

"I am."

Why had this stranger bothered to call and tell her she'd done a bad job? Was he taunting her or angry she had a few details wrong?

Her breath came out in short bursts. Her hand stilled as a slow trickle of fear drained into her belly. Her throat turned dry and she took a sip of her cola. Could he have been... She couldn't finish her thought.

After carefully placing the tumbler on the counter so she wouldn't knock it over, she raced into the living room to find her purse.

"Kerry?" Grandpa called.

"Be right back." After she searched her bag to locate the detective's card, she scrambled back into the kitchen. She refused to believe the caller might be the killer—a killer who knew her name, knew her number.

She dialed Detective Markum and tapped her fingers on the handset, waiting for him to answer.

"Markum."

The breath whooshed from her lungs. "It's Kerry Herlihy."

"What's wrong?"

Was the fear in her voice that evident? "I received a call a few minutes ago at my grandfather's house about the news broadcast."

"From someone you know?"

"No. I don't know who it was. He wouldn't give me a name."

"Tell me what he said."

She detailed the one-sided conversation as precisely as she could. "Do you think it could be the creep who killed these women?"

"It's possible. I'll be right over. What's your address?"

She told him, and he hung up. Damn him.

Kerry downed her soda before she told Grandpa the detective was on the way. She pressed her palm over her chest, hoping to calm the pounding, but it didn't work. "Why wouldn't he tell me the woman's name," she mumbled to herself.

"Some people don't like to be involved."

She slid over to the seat across from him. "I don't buy it. This guy was angry and mean. He didn't want me to be involved, not the other way around. If he knew our number, he might know where I live." Fear choked off her air.

"True."

"Oh, that helps. You could have lied."

"It won't do any good to hide your head in the sand."

She didn't need anymore of Grandpa's sayings. Kerry dropped her head in her hands and didn't move for the next twenty-five minutes until the doorbell rang.

She raced to answer, but not before looking through the peephole first to make sure it wasn't some stranger at her door, or *the* stranger. It was Hunter, face drawn with worry. She unlatched the door and opened it. "Come in."

He stepped into the foyer, grabbed her shoulders and ran a gaze down the length of her. "Are you okay?"

His strong hands reassured her. "Physically, yes. Mentally, no. I can't help but wonder how the man found my number."

Buster came skidding into the living room from the kitchen, nails slipping on the hard wood floor, and whimpered.

"Buster, it's okay." She picked him up, and he calmed down immediately.

Hunter moved past her into the living room, his gaze scanning the room. "Right after you called, I had one of the men attempt to trace the number. He just contacted me on my cell as I was heading down your street. No luck. The guy probably used a burner phone." He spun back to face her. "They're impossible to trace."

Damn. "But he knew me, called me by name."

He was by her side in a second and lifted her chin. "Kerry, it's not hard to find someone's number. And as for knowing you, you were on television."

She swallowed hard. "But I don't live here. It's Grandpa's house." She turned her back to him, not wanting him to see the tears in her eyes. "It isn't as though he could have looked up my name in the phonebook."

"There are ways to find your number. Trust me."

She turned back around. Trust. Ha. The last time someone had said, "Trust me", her sister had run off and left her alone to fend for her seven-year-old self. Susan, her mom, her dad all had done the disappearing act at one time or another.

Her grandfather, the one person who'd always been there for her, padded out of the kitchen.

"Saw you on the news tonight. I'm Kerry's grandfather, Tom Hardy." He stuck out his hand.

"Hunter Markum."

Grandpa waved a hand toward the sofa. Kerry and Grandpa took the loveseat while Hunter dropped down on the chair opposite them. He looked more confident than comfortable, which was a good thing.

"I'd like to tap your phone," Hunter said looking from her to her grandfather.

Kerry glanced at Grandpa. "No problem," he said.

"I'd also like to have an officer patrol your street. If the caller is dangerous, we can't take any chances."

An avalanche of anxiety slammed into her. "You think he'd harm me? In the house?"

Hunter propped his elbows on his knees and clasped his fingers together. "We don't know anything about him, so it's better to be safe than sorry."

"I'll watch out for her," Grandpa said. "I still have a revolver someplace around here. My eyesight's not so good anymore, but if some guy came in here, I could take care of him."

A hint of a smile lifted Hunter's lips. "I'm sure you could."

Kerry felt the need to explain. "Grandpa was with the Tampa Police Department many moons ago."

"That makes me feel a whole lot better," Hunter said.

Kerry respected Hunter for making her grandfather feel important, though they all knew if someone with a gun burst through the door, her grandfather, at his age, wouldn't be able to stop the attacker.

"However," Hunter went on, "I'd be a lot happier if someone stayed with Kerry, twenty-four seven." Hunter looked around. "Is your husband here?"

The look of anticipation almost made her laugh. Too bad the seriousness of the situation weighed too heavy on her mind to experience amusement. "No. I don't have a husband."

"Oh." He coughed as though he needed a moment to regroup. "I'll have to see what the department can do then."

"Are we talking bodyguard here? If you are, I think you're overreacting. A police presence outside the house at night should be sufficient to scare someone away. I don't need round the clock protection. It was only a phone call."

"Kerry, I'm sure you've seen a lot in your line of business, but your skeletons have a look of death removed from their eyes. I know what evil lurks out there. You need protection. If anything happened to you, I'd never forgive myself."

She was surprised at his concern. "Then I guess a bodyguard it is, but where would he stay? Here?" Surely, Hunter wasn't volunteering?

"Once I figure out the logistics, I'll let you know." He tapped his knee. "On a different note, I did follow up on the photo you gave me of the ship tattoo on the woman's ankle." He pulled a piece a paper out of his top pocket. It was the fax she'd sent.

"Did you find the boat?"

"I searched Harbor Island, Davis Island, and the St. Petersburg marinas, but came up empty. Then my luck turned. There's a boat at the Tampa Yacht Club named 'Brandywine.'"

She mentally pictured the letters. "That could be it!" Finally, a ray of hope.

"We haven't turned the corner yet. I found the owner of the sail-boat, but he doesn't have a daughter."

"What about a wife, or an ex-wife?" she asked.

"I asked him. His current wife is alive and well. All other female relatives are accounted for. However, he told me he purchased the boat six months ago."

The usual ramping up of adrenaline dragged her out of her misery. She did the math. "We need to find the former owner."

"I'm one step ahead of you."

"You found him?" Her stomach fluttered.

He smiled as if they were a team. "Yes, only he wasn't home. The maid, who's English wasn't the best, said he'd call me back. When is anybody's guess."

"That's great. Do you have his address? Maybe we can go over there and wait for him to return."

He held up a hand. "Not so fast. I'll stop by soon if I don't hear from him."

She wanted action now. She needed a diversion to take her mind off the phone call.

Detective Markum slapped his thighs and stood. "From now on, Dr. Herlihy—"

"Kerry, please."

He nodded. "Kerry. Until I figure out how to protect you, please don't go out alone. When you're in the house, don't answer the door unless you—"

"Look in the peephole," she finished. "I know." Her mom had drilled in that particular life lesson. "What about driving to work?"

"I can take her," Grandpa said.

"With all due respect, I'd feel more comfortable driving her." Hunter's cell phone rang and he held up a finger. "Markum." After a moment, he mouthed, "Sailboat owner."

She leaned forward, searching his face for a clue.

"I see... I'd still like you to take a look at something that might belong to your daughter...Yes, I can come over now if that would be convenient." He patted his empty top pocket. He looked up and drew letters in the air.

She pulled open the drawer of the coffee table and handed him a pen. He sat back down and scribbled an address on the back of the fax she'd given him. "Thank you, sir." Hunter tapped the phone to disconnect.

"That was Chris Norwood. He said he hasn't heard from his daughter for over a year, but added they'd been estranged for as long. I'm going to interview him."

"I need to come with you," she said.

Her grandfather coughed. "You're a civilian, sweetheart. You can't go."

"Your grandfather's right."

"I'm not about to sit home while a maniac is on the loose. I can help. If the man has a photo of his daughter, I might be able to identify her. I'm the only one who's memorized her facial features."

Much to her surprise, she didn't want this time with Hunter to end. Like a warm, fleece blanket on a cold night, being with him made her feel safe—something she'd longed for, but had never found.

The detective stabbed a hand through his hair. His gaze bounced from left to right, obviously trying to weigh the odds of taking her.

"Fine. It's not like we're talking to a criminal. At least I hope we're not."

"I don't like it," Grandpa grumbled.

Hunter's lips pressed together. "I'll make certain nothing happens to her, sir. By working at the city morgue, indirectly, Kerry works for us."

"That's a stretch, but I know Kerry. She doesn't understand the word no."

Kerry's shoulders sagged. He made her sound like an inflexible person, an image she didn't like.

Hunter's cell rang again. He looked at the display. "Excuse me. It's my daughter." He stepped toward the foyer.

Daughter? So he was married. She refused to address the churning in her stomach.

She turned to Grandpa and kept her voice low. "Don't forget to lock all the doors, including the back door." After he took Buster for a walk, he often left it open. "And find that revolver. No telling what the maniac might do."

His spine stiffened, acting as though she'd tossed an insult at him. "I can take care of myself."

"Not at eighty-one, you can't."

"You don't know what I can do. I'm not so old I can't hit what I aim at. I'll do anything to protect you."

Now who was the stubborn one? "Fine."

She straightened the magazines on the coffee table and strained to hear what Hunter was saying on the phone, and how he said it.

"This detective is something else, isn't he?" Grandpa said, interrupting her eavesdropping. She turned. He had a gleam in his eye Kerry didn't care for.

She held a finger to her lips. "He'll hear you!" Grandpa's hearing wasn't the best, and he talked louder than most. "Besides he's married."

She returned her attention back to Hunter's conversation.

"Do what Aunt Jen says, okay, sweetheart? I'll be home soon...Love you too."

Her eyes widened. Aunt Jen? Did that mean Hunter didn't have a wife?

CHAPTER NINE

KERRY SHIFTED ON THE SOFA. From what she'd told him, she'd spent most of her time in the lab, not interviewing people.

Mr. Norwood sat ramrod straight, his white knuckles gripping the sofa arm. His jaw clenched. "How can you be sure the girl you found is my daughter?"

Hunter handed him the photo of the woman's ankle tattoo. "Sir, I'd like you to take a look at this. For confirmation."

"Oh my God. No." Mr. Norwood clasped the photo to his chest and squeezed his eyes shut. His breaths turned rapid and his lower lip trembled. A sob escaped as tears streaked down his cheeks. "I can't believe this is happening. My little girl can't be gone."

Hunter leaned forward. "Are you certain the image belongs to Janet?"

"Yes. My daughter had that tattoo done after the two of us took a two-week voyage together on my boat, the Brandywine."

"When was the last time you saw her?"

He swiped a handkerchief over his eyes. "Over a year ago, maybe? She and I, um, had a falling out."

"About what?"

He shook his head over and over again, clenched his teeth and inhaled. "I can't believe I never had the chance to say goodbye." He dropped his head into his hands and sobbed.

Hunter shot Kerry a glance. The man was hiding something.

Hunter's shoulders hunched and his lips pulled into a thin line. "Mr. Norwood, do you have a photo of your daughter?"

Norwood swallowed hard, dried his tears and stood. "Yes. I'll get one."

Head down, the man with the sleek silver hair and tailor-fitted suit lumbered down the long corridor lined with photographs. He slipped into one of the rooms and returned a moment later stroking his thumb on the frame.

He handed Hunter the photo. "This was the last picture I have of her. She'd been divorced for about two years from Stanton Grayson when I took it. She was twenty-five at the time."

"She's lovely." The daughter was balancing on the bow, holding onto the mast, the blue ocean sparkling behind her.

"Thank you. She was happy in that picture. She'd finally found another man to marry—David Kopetski."

Hunter handed the picture to Kerry. The girl's long hair flowed in the wind, and her bronzed skin and broad smile seemed to take Kerry's breath away. It was such a shame.

"I know this is a difficult time for you," Hunter said, "but what can you tell us about her physical abuse?"

Mr. Norwood's body went rigid. "I can't talk about it. I don't want to remember Janet in that way."

Hunter leaned forward. "I know this is hard for you, but your daughter wasn't the only body we found, sir."

Mr. Norwood's eyes widened. "There were more?"

"Three others. If we can understand what happened to her, perhaps we can help with the identities of the other victims and catch the person who did this to your daughter."

Norwood stared across the room before his gaze slowly reached the ground. "How am I going to tell my wife our daughter is dead? Sharon's in Europe right now. Oh, God. This will kill her."

"Please, Mr. Norwood. Anything you can tell us would be a great help," Hunter said.

He sniffled. "My wife knew more about Janet's first husband than I did. Stanton hit out daughter. Once my wife returns from her trip, she can give you more of the details." His lower jaw trembled. "Seems the women of the family liked to keep me out of the loop."

Kerry caught Hunter's eye. With raised brows and a nod in Norwood's direction, she silently signaled she wanted to ask a question. As if they'd known each other for years, he lifted his hand in a go ahead motion.

"When I looked at her bones, I noticed she'd had jaw reconstructive surgery. What can you tell us about that?"

Mr. Norwood tugged on his tie, and then swiped a handkerchief across his mouth. Poor man. Confirming a loved one had died was always the hardest part of her job. However, telling the family she'd identified their family member often brought them needed comfort, but apparently not in this case.

He took a deep breath. "We thought Stanton was the perfect man for Janet. Successful and part of a good family, he seemed to adore her. She married him when she was only twenty and still in school." He licked his lips and dragged a hand over his mouth. "Stanton was heading up the corporate ladder. They were happy at first, until she announced she didn't want children. Janet told her mom Stetson had gone berserk. She implied he'd gotten rough with her, though she refused to tell us much more."

Kerry guessed the getting rough part involved breaking her jaw. "Did she live nearby?"

"No. She and Stanton lived in Connecticut. You have to understand, my daughter was the independent sort. She attended Yale and graduated at the top of her class. Stanton needed to control everything around him, including my daughter."

"How did Janet react to her husband's demands?" Hunter said.

"React? Hell, she fought back against the constraint." Norwood shook his head. "After being pushed around too many times to count, she left him, left his money, and came home."

"I bet that pissed off Mr. Grayson," Hunter said.

"That's putting it mildly. Nobody makes a fool of Stanton Grayson III. The bastard followed her here and attacked her one night when

Sharon and I were attending the symphony. That's when he broke her jaw."

Just as Kerry was about to ask a question, Hunter placed a hand on her knee, indicating he wanted to continue. His touch jerked her out of the conversation for a minute. *Stop reacting to his every contact.*

"Mr. Norwood, where is her ex-husband now?" Hunter asked.

Was he thinking Stanton Grayson could be the serial killer? Her muscles froze.

Norwood shook his head. "I haven't heard from him since the incident. I imagine he's back in Connecticut. Why? Do you think he killed my little girl?"

"I may need to contact him." Hunter wrote something in his pad, and then looked up. "Were charges filed for battery?"

"No. We made a deal. He promised to stay away from Janet if we didn't press charges. As much as I hated him for hurting my daughter, he and I both understood his career would have been ruined if we had filed."

Norwood should be thinking more of his daughter and less about something bad happening to her abusive ex-husband.

"And did he?" Hunter asked. "Stay away from her?"

"As far as I know, he did."

Kerry believed Norwood wasn't telling them the whole truth, especially in regards to his strange reason for protecting Stanton. "You mentioned Janet and you were estranged. What happened?" she jumped in. Seems like the assault would have brought them closer.

His jaw hardened. He remained silent for so long, she wondered if he would answer.

"Janet was a bright girl. She worked at a bonds desk at a large bank here in Tampa and did very well for the two years after her divorce from Stanton. As a matter of fact, that's where she met her second husband, David Kopetski. He seemed like a real nice guy—at first. He was nothing like Stanton, I'd thought." He loosened his tie. "Boy was I wrong."

"How so?" she said, keeping her tone soft.

"Sharon started noticing the bruises on Janet's arms, legs, and neck about five months into their marriage. Janet figured out long before my wife or I that David was as manipulative as her first husband. My daughter decided to leave before he seriously hurt her." He hung his head and ran both hands over his head. "God, it sickens me. I should have helped her, should have seen how desperate she was."

"Sir?"

"Instead of coming to me for the money to leave David, she embezzled the bank's funds. She was desperate to escape the vicious cycle of abusive men and knew how much it would cost to start a new life someplace else." He tunneled his fingers and touched the index fingers to his lips.

Kerry could guess the result. "And she got caught."

"Yes."

"Is that when you lost contact with your daughter?" Hunter asked.

"I'm ashamed to say, yes." He locked his gaze with Kerry. "I'll never be able to tell her I'm sorry." Norwood leaned back in his chair. His cheeks sagged. "You have to understand. I'm a lawyer. I was too embarrassed to let my clients or my cohorts know I had a daughter in prison. What kind of father would that have made me?" He dropped his head into his hands, and his back heaved. Mr. Norwood sat back and wiped the tears from his cheek. "I never should have turned my back on her."

Kerry agreed. Someone needed to protect Janet after Stanton hurt her. She wondered what information the ex-husband held over Mr. Norwood's head.

Norwood cleared his throat. "I knew the exact date and time when Janet was scheduled to be released from prison, but by then, she wouldn't talk to either me or my wife. In fact, she demanded we stay away. When I didn't hear from her after her release, I figured she was still mad at us and had moved on. My wife and I never even knew if Janet succeeded in divorcing him. When David Kopetski wouldn't talk to us, we just figured Janet finally disappeared like she'd wanted to."

Poor Mr. Norwood. "That must have been tough."

"Deep in my heart," he continued. "I knew something bad had happened to her." His chin trembled. "Now I know why she never answered our calls or letters."

"I'm so sorry, Mr. Norwood," Kerry said. "If I could ask you one more question. Recently, Janet had a broken collarbone. Do you know how that happened?"

His mouth dropped open. "A broken collarbone? No, I knew nothing about that. Perhaps she injured herself in prison."

Hunter kept writing. When he finished, he looked up. "We'll check it out. Thank you for your time." He handed Mr. Norwood a business card. "I put my cell phone number on the back in case you think of anything."

Kerry touched Hunter's arm. "One more question if you don't mind? Do you know the name of Janet's dentist? I'd like to compare her dental charts with the X-rays of her mouth to be sure we have a match."

Mr. Norwood took a moment before he answered. "No, I'm sorry. There wouldn't be two women with that tattoo, would there? It's so unique. There's no other boat with the name of Brandywine in the area. At least, not that I've seen."

"We want to be sure."

"Okay." He checked the time. "I'll contact my wife tomorrow morning—time zone differences—and see what she can tell us."

Hunter thanked him again for his help and led Kerry outside. The air was muggy and warm, but a refreshing spray from the driveway fountain blew over her face as they headed to the cruiser.

"There's something funny about that guy," she said.

"How so?"

"It's almost as if he's in cahoots with his former son-in-law. He should have reported the abuse to the authorities. Do you think he had anything to do with Janet's death?"

"The father?"

She wanted to strangle Hunter. "Yes, the father."

"Everyone is a suspect until proven innocent."

Good answer. "So now what do we do?"

He glanced over at her. The moonlight reflected off his strong face.

"I take you home."

"Oh." She liked being with Hunter in search of the horrid person who killed these innocent women. Hunter seemed so in control, so safe, so comforting. "I appreciate you letting me come with you. I know it was against the rules."

The entire time they were interviewing Mr. Norwood, she'd completely forgotten about the angry caller.

"You were a help," he said. "Thank you."

Embarrassed by his unexpected compliment, she changed the subject. "What happens tomorrow? Are we going to follow up with Kopetski?"

He opened the cruiser door for her and she slid in. Once she snapped on the seat belt, he leaned his head in close enough for her to kiss him—not that she would. It might be nice to taste his lips though. Just once. But not until she knew for sure he didn't have a wife.

Ask him, ask him. She wished the annoying person in her head would take a chill pill.

"—check out Janet's second husband. Alone. He might have been the last person to see her alive. He also might be dangerous."

Before she could remember what she'd asked him, Hunter clicked the door closed and raced around to the driver's side. Once he was seated, Kerry broached a safer topic. "I believe I can help." She flipped a strand of hair out of her face. "Let me rephrase that. I want to help, need to help with this case."

"You're not with the department. I don't bring civilians with me if I can help it."

"You said I was indirectly with the department since I work at the medical examiners office. You let me come here."

"That was different." His response came without delay. "I didn't want to argue with your grandfather. Besides we know nothing about this Kopetski guy. It's too dangerous."

He had a point. "We knew nothing about Mr. Norwood either." David Kopetski might be as dangerous as her angry caller. Hell, he might *be* the angry caller. "If you're there, what harm could there be?"

"Kerry, I won't chance it. I can't stop a bullet."

"O-kay. Can I make the call to the prison to see if Janet injured herself before her release?"

His face relaxed. "That you can do."

He seemed focused on his driving, not saying another word for the next ten minutes, and the silence was making her crazy.

"Hunter?" He didn't answer. Here goes. "It's rather late. Isn't your wife worried where you are?"

The planes of his jaw tightened. "My wife is... dead."

"Oh." The air pressed down on her, squeezing the life from her lungs. "I'm sorry."

"So am I."

She coughed into the crux of her elbow. "Will you let me know what happens after you speak with Kopetski?" She kept her voice upbeat, though the embarrassment cut her to the core.

Hunter glanced at her and smiled. Actually, smiled, and her pulse sped up. "Don't worry. I promise to keep you in the loop if that's what's bothering you."

"Thanks."

Her body nearly floated off the seat. Hunter Markum was single. Not that she'd get seriously involved with him, but a fling might make her stay here more pleasant.

You're kidding yourself. Since when did you do one-night stands? Never. But that didn't mean she couldn't start, right?

His smile disappeared and changed into a frown. "I want to pick you up tomorrow morning, drive you to work, and then take you home." He reached over and gently clasped her arm as he kept his gaze on the road. "No arguing on this point. I was serious when I said I didn't want you out alone."

"Grandpa said he'd drive me."

"And give someone a chance to sneak into your house?"

Her delightful daydream evaporated. "You think I'm in that much danger?" Her stomach twisted.

"Why take a chance?"

Having a personal bodyguard would give her peace of mind.

Right. Peace of mind? Who was she kidding?

* * *

"I'M BEGINNING to think this Willie Wyble guy is a figment of Mr. DeMarco's imagination," Phil said as he pulled into the cemetery lot.

He'd come here every day for the last week. No Willie Wyble.

"Did you run his prints in AFIS?" Gina asked.

Phil chuckled. "You're really liking all this police stuff, aren't you?"

"I think it's exciting."

She tucked her left leg under her butt and twisted toward him, making her skirt ride high on her thigh.

Phil swallowed. "That so?"

"Compared to teaching fourteen year olds about Alexander the Great for four hours a day, police work is like being in Disney World."

Boy, did she have a lot to learn. "Personally, I couldn't stand history. Math and science were more my thing." Phil cut the engine and jumped out in front of the cemetery building. The intense heat nearly melted his badge.

Gina slid out and stretched, her breasts straining against her top. Man she was something else. He looked away. He didn't need the distraction, and sure as hell didn't need the trouble.

Gina sidled up to him and ran a finger down his arm. "I bet if you'd been my student, you wouldn't be so disdainful about the subject."

He wished she'd stop flirting. His defenses were already on shaky grounds. "You might be right."

She smiled. "Do you hear that?"

Birds chirped, and car engines sounded behind them on the main road. "Hear what?"

"I'll be right back."

Without asking his permission, she rushed around to the side of the cemetery building where they held services. A moment later, she peeked her head back around and waved. "I see a tractor."

Don't tell him their luck had changed. He raced next to her. "Where?"

She pointed off to the right. "He went behind those trees a second ago."

Phil strained to hear the grumble of a far away engine. He looked down at her sandals. "Mind walking?"

"No. Just make sure you keep up."

This time he laughed. Compared to Hunter, Gina was a breath of sunshine. She raced ahead and he had to jog to catch up.

By the time they reached the tree line, sweat had stained his shirt. Even Gina looked like she was ready to drop, but to her credit, she didn't complain.

They neared the Caterpillar backhoe, which was a blend of yellow and rust. "When the cat's away the mouse will play," Phil said, recalling that DeMarco claimed Willie was only allowed to dig at night. It wouldn't turn dark around here for another three hours. He wondered if Jeff Lamont, the cemetery owner, knew what Willie was up to right now.

Phil waved his arms, but the driver ignored him. Phil practically had to jump in front of the scoop before the operator cut the engine.

"Hey, you're in my way, Mister."

"You Willie Wyble?" Phil asked.

"Maybe. Who's asking?"

"Phil Tedesco." He didn't need to mention he was a cop. That might shut him up. "Can I talk to you for a minute?"

Willie scrunched his hat on his head. "You here to buy worms?"

"Wish I had the time to go fishing. No, I need to ask about Mr. DeMarco."

Willie looked around as though Demarco, or perhaps Mr. Lamont, were hiding behind the trees, spying on him. "What about him?"

This was not the best setting to discuss whether Willie had anything to do with the theft of the body, but beggars couldn't be choosers. "Are you digging this hole for one of his...customers?"

Willie pressed his lips together.

"Are you?"

"You gonna tell Mr. Lamont?" Fear rolled off Willie.

"No. I was just curious." Phil shifted to the left to move out of the low-lying sun's path. "Do you dig a lot of holes just for the hell of it?"

"Sometimes. Usually late at night when no one can see me, but tonight I got another job. That's why I'm digging now."

Phil bet Lamont would be pissed if he ever found out. "Doing what?"

Willie's lips curled up. "Not telling."

Gina moved up next to Phil. "Hi, Willie."

Willie studied Gina. "Who are you?"

"Just a friend." She took a step closer and put her hand on the trac-tor. Phil wanted to pull her away, to keep her from harm, but Willie didn't move a muscle.

"I don't have any friends." Willie's lips turned into a frown. "Well, maybe one."

She glanced at Phil, and then back at Willie. "You said you like to dig holes. Did you dig any over at Westchase a couple of months ago?"

"Maybe."

Phil was beginning to lose patience, and the hot, muggy evening wasn't helping his mood. "Maybe yes, or maybe no, Willie?"

Willie started the engine again and put the tractor into gear. Gina jumped out of the way. Phil shouted at him to stop. About a minute later, Willie cut the engine again. "I can't go to prison. I have to be outside. Digging. People need the worms. I have to dig."

"Willie, you didn't do anything wrong if that's what worrying you," Phil said. No law against lying.

"Wrong?" He shook his head. "Willie didn't do nothin' wrong. I have to make a livin' you know."

Gina looked like she was going to jump on the tractor next to Willie and beat the truth out of him. Phil took her hand and squeezed hard, and that one touch shot his mind off on a tangent. "Do you dig holes for people other than Mr. Lamont or Mr. DeMarco?" Phil kept his tone even despite the erotic thoughts running through him at the moment. He released her hand.

"Sometimes."

"So you dig holes when people hire you. Do you know what goes in the hole after you dig it?" Phil wasn't sure about his mental capacity.

"Shit yeah, I do. A body."

Willie wasn't all that dumb, despite the fact they were having this discussion at a cemetery. "Let's get back to Westchase. Who did you dig the hole for?"

"I can't say."

"Willie, do I need to subpoena you?"

Willie ran his hand up and down the lever that controlled the scoop. "What's subpoena?"

"It means if I ask you a question, you have to tell the truth." He didn't add that Willie might have to go to court. He didn't want to scare the poor guy to death.

"It was some foreigner."

"Mr. Hakeem?"

Willie looked around again as if he expected the cemetery owner to catch him doing something he shouldn't. Phil asked again. "Willie?"

Willie turned on the ignition and began to dig again. Gina stepped forward, grabbed hold of the tractor and placed a foot on the step.

CHAPTER TEN

PHIL DRUMMED his fingers on the conference room table and leaned toward Gina. "You can't just go off half-cocked around a person of interest."

His head pounded with *what if* scenarios. What if Willie had harmed Gina? What if Willie had run them over? God. He'd given her free reign for a moment, and she'd abused the power.

Gina leaned back and rubbed her eyes. "You keep saying that. Get over it. Nothing happened."

"This time. Willie Wyble could have had a gun."

She crossed her arms over her chest. "He was harmless. If he'd been armed, he would have shot you on sight."

"Me? You're the one who tried to sit next to him. What were you thinking?" His voice shook.

"I told you in the car. I was trying to extract more information from him. Ever heard the phrase, you can catch more flies with honey than vinegar."

"That's not the point."

"Whatever. I'm fine. You're fine."

He'd confiscated one of the rooms at the station for some place quiet while they searched for Mr. Hakeem's photo in the police logs and make phone calls to all the Hakeems. Some quiet.

She pulled the phone book closer to her. "I thought you wanted me to continue calling."

"I do. I also want you to admit what you did was stupid."

"Okay, I'm sorry, but if you hadn't pulled me from the tractor, we would have learned something."

"It's not how we do it here." Phil forced calm into his tone.

"Whatever." Gina opened the book, thumbed through half the pages, grunted and slammed the book closed. "We'll never find this guy. There are a million Hakeems in here."

Hardly a million. "Try eight."

From her subdued tone and her slumped shoulders, perhaps he'd been too hard on her. She wasn't totally at fault. She didn't know police procedure. Hell, he should have given her a heads up about interviewing techniques.

Actually, he blamed himself for even bringing her with him to talk to Willie in the first place. The old guy probably was harmless, but she shouldn't have interfered with the interrogation.

Phil shoved a box of blueberries toward her as a peace offering. "I'm sorry I yelled."

She smiled and straightened. "That's okay. Does that mean I can stop calling?"

"Police work is about never giving up. Try a few more names." Phil failed to keep his tone stern. Man, the woman had a way of getting under his skin.

"Why can't we ask Samson DeMarco's brother about the files? They might contain this man's contact information."

He had to hand it to her. The woman was bright. "I already tried to get a hold of the brother, but he's out of town for a few more days."

"Let's go back and make Willie talk." Her adorable lips puckered.

"I understand your frustration. I'm frustrated too, but we can't make someone confess if he doesn't want to."

"I think he knows something about the body."

"I agree, but we have no evidence to bring him in." He didn't have time to teach her everything about police regulations.

She leaned forward and her breasts nearly popped out of her top. Dear God in heaven, it was hard to look at her and not drool.

Phil pulled his cell phone from his pocket. "I'm hoping Lefevre is back. He handled the DeMarco case." He turned his back to the enticing hottie and punched the number for the front desk. Mac Gibbons answered.

"Say, Mac. It's Tedesco. Is Lefevre back yet from vacation?"

"Yeah, he's about twenty feet behind me. He came back today."

"Thanks."

Phil disconnected and turned to Gina. "I'm going to see what Lefevre knows about this Hakeem guy. There's no use wasting our time reinventing the wheel."

She huffed. "Why didn't you think of that before you made me do all this work?"

God, she looked so cute when she was angry, but that didn't mean he wasn't still pissed at the stupid stunt she'd pulled today in the field. "I thought you'd like to practice the investigative techniques."

"Fuck you," she said with an engaging smile.

Love to.

* * *

FOR THE FIFTH time in the last half hour Hunter passed by Kerry's house. An old couple walked across the street with their dog, and two teenagers raced down the middle of the street on bikes.

If the angry caller was smart enough to find Kerry's phone number, he could figure out her address. There were plenty of places to hide in this tree-lined neighborhood.

Damn. The queasiness that crawled around in his stomach every time someone he knew was in danger came back full force. That's why he'd picked Kerry up for work and dropped her home again. At least when she was in his car, the killer had little chance of harming her.

Kerry's grandfather said he and his friends could stand watch at night. Hunter appreciated their offer, but he couldn't trust men in their seventies or eighties to have the best reflexes. It didn't matter they used to be cops.

As he circled her block again, his cell rang. He glanced at the display and tensed. The number wasn't a familiar one.

"Markum."

"This is David Kopetski. You left a message to call you?"

Janet's husband. Hunter eased over to the shoulder, his mind racing with questions. "Thanks for the call back. I wanted to ask you about your wife, Janet."

There was a long pause. "What about her? I haven't heard from her in a long time."

No shit, since she died a year ago. "Can we meet someplace to discuss her?"

"Who the hell are you?" The man had definite anger management issues.

Hunter had told him he was with the sheriff's department when he'd called the first time. Apparently, some people don't listen. "Hunter Markum. Hillsborough County Homicide."

"Homicide? Is she dead?"

The man's lack of concern caused a cold knot to form below Hunter's ribs. "We believe so, Mr. Kopetski. I'm sorry."

"Shit. She probably got what she deserved. Did you know she was an ex-con?"

So he knew of her release. "Yes. Could we talk? This won't take long. I can swing by your place if you'd like."

"I have nothing to hide." He gave Hunter his address.

Leaving Kerry's neighborhood to speak with Kopetski bothered him. Not that he planned on driving around until she went to bed, but he wanted to make sure if someone was watching, they'd know she was under surveillance.

If he took Kerry with him, she'd be able to add detailed information about the woman's abuse. If by some chance Kopetski turned violent, Hunter would make sure nothing happened to Kerry.

Who was he kidding? He shouldn't take her on a police matter even though she was involved in the case, but he worried about leaving her alone, unprotected. She'd be safer with him. Or so he told himself.

To be honest, he liked being with her, became lost in her warm green eyes and dreamed of touching her soft skin. Today, when he'd driven her home, he'd caught her glancing his way a couple of times. The moment he caught her eye, she tossed him a little smile before looking away. Man did his heart skip a beat or what.

Fuck it. He dialed her number before he changed his mind.

"Tom Hardy."

"Tom. Hunter Markum. Is Kerry around?"

"Sure. I'm not letting her out of my sight if I can help it."

Hunter smiled. He liked Tom.

A moment later she was on the phone. "Hunter? Did someone call about the reconstruction?"

He hated to dampen her hope. "No, I'm sorry. Janet Kopetski's second husband just returned my call. He's willing to meet."

"That's great."

"Do you want to come with me? I thought maybe having—"

"Yes. When?"

He chuckled at her enthusiasm. "How soon can you be ready?"

"I'm ready now."

"I'll be there in two." He hung up before she questioned why he was nearby.

She wouldn't be happy he was circling her house, but too damned bad. The caller was a potential killer and posed a threat to her.

Hunter pulled into her drive and smiled at the picture she made standing outside her front door. He liked how the lamps around the base of the trees illuminated the leaves and cast a nice glow on the single-story home. It was harder for someone to sneak up to the place.

When Kerry climbed into the cruiser, a mixture of sweet and sour hung in the air—like lemons and cinnamon, a scent he'd remember a lifetime as Kerry's.

"Thanks for inviting me."

The chocolate richness of her words pulled him out of his sensual journey. He inhaled, needing to move back to safer ground. "You didn't receive any more calls, did you?"

"No. Why?"

"You never know with some crackpots." He didn't want to scare her too much. "I did some digging into Janet's first husband, Stanton Grayson. Seems he was, or rather is, an accomplished lawyer. While they lived in Connecticut, she filed for divorce and stated abuse as the reason. It was thrown out of court for lack of evidence."

"That doesn't surprise me. The husband probably pulled enough strings to get the court case tossed." She crossed her arms over her chest.

"Probably."

"Did you find any evidence hubby tried to reconcile?"

"No."

"I wouldn't be surprised if Grayson wanted to see her one more time after he'd broken her jaw." She set her purse on the floor between her legs. "Maybe he feared she'd try to reopen the lawsuit. A lawyer wouldn't like to be exposed as a wife beater."

"That's true." Hunter backed out of her drive. "Let's see what Kopetski has to say before I contact Stanton Grayson."

"Good idea." Kerry leaned her head back against the seat. She looked as exhausted as he felt. He wished the police had the manpower for around the clock surveillance, but until Kerry was physically threatened, he'd have to be content to motor past her place himself.

He handed her the directions to Kopetski's place. In less than twenty minutes, they were at the man's home, or rather his shack. His living accommodations were not what Hunter had expected, given Janet had married well the first time around.

In the dark, it was hard to see how much the paint had faded on the one-story wood-framed house, but the missing shutter on the front window told him Kopetski didn't visit Home Depot on a regular basis. The grass, or maybe weeds, hadn't been cut in weeks. The trashcan by the curb had been knocked over and its contents littered the drive. The heat mixed with the rotting food filled the air with a rancid stench.

Kerry stepped around the strewn beer cans and other unidentifiable contents but didn't comment.

Kopetski jerked open the door on the first knock. Legs wide, he scowled, narrowed his eyes and planted both hands on the doorframe. The odor of alcohol rolled off him. The stained wife-beater T-shirt only added to the cliché of an abuser. At least the elastic-waist nylon shorts, flip flops, and too tight shirt gave him no place to hide a weapon.

Why had the man returned his call? To see how much Hunter knew?

"Mr. Kopetski?" Hunter asked, flashing his badge.

Kopetski grunted, turned around, and headed toward the living room. The guy didn't stagger. Good. Nor did he acknowledge Kerry—a good sign he might not be the one hunting her.

Hunter and Kerry followed him into a musty, smoky living room. He debated asking Kerry to return to the cruiser to wait until the interview was over, but right now, he needed her expertise.

Without waiting for an invitation, Hunter sat on the sofa, leaving the cleaner-looking chair to Kerry. A dirty plate and half empty coffee mug sat on a table between the sofa and the two chairs. The slob had tossed two pairs of Jockey shorts on the floor in the corner.

"Mr. Kopetski, when was the last time you saw your wife, or rather your ex-wife?"

He scratched his chin. "Must be over a year now."

"Why did you two divorce?" Hunter wondered if he'd admit to the abuse.

"Irreconcilable differences."

"Was that before or after she landed in prison?"

"Before."

"Did you talk to your ex-wife after she was released from prison?"

The man's shoulders stiffened and his lips firmed. "And if I did?"

Hunter scribbled a note in his pad about Kopetski's belligerent response. "I'm here only to gather information. We found the remains of a woman with a tattoo on her ankle. The particular shape led us to her father who identified the tattoo as belonging to your ex."

"So?"

So? What an asshole. "Did you stay in contact with Janet throughout her incarceration?"

Kopetski swiped a hand across his mouth. "I tried, but she wouldn't talk to me."

Hunter didn't buy the guy's story. "When she was released, did you contact her?"

"Maybe."

If Kopetski had nothing to hide, why wasn't he more cooperative? And why call back? Disgusted, Hunter caught Kerry's attention, jerked his head in the direction of the door and raised his brows.

Kerry held up a discreet finger. "Mr. Kopetski, I'm a forensic anthropologist, which means I examine bones. Janet had a broken right collarbone shortly before her death. Do you know what happened?"

Kopetski looked to the right, then to the left. "Yeah. She was carrying a heavy suitcase downstairs from the bedroom. She was almost to the bottom when her foot caught, and she fell." He glanced to his feet, then back at Hunter. "Say, do I need a lawyer or something?"

"Only if you killed your wife."

Kopetski jumped up from the couch, his lips pulled back in a sneer and his fists clenched at his side. "Fuck that. I didn't touch the bitch. She fell on her own."

Hunter shot to his feet and stepped in front of Kerry, his hand on his weapon. "I merely asked a question."

"Fuck the question. I didn't do shit."

Hunter wondered how he could get Kerry out of there without a confrontation. Before he formulated a plan, Kopetski crumpled back to the sofa.

Hunter released his breath but remained standing. "What were you doing with her the night she fell?"

"I found some stuff of hers in my garage, so I called her to come pick up her crap."

This place didn't have stairs. He must have been living somewhere else—or else he was lying. "Did you take her to the hospital after the accident?" There'd be a record if he did.

"She wouldn't let me. She called a friend who came and picked her up, along with her stuff."

"Do you know the name of this friend?"

"No." Kopetski stood.

Enough was enough. "Thanks for your time. If you leave town, let me know." Hunter dropped his business card on the coffee table.

He grabbed Kerry's hand and hurried her outside. The last thing he wanted was her around if a fight broke out.

Even heavy with moisture, the warm, fresh air was a hell of a lot better than the cigarette-laden house interior. Hunter cut across the lawn to avoid the stinking trash in the drive. He held Kerry's hand long after they were safely outside, and a feeling of comfort blanketed him. It was the first time since Amy had died he'd been at ease.

He released his grip to open the car door and said nothing until he'd pulled out of Kopetski's drive. "So what do you think?"

"Think? He's a drunk, he's angry, and I wouldn't want him for a husband."

Hunter chuckled, but his laugh contained little joy. "You got that right."

Kerry twisted in her seat and tucked her leg underneath. "Mr. Norwood mentioned Janet met this guy at work. Brokers usually make a fairly good living. This guy looked like he barely had enough money for food and certainly not enough for cleaning help."

"I agree. With his temper though, I wouldn't be surprised if he lost his job though. His anger could have stemmed from the rejection from the wife or because the market wasn't doing well. I'll check out the case file for Janet's arrest. It might give us a clue about what kind of man we're dealing with."

"Good thinking, detective."

Her compliment lightened his anxiety. "The break in the collarbone. How severe was it? Would it require something other than a sling and some ibuprofen?"

"Hers was bad. Enough to require some screws and a small plate."

Hunter pulled onto Dale Mabry Highway, away from David Kopetski. "This woman had a broken collarbone and a broken jaw." He shook his head in despair. "I don't understand how a man could hit a woman."

"Me neither. Her jaw injury was older than the collarbone break, which fits with the story her father told us." She slapped the dash. "Damn. Janet had a nick in the bone of her right index finger."

Hunter braked at the light and looked over at her. "So?"

"A collarbone break is a routine operation, probably done by someone in Emergency. I could tell from the coloration of the bone in the finger her injury was right before her death."

Someone behind him honked and he diverted his attention back to the road. "How could that lead us to a suspect?"

"In order for the bone to be chipped, the finger would have been close to being severed."

"Go on." Was she thinking the killer did this?

"If she didn't get immediate help, she would have bled to death."

"And how do we know bleeding to death wasn't the cause of death?"

"From the smoothness around the bone chip, her finger had been repaired."

"Could someone in Emergency have handled it?"

"The hospital would have called in a vascular surgeon to reconnect the tiny blood vessels. It's exacting work and takes a specialist. I've also known plastic surgeons who do this type of vascular work. One doesn't rule out the other."

He slapped the steering wheel. "Why do we always come back to doctors?"

"Because we believe they are there to help."

CHAPTER ELEVEN

HUNTER WALKED Kerry to her front door. She liked being around Hunter, liked his chivalry. She couldn't remember the last time a man had worried about her so much—other than her grandpa.

"I'll pick you up at quarter to eight Monday morning," Hunter said.

"I feel bad you're taking so much time out of your day. If I park in the garage, I'm sure I'll be safe to drive to work. I wish I could have Grandpa to take me, but he's kind of a scary driver."

"It's no bother. Really."

A small thrill lightened her step knowing someone was watching out for her—and not just anyone, but Hunter Markum.

Once she threw the deadbolt on the door, she peered through the peephole and watched him trail back to his car.

She turned around. "Hi, Gramps."

No surprise, Grandpa was waiting up for her on the sofa reading a frayed-edged magazine. He wasn't reading a word if the speed with which he flipped the pages was any indication.

The Jack Russell jumped at her legs, and Grandpa clapped his hands. "Down Buster. Come here, boy."

The dog obeyed. Her cell phone rang, and she smiled. It was Hunter. "Yes, Detective?"

"I had a thought. Could Kopetski have been your angry caller?"

Kerry's joy evaporated. She'd rather have spiders crawling over her body than be in a room with a man vicious enough to kill those women.

She stepped over to the chair across from the sofa and slid onto the seat, grasping the arm. "I'm not sure." She tried to replay the stranger's voice in her mind but couldn't come up with any distinctive accent or odd speech patterns. "The man on the phone hadn't spoken more than a few sentences. To be honest, I didn't pay attention to Mr. Kopetski's voice, but it's possible. Both men were angry." She bit down on her lip. "But what would have been his motive? Murdering his wife, Janet, I could buy, but would he have killed Jane Doe #1?"

"Who's to say, until we know who #1 is." A horn honked in the background. "Try this scenario. Maybe #1 worked at the same firm as Janet, or perhaps she was a neighbor who witnessed the abuse."

"You're blowing this situation out of proportion." At least she hoped he was.

"I'm worried this guy might come after you."

She swallowed hard. "Why would he do that?"

"Kopetski knows you can learn things from his wife's bones."

"So?"

"Kerry, I've seen too many times when witnesses get harmed."

"I'll be fine. Besides, I'm not a witness, per se. I promise I'll lock all my doors. If our weirdo calls again, I'll let you know. And this time, I'll listen to his cadence, memorize how he sounds." Buster rushed over to her and licked her hand. She ran a hand down his back.

"Let's hope it doesn't come to that. Call me if you plan to leave your house tomorrow, okay? If you have to go to church even, take your grandfather with you."

"Goodnight, Hunter." She disconnected and slipped the phone into her top pocket.

"What did he want?" Grandpa asked, as he flipped through the torn magazine, again without looking at the pages.

"Just making sure I was safe."

"If you ask me, it sounded more like he thought you were in some kind of danger."

"Hunter is a worry-wart, that's all."

"I like that young man."

She half-smiled. "Me too." Hunter was a sweetie, even if he had a wild imagination.

Her phone rang again. She rolled her eyes and swiped on the phone. Hunter needed to get a life. "Yes, Hunter."

"Kerry?"

It wasn't Hunter. It was a woman's voice. "Yes."

"Oh, Kerry, I'm so glad I got a hold of you. Didn't Grandpa tell you I wanted to speak to you?"

Susan. Her stomach rolled. "Yes, he did. I've... been busy."

"Grandpa told me about your cases. I wished I could have been there to watch you on TV. Was it exciting?"

Exciting? "No, Susan. Four women and an infant are dead. Nothing about that is exciting."

"I'm sorry."

Susan paused so long, Kerry thought they'd been disconnected. "You there?"

"Yes. Look, I know I screwed things up between us, but I had my reasons." Her voice shook. "I was thinking about coming for a short visit. Would you meet me if I came?"

Susan would come whether Kerry gave her permission or not. The hurt swirled inside her, and Kerry tamped it down. Maybe if she were able to admit to her sister how much Susan's actions had torn her apart, Kerry might be able to heal. "Sure."

"That's wonderful. I'll call when I get into town. Bye."

She hung up just like that. Kerry shook her head. Good ole Susan. Some things never changed. How much time would Susan allow her to prepare for this uncomfortable trip?

Grandpa looked up expectantly. "So you finally connected. What did Susan say?"

"She's coming to visit."

Her grandfather stilled. "I don't know if that's such a good idea." He looked away.

Kerry moved from the chair to the sofa, and Buster snuggled next to her. "Time out. You've been pushing for the reunion since I came here. What are you hiding?" Kerry didn't like the idea of seeing her sister again, but Grandpa apparently had a different reason for not wanting her to come.

He ran his gnarled fingers along the front cover of the ragged magazine. "I, ah, probably should have told you this a long time ago, but when Susan lived here, she had a boyfriend who abused her." His eyes watered.

"Abused her?" Guilt waved its ugly head, followed by a rush of anger. "Why didn't she tell me?"

"She wasn't proud of how she'd handled Brad. Actually, she left Tampa because of him. Had to run away in fact and disappear for good. Even I don't know where she went. She uses a pre-pay phone card when she calls so it can't be traced."

The horror of the situation took Kerry's breath away. "Was he that bad?"

"She never gave me any details. I'm sure she has a lot more to tell you."

"What else?" He dropped the magazine on the table and looked away. "Oh, no you don't. You can't drop the bomb then not tell me."

"It's Susan's story to tell." He eased off the sofa. "Let's go for a walk, Buster."

Damn him. She hated when he clammed up. It wouldn't do any good to question him though. The man could keep a secret better than an angry pit bull could hold onto its victim.

* * *

KERRY DIDN'T HAVE the luxury of a relaxing weekend. The clock was ticking. She needed to identify the three women and the infant, make more reconstructions, find little oddities in their bones that would help her find out who they were, and learn how they'd died.

She'd arrived at the lab over an hour ago but had managed to place only a few markers on #3's skull. Her mind still reeled from what Grandpa had told her about her sister. My God. What if Brad had hurt Susan enough to kill her? Her sister could have been one of these women.

Kerry couldn't image the horror of someone knocking on her door and telling her Susan was dead. Kerry shivered and forced herself to get to work. Wouldn't Hunter be pissed she'd driven herself to work instead of him chauffeuring her? Grandpa didn't want to sit in the lab all day, especially on a Saturday when the place was dead—no pun intended. She had no choice but to come alone. Hunter would yell and complain about her being careless and not following his directive, but too damn bad.

If he found out, he'd repeat the litany about how she needed to make sure she checked the back seat of her car before getting in, locked her car doors before she started the engine, and not to become distracted when she went from the parking lot to the office across the street.

He acted as though she'd come from the boonies. Okay, maybe she had at one time in her life, but she'd lived several years in Baton Rouge and that was no small town.

When her phone rang, she shuffled through her purse to find her cell, and then checked the display. Gotta love caller ID. "Hi, Hunter. What's up?" *Please don't let him ask where I am.*

"I've been doing research on Janet Kopetski."

"Find anything out?"

"Seems she was a model prisoner. The bonds desk where she worked told me she was a top-notch investor. I also spoke with two of her coworkers and neither one even knew she was married."

He gathered some amazing information for a weekend. The man must have major contacts. "Abuse is not only terrible but embarrassing. I can see why she kept quiet about her ex."

"You haven't figured anything else out about the case, have you?"

She stilled. Did he know she was at work? "No, but you'll be the first to know when I do."

"Okay, I'll see you Monday morning."

The moment the connection died, disappointment hit. She'd wanted to ask him how he was holding up, if he was sleeping okay, and eating enough—like everyday conversation between two people who cared.

Kerry moved back to the half done skull, and a renewed sense of anticipation and energy filled her. Talking with Hunter helped center her attention on these women, in part because he was a non-stop whirlwind of information and in part because his passion for justice was infectious.

She'd wondered more than once when he had time for his six-year old daughter. With his wife dead, she imagined taking care of the little girl was doubly hard.

Kerry pushed aside the thoughts of the dedicated man and returned to work on #3's face. She didn't want to let Hunter or the families down.

Discovering patterns drove Kerry to work harder. She'd loved puzzles as a child and became a whiz at cryptograms and crosswords by the age of fourteen. When Sudoku came on the scene, she knew she couldn't even try one for fear she'd get nothing done once she started to arrange the numbers.

These four women were a puzzle in their own right. If she studied them enough, she might learn how their deaths were connected.

Kerry measured and cut more clay strips that would give life to #3. Hunter's partner was working on the theory that an undertaker had dumped the bodies. She admitted these women could have been runaways, like Janet Kopetski. Janet's dad hadn't spoken to her for quite a while before she died. Perhaps phone calls went unanswered when the undertaker tried to contact the families, and not wanting to foot the bill for the burial, decided on dumping rather than burying. It was far-fetched, but not outside the realm of possibility.

Kerry finished gluing the markers on the skull before placing the first piece of clay on #3's forehead.

"Dr. H?"

She jerked at the voice. A young man stood at her door staring at the floor. He worked at the ME's office. What was his name?

"Yes?"

He waited a moment. "I'm Dr. A's autopsy tech, Steven." He made eye contact, something he hadn't done before.

Her shoulders relaxed. "Ah, yes. I'm sorry. You helped with the infant we brought in a couple of days ago."

"Uh, huh. I, ah, wanted to see if you needed anything." His grin had a boyish charm.

"Actually, yes. Do you know if Dr. A is around?" John Ahern's nickname sounded funny, but then again, so did Dr. H.

"He just left. He has the Monday to Friday shift. He only came in today because he had some paperwork to do. I don't think he knew you were here or he would have stopped by."

She wished he had. Kerry enjoyed this short interruption in her day but couldn't for the life of her figure out the point of the visit. Certainly, he wasn't flirting with her. He was a good five years younger than her.

"I'll let you know if I need anything."

He shifted his weight from one foot to the other, and then smiled. Cute guy, but not her type. He was too GQ. An image of Hunter flashed in her mind. She liked his more serious attitude toward life.

"Well, take care. And be safe," he added as he slipped out.

Hell, maybe he was a friendly guy who wanted to welcome the newcomer. But why the shy act when she first encountered him? She shrugged and returned to work reconstructing #3.

Two hours later, hunger stopped forward progress. She needed food bad. Those who were working today had probably already eaten. Hunter warned her to stay in the building. Walking downtown alone to catch a bite would really piss him off, so why tempt fate?

On the other hand, there was no reason why she couldn't work from home. No one would bother her at Grandpa's, and the thought of the leftover chicken Parmesan Grandpa had fixed made her stomach grumble.

She packed up her gear and placed the skull in a cushioned box. She was glad to be leaving the cold morgue and returning to the comfort of her home, or rather Grandpa's house. The longer she stayed there, the more she believed this was where she belonged.

On her way out she called Hunter. Shielding her eyes against the bright sunlight, she stepped onto the sidewalk in front of the Medical Examiner's building.

"Where are you?" he asked.

"I'm about to go out." Technically not a lie.

"Is your grandfather with you?"

In her heart he was. "Yes."

"Don't talk. Focus on your surroundings."

"The neighborhood's safe."

"I meant once you arrive where you're going."

Now he was scaring her. Kerry looked around. No one was within several hundred feet. "I'll be fine."

The door to the main entrance of the lab's office creaked opened behind her and she spun around. Steven.

He waved and stepped back inside.

CHAPTER TWELVE

AFTER WOLFING down the leftover chicken, Kerry worked non-stop the remainder of the day on the clay reconstruction, taking only a small break to whip up a protein shake for dinner.

After seven hours of work, her accomplishments weren't impressive. All she'd done was place the strips of clay around the skull's forehead, cheek, and mouth area. At this rate, it would take her two weeks to finish the face.

Grandpa shuffled into the kitchen. "Don't you think you've done enough for one day?" He looked through his bifocals at her work. "Hmm."

"Does it look bad?" She thought this face was coming out better than #1 had at this stage, but she was not a good judge of her creations.

He touched one of the markers on the chin. "This one's wobbly. You must be rushing. How about coming to bed? You can get up early and continue tomorrow."

She jiggled the rubber. Crap. It did sway but only a little.

"Maybe you're right." Her fingers were having trouble keeping steady.

Kerry put the clay back into the plastic bag so it wouldn't dry out, and then closed the box that contained the eyes and teeth. Jane Doe #3 was missing her number thirteen maxillary canine, her maxillary first molars, sixteen and twenty-six, and both of her mandible third molars. The rest were in good shape.

She yawned. Her grandfather was right. She was too exhausted to do a good job.

After Grandpa called Buster to bed, Kerry flipped off the kitchen light and jumped in the shower. The hot water pounded her back. It was pure heaven. Exhaustion dampened her defenses, and for a brief moment, she pictured herself sharing the watery paradise with a certain homicide detective.

She'd done the two-at-a-time wash-each-other experience only once, and Rod had turned out to be married. Her luck with men had always sucked. She'd moved to Tampa in part to be away from him. She also wanted to escape the pain of having lost her unborn child.

Hunter might be single, but from the way his face pinched when he spoke about Amy, she knew he was still deeply in love with his dead wife. Maybe that was a good thing. Kerry certainly didn't need any more distractions surrounding this case.

Guilty about wasting water, she turned off the shower, towel dried, and pulled on a cotton nightgown. She slipped into bed, hoping for much needed recuperative sleep.

Instead of the deep sleep she craved, she would doze off, only to wake up a short while later, uncomfortable with the temperature. Her sheets were too hot, but when she'd kicked the top sheet off, she became too cold. *Aargh*.

She fell into a fitful dream state. Dark, scary images of someone in the backseat of her car with gleaming, wild eyes peering back at her in the rear view mirror darted through her subconscious. Then she dreamt of someone grabbing her by the ankles and dragging her into the woods while her face scraped against the rocky ground. When the mad man raised his arm to hit her, Kerry forced herself to wake up. Sweat drenched her nightgown.

She looked around to make sure no one was in her bedroom. Only eerie shadows from the moon danced on her wall. She listened for the sound of someone breathing but heard her own heartbeat pulsing in her ears.

It's only a stupid dream. Go back to sleep.

Again she drifted off. This time, she dreamt someone in a red pickup truck was following her down a dark, narrow road and forced her off the road onto a muddy field. As he approached her car on foot, she tried to speed away, but the tires spun on the soft shoulder, trapping her. Damn. He pulled out a knife and pounded on her driver's side window with the hilt.

Kerry sat straight up in bed, shaking. She debated working on her creation, but her mind was too frazzled to be effective.

Scratching sounds drifted in from the kitchen. She stilled. Buster? It must be. Yet she could have sworn she'd seen Grandpa take him into his bedroom, and he always closed his door to keep the dog from roaming around at night and waking her up. Maybe Grandpa had failed to shut it all the way. Yes, that was it.

Go to sleep, Kerry.

Aw hell. When her stomach was full, she often slept better. A protein bar would help with that.

She tiptoed out of the room into the hallway. Not wanting the light to leak under Grandpa's door, she left it off.

Once in the kitchen, she went past the refrigerator and headed into the pantry. The scant light from the glowing microwave clock was enough to light her way. The protein bars sat on the back shelf in a plastic bin. Thank goodness for Grandpa's insanely neat pantry, because she knew exactly where to reach. He'd even arranged his spices alphabetically.

She grabbed a long smooth bar, turned around, and headed back to the hallway, careful not to bump into the kitchen table on the way out. She ate her feast on the way and dropped into bed the moment she returned.

A loud knock sounded on her door, and it took a moment to realize she wasn't dreaming. She opened her eyes. Soft rays of daybreak had filtered into her room. "Yes?"

"Kerry, you need to come see this." Grandpa sounded scared to death.

"What's wrong?"

"Come quickly."

Oh shit. She moved super fast, not bothering to change out of her nightgown.

A minute later, she stared at a note on the fridge written in red magic marker. The handwriting was shaky. "Be happy it was dark."

"What does that mean?" Grandpa asked.

Kerry's breath sucked right down to her toes, and her legs trembled. "I d-don't.. know. I didn't write it." Her mind raced. "I came in here last night for something to eat. I didn't turn on the light when I grabbed a protein bar." Her eyes widened as she clasped a hand over her mouth. Oh, shit. "Could someone have been in here when I was here?" Bile threatened to erupt.

"That's who Buster must have been growling at. I'm sorry. I thought you were prowling around and Buster was confused. Oh, my God. I should have seen what upset him."

"It's not your fault."

He twisted her shoulders toward him. "Are you okay? The prowler didn't harm you or anything, did he?"

"No. I never saw him." She couldn't bring in enough air.

Grandpa wrapped his arms around her. "If anything happened to you, it would kill me."

"I'm fine." Physically. "If only I'd turned on the light."

Grandpa held her at arm's lengths. "My God, no. He would have harmed you for sure."

Kerry swallowed hard. Grandpa lowered his arms, and she looked over his shoulder. Her heart stopped. "Where did you put my skull?" Her case with the eyes and teeth remained where she'd left it.

"I didn't touch anything." Grandpa looked around in confusion.

Goddamn it. "He stole it." Acid burned in her stomach as she raced to the table, praying she set the head on the floor, only it wasn't there either. "It was the only evidence I had to identify her." Sweat beaded on her forehead. "Now #3 will never have a name."

He patted her back. "As long as you're unharmed, that's all that matters. We'll find the skull."

"How?"

"Sit down and call Hunter. I'll locate a locksmith to see if he can replace the locks. I'll have an alarm system installed. I won't let anyone hurt you."

The ramification hit her. This maniac could have killed Grandpa.

Or her. But he hadn't.

This time.

Hunter would figure this out. She grabbed her phone. Crap. This was a crime scene. She jumped up. "We need to leave the kitchen. The forensic team doesn't need us messing with trace evidence."

"I agree."

She paced the living room as Hunter's phone rang. *Come on.* She didn't like waking him early on a Sunday morning, but she had no choice.

"Markum."

His voice came out calm, helping her breath. "It's me, Kerry." She couldn't control the sob that bubbled up from her throat. "Someone broke into our house."

"Shit. Are you hurt?"

"No. No. He stole the skull!"

"The what?"

"The #3 reconstruction I was working on."

"Lock your doors. I'll be right over. And Kerry?"

She swallowed hard. "Yes?"

"Don't answer the phone or the door unless it's me, okay?"

Like she would? "Okay."

They waited for Hunter in the living room. All she could do was stare into space.

"Everything will be okay, Kerry. We'll lock this place up real tight."

The doors had been locked up *real tight* last night. That didn't stop the thief. Frustration made her want to pound something, scream at someone, but the horror kept her too numb to act out her anger. She wasn't worried about herself though. She was worried about Grandpa being alone when she was at work, and she worried Jane Doe #3's family would never have closure. Yes, she could have a forensic artist do a 2-dimensional drawing of the photograph of the skull, but it wouldn't be as good as the real thing.

After what seemed like an hour, a loud rap sounded on the door. Hunter. Kerry raced to answer his knock. She checked the peephole, saw his worried expression and opened the door. Without giving any thought to the consequences, she stepped close to him and leaned into his chest. Hunter wrapped his arms around her, bringing her great solace.

She backed away and wiped the tears that had trickled down her cheeks. "I can't believe he stole the skull. I never should have brought it home."

"Don't beat yourself up. You couldn't have known. Listen, I've called the crime scene unit. They should be here any minute." He placed a warm hand on her waist and led her over to the sofa. "Sit down."

As if he were psychic, a van pulled into their drive. He stepped over to the bay window. "It's them."

Hunter greeted Crandall Pickford, the same person who'd been the lead CSU person on the Jane Doe cases, and his four assistants. Hunter introduced them to her grandfather.

"Kerry, can you show us what was disturbed?" Hunter used a soft, soothing voice.

She nodded. Only then did she notice her rather see-through night-gown. "Can you wait a sec for me to put something on?" She crossed her arms, but when Hunter's gaze dropped to her breasts, she refused to address how warm and powerful that made her feel.

"Sure." Hunter stepped in front of her, blocking the men's view as she raced to her room.

She threw on a pair of jeans, a sports bra and T-shirt. So as not to gather any additional evidence on the soles of her feet, she slipped on a pair of sneakers. She marched out of her room and hurried to the kitchen entrance. "He came in through there." She pointed toward the back door.

"How do you know he came in through the back?" Hunter asked.

"The deadbolt on the front door was still locked this morning."

The technicians went to work, photographing and dusting every conceivable surface, measuring distances as they went.

Hunter stayed with her at the kitchen entrance. He leaned in close. "Are you okay?" She looked up at him. "I mean really okay?"

"I'm so angry I could spit. Why did he have to take the evidence?"

"It tells me we're getting near, and that one person probably perpetrated these crimes. He's scared to death we'll find the identities of these women and then find him."

Grandpa stepped behind them. "I'm going to ask Frank, Chuck, and Richard to begin twenty-four hour surveillance on the house."

"Great," Hunter said.

Hunter placed a gentle hand on her waist, and another tingle of anticipation took her mind off her despair for a brief moment.

"Can I talk to you?" he asked. She could smell his minty mouthwash.

"Sure."

With her grandfather transfixed watching the technicians, Hunter sidled over to the front door. "I'm sure your grandfather's friends mean well, but if this guy was able to get into your house without your knowledge, he could probably pick off the old men one at a time."

Another wave of fear skittered up her spine. "If you're trying to scare me, you've succeeded."

"I'm sorry, but you need to face reality. You're obviously not safe in this house. I know you won't like this suggestion, but I think you should move in with me."

CHAPTER THIRTEEN

"Daddy, is she going to be our new mommy?" Melissa looked up at Hunter with adoring eyes.

Kerry smiled at the innocent question while forcing her heart not to break. Her daughter, had she lived, would have been almost two.

No, sweetheart." Hunter knelt eye level to Melissa and ran a gentle hand down the little girl's blond curls. "Kerry is working on a case with me. There's a bad guy after her. I want her to be safe, so I brought her to the safest place in the world."

"You mean here, Daddy, with us?" Melissa's eyes widened.

"Yup."

"Okay." His daughter slipped from his grasp and skipped over to Kerry. "You want to see my room?"

Kerry laughed at Melissa's acceptance of everything her father said. "Sure."

Hunter raised his brows and smirked. "I'll put your things in the guest room."

Melissa grabbed Kerry's hand. Baby powder and sweet shampoo floated upward. What she wouldn't give to have her own little girl back.

Melissa led Kerry past the room where Hunter was stashing her suitcase and into the last room on the right.

The little girl halted at the entrance. "Isn't it beautiful? Aunt Jen and I decorated it."

Kerry smiled. "It sure is."

A blue ceiling, complete with white puffy clouds, hovered above a four-poster bed with a pink and white checkered bedspread. Sitting in one corner was a large bin filled with toys, and off to the side was a bookcase that spilled over with dolls of every kind.

"Come see this." Melissa pulled her toward the desk. A small laptop glowed. "Daddy gave this to me. I can play games on it and everything."

Hunter's daughter was well loved.

The object of Melissa's adoration appeared in the doorway. "Melissa, let's let Kerry get settled. You can play with her later. She's already had a hard day."

"Why did she have a hard day?"

"Why don't you play with your dolls while Kerry and I talk about our case?"

"Okay." Question forgotten, apparently.

"Come here." Hunter opened his arms and Melissa ran toward him. He lifted her up, gave her a kiss, and then spun her around. "You're such a good girl. Love you."

"Love you back, Daddy."

He set his daughter down and then flicked his head toward the living room.

Kerry followed. "You've done a wonderful job with Melissa. She's delightful."

"Thank Jen. I don't know what I would have done without her, especially with my hours." Wrinkles etched around the smooth area of his eyes.

"Ever think of quitting the force?"

His jaw twitched. "No. Too any criminals still to put away."

Oo-kay. She wouldn't bring up that topic again. His pinched mouth made her want to hug him, but she didn't dare. She needed to stay objective and couldn't chance not solving this case.

"Let me show you to your new digs. I'm afraid it isn't fancy. The room is actually my office, and you'll have to sleep on a pull-out bed."

She smiled. "That's wonderful. One can't put a price tag on peace of mind." A jolt of apprehension jerked her to attention, and she grabbed Hunter's arm. "Ohmigod. Whoever stole the skull doesn't know I've left Grandpa's house. He may come back and harm him."

Hunter turned and ran his hands down her arms. "I've thought of that. Now that a crime has been committed, we'll have a squad car outside your house at night. At least until our killer realizes you aren't there."

Kerry let out a breath. "Thank you."

Hunter shifted his stance, tucked his thumbs in his pockets and straightened. He cleared his throat. "Let me show you to your suite." Her heart thawed under the heat of his smile.

He led her into a room measuring about twelve feet by ten feet. All the office furnishings were a boring brown down to the desk, two bookcases, one five-drawer file cabinet and a sofa.

"I'm sorry," he said. "It's all the space I have."

Had the disappointment she'd tried hard to bury color her face? At least there was a closet for her to hang her things. "No. It's perfect."

"Unpack, then meet me in the living room. I want to go over your statement again."

"Why?"

"Sometimes witnesses recall things after they've had time to reflect."

She shrugged. "You're the expert."

* * *

HUNTER LEANED against the back of the sofa and slapped his notebook closed. "I appreciate your willingness to talk about this nightmare one more time."

"I wish I could remember more," Kerry said. "I know how much one sound, one smell, one thing out of place can help." She dragged a hand through her hair. "It feels like someone erased my memory after I went back to sleep."

"You did fine."

She leaned forward on the recliner across from him. "Let me make it up to you by cooking dinner."

"You don't have to do that. You've recalled more than most witnesses I've interviewed."

Her lips pressed together. "That may be, but I need to do something with my hands or I'll go crazy."

"You sure? I suck at cooking, so you won't get an argument from me." He mentally raced through what he had in the cupboard and in the refrigerator. "I don't have much in the way of fancy ingredients."

She smiled and his other brain reacted.

"Leave everything to me and your daughter."

"You're the boss."

Hunter gathered Melissa and let the two of them do their thing. His daughter was overjoyed when Kerry asked her to choose the menu. Her pick was spaghetti and meatballs. He could have guessed. It was his daughter's favorite.

As they searched the kitchen for the pots and pans to prepare the meal, he squeezed his eyes shut when Kerry guided Melissa's hand in stirring the pot.

He wasn't wishing for an Amy replacement. Far from it. But someday he dreamed of a mother for Melissa and a wife at his side— someone who would understand the rigors of police work. That was one area where he and Amy had disagreed almost nightly. She never understood why he couldn't just walk away from an assignment when she wanted him home.

"Melissa," Kerry said, "would you mind setting the table?"

"Sure." She spun around toward Hunter. "Can you help me, Daddy?"

Hunter pushed away from the doorjamb and hustled toward her. He pulled the dishes from the cabinets and placed them on the table. Melissa took over and lined up the silverware next to the plates.

Ten minutes later, Kerry brought over the meal to the table and smiled. "Dinner's ready."

Her smile almost made him forget why she was here.

They ate in silence for the first few minutes. He hadn't realized how hungry he'd been.

Melissa broke the quiet. "This is great, Kerry. Daddy's not a very good cook."

"Hey, watch it, Pumpkin. I can boil water with the best of them." He reached over and ruffled her hair.

"Aw, Daddy, I was only kidding."

Little stinker would be a major man-eater when she grew up. She was sprouting up way too fast for him as it was.

Just as they finished, his phone rang. "Excuse me." He glanced at the caller ID, but didn't recognize the number. "Markum."

"Detective... Markum?"

"Yes."

"This is Jamal Wilson. I saw you on the news. I think the clay model might be my fiancée. She disappeared seven months ago."

His pulse jetted into overdrive. Hunter recognized the name. Jamal had been questioned when his fiancée went missing. "Would you mind coming to the police station? You can get a closer look at the model."

"Sure. When?"

"Say, in forty-five minutes?"

"I can be there."

"And bring some photos of your fiancée. They'll help our forensic anthropologist determine if our body is hers."

Jamal let out a small gasp that sounded fake.

"I'll, ah, see what I have. Bye." Jamal disconnected.

Hunter put his cell phone away. Every muscle in Kerry's body tensed. Because Hunter didn't want to discuss anything in front of Melissa, he lifted his daughter's chin. "Sweetheart. I'm afraid—"

She moved out of his reach and his throat clogged. Hunter swallowed. "Melissa?"

"I know. You have to take care of something." She rolled her eyes and sighed. "I'll get ready to go over to Aunt Jen's."

Her small cracking voice ripped him up inside. "I'm sorry, hon."

"That's okay. You have to save the world. I understand."

Jen must have told her that tale. He leaned over and kissed her. "Get ready then."

When Melissa had left the kitchen, he told Kerry about the call.

Her eyes brightened. "I don't want to get my hopes up, but I can't help but be excited. We might have identified our second victim."

* * *

AFTER THEY DROPPED Melissa off at Jen's house, Hunter drove them to the M.E.'s office to pick up #1's reconstruction for Jamal to study up close and personal. Good thing Kerry had the key code to get in.

The head-on-a-stick, as Hunter dubbed it, now sat in front of Jamal Wilson at the conference table.

"I'm not sure," Jamal said, shaking his head at the model.

"Why did you wait so long to call?" Hunter asked. They'd displayed the case three days ago.

"The face only kind of looked like Tameka, you know what I mean?"

Kerry leaned forward. "Reconstructions aren't exact science, Mr. Wilson. I had to guess the shape of the lips, ears, eyelids and other parts that are formed by fatty tissue rather than by bone." Kerry tapped the pile of photos he had sitting in front of him. "May I see what you brought?"

"Sorry." He slid the pictures over to her. "I had to get them from her mom."

He didn't have any photos of her? Something didn't fit.

Kerry flipped through the pictures. "May I keep these for a little while? I'd like to scan them into the computer to compare them to the X-ray of her face. This might give me a better idea if we have a match."

"Sure, whatever."

Hunter opened Wilson's file. "It says here you were brought in for questioning in regards to Tameka's disappearance."

"Yeah, but they got nothin' on me." Cocky SOB.

Hunter leaned back. "You and I both know, Mr. Wilson, that if this is Tameka's body, we could bring formal charges against you."

He waved a hand, but Hunter could tell it was all bravado. "I got nothing to hide. I didn't kill her. I loved her."

That was why he'd hit her. "Says here there were four domestic violence calls against you."

Wilson crossed his arms. "I didn't come here to get fucking interrogated. I wanted to make sure this was my woman, that she hadn't run off."

He probably meant he wanted to make sure his slave hadn't left on her own free will. Most likely he missed having her cook and clean for him.

Hunter's avenue of questioning wasn't getting him anywhere. "Why don't you start with the last time you saw Tameka?"

Jamal shrugged. "I don't know the exact date. It's been a long time, ya know?"

"What were you doing right before she disappeared? Surely, you can remember the day Tameka didn't come home. After all, you were engaged to the woman." Acid burned in Hunter's gut. The man didn't deserve Tameka.

"Sure. I was at work. She had some kind of doctor's appointment or something after she finished her shift. I never saw her again after that."

Hunter straightened. "What kind of doctor's appointment?"

Jamal skewed up his lips. "What do you care?"

"It may be important." Hunter forced his tone to be civil.

Jamal rolled his eyes. "I think it was a plastic surgeon. She'd had to have some work done to her face and all."

"For what kind of procedure?"

"Shit, I don't know, man."

Hunter leaned forward and leered at him. "Try to remember. It could be very important."

"Don't get your pants in a wad. Her ex-husband beat her up pretty bad. Got lots of cracks in the bones right around here." He ran a finger down the right side of his face. "One cheek had become lopsided. Made her ugly."

Jamal was no looker himself. "Go on."

"She figured as long as the doctor agreed to do the work kind of cheap, she'd ask for a chin implant. Said it would help her self esteem. Hell, I was all for it."

Hunter looked over at Kerry who sat perfectly still. She'd grasped the hem of her blouse and bunched it tight.

Hunter glanced back to Jamal. "How long ago was she injured by her ex?"

"Maybe a couple months before we met." Jamal slapped the table. "What does this have to do with anything?"

Hunter wouldn't answer his question. "Do you know the name of the doctor?"

Jamal stretched out his legs and leaned back in his seat. "Hell no. I couldn't keep track. Once she found a job that gave her health insurance, she was going all the time to dermatologists, eye doctors, you name it." He waved a dismissive hand.

"Where did she work?"

"Wal-Mart."

Kerry straightened the photos on the table. "Do you by any chance have a hair brush she might have used? I'd like to compare her DNA."

"Lady." He laced his fingers on top of his head. "I tossed all her shit out once she left. Her old lady might have kept her stuff. Ask her."

* * *

KERRY LEANED CLOSER to the computer for a better view of the image. Her desk sat in the corner of her lab and rays of the afternoon sun streaked across her screen. She'd scanned the pictures Jamal had lent her into Photoshop. Using the Transform Tool, she rotated and resized the images to match the size of the skull's X-ray. One at a time, she laid the X-ray of Tameka Dorsey's skull over each photo.

"Crap." Too many of the pictures were either blurry or the angle of the head couldn't be corrected effectively.

"Wait a minute," she mumbled to herself. Two photos looked like they might line up, and excitement coursed through her. Using the arrow keys, she nudged the photo to the right. While the photo wasn't a perfect fit, Kerry wasn't ready to rule out she wasn't Tameka Dorsey.

Thank goodness she'd asked Hunter to reach Tameka's mother for her daughter's dental X-rays along with a hairbrush or toothbrush. Kerry needed just one item to extract her DNA.

Tameka had no filings or crowns, which might imply she hadn't gone to a dentist in a while. That could hinder the identification.

Her cell rang. Her pulse quickened as she raced across the room to where she'd left her phone. "Hello?"

"It's Hunter. I was able to locate the dental X-rays and dental report for Tameka Dorsey."

Hearing his voice brought her relief. "That's wonderful."

"The doctor's office is on my way to your lab, so I thought I'd pick them up and drop them off."

How sweet. "I appreciate that, but don't you need a warrant or something for them?" He'd only spoken to Tameka's mom today. When did he have the time?

"I had her mom sign a consent form for her release. You know, all that HIPAA stuff."

"Good thinking."

"Give me about fifty minutes."

"Okay, bye."

The wait to discover the identity of #1 was almost over. She might finally have a name on her grave marker.

With her stress level lowered for a moment, Kerry sat on her chair and closed her eyes, hoping for a short power nap before Hunter arrived. She'd spent a restless night on his pullout sofa. Each little noise had woken her up. First, the air conditioning clicked on, then Hunter or perhaps Melissa, had risen in the middle of the night. Strange houses had strange creaks.

At first she chalked up her sleeplessness to the fear of another intruder attack, but Hunter had insisted she lock the office door from the inside. That helped give her some peace of mind, but she kept imagining the creep crawling in through the bedroom window.

Having Hunter down the hall only added to her inability to sleep. Her fertile mind conjured up all sorts of erotic scenarios. Did he sleep naked? What would he be like to sleep next to? Was he a cuddler? She figured her carnal thoughts had to be the result of anxiety since she'd never dreamt about a man like that before.

A knock on the lab door roused her from her daydream. She bolted upright. Hunter walked in with a packet in his hands. "Power napping?"

She must have left the door ajar. She swiped a hand over her eyes to clear them. "Sorry. I suddenly couldn't stay awake." Thank God, he couldn't read her mind.

"No need to apologize."

Hunter dragged a chair from one side of the room, sat next to her at the computer and handed her the information.

When she fumbled with the clasp, he slipped the envelope from her fingers. "Let me."

In a flash, he'd pulled out the X-rays, and then passed them to her. Kerry studied the report. "No filings or crowns. We may have our girl." She looked up and smiled.

"Are you sure?"

The report was sparse, but it did contain a single radiograph that spanned both the upper and lower dental arcades. "Give me a sec." Kerry placed the dental X-ray over the X-ray of the skull. The tooth roots fit perfectly. "I'd say we have a match."

Hunter grinned. What she would give for a camera now. "Good job, Doctor Herlihy."

She prayed her beating heart didn't show through her surgical gown. "Did you happen to ask Tameka's mother the name of her plastic surgeon?" She needed to take her focus off Hunter's handsome face and concentrate on her job.

"Sure did."

"And what did she say?"

CHAPTER FOURTEEN

KERRY RUSHED BACK into her lab with a Tampa phone book she'd borrowed from the reception desk. "Knock yourself out." She tossed the heavy tome on the desk and it landed with a thud.

Hunter chuckled at her antics and looked up the number for Tameka's surgeon. An expert in facial reconstruction, Dr. Paul Dalton was a renowned plastic surgeon.

Hunter dialed the office in the hopes of setting up an appointment with Dalton.

"Dr. Dalton's office, how may I help you?" a sweet-voiced female answered.

He asked to speak with the doctor, and she told him Dr. Dalton was doing consulting work at the River of Hope shelter. Could he call back tomorrow?

"No problem."

Kerry looked up. "He wasn't there?"

"No. He's doing charity work at the women's shelter."

"Really? I admire people who give of themselves like that." Her eyes narrowed. "Battered women need an advocate."

Had Kerry or someone close to her experienced abuse? "You know

Jamal claimed Tameka had an appointment with Dalton the day she died."

Her eyes widened and her pretty face paled. "All the women we found were battered."

"I know." Hunter let her sift through the facts. Sometimes another point of view could unearth a clue he hadn't noticed.

Kerry paced the floor, her paper covered feet making a soft swishing sound on the tile. "Okay. We know Tameka went to Dr. Dalton to repair her face. What about Janet Kopetski?" She spun around to face him.

Her brows rose and her lips pressed firmly together. If only he knew for sure how these women had died, he'd tell her in a heartbeat. "What about her?"

"Did she go to Dr. Dalton? If she did, and if both disappeared after their appointments then—"

"Whoa. Who said they had the same surgeon? Besides, we have no idea when Janet Kopetski disappeared. All we know is that she'd cut her finger sometime before her death."

"Then call Janet's father to see if he knows who worked on her broken jaw and finger." Her breath came out ragged.

"Okay." Hunter wanted to help these women too, maybe as much as Kerry, but right now, he wanted to help relieve Kerry's anxiety. He'd never met a woman who cared so much for the dead.

He flipped open his small notebook and scanned the pages detailing Norwood's interview. "According to my notes, Mr. Norwood wasn't in the know about his daughter's medical issues."

"He did say that." She dropped into the seat next to him. "He said he'd ask his wife."

Kerry touched his arm and heat shot straight to his groin, but he refused to admit his racing pulse was attributed to the fact Kerry stirred a long dead emotion inside him.

"So he did."

Hunter admired her tenacity. Kerry leaned closer to him, and her scent shifted his focus to her as a woman instead of her as a professional.

"What's wrong? You look like you've seen a ghost."

Hardly, a ghost, more like a goddess. "Nothing." Heat raced up his face. He turned his head, flipped to Norwood's number, and punched it in his cell. Thank goodness Kerry wasn't a mind reader.

Ten seconds later, the answering machine clicked on. Dumb move. He should have asked for Norwood's work number when they interviewed him. He left a message regarding Janet's surgeon and asked Norwood to call him back.

"Let me guess. He's at work," she said, her shoulders sagging.

"That would be my guess, but I don't have that number." He leaned back in the chair. "On a slightly different note, I did a little research on our charming Mr. Kopetski."

Wide eyes stared at him. "What did you find?"

He cleared his throat, trying to keep his mind on the task at hand. "Seems Mr. Kopetski worked for the same financial institution as Janet for about six months. According to one of the coworkers, Kopetski was a hot head. He hated to lose money—his or his clients. He literally was in a fight with one of the brokers and got canned. It was about then he took out his frustrations on his new wife, Janet."

She flinched and Hunter's gut clenched. Stupid. He should have delivered the news with more subtlety. Kerry was a woman of great empathy, which was one of the reasons he found her so attractive. But dammit. She dealt with ugliness everyday. He thought she'd be desensitized.

"I trust the police have a record of his domestic violence against her?" she asked.

Hunter was impressed with how fast Kerry picked up the pieces of the puzzle and ran with them. "Yes. As a matter of fact, the cops were called to his house twice during their short marriage."

Her lips firmed. "It's hard to believe she would have put up with him after the first incident. What was the date of the last call?"

Hunter flipped through his notebook again. "Shortly before she was arrested for embezzling funds."

Kerry's face fell. "Oh."

He leaned forward, resting his elbows on his knees. "That doesn't mean he didn't harm her after she was released from prison or that

Kopetski didn't push her down the stairs for that matter. It just means she didn't report the crime because she was dead."

"You're probably right."

"What I don't get," he said, "is the shelter connection."

"She might have done volunteer work there."

"It's possible. I figured Janet would have had the money to pay for a good surgeon, assuming both she and her husband were pulling a decent salary."

"Maybe she went to Dr. Dalton's regular office and paid like a normal person."

"Good thought, but why embezzle the funds if she could afford surgery on her own?"

"Surgery isn't cheap."

"True. I'll draw a time line to make sure our dates and facts line up." He shoved a hand through his hair. "I don't know why we're even speculating. We don't know if they had the same doctor."

"Knowing you, you'll find out. When you do, don't stop at the surgeon. See who the anesthesiologist was and other medical attendants. There could be a commonality there."

"You're good." He loved how their minds reinforced each other's.

Kerry shifted in her computer chair, and the metal leg squeaked. "Are you going to tell Jamal about identifying his fiancée or do you want me to call?"

"I'll call both him and Tameka's mother and tell them we have a match."

"To be absolutely sure, I want to compare the DNA. It'll take a few months to get the results back, but they should know I'm ninety-five percent sure it's Tameka."

He snapped his fingers. "Tameka's mom gave me a hair brush. I put it in an evidence bag and locked it in the cruiser's trunk."

"Great."

He raked his hands down his face. "There has to be some way to tie Janet Kopetski to Tameka Dorsey. I wish I knew what I was missing."

* * *

HUNTER WANTED to wait until after Melissa had finished eating before he called Mr. Norwood again. He wouldn't have to leave her with Jen if he could conduct business over the phone. Nothing gave him greater pleasure than to spend time with her. Unfortunately, his life was dictated by criminal activity, and Melissa often suffered because of it.

He polished off the rest of his coffee while Melissa and Kerry had some foreign conversation about the newest clothing styles. They giggled, and he just kept quiet.

When they finished dinner, Melissa and Kerry cleared the table and cleaned up. He was amazed. Every time Kerry asked Melissa to help her, his daughter beamed. She never pouted like she often did when he asked her to do chores.

Damn. He should have looked for a mother for his daughter. Between his job and taking care of her, he hadn't found anyone he wanted in his life or Melissa's.

From his vantage point at the dining room table, he studied Kerry bent over the sink washing dishes and Melissa carefully drying them. He shook his head, willing the blood to flow to his brain.

Yes, he could have Kerry watch Melissa tonight should the need arrive, but he didn't like leaving them alone. With a possible serial killer on the loose, there was no telling what might happen, and he refused to put his daughter or Kerry in harm's way.

Imposing on his sister was his only choice.

He turned his back to them and flipped through the pages of his notebook to contact Mr. Norwood. Before he finished his search, his phone rang. Speak of the devil. He gave himself a psychic point.

"Mr. Norwood. Thanks for calling me back."

"I have the name of Janet's surgeon you asked for. My wife said he'd done a wonderful job."

Hunter waited a beat. "Who was he?"

"Paul Dalton."

Adrenaline pumped through his system. "When was that?"

"I don't have the exact date, but it was after Stanton broke her jaw."

Hot damn. "Thank you, Mr. Norwood, you've been a big help."

He disconnected and turned to Kerry. "Dalton."

She turned off the water and faced him. "What about Dalton?"

"Sorry. That was Mr. Norwood on the phone. He said Paul Dalton was Janet's surgeon."

She smiled and pumped her arm once. "Yes!" Soapsuds flew off her hands. "I was hoping it was him. I thought it might make things easier, but I never expected our luck to hold up."

"Who's Dalton?" Melissa asked.

"He was a doctor who operated on one of my clients, that's all."

Some day, Hunter would have to speak freely in front of her. When she was older, he wanted her to understand how cruel the world could be, but right now, he wanted to protect her from the underbelly of society.

Hunter crooked his finger, and Melissa trotted over and climbed onto Hunter's lap. He gave her a big hug and a kiss. "Why don't you go boot up your computer, sweetie. I'll send in Kerry in a few minutes and you can show her the new game Aunt Jen bought you."

"Okay." Melissa scooted off his lap and skipped out of the kitchen.

Hunter twisted back to Kerry. "Considering Dalton did pro bono work, it makes sense he'd have dealt with women from different walks of life. Janet probably was quite poor after her release from prison. If Kopetski pushed her, maybe she sought out the shelter to get away from him."

"That makes sense." Kerry tucked a loose strand of hair behind her ear, and the soap clung to the side of her face. Cute.

Hunter leaned forward, elbows on knees. "Dalton might know of a connection between the women. I want to speak with him."

"I'd like to come with you when you do."

"Why?" He couldn't take any more chances one of his calls could turn deadly.

"I thought I could show him the X-rays of my other two Jane Does and see if he recognizes them."

Her logic always cut through the best of his intentions. "You think he could look at an X-ray and identify the person?"

She hesitated. "I bet if we described each of the women's injuries, he might remember them. Besides, these women have been dead for six months to a year. You would think he'd have wondered why they never showed up for a follow up appointment."

"That would make sense if they'd had surgery right before their deaths. It's possible Dalton could have treated them and not have planned to see them again once they healed."

"True."

Her pressed lips and slumped shoulders tugged at a vulnerable spot. "I'll take the X-rays and show them to Dr. Dalton. You can write down all the information you know about these women and give him the rundown." He smiled, hoping a little charm would convince her.

Kerry's hands shot to her hips. "Why are you shutting me out?"

"Keep your voice down. Melissa's down the hall."

"Sorry. I still think I should be there," she whispered. The moment she stepped toward him he feared he'd cave.

"I understand your passion for finding the identities of these women. I even admire you, but this is my case. I won't put you in harm's way for anything." *Please let her be reasonable.*

"Harm's way? You just said this guy was the angel of mercy. He had no connection to them other than to have treated them. Isn't that what you implied?"

Big mouth_. Maybe he was being overly cautious. "After I see him, I promise to tell you everything he said."

Her jaw tightened as she ran her gaze over him. "You'd better."

Melissa called Kerry's name and her whole demeanor softened. "I have to go."

* * *

AFTER HUNTER DROPPED Kerry off at work and his daughter at his sister's house, Hunter headed to Dr. Dalton's office. His secretary showed Hunter to an office in the back of a three-story, all glass office building. Nice digs. The floor looked like polished granite and the artwork was worthy of being in a museum. No wonder the guy could afford to do charity work.

When Hunter entered the plush office, Dr. Dalton stood to greet him. The doctor was tanned, about thirty-five to forty, small of stature and dressed in what looked like a tailor made suit. Handsome, almost to the point of being pretty.

"Please, Detective, have a seat." The dark blue, leather, high-backed chair went well with the gray carpet and light gray walls. Hunter eased down. Man, he'd never experienced a more comfortable seat in his life.

Dalton sat behind his desk instead of in the seat next to Hunter. The doctor was obviously into proving his superior position. The many diplomas on the wall were enough to convince Hunter the doctor was as good as he'd heard.

"I'm here to discuss two of your former patients, Tameka Dorsey and Janet Kopetski." Hunter concentrated on Dalton's eyes. They never lied.

"Lovely ladies." Dalton's smile was engaging, and his teeth were so white and straight, they looked veneered. "But surely you know I can't give out information about my patients. Doctor-patient privilege and all that." Dalton chuckled and appeared relaxed, but his eyes twitched. What was he hiding?

Hunter was prepared for the runaround. "They're no longer your patients. Both are dead."

Dalton clasped a hand to his chest. His mouth gaped open. "My God. When, how?"

Hunter didn't want to give too many details. "Their bodies were found in shallow graves not far from here. Perhaps you saw me and the forensic anthropologist who created the clay model on TV."

"No, I didn't, I'm sorry. I can't tell you how upset I am to learn about their deaths. Tameka was engaged and so full of life. I believe Janet had had some trouble with her ex-husband but was trying to start her life over again."

"Would you mind if your secretary showed me the dates of their last visit?"

He waved a hand. "By all means. I'll let her know to give you the information on your way out."

"Thank you." Hunter didn't move as Dalton stood.

"Anything else, Detective?" Dalton's jaw clenched ever so slightly.

"Yes." Hunter handed the doctor the X-rays Kerry had prepared for him. "We also found two other females at the gravesite. Both had had plastic surgery of some kind. One was a thirty-five to forty-five Caucasian with a broken ulna that had pins and plates. She also had had a broken nose that required surgery. The second female, of white European descent, had been dead approximately six months when we found her. She was a bit younger. Her right eye socket had been damaged, and then repaired. Do any of these women sound familiar?"

Dalton slapped the X-ray onto the light board. He stared at the images, cupping his chin with his hand. "This doesn't look like my work. I'm sorry." Dalton glanced at his gold watch. "I'm afraid I have several patients to attend to. So if there's nothing else..." Dalton's gaze bounced around the room as he dragged a hand down the front of his neatly pressed suit.

"Just in case something comes to you, I'll leave these X- rays. We have duplicates at the M.E.'s office."

"That's fine."

Hunter stood and shook Dalton's hand. Hunter never understood why a man would polish his nails.

* * *

KERRY'S LAB door squeaked open. "Here ya go, Dr. H." Steven rolled a body bag on a gurney into the room.

"Who is it?"

"Jane Doe #4. Dr. A said to tell you he'd finished the autopsy and she's all yours."

"Tell him thanks."

Kerry wasn't excited about having to remove what was left of the decaying soft tissue from #4's body to make an identification, but the process required it.

She dragged the large stainless steel pot from the maceration station, filled it with water from the sink, and then added a tablespoon of Adolph's Meat Tenderizer to speed the cleaning process. She then dropped it back on the burner under the hood and set the temperature to one hundred eighty degrees.

Her back screamed from the exertion, and a layer of sweat covered her brow. She'd have to cut away the large pieces of flesh first before soaking them in soapy water.

Fully suited up in hairnet, facemask, and gown, Kerry zipped open the bag. The fetid smell of decomposed flesh hit her hard. She should be used to the odor, but each body smelled a little different. And #4 was particularly foul, although she should be happy the maggots weren't grabbing a bite.

Once she extracted the female from the bag, she carefully cut away the flesh with a scalpel. The tedious job would take hours.

Less than fifteen minutes into the chore, the door banged open. "Dr. H. You gotta come." Steven was out of breath.

"What's wrong?" Her heart jetted into overdrive.

"The cops just fished a body out of Tampa Bay. She's pretty badly decomposed. Dr. A called and said he needs you."

She held up her gloved hands. Bits of flesh dangled from her fingers. "I'm kinda in the middle of working on this woman."

"Sorry. She'll have to wait."

CHAPTER FIFTEEN

ONCE KERRY and Steven hit SR 60, they headed east, parallel to I-4. The crime scene area wasn't hard to find. Police cars with flashing lights lined the road leading to the Bay.

A guard stopped them at the entrance. Once Steven showed his ID from the Medical Examiners' office, the guard waved them through. Because the place was swarming with cops, she scanned the area looking for Hunter. Disappointment grabbed her when she realized he wasn't there.

Kerry pointed to John's van and Steven pulled in next to him. "Thanks for the ride. I'll have Dr. A take me back."

"Sure. Have fun and stay safe."

Have fun? She doubted it. Staying safe was easy among a mob of police. She waved goodbye to Steven and headed to the scene with her equipment in tow.

John was on his knees looming over the victim's body. She walked up behind him and looked over his shoulder. Apparently, he was so engrossed in taking notes, he didn't notice her shadow hanging over him.

Kerry studied the female. Her face was flat, her skin decaying. The woman looked like she'd been in the water a good month. Small holes and tears appeared at random intervals in her mostly intact clothes. Those might have been the result of fish feasting on her. The sea creatures had already had a celebration with her eyeballs.

Kerry stepped to the side and her shadow moved. The medical examiner jerked around. "Hey. Thanks for coming. I thought you'd like to see what a dead body with her soft tissue looks like." He smiled.

"Thanks, but I think I'd rather stick to skeletal remains. They're cleaner and easier to handle."

"Your loss." He chuckled. "Hey, at least she only smells like salt water."

"Agreed. Any identification on her?"

He shook his head. John adjusted the female's light brownish-red hair, which had begun to slip off her scalp. Kerry placed her case on the ground and knelt beside him.

"How can I help?" she asked.

"Tell me what you see?"

John was the expert. She only did bones, but there was a small thrill in being asked to give her opinion. "I'm afraid Steven filled me in on her age. He told me the vic was between thirty and thirty-five, but I'm betting the bloating would help reduce the facial wrinkling somewhat, which would give her a more youthful, if not dead, appearance. I'd say she's closer to forty than thirty-five."

He gave her a small smile. "Quite good. What else?"

Kerry took her time studying the body. "From the shape of her face, I'm guessing Hispanic."

"I agree. And her height and weight?" John seemed to enjoy her impromptu evaluation.

"Taking the bloating into consideration, I'd say five foot three and weight about one seventy." Kerry gloved her hand and tilted the head to one side, and then the other. A fresh, red scar went from the victim's right ear to half way under her chin. "From the neat stitch job, I'd say she had some kind of plastic surgery quite recently."

Her gut reacted in a bad way. Maybe the heat was getting to her.

Hunter's comment about plastic surgeons raced back to her. Surely there wasn't a connection between this woman who'd been dumped in the Bay and those she'd found buried in the construction site. Killers didn't usually change their MOs, or so Hunter had claimed.

"Good catch." John lifted the vic's shoulder and leaned the body away from Kerry. The woman's cause of death was evident. "One shot to the back of the head probably killed her. If she wasn't dead when she hit the water, she was shortly thereafter."

Kerry sat back on her haunches. The effect of the salt air mixed with the heat made her stomach queasy. Next time, she'd bring a large brimmed hat to help keep the sun off her face. The cap she wore to prevent leaving any trace at the crime scene was enough to raise her core temp by a couple of degrees.

Once the crime scene techs finished measuring and photographing the area, John zipped up the victim. "Let's bring her back to the morgue for an autopsy," he said to one of the techs. His gaze remained on the men until they'd finished loading the body into a van. He swiveled back to her. "Anything else you noticed?"

"It's hard to be sure, but I'd say the woman spent little on her wardrobe. The wear pattern on the soles of the sneakers implied she'd owned them for quite some time."

"I noticed the clothes didn't match either. From the workmanship, I'd say she was wearing hand-me-downs." John closed his med kit and ratcheted his body to a stand.

"Your arthritis getting to you?"

"A little."

Kerry gathered her instruments. "Are you thinking she might have been a regular visitor to Goodwill or maybe even a women's shelter?"

"Shelter?" He shielded his eyes with one hand.

"I guess I'm having difficulty separating my four buried bodies from this one." Kerry gave him the rundown of possible theories.

He walked toward his van, his job over for now. "I'll keep your idea in mind when I autopsy her. I guess she's Jane Doe #5."

* * *

KERRY WAS QUITE happy to be back at the morgue. At least in the cool room, she wouldn't suffer from heat exhaustion. While John began the autopsy on the new victim, Kerry pulled #4 from the body bag and turned the burner to low.

As she cut and scraped the dead tissue from the bones, she dropped the finished bones in the warm, soapy water. The chore required concentration since she had to cut close enough to remove the skin, but not so close to mar the bone.

Before she knew it, over an hour had passed. Not wanting to keep Hunter from Melissa any longer than necessary, she called it a day. Kerry phoned Hunter to tell him she was ready for him to pick her up.

She turned off the burner and decided to let the bones soak overnight. The stench of the cooked flesh gagged her, forcing her to adjust her mask and closed the hood.

Next she rewrapped what was left of the body and placed #4 in the morgue cooler. Tomorrow, she'd finish the bone cleaning. Only then would she have time to work on the plaster mold of the skull. No way would she chance losing the original head again to the thief.

The clean up took close to a half hour. As she wiped the last of the counters, someone knocked on her autopsy door and the pushed it open.

Hunter. Though he looked tired, his broad shoulders and chiseled jaw sent her hormones soaring. Her face heated.

"What's wrong?" he asked.

Good Lord. Could he tell she'd had a momentary fantasy? "Wrong? Nothing. I was outside in the heat for a long time. Do I look pink or something?" She was proud of her good catch.

"No, you look…"

Her mom always told her she never could hide her deepest emotions. "Sad perhaps?" she asked.

"I am. The police found a body floating in McKay Bay today. The female victim had been shot once in the back of the head and dumped in the water with a cement block around her waist to cover the crime." Kerry pushed back the despair. "Her death seemed so senseless."

"Welcome to Tampa. You ready to go?"

Apparently, he wasn't the type to become personally involved with every victim. She needed to learn that skill.

"Hunter, there was something about this woman that made me think she might be related to my Jane Does."

"Why don't you tell me on the way home?"

Kerry grabbed her purse, shut off the light, and locked the door. She trailed after him.

"The victim was dressed poorly." He turned around, and when he opened his mouth, she rushed on. "John and I believe she might have been a recent visitor to a shelter. And get this. There were fresh scars behind her ear, which implied she'd had surgery. Plastic surgery perhaps."

His face showed no reaction. In fact, he didn't seem to get the connection. Aw hell, maybe her imagination was getting the best of her.

He lifted a hand and placed it on her shoulder. Warmth spread straight to her groin. "We'll take her photo to the shelters to see if anyone can identify her."

"Really? So you think the same person might have killed all five women?"

He opened the front door of the building. "Now that's a stretch. If she was shot in the head, then dumped in the Bay, the MOs aren't anything alike. But I won't discount your gut feeling."

They exited the building. Even though it was close to six at night, the heat blasted her. "Thank you."

"I received the lab results back on the break-in at your house." Hunter placed his hand on the small of her back to guide her across the street.

Kerry looked up at him. "Did they find anything?"

They reached the other side of the street and walked to the parking lot. "The thief used a bump key to get in your house. That's why we couldn't tell there was any forced entry."

"A what key?"

"Get in the cruiser and I'll tell you." He closed the door and rushed over to his side. "A bump key. Most people buy only a few brands of locks, like the ones found at home stores. This makes it easy for the thief to make a key that unlocks the door."

"I don't understand."

Hunter started the car and immediately flipped the AC to high. "In a nutshell, the thief purchases an uncut key that fits the particular brand of lock and cuts all the ridges the same height. It takes a little practice, but when he inserts the key into the lock, and then pulls it out just a little, it makes a clicking sound. He'll use a hammer or even the handle of a screwdriver to tap this new key just so. This allows the key to *bump* the tumblers into place."

"That's horrible. Are you saying anyone can break into any house at will?" That must have been the scratching noise she'd heard coming from the kitchen. And here, she'd thought Buster had gotten loose.

"Not if they have an alarm system or more distinctive locks."

"That gives me the chills thinking about it."

"Come on. I promise no one is going to break into my house. I have state of the art protection."

It didn't hurt to have a gun-toting Hunter around either. She'd have to call Grandpa to see what kind of new locks he'd installed on the doors.

"Did the lab find any fingerprints or trace elements to connect them to a particular person?" she asked.

"No. This person was careful, but not perfect. He dragged in little pieces of seashells on your kitchen floor."

Seashells? "Grandpa's house is miles from the beach."

"Testing showed no trace of salt on the shells either. We're now looking for someone who walked on a shell drive." Hunter slipped onto Morgan Street.

"That's a long shot."

"True. But that wasn't the only piece of evidence. While we didn't find any discernable fingerprints inside the house, we found a footprint outside the back door."

"Did you check to see if the print belonged to my grandfather? He goes out that way to walk the dog twice a day."

"We checked his shoes, and they weren't a match. The lab techs came out and made a mold of the imprint. Turns out it belongs to a Nike shoe, about size 10."

"So all we need is to find someone with that shoe size who has a shelled drive."

"You've got it."

* * *

KERRY FINISHED WIPING down the morgue counter for the tenth time this morning. She was ready. Ready to show the world her second facial reconstruction.

This creation had taken more than a week to complete because of the work she'd had to do to prepare #4's body for analysis. Kerry hadn't been willing to work on the face at Hunter's house. Melissa might have been upset to see a dead woman's skull. After all, she'd only lost her mom two years ago. Knowing how a six-year old mind worked, Melissa would have asked a thousand questions, questions Kerry didn't feel comfortable answering.

She checked her watch again. She had a few minutes before she had to leave for her TV interview.

Wanting to show off her creation to John, she carried her clay face across the hall, holding onto the base with both hands. She opened the door with her hip and stepped into his autopsy room. God, but the man kept this place colder than a freezer. He looked up over his mask, his eyes sparkling.

"You finished!" he mumbled under the surgical mask. He slipped off the mouth covering cloth, set his scalpel on a metal tray, and walked over to her. He took the base from her hands and twirled the sculpture around. "It looks wonderful. We may have to use you in the future to do other clay reconstructions."

She hadn't known she'd done that fine of a job. "Thanks. Hunter's on his way to pick me up. A reporter will interview Hunter and me at the sheriff's department."

"You less nervous this time around?"

"Much. Hunter will do most of the talking anyway. I'm just there to point out a few interesting characteristics that might help a relative identify her."

Kerry glanced over at the table. "Is that the woman from the bay?"

"Yes. The bullet killed her." He handed the skull back to her. "Here's the sad part."

Kerry stepped over to the table. While her stomach and nose could handle the decomposition, her heart ached at seeing the woman cut up.

John pulled apart the abdomen. "Look here."

"She was pregnant?"

"I'm afraid so."

Now the police would have to tell her relatives both the woman and her unborn child were dead. "Let's hope we can identify her soon. The father of the child must be out of his mind with worry."

"Or he did the deed."

Kerry increased her hold on the base. "I have to go. The television crew won't wait forever."

"Good luck."

"Do you mind?" With both hands clasping the #4 model, Kerry angled her head forward for John to open the autopsy door.

As she walked back to her lab, another door whipped opened and smashed into Kerry's shoulder. She faltered. Her foot caught, causing her to stumble.

Someone behind her jerked her arm back to steady her causing her fingers to let go of the base.

"Steady," a familiar voice said.

The clay model flew out of her hands. As Kerry opened her mouth to tell him to let go of her arm so she could catch the head, the damned thing landed with a thunk before she got the words out. "Noooo!"

On its base, the model teetered, then rolled over onto the side of the face.

Kerry spun around. "Look what you did!" She hadn't meant to blame Steven for the accident. He hadn't been the one to open the door, but he had pulled back on her arm.

"It's my fault," a young girl said, her mouth half open. "I just opened the door. I'm sorry."

Kerry took a deep breath. "It's okay. It's okay. I can fix the damage."

Heart pounding, she picked up her precious model and raced back to her lab. One cheek and part of the right lip had sagged. With her sculpting tool, she repaired the damage, then immediately placed the item in a safe cardboard box.

She needed to make sure the model was steady on the ride over. Hopefully, bubble wrap would do the trick. The last thing she needed was for Jane's face to fall over again in the car and get smashed. Just in case, she brought a few tools to do damage control. Heat wasn't kind to clay.

Hunter was waiting for her outside. Once again, she was struck by how handsome he looked in his midnight blue uniform.

"Hey," he said.

His gaze held steady on her face. For a moment she thought the quick makeup job she'd done right before she left looked uneven. "Something wrong?"

He laughed. Actually laughed. The spurt of joy surprised her. "No." He started the engine and left.

In relatively light traffic, they arrived twenty minutes later. "We need to hurry," he said.

The same cameraman, Josh something, was in the conference room doing lighting checks. Liz Culbertson greeted Kerry like an old friend, helping to relax her.

Liz asked the same questions as before, and the interview lasted less than fifteen minutes. A second after the last answer, the two News Channel 8 people disappeared.

Hunter lifted the head from Kerry's hands. "I think we better keep this in our evidence room. We can't chance losing this one."

She believed the head would be safe back at the morgue, but why take the unnecessary risk? "Fine." Hunter had half turned around when she decided now would be as good a time to ask him the question that had been burning in her brain all day. "I'd like to watch the news at my grandfather's house tonight. Do you mind?"

His jaw tightened. "That's not a good idea. Look what happened the last time we went live."

Damn him. She knew he'd bring up the phone call. "If the angry man needs to reach me, he'll call me at Grandpa's. He doesn't know I've been hiding at your place for the last two weeks."

He hesitated. "I don't want to leave Melissa with Jen again tonight, and I don't want you to be alone in case the man calls."

"Then bring her! I'd love for my grandfather to meet her. The two of them would get along wonderfully. And I'll make dinner. I'll ask Grandpa to pick me up. I'll leave work early and stop by the store."

His lips firmed. "You know the thief knows where you live. If he's also the killer, you don't want to be running around unprotected."

She smiled. "Don't worry. I'll have Grandpa carry his gun."

* * *

HUNTER WAS proud of Melissa as she watched the beginning of the news. She didn't whine or squirm in her seat. More surprising, she hadn't clung to his side when they arrived at Tom Hardy's place. Maybe sitting next to her new best friend, Kerry, helped. His daughter was turning into a wonderful young lady.

The broadcast switched to Kerry holding the head standing shoulder-to-shoulder with him.

"That's you, Daddy."

Kerry ran a hand down Melissa's head. "It sure is. Would you do me a favor, sweetie?"

His daughter looked up at her. "Sure."

"My grandfather locked the puppy up in his bedroom. I can hear him cry. He's lonely. Would you mind playing with him for a bit?"

She swiveled around. "Can I, Daddy?"

Why hadn't he thought of that? Little girls shouldn't watch all this death. Besides, how could a father say no to her bright smile? "Sure."

"I'll show her where it is," Tom said.

"Thanks."

Hunter had only glanced at the first newscast that showcased #1. This time was different. He concentrated on Kerry, on how pretty she looked and how elegantly she spoke. Kerry looked more relaxed tonight, both on and off screen, than she had the first time she'd appeared on camera.

Once their presentation concluded, Kerry flipped off the TV just as Tom and Melissa came back with Buster at her heels.

Kerry stood and smiled down at his daughter. "Are you ready to help me get dinner?"

"Yes!"

Hunter's pulse spiked at the sparkle in his daughter's eyes. Melissa missed her mom, needed a woman's touch.

He couldn't help but stare long after the two disappeared into the kitchen.

"Sweet little girl you got there, Hunter," Tom said.

He jerked to attention. "Yes she is. I wish I had more time to spend with her, but the job takes a lot of my focus."

"I hear ya," Kerry's grandfather said.

They sat in awkward silence for a long moment. "I wanted to thank you for letting my Kerry stay with you. I can't protect her like I used to." The sadness in the old man's voice tugged at his heart.

"I don't think I'm doing much in the way of protecting. It's more like I'm letting her hide at my place."

"Well, I'm glad she has you to look out for her. I miss her cooking though. She's a fine chef."

"Kerry's a remarkable woman." Her culinary skills weren't what drew him to her. Her passion in needing to identify the dead told him a lot about Kerry as a person. She had a lot of inner strength, spunk, and sincerity.

As long as they were talking about Kerry, now was Hunter's chance to learn more about her. "What made her leave her job in Ohio and come to Tampa?" He wasn't about to ask about any exes floating around.

She'd not been willing to share much with him. Kerry answered only when Melissa asked a question. Share, hell. When Hunter had touched her waist to help her reach a bowl in the top cabinet, Kerry had stiffened. Hunter wanted to find out who'd done a number on her.

Her grandfather wagged a finger. "You'll have to ask her yourself, young man. I stay out of her affairs."

Before Hunter could formulate another question, the phone in the kitchen rang, and every muscle in his body tensed. He sprang up from the chair and rushed into the kitchen. Kerry seemed frozen at the stove, staring at the phone. Melissa was at the sink washing her hands.

He wiggled his fingers for Kerry to answer the call. Hunter side-stepped to the sink. "Come on, sweetheart. Let's give Kerry some privacy." The phone kept ringing.

"Why can't I stay, Daddy?"

"Kerry's grandpa wants to show you something." The sharp shrill pierced his heart. *Answer it, Kerry!*

"Okay!" Melissa skipped out. Not wanting the caller to hang up, Hunter strode to the wall phone, picked up the receiver, and held it to Kerry's ear, leaving enough space for him to listen. Their cheeks practically touched, as did their fingers. He held his breath, waiting for the caller to speak.

CHAPTER SIXTEEN

IT WAS SUSAN. Kerry felt Hunter's shoulders relax against her body the moment her sister's voice boomed. He gave a gentle squeeze to her waist and walked back into the living room.

"Hi, Susan." Kerry wasn't certain she wouldn't have been happier speaking with the stranger. To be fair, Kerry hadn't seen her sister in over ten years. Maybe her older sister had changed.

Laughter floated in from the living room, barely louder than her racing heart. Kerry would have given anything to be with Hunter and Melissa rather than conversing with her sister. Seeing Hunter play with his daughter with patience and love would have helped erase her dread.

"I just arrived in Tampa," Susan announced.

With all the recent turmoil, Kerry had forgotten Susan's planned visit. She didn't need to be dealing with a killer and her sister at the same time, but she was curious to find out what was so important to make Susan creep back into town and chance running into her abusing ex-boyfriend.

"I wasn't expecting you so soon."

"I won't keep you, but could I stop over tomorrow night? We really need to talk."

"Where are you staying?"

"At the Holiday Inn on Fowler."

Thank God Susan didn't say she planned to stay with Grandpa. Uncharitable, but her sister had never been trustworthy.

"What time do you want to come over?" Kerry grabbed her stomach to stop the ache.

"After dinner. Around seven, okay?"

Hunter could drop her off at Grandpa's after work, pick her up and drive her back to his place afterwards.

"I'll be here."

Susan hung up without saying goodbye. Her sister must be uncomfortable with long conversations. Maybe she believed someone might trace her call—someone like the creepy boyfriend who'd harmed her. But then why come? And why call?

Kerry checked her watch. If Susan were in town, why not ask to come over now? Not that it mattered. Tonight, tomorrow, whenever, the two sisters would meet. Hell. It might not hurt to spend a few hours with her. Maybe Kerry would learn why her sister had acted so strangely when they were growing up.

Stepping over to the wall, she placed the receiver on the hook. Her fingers curled into a claw. She didn't need this visit right now, but she couldn't change it now.

Melissa. She needed to be with Miss Cheer. The little girl was the perfect antidote to the tension crawling up Kerry's shoulders and stabbing her at the back of her head.

She poked her head into the living room. "Who wants to help me cook?"

"Me! Me!" shouted the little girl.

Kerry had fallen hard for Hunter's daughter. Something about the way she lit up a room helped soothe Kerry's heart.

Together, Melissa and she prepared a very simple meal—tuna casserole, which was another one of Melissa's favorites.

"Don't forget to put the 'tatorchips on top," Melissa chirped.

Kerry smiled. "I wouldn't think of forgetting." She grabbed a small bag of chips from the pantry, opened it, and handed the bag to Melissa. "You can crunch them."

"Yes, ma'am." Melissa took the bag and pressed it between her small palms. "I can't wait to tell Katie I helped you, just like she helps her mommy."

God, she was cute. As comfortable as Kerry felt playing mom, her nerves were getting the best of her, and not all because of Susan's imminent visit. Kerry's gaze shot to the wall phone. The second news story had appeared less than ten minutes ago. Would the mysterious man call and berate her again? Or would she have another sleepless night wondering if a family member would recognize #4?

What's your problem, Herlihy? If the man calls, you'll have to hide out at Hunter's again for who knows how long. Do you want that?

Yes.

She refocused on the meal preparation. Kerry mixed the casserole and popped it into the oven. "While the dinner's cooking, let's go back and talk to your dad and my Grandpa."

Anything to keep from watching the phone. Being in the same room with the instrument of torture only ratcheted up her anxiety.

Melissa reached up and grabbed Kerry's hand. Her heart melted.

The hour-long news was wrapping up when the phone rang again. Hunter jumped up, but Kerry waved him off as she stood. "It's probably my sister calling me back. I'll get it."

She only half believed her statement. As calmly as she could, she walked back into the kitchen, each ring shredding her composure.

Hands trembling, Kerry picked up the receiver. "Hello."

"Did you expect me to call you at the detective's house?"

The man's words sunk in. How did he know she'd been staying at Hunter's? Spikes of fear marched up her spine. Violation and exposure made her mouth turn dry.

"Wh-who is this?" Her voice cracked. Damn.

"Stop... looking... for... these... women. They deserved to die. They're better off dead." His cold tone sent ice down her throat, cutting off her air.

With the phone to her ear, Kerry stumbled to the kitchen's entrance. Hunter must have followed her for he was by her side in a moment, listening, ear-to-ear.

Hunter's warmth and strength gave her the courage to ask, "Did you kill these women?"

"Tsk. Tsk. Ask any more stupid questions and you'll be next."

He disconnected with a sharp click, and the deafening silence rang in her ears. The trembling began in her hands and shot down her legs. Her fingers remained locked on the handset.

Hunter pried the receiver from her grasp and led her over to the chair. What had the caller wanted? Did he really think she'd stop looking? Who the hell was he?

Hunter gently placed the phone on the hook, and then squatted in front of her, taking her hands in his. "What else did the man say?"

Even Hunter's warm voice couldn't prevent her breath from pumping hard in her lungs.

"He...he knows I, ah, am staying at your house." She hiccupped.

Hunter leaned back on his heels and blew out a breath. "Shit. What else?"

"He told me not to try to identify the women."

"Did he say why?"

What had the man said? "I can't remember. I'm so sorry." He rubbed his thumb over her palm, and the pressure helped level out her breathing to a near calm, but she still had to fight the jumble mass of fear rushing through her brain.

"Did you recognize his voice? Was it Kopetski? Or Norwood?"

She'd promised herself she'd be more aware of his tone, his accent, how he spoke the next time he called. All rational thought disappeared the moment she heard him speak. "I don't know." He cast his gaze downward, but she couldn't lie. She had nothing concrete to tell him.

He squeezed her hand. "We need to find a safer place for you to stay."

A safer place than with Hunter? "Why can't I stay with you?"

"You said he knows where I live. It won't be safe for any of us there. I'll have to warn Jen, too. If he knows where I live, there's no telling what else he knows."

"Hunter, I'm so sorry. This is all my fault. If I hadn't made the clay—"

"No. Don't think that. It's your job to identify these women. You can't let him intimidate you. We'll take precautions to keep you safe. Without the clay reproductions, we may never learn who killed these women." He stood and slipped his hands from hers. "I'm going to make some calls. After dinner, we'll pack. Okay?"

"If this man knows I'm staying with you, he must know where I work." Panic gripped her hard. "He'll find me."

A reassuring lift of his lips made the ache in her head subside. "We'll let Dr. Ahern know he needs to keep an eye on you. You'll be safe with him."

"Okay." John Ahern was like the father she'd never had. He'd protect her. If Hunter drove her to work, she'd be safe as long as she didn't leave the building.

"I spoke with one of the men I work with, Cade Brentwood, who owns a remote cabin in Odessa he uses on occasion. He was planning to go there this weekend but said he'd go another time if we need the place. It'll be a long commute, but no one could follow us out there without me knowing."

"Is it safe?"

"Don't let its location fool you. He had a state-of-the-art security system installed."

Hunter ran a knuckle down her cheek.

The tender touch nearly made the dam of tears break loose. "Thank you."

"I wanna check if my men were able to trace the call."

She shook her head. "He wasn't on the line long enough, was he?"

"I can't say just yet. It'll be moot if he used a burner phone."

Kerry searched her mind for an article she'd read months ago. "Maybe the cell has a GPS? Can't we locate him from that?" Her voice rose to a screeching pitch.

"It's not as easy as it's made out, but we'll give it a try. If we do find where the signal originated from, I wouldn't be surprised if the phone's in a dumpster far from our caller."

Kerry wrapped her arms around her stomach, the sour sickness in her gut rising in her throat. She covered her mouth, slowly inhaling and exhaling until the feeling faded. What had she gotten herself into?

The oven timer dinged. Dinner. No way could she eat now, but for Melissa's sake, she'd have to put up a cheerful front.

Melissa came running into the kitchen and plopped down at the table. "I'm ready. Grandpa Hardy made me wash my hands again after I petted the dog." She held up her clean hands as proof.

Mustering as much composure as she could, Kerry served dinner while Hunter remained out of sight. His tense voice filtered in, but she couldn't make out the words.

He returned just as she piled food on Melissa's plate.

If Hunter's daughter hadn't asked a million questions, the dinner conversation would have been nil. Thank goodness, Grandpa ran with the ball and satisfied Melissa's curiosity about life. Kerry wished she could have given Melissa her full attention, because the little girl deserved so much more.

Once everyone finished, Kerry dumped her uneaten meal into the disposal. "Let's clean up, Melissa, so we can take you home." She hated how her voice wavered. She could only keep up the upbeat mood for so long.

After she and Melissa finished, Kerry slipped into her bedroom to pack for a longer stay. She hadn't brought much to Hunter's on the first go around—wishful thinking on her part that Hunter would catch the guy within the week.

On autopilot, she stuffed her clothes into two suitcases. She refused to think how long she needed to be away from her grandfather.

She dragged herself out to the living room, lugging both her large cases.

Grandpa and Hunter were shaking hands. "Take good care of her, Hunter."

"I will."

Kerry kissed her grandfather's cheek. "I'll call you."

Hunter brushed his fingers on her arm. "If you do call, it'll have to be from work. We don't want anyone tracing your calls to our new location."

* * *

AFTER THEY STOPPED BACK at Hunter's house for his and Melissa's clothes, they headed to Jen's. Kerry watched Hunter check the rear view mirror time and time again, his thumb and fingers playing some silent tune on the steering wheel.

Damn. Her confidence melted with each of his glances. On red alert, Kerry too, eyed every driver who passed by. It didn't matter no one paid attention to them. Her anxiety refused to go away.

They'd driven about fifteen minutes in silence when he reached across the seat and touched her hand. "You going to be okay?"

She swallowed the lump in her throat. "Sure. Why wouldn't I be?" She didn't need to let him know how scared she was. He'd probably insist she stay away from work, which she'd refused to do.

More than ever, Kerry was determined to identify these women—even if it was the last thing she did.

"It's okay to be afraid, you know. Actually, it's a good thing. It keeps you on your toes. Keeps you smart."

The man was a mind reader. Talk about scary. She turned her head toward the side window so he wouldn't see the tear trickle down her cheek.

Five minutes later, Hunter pulled into his sister's drive, and cut the engine. "Come on."

"I can stay out here. Are you going to be long?"

"No, but there's no telling who's out there."

Kerry swiped her cheek dry. She twisted around and checked the back seat. The precious child was sound asleep.

"Do you think Melissa is safe at your sister's?"

"Jen's husband is with the Special Forces. He's on leave for the next month and promised he wouldn't let her out of his sight."

He opened the back door of the cruiser and picked up his sleeping daughter as Kerry grabbed Melissa's small suitcase. His daughter snuggled in Hunter's arms. Kerry was going to miss the energetic little girl.

Before Hunter's finger reached the bell, Jen pulled open the door. Worry lined her face. Her gaze shot to Kerry and smiled.

The resemblance between Hunter and his sister was remarkable. Both were tall with a golden skin tone. Each had an athletic build, though Hunter was all muscle and Jen's weight was more evenly distributed.

"You must be Kerry. Come in."

For the first time in days, Kerry relaxed.

* * *

KERRY DECIDED Cade's cabin and the surrounding acreage was probably beautiful, but in the dark, the moss hanging from the trees looked like evil fingers reaching out to grab her. The area gave her the creeps, but she didn't want to make Hunter's life more miserable by complaining.

Thank goodness he'd parked in front of the house and not by the large barn that sat off to the side. A bare bulb glared from the top of the large wooden structure, casting spooky shadows on the building.

"What's in there?" she asked, pointing to the barn. Kerry climbed out of the front seat not letting her gaze wander from the mystery building. She had no idea why she needed to know, but the old place reminded her of Halloween—not the candy part, but the bad part.

"Cade is an old car buff. He restores classics."

"Oh."

Not evil at all. The dark must be making her mind imagine all sorts of things. Rather strange for a person who digs up bones for a living. She should be used to creepy things. Kerry inhaled deeply to help her relax. The air was sweet with jasmine, along with a hint of pine.

Her eyes adjusted to the darkness as she studied the large lake that bordered the property. The half moon glinted off the water and a few well-lit homes winked in the darkness far across the lake.

Hunter said nothing more as he carried his suitcase and one of hers into the house. She followed, lugging the other case.

Once inside, cool air met her. The relief of being out of sight helped calm her.

Hunter pointed to the small galley style kitchen they passed as they entered the cozy living room. "Cade told me he stocked the kitchen already. He made an extra trip up this evening and bought more food. Remind me to buy him a good bottle of scotch."

"That was very generous of him, especially since you only called him a few hours ago."

"That's Cade for you. He's the most proactive person I know."

Kerry put her suitcase on the scuffed wooden living room floor and looked around. The furniture was old but functional. One plaid couch, two leather chairs, a coffee table and two bookcases, filled to the brim with books, took up the entire living room. A small television was perched on top of a metal stand.

"You can stay in Cade's sister's room. I'll take Cade's room."

"I don't care if I have to sleep on the floor. Right now, I'm having a hard time standing."

"Come on. I'll show you where you can put your things. You can freshen up first if you want. There's only one bathroom."

One bathroom? Yikes. That might put a bit of a strain on their relationship.

* * *

PHIL LEANED BACK in his office chair and glanced over at Gina talking to Janet Hill, a vice squad detective. He had to hand it to her. During the first three weeks of her internship, Gina hadn't once mentioned she wanted to quit. He admired her spunk. However, she had yet to be exposed to the nasty side of death.

Harold Reismann, a gawky new recruit, dropped a folder on Phil's desk. "Lab results from the tool mark found at the gravesite just arrived."

"Oh yeah? What does it say?"

"I dunno. Boss just asked me to deliver it."

"You didn't peek?" Harold already had proven himself to be the department snoop. "You know the case has earned quite a lot press. It isn't every day we have a possible serial killer on the loose."

"I know." Red rushed up his face. "Okay, I did look, but only a little. The report mentioned something about a shovel, but that didn't seem very earth shattering."

Gina was convinced the long, smooth mark on the side of #1's grave belonged to a shovel owned by Willie Wyble. Not that she'd seen Wyble anywhere near a shovel, but her gut told her he'd dug the grave. She wasn't willing to go so far as to claim he'd killed anybody. She liked him for some reason. It was the whole cheer for the underdog thing, she'd said.

Phil grabbed the envelope from his desk, undid the clasp and read the report. Apparently, the shovel used to dig the grave had a bent corner. Other than that, it had no distinguishing marks. No brands were listed. It sounded like a dead end to him.

"Does it help?" Harold asked, as he shifted his weight from side to side and shoved his hands in his pockets.

"Doubt it." Phil skipped to the next page. "Oh, here we go. They processed a belt loop I found near #3's grave."

"Do you think it belonged to the killer?" The guy's voice rose half an octave.

"No telling. It came from a pair of Wrangler Jeans though."

"Oh. So nothing real good."

"Nope."

Pimply-faced Harold dragged back to the hole he'd come from just as Gina walked over. Phil had been angry about the babysitting job at first, but she was proving herself rather astute. Not to mention hot.

"What's up?" she asked, leaning a hip on his desk. Her skirt rode up on her thigh.

He'd reached his limit. She was a siren determined to get him in bed, but Phil was no dummy. Sleep with Gina—lose his job. He tugged on her skirt, but the fabric didn't budge.

"Hey." She swatted his hand away and leaned over. "You sure you want to go there?" One eyebrow lifted. "Taking my clothes off in public, Detective Tedesco, can be quite dangerous."

"I was doing quite the opposite."

Her sly smile almost made him forget about the shovel and the belt loop. "You are incorrigible."

As he was about to toss back a comment, Phil glanced up at the sound of pounding feet. "Ah, Gina. I think there's someone's here to see you."

Gina's uncle slipped around some desks and barreled right up to her. Jack Andries tapped her shoulder. Gina turned around and lost the color in her face. She was on her feet in a flash.

"It's not what you think," she blurted out.

Jack's lips curled downward. "We'll talk later. Right now, I need to speak to Phil. Alone."

CHAPTER SEVENTEEN

JACK ANDRIES FACED PHIL, his neck muscles straining. "We found Willie Wyble with a bullet in his head. I want you to be principal on this one."

Oh shit. "Tell me what you have."

"The cemetery owner, Jeff Lamont, found the body under some trees. I don't have any other details".

"Thanks, Captain."

The moment his boss slipped out of sight, Gina rushed up to him. "So?"

"I have a DB I need to investigate."

"I want to go."

"No."

She clung to his arm. If Jack Andries happened to come back, his boss would have a fit if he found his niece all over him.

"How am I supposed to learn anything if you keep me away from all the fun?"

Phil figured one look at a smelly dead body and she'd puke. It would be the end of her short career, and his boss would be happy. "Fine."

The moment she climbed in the cruiser, Gina started in on him again. "What did Uncle Jack say when I left? He was pissed, wasn't he?"

"Ya think? You're lucky he didn't chain you to the chair because of what you're wearing." Phil glanced over at her. She tugged on the neckline of her top and pulled down her skirt. Enough said. "You sure you want to see a dead guy? It could be gruesome."

"I'm not some delicate flower."

He refused to comment and would reserve judgment for after the viewing.

In light traffic, they made it to the cemetery in under twenty minutes. Three cop cars were sitting in front of the main building, lights swirling. Jeff Lamont, the proprietor of the cemetery, was talking to Quay Desmond, Phil's former partner. Good guy, but a little over the top in interrogation tactics.

"It's show time," Phil sang as he crawled out of the driver's seat.

The blistering heat caused instant sweat to pool under his arms. Gina smiled as she oozed out of the car. "So where is he?"

"Gotta ask first." Phil approached Quay. Gina followed right behind. "Whatcha got?"

"Why don't I let Mr. Lamont tell you?" Quay said. No rancor in his tone, but Phil wasn't naïve enough to think their rift was over.

Phil directed his gaze at Lamont. "The report said you found the body."

"Yes. I saw the front loader at the edge of the cemetery. That doesn't look good for the digger to be in plain sight, especially when we were about to have a viewing, so I went over to investigate. I admit I kind of panicked when I saw a foot sticking out from under some low lying branches."

Understandable. "Did you touch the body?"

"Kind of. There was a lot of blood, so I felt for a pulse." He shook his head once. "I was hoping he'd cut himself and had just passed out, but I didn't find any signs of life.

"Can you show us where you found him?"

"Sure. Let me get the golf cart. It's quite a walk." The cemetery proprietor whipped out a handkerchief and wiped his damp brow as he headed toward the large cement building. Being excessively overweight must be a bitch in late June.

"Mind if I tag along?" Quay asked.

"Sure. I can't quite get a handle on Lamont's agenda. You know Jack Andries' golden rule—safety in numbers."

"Oh, yeah, and you always did follow rules."

Phil caught the sarcasm in his tone. "I do when it suits me."

Quay chuckled. "By the way, I talked to the gardener. He didn't see or hear anything."

"Maybe the shooter used a silencer."

Quay shrugged. "The lab will be able to confirm or deny that theory."

"Did you call the M.E.?"

"On his way."

"Good."

Quay seemed to have overcome his two-year snit. Had Phil known Courtney was dating Quay, he never would have asked her out. Friends didn't snake dates from each other. He'd apologized, but Quay wouldn't forgive him.

Lamont rolled up in a golf cart, and the three of them climbed in. The bumpy drive took only a few minutes to reach the crime scene. Yellow police tape ringed the backhoe and small wooded area.

Arms crossed, Officer Ricardo stood watch, his face sheet white. Phil nodded to his fellow officer. "Jose."

Ricardo stepped into the shade. Gina stayed on the cart while Phil and Quay examined the backhoe. Blood spatter on the seat neatly outlined the shape of a head. The shattered front glass implied the shooter stood in front of the victim when he took aim.

"If he was shot here," Gina said, "why move the body?"

Phil whipped around. He hadn't heard her approach. "You'll have to ask the killer, though it's possible he wasn't dead on impact."

Gina slinked closer, looking cool and calm, despite the heat and the blood bath on the tractor and ground. "Unless the killer thought someone might come and investigate. If Willie Wyble was slumped over the wheel, it might draw more attention."

"I think the blood spatter would be a dead giveaway something was wrong."

She punched him in the arm. Guess she didn't like sarcasm. Welcome to the force.

Wanting to examine the body, he stepped over to the prone corpse. No need to ask Gina to join him, she'd be right behind him.

They ducked under the low-lying magnolia tree branches that gave some relief from the heat. Wyble's body was half under the tree, half out. From the body's position, Wyble could have fallen off his seat, and then crawled ten feet to his death.

Phil squatted behind the body. "These look like claw marks, like he pulled himself under the tree."

Quay joined him. "We'll need forensics out here, but I have to agree with you on this one." He shook his head. "How Wyble could move after being shot in the head is a mystery to me."

"The body can do some amazing things."

Gina knelt next to the body. Willie's right eye was dangling out of its socket where the bullet had entered. How could Lamont have thought Willie might have survived such an injury?

Dried blood covered the top part of Wyble's face, and flies were swarming around the gapping holes, enough to gag a seasoned cop. Phil expected her to puke. Instead, she reached toward Willie's fingers. On reflex, Phil yelled, "Don't touch him. As a matter of fact, we need to stay away from him until the medical examiner and crime scene unit do their thing."

She looked up at him. "I wasn't going to touch him. I wanted to see what he'd written."

"Written?" Phil and Quay inched closer.

Gina pointed to the ground. "Looks like a *D* and then an *o*."

Phil had to agree. "Let's let the CSU team photograph it. With the enhancement software, they might be able to make out the third letter. Good catch."

Gina smiled and lust grabbed him hard. Not the right response in this situation, but God, she was getting to him.

* * *

KERRY WALKED down the hallway to Dr. Quentin Dobbins' autopsy room. John had mentioned Dr. Dobbins had agreed to do the workup on the infant they'd found. Now that Tameka Dorsey and Janet Kopetski had been identified, and #4's face was in front of the public, Kerry wanted to focus on the remains of the little girl. If John couldn't confirm #4's cause of death, she'd investigate the woman's bones more thoroughly.

It sickened her to think she might never be able to identify #3. The killer had stolen her skull.

Nothing she could do about the theft now. The sheriff's department was working on the case. Her job now was to identify the baby. No mother should wonder about the fate of her child.

Hunter had pulled all the missing person files of infants for the past year, but none came close to the description of Baby Doe. She couldn't help but wonder if someone had smothered the girl in order to keep her from crying. Or had the baby died of some horrible disease? Had the parents wanted to cover up her death because they'd failed to act in time to save her?

Only good old-fashioned forensics would supply the answer.

Dr. Dobbins was busy working on a mature male when she slipped into his cold room. "Knock, knock."

The tall, thin man looked up. "Yes?" His hands continued to probe the body, and blood streaked his goggles and rubber gloves.

They'd never met, but John claimed Quentin was one of the best pathologists he'd ever worked with. "I'm working with John Ahern on the four women found in the field in North Tampa."

He plopped a liver into a tray and removed his mask. "How can I help you?" Not the most friendly greeting, but given the chore in front of him, she couldn't blame him for being a bit testy.

"We brought in an infant about three weeks ago. John said you'd be doing the autopsy, and I haven't gotten the results."

Dobbins removed his gloves and goggles and stepped over to a file cabinet. "Oh, yes. Sad case. John requested a rush on her. I finished running the tests quite some time ago and sent the report over to him." He lowered his chin and glared over his glasses. "Were you with him when the body was discovered? I don't recall seeing you before."

She didn't care for his accusatory tone, but she was the beggar here. "Yes. I'm Kerry Herlihy, a forensic anthropologist consulting for the summer."

He half smiled. "Oh, you're the one from Brahman University that John found."

"Yes."

"Welcome on board." His tone came out civil this time. "I usually work the late shift, so that's why we haven't crossed paths."

"Ah." Kerry straightened her lab coat. "I just assumed someone would have handed the little girl's remains over to me for identification purposes. I hadn't realized I needed to ask for them."

"No problem." He pulled open his desk drawer and leafed through a stack of folders. "Here is a copy of the report." He handed her the paper.

Kerry read what he'd given her. "Natural causes?"

"Nothing else was conclusive. I ran a tox screen but came up with nothing. The pathology showed only healthy tissue." His posture softened. "We only had the lower part of her body and nothing pointed to a violent COD."

She wondered if he'd studied the bones for fractures. "Where's the body now?"

"In drawer number three. Help yourself."

"Thank you."

"I'd like to do a facial reconstruction on her and scan her face into our age progression software. I'm sure someone has to be missing her."

"Given she was buried without a casket, I'm guessing that someone didn't want anyone to find her."

How could someone dump a baby in a grave in the middle of the woods? "Did you send her DNA in for testing?"

"No. I didn't see the need given we have nothing to compare it to. If you can get a possible identity, then I'll go ahead with the matching process. However, don't hold your breath for an answer from the lab for a few months. They're backed up right now."

"If Tampa's labs are anything like the ones in Cleveland, they'll stay perpetually backed up."

"Sad but true." He pulled out the morgue drawer, removed the tiny body bag and placed her on a gurney. "Knock yourself out."

Kerry's heart ached for what she was about to do. She wanted to clean the bones to see if she could determine evidence of violence. "Thank you."

"Just let John know you have her."

"Will do."

With a heavy heart, Kerry wheeled the young female down the hall. The edge of her gurney knocked into Steven's thigh as he breezed out of John's lab.

"I'm so sorry. Did I hurt you?"

"No I'm fine," he said rubbing his leg.

Thank goodness he wasn't hurt, but he did always seem to be under foot. "I must have been off in la-la land."

Without asking permission, he grabbed the cart and steered it into her lab. "Who you got here?"

"The little girl John and I processed about three weeks ago. I want to do a facial reconstruction on her."

"You have any luck with the other faces you did?"

She held open the door, and Steven pushed the gurney into the lab. "Actually, yes. Jane Doe #1 was identified by her fiancé. I'm still waiting to see whether anyone recognizes #4."

"But a baby? They kind of look alike. Won't it be hard?"

"Yes, very hard, but I have to try. Can you imagine the pain the parents must be in?"

"No, I can't."

Once he parked the cart under the overhead light, Kerry lifted up the maceration station hood and grabbed the large stainless steel pot.

"Here, let me help you." Steven took the pot from her and placed it in the sink. "Dr. A told me some crank caller threatened you after he saw you on TV."

"Yes, can you believe it?"

She filled the large container with water, and then added some mild detergent, along with some bleach. No use subjecting herself to more smell.

"Here, let me put this back on the burner for you." Steven carried the filled pot to the station and set it on the burner. "That's a heavy mother."

"I know." She'd hurt her back the last time she had to lift the water.

He swiveled to face her, his back blocking the burner. "I didn't see your car in the lot when I drove in."

"Excuse me." Steven moved out of the way. "Detective Markum is driving me to work. He's afraid my caller might come after me."

His brows rose and the ends of his lips turned up. "I didn't realize the police offered door-to-door service."

Kerry face heated. "I think it's more than the usual police concern." She added the meat tenderizer, keeping her back to Steven, not wanting him to see the blush that colored her face.

"He likes you?" Steven hopped on the counter next to the station. "You want to talk about it? I'm a good listener."

She turned back to him. "Some other time maybe." Kerry smiled. "I really do need to work."

The guy was sweet, but she couldn't afford the time to chat. She was, after all, on temporary loan from Brahman University. If she ever expected more jobs from the M.E.'s office, she had to perform well.

He jumped down and saluted, nearly knocking her purse off in the process. "My bad." He pushed her purse to the back of the counter, safely out of the falling zone. "Then I shall leave you to the infant."

Before she could unzip the body bag, Steven disappeared out the door. She sobered the moment her fingers touched the body. The chore ahead would test her resolve to the max. This could have been her child had her baby lived.

Don't do this to yourself. The only way to bring comfort to the parents was to find the identity of the child.

With a plastic utensil, Kerry scraped the soft tissue from the bones, forcing her mind on the technique, not on the person beneath. Next, she brushed the bones clean and placed them in the pot of warm, soapy water.

With the worst of the job complete, she studied the cranium, hoping to find a clue as to the baby's cause of death, brushing away her tears with back of her hand. The skull had been broken into a few pieces, but with a little glue, she'd be able to recreate the whole cranium.

While she couldn't tell what the baby looked like from the bones alone, she bet the child would break the most calloused of hearts.

It was such a horrible, horrible tragedy. When the tears blurred her vision, she closed the fume hood and placed the dried bones in anatomical order. Before she'd managed to put the hand together, her door creaked open. Hunter?

She looked up and froze.

CHAPTER EIGHTEEN

"Susan?" Kerry's jaw tightened, and her stomach swirled.

Kerry almost didn't recognize her sister standing in the doorway. The security guard was behind her. "She said she was your sister," he said. "She wanted to surprise you."

"She did at that. Thank you."

He nodded and closed the door.

Why was Susan wearing red glasses instead of her customary contact lenses? Not that it mattered.

Kerry studied her. Something else looked different—out of place. Sure, Susan's hair had streaks of gray and her hips looked much wider than they had ten years ago, but those signs of aging were normal.

Her sister's nose looked as though she'd broken it, and the cartilage hadn't healed properly. That's what was different. Had Brad done that?

Susan rushed in. "I know I said I'd meet you at seven, but Grandpa told me you had to move out because of some psycho. I came to Tampa just to see you, and I didn't want you to disappear on me like I used to do to you." She chuckled, but the tight lines around her mouth told Kerry that Susan saw nothing funny in her statement.

"What a minute. Did you say disappear?" Queasiness grabbed her. "You're admitting you abandoned me when we were growing up?"

Susan avoided eye contact by glancing over at the bones on the metal gurney. She wrinkled her nose and pointed to the remains of Baby Doe. "What are those?"

Everyone knew what bones looked like. What game was Susan playing now? "They're the skeleton of an infant, a baby girl, or at least most of the bones." Kerry forced her tone to be even.

Susan's face turned ashen. She grabbed the top of the desk chair next to the gurney and slid onto it. "How did the baby die?"

Kerry couldn't figure out if this was some kind of ploy to soften her up or if the appearance of the small bones truly distressed her sister.

"I'm not sure. Florida had some pretty heavy rains last fall that washed the dirt away from the grave site and exposed the body bag." Susan didn't need the grim reality of the dog ripping apart the heavy plastic. "We're still trying to determine cause of death."

Susan covered her mouth for a moment. "How terrible. She wasn't in a casket?" Her eyes brimmed with tears.

"No. Someone buried her in the woods. Why the interest?"

"How old was she?"

Susan's quick change of focus more than hinted she wasn't ready to address Kerry's questions of abandonment. "Susan why did you come? I don't think it was because you were interested in my work." Yes, she sounded bitter, but Kerry's pent up anger got the best of her.

"I wanted to tell you my side of the story of what happened years ago. I've kept my secret way too long."

"Secret?"

"Yes. Secret. I know I've hurt you, and I want to right that wrong."

Kerry didn't have time for some phony confession, or some made up secret for that matter. "I'm busy right now." Another harsh comment, but her sister had never been straight with her.

Susan leaned forward. "I know you hate me." She reached out and grabbed Kerry's hand. Kerry flinched, but didn't pull away. "Trust me, I only did what was best for you when you were young."

"That's rich." She slid her hand from Susan's tense grasp and fiddled with the bones on the cold, metal tray. "Why should I believe you now?"

"Maybe because it's the truth."

Kerry was tired, irritable and pissed, but Susan's words rang true. No doubt her stubborn sister wouldn't leave until she vented. "Fine. Tell me about this secret."

"Do you want to sit?"

"No." She wanted to pace, stomp, kick something. Instead, she stood still.

Susan let out a long breath. "I'm not sure where to begin."

"Don't do this, Susan. Just start at the beginning."

She sucked in an audible breath. "I know you think I always ran off when Mom left town, but it's not what you think."

Kerry's hands flew to her hips. "That's because you always did."

Susan slipped a strand of hair behind her ear, a habit Kerry always adopted.

"I realize now how terrible and frightening my disappearing act must have been for you."

Took her long enough to figure that one out. "I was only seven. You were supposed to stay with me, watch me, make sure I was taken care of. At least that's what Mom told you to do. What was I supposed to think when you took off and stuck me with the drunk neighbor?"

"I know. My leaving was inexcusable." Susan studied her lap. "I used to visit Dad whenever Mom left town for one of her auditions. He didn't like picking me up when she was around."

"You spent alone time with Dad? I always thought we visited him together."

"I didn't want you to know. That's why I told you I was out with my friends."

This was getting them nowhere. "Yeah, you always had some reason why I couldn't come. I asked Mom about that once, but she said teenagers needed to be away from their sisters sometimes. I believed her."

Susan bit her lower lip and sniffled. She surveyed her hands. "Daddy and I did more than visit. I never told you. In fact, I never told anyone." Susan twisted her fingers together.

Something wasn't right. Oh, shit. A two-by-four could have smacked her across the back of her head, and Kerry wouldn't have been more surprised. "Are you saying Daddy *molested* you?" Kerry's pulse zipped to warp speed. That couldn't be true.

Shame slammed across Susan's face. "Yes. If I hadn't agreed to service him, he said he'd...he'd come after... you."

Kerry's mouth dropped open. "When I was six or seven?" Her legs weakened and bile rose up her throat.

"Yes. It was unthinkable, is unthinkable, but I was fourteen when the abuse began. He was our dad. I believed he'd harm you if I didn't do what he said."

From Susan's shifting eye movement, Kerry knew her sister was telling the truth, and a wave of disgust blasted her. "Couldn't you have told Mom?" Kerry slipped down in the seat next to Susan.

Her sister leaned forward. "You don't understand what it was like. He made me promise not to tell anyone. I know he would have hurt you if I hadn't done what he'd asked. Besides, do you think Mom would have believed me? She claimed Dad could do no wrong."

"Until he took up with another woman and left us."

"She always became angry when I bad mouthed him."

Mom was a wonderful, warm woman, but she was often in denial about most issues. Too bad she had more prescription drugs than a pharmacy, which made their mom less than coherent at times.

Reality stabbed Kerry in the heart. "You protected me and never told me?" How could she have been so blind for so long?

Susan cocked a brow. "At seven, would you have understood?"

Kerry's mind took a trip back in time. "I guess not." She wanted to forgive her sister, but Kerry recognized there was a lot more to the story. "When Daddy died, why didn't you tell me about the abuse then?"

Susan pushed her glasses up the bridge of her nose—a definite stall tactic. "Shame maybe. Besides, you were in high school and able to fend for yourself. Why ruin your year? Even after the abuse ended. I wasn't ready to face what I'd done." Susan stared off into space for a moment.

"Couldn't you have spoken to a shrink or something?"

"Maybe, but I thought if I just left town, I'd be fine. I wasn't ready to confront Mom with the accusation Dad abused me while she did her thing. Knowing her, she would have pushed me even further away, so I came to Florida. Grandpa was someone I could count on."

"At least we agree on one point." Kerry had missed so much of her sister's life, and sadness replaced bitterness. "How could you leave Ohio though? It was our home."

"You left too."

"But I had a good reason."

"So did I."

She'd give Susan a chance to explain. "I'd like to hear it."

Susan studied the hanging light in the ceiling before fixing a look at Kerry. "You were in school when I met a guy who I thought would solve all my problems and help me get away from Dad. Only Brad was as bad as our father. Eventually, I had to hide from him too, had to leave."

Ohmigod. "He abused you, didn't he?"

She nodded as her lower lip trembled. "I didn't want to leave you or Mom, but I had no choice. You think I wanted to quit my teaching job and sever ties to everything I held dear?"

"That would be hard." If Kerry ever had to stop working with bones, she'd go crazy.

"Damn right it was hard, but if I hadn't, Brad would have hounded me. Trust me, I moved three times and he still found me. He even showed up at work." Susan shook her head. "I finally had to pay a skip tracer to help me hide. I had to give up my career, my friends, my church group, everything. Only Grandpa knew I was in Florida. Even then we had to be super careful anytime we contacted each other."

"You couldn't have called me? Even once?"

"Back then, they didn't have burner phones. I always believed somehow I'd slip up and Brad would trace my call. He was a computer programmer, and well-trained in all the latest technology. You were in college and happy. Grandpa kept me informed what was happening in your life. Why ruin things?" Susan shifted in her seat. "Would you have welcomed my calls back then?"

"Maybe not." Kerry swallowed hard, thinking of the trauma Susan had suffered. "Grandpa said you'd met someone in Florida."

She shook her head. "I told Grandpa that. I was pregnant with a little girl and had to make up an imaginary man. Brad was the father."

The first hint of excitement raced through her. "You have a baby?" Without thinking, her own hand shot to her belly.

"I *had* a baby. Eventually, Brad found me. I called you when Grandpa told me Mom had died."

"I remember."

"I was careless with my landline. Brad arrived on my front doorstep about a week later."

Kerry couldn't imagine her sister's pain. "And your daughter?"

Tears streaked down Susan's face. "He stole her."

"Stole her?" Kerry could only imagine the trauma. When her unborn child had died, devastation kept her company for months. "Why didn't you report him?"

"I did, but what could the police do? They couldn't find him."

"Didn't you look for Brad and your baby yourself?"

Choked up, Susan couldn't speak for a moment. "Yes, but I never found them. I went back to Ohio, thinking he may have gone back there. I've been looking ever since."

Susan's story explained everything. How could Kerry have been so angry that she didn't search deeper for the truth? She'd dismissed her sister, thinking she was evil.

Who else had she misjudged?

* * *

PHIL SHADED his eyes from the strong sun. "Mr. Lamont, would you mind if we look in the cemetery's storage shed?"

Lamont swiped a clean handkerchief over his forehead. "No, but whatever for?" His shoulders straightened. "You don't think *I* had anything to do with Willie's death do you?"

A yellow jacket buzzed near Phil's head. He stood still, not wanting to piss off the pesky insect. "We have no cause to suspect you."

Lamont's muscles relaxed. "Look away. The shed is unlocked." He pointed to the small storage unit.

Unlocked? Great. Anyone could have accessed the lawn equipment. "Come on, Gina, let's explore."

She lifted the edge of her shirt, dipped her head and wiped her brow. "Aren't you hot in those long pants?"

Hot for her, maybe. "I'm used to the heat." Not really, but wearing shorts was unprofessional.

"Can't we use the golf cart?" she whispered. He could tell she was trying to keep the whine out of her tone, but she had failed.

"The walk's less than the length of a football field."

He took off and Gina followed. "What are you hoping to find in that dirty old building?" she yelled after him.

"A shovel with a bent edge."

She rushed next to him. "You think Willie Wyble had something to do with the murders?"

Phil chuckled. "Let's not jump to conclusions so fast. There are probably a hundred bent shovels in Tampa alone, but I need to make sure there isn't one here."

Gina jogged next to him to keep up. How did she stay so upbeat? Looking at Willie should have made her sick. Women. He'd never understand them.

As Lamont had claimed, the shed door was unlocked. In fact, it was half-open, which would give easy access to anyone.

Once inside, he squinted to adjust to the darkness. Gina extracted a small Mag light from her purse and flicked it on. Her level of preparedness impressed him. She was a real girl scout. The thin wash of light allowed them to maneuver in the cramped space without tripping. Bags of fertilizer, rakes, mulch, and a riding lawn mower took up most of the space.

Gina swung the light around the fifteen by ten foot room. "There are a bunch of shovels," she said, pointing the light to the far corner.

Phil pulled on a new pair of latex gloves from his pocket and slipped them on. "Gimme the light."

She obliged. "What is it?"

Phil lifted one of the shovels. "See here. The tip is bent. Looks like it might match the Jane Doe case Hunter's working on."

"Cool."

"Or else I'm desperate to find something." Phil returned the light to Gina. They left with the shovel, hoping Lamont wouldn't mind if they processed it. The CSU team was finishing up across the grassy lot, and the medical examiner and his technicians were loading Willie's body into the van. Time to see Lamont.

A slew of cars were pulling into the half-full parking area, indicative of a viewing. He turned to Gina. "Why don't you wait in the car and start the AC? I'll be out in a minute."

"I'd rather come with you," Gina said.

He didn't have time to argue. "Wait in the car. Please." He held out the keys.

She snatched them and shuffled back to the vehicle. Phil entered the chapel and asked for Mr. Lamont. A young woman directing the grieving relatives and friends to the chapel, pointed to an office down the corridor.

Phil knocked and entered. Lamont lifted his head. "Yes, Detective?"

Phil raised the shovel. "Do you mind if we process this?"

His lips pulled back into a thin line. "Whatever for?"

"Willie, or someone, might have used this in another crime."

"I think you're grasping at straws. Willie would never harm anyone." He waved a hand. "But go ahead if you think it will help. I have nothing to hide."

"Do you know Mr. Wyble's home address?"

Lamont huffed out a laugh. "Willie didn't even have a home that I knew of. I'm not sure where he went when he left work."

"Did he have any relatives?"

Lamont's focus shifted down to the right. A moment later, he pulled open a desk drawer. "I did have him fill out an application. Or rather, *I* filled out his application for him. Willie said his hand shook too much to write, but I don't think he knew how."

"If the letters in the dirt by his head are any indication, he did."

Lamont opened a file and handed Phil the paper. "Home address is blank, but he does give an address for a sister."

"Could you make a copy for me?"

"You can have this one. I have no use for his information anymore."

"Thanks."

Phil and Gina left with the shovel in hand. Phil wasn't sure if there was any connection between Willie Wyble's death and the four Jane Doe murders, but he needed to follow every clue. Right now, it was all they had to go on.

On the way out of the cemetery, Phil called Willie's sister's cell phone. She said she wouldn't be home until five thirty. "We've got an hour to kill. You up for a bite?"

"Sure, why not?" While her words sounded chipper, her tone did not. Gina's enthusiasm for crime solving seemed to have dried up.

In fact, instead of blasting him with a thousand theories about Willie's death and the connection to the shovel, she stared out the cruiser window. She appeared to be more affected by the corpse than he'd realized, so Phil let her mull over her thoughts in peace.

Once they were served at the restaurant, Gina picked at her food, but he wisely didn't razz her about her reaction.

Phil swiped a napkin across his mouth and signaled the waitress for the check. "Time to interview the sister."

They followed Ella Wyble Jones' directions to her home in a posh neighborhood in South Tampa, which came as quite a surprise given Willie's homeless state.

A Hummer sat in Mrs. Jones' drive. Phil estimated the house to be about thirty-five hundred square feet and the lot about seventy-five by one hundred. The zero lot line was too claustrophobic for him. The rows of colored flowers that bordered the walkway were a nice touch, but he wouldn't live on such a busy street. He liked a neighborhood where kids could run down the middle of the road and play ball.

"Nice place," Gina said. She tugged on her skirt as they neared the front door.

"If you like the up tight, money kind of place. I'd be surprised if she ever let Willie in her house."

Mrs. Jones answered after the first ring. He flashed his badge.

"Detectives. Please come in."

He guessed her to be in her mid to late forties. Although her makeup was perfect, it didn't hide the red color rimming her eyes.

Mrs. Jones directed them to two leather chairs facing the screened-in pool. She sat opposite them on a new-looking suede sofa.

"We're sorry for your loss, ma'am," Phil said.

"Thank you. As you might have guessed, Willie and I didn't come in contact with each other very often, though God only knows I tried. Willie had...issues."

"Yes, ma'am." He could only imagine what plagued the man. "Do you know of anyone who would have wanted to harm your brother?"

She blew her nose. "No."

"Did he ever mention any friends or acquaintances he might have spent time with?" Somebody had to know the company Willie kept.

She shook her head and her cheeks sagged. "Willie was a loner. He did odd jobs for people. My brother liked to dig. Dig dirt, dig for worms, dig for the sake of digging. As you probably know, he worked for Mr. Lamont at the Fair Lawn Cemetery on a regular basis."

"We spoke with Mr. Lamont. Do you know of anyone else Willie came in contact with?"

"He shared a *space* by the Crosstown with Tanner Nash. His favorite spot was under the overpass on Willow Avenue."

Hunter questioned her further about Willie's mental state, but he didn't learn much, other than the fact Ella Jones cared for her brother.

"If you think of anything, give me a call." Phil handed her his card and stood.

Once outside, spunk came back into Gina's step. She'd said nothing during the short interview.

Gina jumped into the cruiser and slammed the door. "If I ever buy a house, it won't be formal like this one. I was afraid to sit on the furniture."

"Then I think you might feel more comfortable where we're going next."

CHAPTER NINETEEN

KERRY HADN'T BEEN able to sit still ever since Hunter had picked her up from the morgue and taken her to the cabin in no-man's land. Susan's visit had diverted her thoughts from yesterday's threatening phone call, but now the man's eerie words, "You'll be next," reverberated in her head.

At first she thought the warning might be purely bravado. Perhaps he wanted people to think he was the serial killer and all he wanted was attention, but his crisp words sounded educated. Not that educated people couldn't kill, but...aw hell, she had no idea what to think anymore.

Still, if he had nothing to do with the murders, why call her? And how did he get her number? And how did he know she was staying with Hunter?

These random thoughts were driving her crazy. Okay. She admitted it. She was turning into a paranoid idiot. In fact, every noise made her jump. This afternoon when someone had dropped a metal pan outside her autopsy room, she'd nearly had a heart attack. If that wasn't bad enough, tonight when a cloud passed over the setting sun and cast an eerie shadow on the window she'd flinched. Twice in fact, she'd sworn she'd seen a face peering in at her.

Too bad Hunter had been doing his thing in the kitchen when the last image flashed by. Without someone else to corroborate her sighting, she had to believe she was losing her mind. After all, Hunter had claimed no one had followed them to this desolate house.

Another shadow zipped by the cabin window, and her blood pumped through her system. She must have whimpered or something because Hunter came racing out with a dishtowel in his hands.

"Are you all right?"

"It's nothing, really." She chuckled. "For a moment, I thought I saw something outside. Can you believe it? A bird must have been flying close to the window and cast a shadow." Though at six thirty, the sun was low in the sky. "Go back to doing what you were doing. I'll be okay." Or not. Her nerves were close to doing her in.

He studied her. "I'll check it out. Be right back."

Before she'd had a chance to tell him her imagination was out of control, he'd tossed the towel on the dining table, slipped his gun from his holster he'd slung on the back of the chair, and disappeared outside.

Kerry waited on the sofa while Hunter investigated, her toe tapping out a beat, and her gaze never leaving the window. Why she didn't want to press her face against the glass and look for herself was anyone's guess.

When Hunter flung himself in front of the pane and made a funny face, her hand shot to her chest. She laughed, and then hiccupped. No pills could have been a better cure for her anxiety than seeing Hunter Markum acting silly—something she never expected from the always-in-control man.

At her smile, he ducked out of sight and returned inside. "The boogie man is *not* outside," he announced with authority. "Wait here. I have something for you."

The refrigerator door banged open and a drawer closed. Hunter jumped out of the kitchen with two beers in his hand. "Ta da." He handed her the cold bottle.

Could she use a drink, or what? The tangy liquid raced down her throat. "That hit the spot. Thank you." She grasped the beer bottle with both hands and settled the drink on her lap. "I can't seem to stop the caller from getting to me. Thank you for looking around." She stood and paced the small strip between the living room and dining room.

"No problem. I didn't see any signs anyone had been here." He took a swig of his drink. "Hey, we'll get this guy. I promise."

Her spine tingled. "I know, it's just..."

He placed his drink on the coffee table, sidled over to her, and put her bottle down. As Hunter ran his strong hands from her shoulders to her wrists, her heart raced.

God, the man was a beautiful creature. Golden skin, blue eyes, and black, wavy hair that fell over his forehead. His musky scent raced to her brain and almost made her forget her anxiety.

"Everything will be fine," he said in the tenderest tone.

"I know I'm out of control and that my worries are irrational, but I have this premonition this madman isn't going to leave me alone."

"Your concerns are real, but if we take precautions, we'll win. Besides, I won't let anything happen to you." He smoothed a knuckle down her cheek.

Her heart warmed at his attention. She wanted him, but she refused to be sucked into a world that could hurt her. Hunter would leave, like everyone else she knew. His job meant the world to him.

"I feel foolish worrying you," she said, breaking the silence between them. Hunter could protect her. At least while they were both in the cabin. "Again, thank you." She reached up to touch him but stopped part way.

His gaze left her face for a moment, and then he cleared his throat. "Just doing my job."

His job. "Right."

Hunter never said whether he was paid to protect her, so maybe something else was going on.

He stepped back. "Why don't you start work on the Baby Doe reconstruction? I'm the principal on the case, remember?" He tapped her nose. "And I don't like cold case files." He flashed her a quick smile before sobering. "I want to solve this one almost more than the murders of the four women."

"Really?" Kerry understood he cared for the dead, deeply, but she hadn't realized he differentiated between victims like she did. "I feel the same way."

"I know."

As if some magical force pressed against her back, she took a step closer. She told herself she only wanted to feel his warmth. Who was she kidding? She wanted to grab his strength and be...well, connected with him. They shared a common bond.

Instead of rushing into his arms, she placed a finger on his chest. "If anyone can find who did this horrible thing to the child, it's you."

He flashed her another smile. "I wouldn't go that far, but I'll try my best to get the perpetrator."

She bet compliments were far and few between in his line of work. "I know you will."

He squeezed her upper arms and dropped his hands. "I'll whip us up something for dinner while you work."

Kerry's mouth half opened. "Wait a minute. You want to cook?" Melissa warned her he'd ruined more meals than he'd made edible. "For my health, maybe I should cook."

"You're taking my daughter's side?" He winked. "Why I make the best mac and cheese in the world. You just wait and see."

She laughed for real this time. "You win. The sooner I begin the reconstruction, the closer we'll be to identifying the toddler. At least I'm not worried I'll receive an angry phone call about *this* case. The man who murdered the woman can't be the same person who buried this little girl. If he wrapped her in a jacket and buried her with a teddy bear, the person cared."

"I'd say you're right on that count. Completely different MO, thank God."

"Do you remember the woman the cops fished out of the ocean that John had me help with?" Talking about any case other than the toddler case helped release the knots in her neck.

"Yeah. What about her?"

"Did you ever show her photo at the shelter?"

His whole body tensed. "Damn. I'm sorry. I haven't had the chance to go. I promise I'll check tomorrow."

"No problem. I know you're not principal on that one."

"I'll check who is and let you know if they've brought in a person of interest."

"Thanks."

Once Hunter disappeared into the small kitchen, she spread her gear on the dining room table. This time she'd taken the time to make a plaster cast of the skull. No way would she chance losing evidence again. Once was enough.

The child's jaw was missing, but she'd been able to put the cranium together using super glue. There were some cracks in the skull where an animal had bitten into the hard surface, but considering where they'd found the remains, she was happy with what she did have. The plaster mold looked good. She hoped she'd guessed correctly on the size and shape of the missing jaw.

Hunter said they were processing the jacket and teddy bear but didn't expect to find much because of the length of time since the infant's burial. Water and dirt had soaked the two items, rendering genetic material unviable. Her hope now was to get DNA from the tiny bones. However, without a parent to donate their own DNA, the chances of finding a match to the child were slim. Hunter had checked the missing children reports, but none matched the sex, age, race and time frame for this infant.

Before she realized how long she'd been working on the face, Hunter waltzed out of the kitchen carrying a bowl of mac and cheese into the living room/dining room area. The rich aroma of strong cheddar filled the air, and her stomach grumbled. Her last meal had been hours ago.

"Here ya go." Pride colored his face.

"That was fast. I'm sorry Melissa isn't here to join us," she said. "I bet she would have loved this dinner."

"Her second favorite meal, but I imagine she's eating real good stuff at Jen's."

Kerry took the bowls from his hands set them down on the coffee table. "My work is kind of taking up most of the room on the table. Mind if we eat over here?"

"I can eat standing up, being shot at, or stuck in the middle of a hurricane. The coffee table is luxury, trust me."

That phrase word again. Trust. Twice in two days. Why was she so afraid to let go of her fears?

Kerry dropped onto the sofa, expecting Hunter to sit in the leather chair off to the side. Wrong. He sat right next to her, their legs touching.

Hormones and adrenaline zinged through her veins. He smelled of kitchen soap with a hint of pine. Part of her told her to scoot over, but the portion of her brain that controlled her hormones told her to stay put.

While she'd never been married, she was no stranger to intense affairs. A short-term fling with the sexy detective wouldn't be so bad, would it? It might even help her focus on something other than her past.

"You okay?" Hunter asked.

Heat zipped up her face. "I'm fine. Was I staring?" *Please don't say I looked dreamy eyed.*

He had the gall to laugh. "I'd say. You looked like you were on some island paradise."

With you. Her body temperature nearly broke the mercury on the thermometer. If only she had paranormal powers, she'd blink or twitch her nose to disappear. No luck on that front. Instead, she stuck a mouthful of food into her mouth and looked away. She swallowed and glanced back at him. Hunter hadn't moved, his gaze still on her. He leaned toward her.

Please don't let him kiss me. I have no willpower to stop him.

* * *

"THIS SUCKS," Gina complained. "Are we going to stay here all night? How do we know this vagrant will even show up? What do you expect him to tell us? How do you—"

"Welcome to the world of surveillance." Given Gina didn't take a breath or stop long enough to hear his response, she obviously wasn't interested in what he had to say.

Phil pulled out a cold bottle of water from a cooler in the back of the cruiser and handed it to her.

"Thanks." Gina slumped back into the seat.

He was about to lecture her on patience and perseverance when a disheveled man in a plaid shirt, stained pants, and matted hair rounded the corner. "I think we may have our Nash character. Stay here."

"Like hell I will. He's not dangerous. Look at him." The man, holding his paper bag with both hands, climbed two feet up the incline, stopped, and then proceeded another two feet, his chest heaving in between steps. Gina pushed open the door and slid out. "He's having a hard time making it up the slope to his mattress. He has to be in his sixties. I'm coming with you."

Christ. If her uncle ever found out about this, Phil would be pushing paper behind a desk all day instead of solving homicides. When it came to Gina, he had a hard time saying no.

"Mr. Nash," Phil shouted.

The homeless man halted once more and turned around. He squinted, turned back and headed up to the torn mattress at the top of the incline.

"Come on," Phil said, as he crossed the street.

The heat combined with the trapped exhaust fumes made breathing unpleasant. Gina didn't look so good either. He grabbed her hand as they began climbing the slope. She was such a rookie. When would she learn not to wear heels on a stakeout? He'd tell her, but she looked too damned good. Why ruin a good fantasy?

"Mr. Nash?" Phil said.

The old man dropped down on his mattress. His breath came out ragged. "Yeah?"

Phil flashed his badge and the old guy squinted. He leaned closer and fear scampered across his face. "I didn't do nothin'."

"I know. I wanted to talk to you about Willie Wyble."

"Haven't seen him."

"That's because he's dead." Phil waited for a reaction, but none came.

"So? I didn't kill him. Me and him were friends."

Phil glanced behind him. Gina wisely kept back, her hand over her nose. Poor girl.

Phil squatted in front of the man. "I'm trying to find out who might have wanted to hurt Willie. Any ideas?"

"No." Nash's gaze shot to the right then left. Liar.

"Can you tell me who he worked for besides the man at the cemetery?"

"How should I know?"

Phil inhaled a couple of slow breaths. "You shared this overpass. I'm betting you two talked. Look, I know Willie loved to dig. Dig for worms, dig graves."

Nash smiled. His teeth were surprisingly even and white. "He did love to dig them graves too. He had a cell phone, ya know, and would get calls late at night for a digging job. Someone would pick him up and take him different places. He'd come back happy. Always brought a bottle with him. Willie was good at sharing."

Excitement raced through Phil. "Did this person drive a black Hummer by any chance?" Could the driver have been Willie's sister?

"Never saw one of them. As I said, there were different cars at different times."

"Okay. Can you describe one of cars that picked him up? It might have been as long as a year or two ago."

Nash took a swig from whatever was in his paper bag. "Nope."

He reached into his pocket, fished out a five-dollar bill, and waved it in front of the man. "Try harder."

Nash swiped the money. "One van. I couldn't forget it. It had Medical Examiner seal on the side."

Oh shit.

CHAPTER TWENTY

HAPPY TO HAVE an excuse to get away from the cabin, Hunter slipped out without grabbing the kiss he wanted. Kerry tempted him like no other woman had. When their legs had touched on the sofa, his thigh almost caught on fire. Thank God he'd held back. Her eyes had widened, and then she'd stuffed a handful of food in her mouth.

He'd almost laughed out loud at her reaction to their contact. She'd wanted him, and he wanted her, too, but now wasn't the time. If he hadn't been working a case with Kerry, he sure as hell would have given her a kiss she would have remembered for a lifetime.

Half the time she acted as if she wanted to jump his bones, and the other half, she pulled away as though he were the abuser. Women. He'd never understand them.

On a good note, he was pleased she'd confided in him about her sister's visit. During her discussion, Kerry appeared more relaxed around him than she had before when they were alone. When he questioned her about her childhood though, she'd closed her mouth tighter than a clam out of water. Can't win 'em all.

Understanding his reaction to her, he wisely decided to leave, at least for a short while. Kerry would be safe, since Cade's cabin was well-equipped with surveillance equipment. As a backup, he'd called a couple of the neighbors and asked them to keep an eye out for any unusual activity.

Fortunately, Kerry didn't even blink when he told her he wanted to do some follow up work on the unidentified woman found in the Bay. She seemed content to work on the reconstruction of the infant while he headed to the shelter with a photo of the murdered victim. For some reason, she believed this case was related to the Jane Doe case. He didn't buy her theory, but he couldn't afford to ignore any clue.

Hunter had called the precinct and learned Jeff Shapiro was principal in charge of the Bay woman's case. According to Jeff, the rope tied around the dead woman's waist, along with the cinder block, were at the lab being tested. No person of interest had been brought in for questioning though. The autopsy had confirmed she'd died by the bullet and not by drowning, thank God.

"Go ahead and ask at the local shelters. I'm swamped with three other cases, and this one is going cold fast."

"I'll let you know what I find out," Hunter said.

A short while later, Hunter pulled into the River of Hope shelter's parking lot. He knew the woman who ran the place and decided to start there.

He jumped out, and the contrast between the cruiser's cold AC and the heat made his face sweat. He patted his top pocket, double-checking he had the photo of the unknown body.

Inside, a twenty-something year old girl, with dyed black hair glanced up from her desk. She looked as though she'd been electrocuted. She raised a finger and finished her rather personal phone conversation. Once she hung up, she turned her attention back to him and smiled. Hunter couldn't help but study her four eyebrow rings, two nose rings, and one cheek ring. They must have hurt like a bitch when she first had them put in, but he shouldn't judge.

"What can I do for you?" From her tone he almost expected her to add, "Big boy."

He flashed his badge, and she leaned back in disgust. He then placed the photo on her desk. "Have you seen this woman?"

The receptionist blew a bubble. "She don't look so good."

Why did people have to state the obvious? The color of the woman's face was a flat, bluish tinge. "Do you recognize her?"

"Nope. Never seen her." She shoved the photo back at him.

The girl had barely glanced at the Bay woman. "Thanks." His comment came out too sarcastic, but his mood wasn't the best today, especially after a sleepless night listening for whimpers to come from Kerry's room. He'd shown her the camera system, but she remained nervous.

The click of heels behind him caught his attention. He swung around, facing a well-dressed, older woman. Hunter stuck out his hand to the woman who ran the shelter. "Evelyn."

"Detective. Nice to see you again. How can I help you?" She tossed a disgusted look at the young girl. Evelyn must have overheard part of the exchange.

"I was hoping you'd help me identify someone."

"Won't you come into my office?"

Hunter followed her into a small room. The bare walls and worn, cheap furniture looked the same as last time he was here. The shelter was always short on funds. Once Evelyn was seated, he showed her the photo.

"Do you recognize her?"

Her face pained. "Oh, my God. That's Nancy Donello-Sanchez. When did she..."

"We're not sure. She appeared in Tampa Bay a few days ago."

"What a shame." Evelyn ran a hand down her face. "A nice woman, but she suffered from depression as so many of them do." Evelyn leaned back in her chair. "Did you speak to her ex-husband yet?"

"No. I didn't know who she was until now."

"How forgetful of me. I'm sorry." Evelyn lifted the photo and tilted the paper toward the light. "She'd come to us several times over the past couple of years. As you are well aware, the women who use the shelter are often abused. Even when they're back on their own, they sometimes find other men who abuse them. The cycle is a deep one."

He knew the stories. "When was the last time she was here?"

Evelyn bit her bottom lip. "Maybe six months ago?"

"Do you have an address for her, her ex-husband, or her last boyfriend?"

"I should have the address for the ex-husband at least." She stood and riffled through a four-drawer file cabinet. "You know I should ask for a warrant, but since Nancy is dead, I guess it won't hurt to give you her file."

"I can get one if it'll help you with the paperwork."

She shook her head and handed him the file. "Let me know what you find out."

"I will."

* * *

HUNTER HAD LOCATED Nancy Donello-Sanchez's ex-husband all right —in the cemetery off Nebraska Avenue. He hated when a clue got snatched out from under him. But such was the life of a homicide detective. One down, one to go.

Nancy's neighbors had given Hunter the name of the boyfriend, a man who every one confirmed was a useless piece of shit—or UPS for short. Finding him would not be easy.

After four false leads, Hunter ended up at a lube station near the Tampa Stadium. A quick flash of his badge and he was directed to Ronald Whipley, Nancy's former beau.

"Mr. Whipley?"

The skinny, bearded man stopped pouring oil into the engine and met Hunter's stare. "Yeah?"

"Is there some place we could talk?" The strong aroma of grease, oil, and body odor was more than he wanted to handle right now.

Whipley put the can down, wiped his hands on his pants, and nodded toward the outside. "What's this about?" He seemed friendly enough.

Hunter had to assume he knew his girlfriend was dead. She'd been gone at least a month.

"When was the last time you saw Nancy Donello-Sanchez?"

"She dead?" No distress showed around his mouth or eyes. Now there was a callous man.

"Why would you ask?"

"Cops don't come around asking questions if the person ain't dead, now do they? Besides, I haven't seen Nancy in over two months."

Figures he claim that. Hunter had to confirm whether the murdered woman and Kerry's Jane Does had anything in common. "Did you know Nancy was pregnant?"

"No shit? Aw, Christ." He stabbed a hand over his straggly hair. "Why didn't she tell me?"

Finally a reaction. "I wish I could answer that." The man's jaw clenched, but Hunter didn't have time to give him couch time for his problems. "One more thing. Did Nancy have any surgery prior to her death?"

Whipley shrugged. "If she didn't tell me about the baby, she sure as hell wouldn't have told me about any surgery. I wouldn't be surprised if she had some work done before I met her. Her ex had done a number on her, or so she said."

How could Nancy afford plastic surgery? "Did Nancy have some kind of health insurance?"

"Before we met, she worked for the public school system cleaning for them and had pretty good bennies."

The school's insurance might have paid for the surgery. "Why did Nancy and you split?"

Whipley looked toward the ground. "We had a whopper of a fight a few months back. She came at me screaming and yelling. Thought I'd cheated on her." He shuffled his feet. "I didn't, I swear, but Nancy didn't believe me. She ran off and I never saw her after that."

If Nancy suffered from depression, other issues might have affected her. "Don't leave town."

Whipley took a step forward and clenched his fists. "You think I had something to do with Nancy's death?"

"I'm just asking questions, that's all."

"Well, ask someone else."

Hunter was losing his patience. "You have any ideas who might have wanted to hurt Nancy?"

"No, but her mom might know."

"This mom have an address?"

"Yeah." Whipley told Hunter where the woman lived before stomping off.

Wild goose chases were not his thing, especially since all he could think of was getting back to Kerry. He was tired and hungry. Tomorrow would be soon enough to follow this lead.

As he piled into the cruiser, his cell rang. It was Phil. "How's Gina?" Hunter asked before Phil got a word in.

"Funny. I've been trying to reach you."

"You got me now. What's up?"

"Gina and I have been following up on the murder of Willie Wyble. We spoke to some guy whose bed is under the Interstate with Willie. Nash said Willie was picked up by the Medical Examiner's van during one of late night digging jobs."

Hunter's blood ran cold.

He had to rush back to the cabin. Pronto.

* * *

"Hey, Kerry," Hunter shouted, as he ran up to the cabin. He raced into the living room, expecting to see her hunched over the table working on the infant's face.

Only she wasn't there. The beginnings of her reconstruction were strewn all over the place, but no Kerry, and a cold dread clogged his muscles.

"Kerry?" he croaked.

After talking with Phil, his imagination had gotten the best of him. He'd even conjured up the idea that someone in the ME's office had murdered these woman, and that Kerry could be next.

He listened for a moment, thinking she might be in the shower, but the house remained deathly still, except for his quick breaths. He checked all three bedrooms, but came up empty. Where the hell was she?

Acid attacked his gut. There had to be a good explanation why she'd seemingly disappeared.

His fogged mind wasn't thinking straight. She probably needed a respite from the back-breaking work of clay reconstruction and decided to sit out by the dock. He sped outside, his adrenaline slowing down.

"Kerry?"

Leaves rustled and a few birds chirped. He sprinted to the lake, prepared to see her sunbathing on the wooden dock, but the place was empty. Cade's dingy still bobbed on the water, tied neatly to the dock.

She didn't have a car, so where could she have gone? The only place left was the barn where Cade kept his refurbished cars, though he saw no reason for her to be exploring.

Shit. If she'd borrowed one of Cades' classics and gone somewhere, he'd... Hunter refused to think of the punishment he'd dole out when he got his hands on her delicious body. Kerry had a stubborn streak, and she didn't obey orders very well—if at all. A bad combination for sure.

As he pulled open the heavy barn door, it squeaked. He flipped on the overhead lamp and counted the vehicles. Damn. One was missing. Cade often bragged about his six restored cars. Now there were five.

Hunter pulled out his cell and called her, preparing his tongue lashing when she answered. He paced as the phone continued to ring. "Pick up, dammit."

What had she been thinking leaving the cabin? Her answering machine clicked on. "Kerry, call me."

From his harsh tone, he knew he didn't have to tell her she needed to call right away. Hunter strode back in the house trying to come up with a plausible explanation.

Her cell phone sat on the coffee table. Blast it. His mind raced. Kerry never left without her phone. She'd mentioned she needed to be available twenty-four seven in case the M.E.'s office needed her. Maybe John Ahern had called her and she'd rushed out, forgetting to take her cell.

That's what must have happened. He dialed the main office. Hunter did a loop around the dining room table while he waited for the Medical Examiners' front desk to answer. Another voice mail. Crap. It was Saturday, so it made sense one would be manning the office phones.

Hunter had one last hope before he called in the troops. John

Ahern might know where she was. Thank goodness he'd programmed John's number from the last case they'd worked on. The assistant M.E. answered on the first ring.

"It's Hunter Markum. Do you know where Kerry is?" He didn't have time for pleasantries.

John waited a beat before answering. "No. We didn't have any need of her today. Why? I thought you were keeping her in some kind of safe house."

"I was, but she's missing."

CHAPTER TWENTY-ONE

"How do you know the baby isn't with Brad's mom or in daycare?" Kerry asked her sister. She turned down the car AC as they idled in front of Susan's ex-boyfriend's house.

"I don't, but it's a Saturday. Teresa should be home, playing outside, having fun." Kerry's sister pushed open the car door. "I'm tired of waiting. I'm going to confront the bastard."

Kerry grabbed Susan's arm. "Are you crazy? Stop and think. Suppose your child is fine. Do you want him to know you're stalking him? Worse case scenario, he could come after you or take out his anger on Teresa."

Susan leaned back into the seat and turned toward her. "I'm not stalking him. I have to find out about my daughter—the daughter he *stole* from me."

"Then let the police handle it. You said you'd sworn out a complaint."

"Two years ago. I don't think the police care anymore."

"Hunter would care."

Her lips pursed. "Hunter this, Hunter that. You make him sound like some goddamn saint."

Kerry flinched at Susan's bitter attack, but she understood where her sister was coming from. Hunter didn't abuse women like Brad had.

"How do you think Brad would react if he knew you've learned where he lives?"

Her lips were pressed together so tight her chin trembled. Kerry had never seen her sister so distraught. "He'd probably hit me."

"Or worse. You need to stay away from him. I don't mind us watching for a little while longer, but there can't be any interaction without the police being here."

"You are such a goodie-two-shoes." She huffed. "Always have been."

Kerry needed to refocus her sister's thoughts. "How old is Teresa now?" Kerry knew to the day how old her child would have been had she'd lived.

"Two years, seven months and three days."

Poor Susan. The hole in her heart must be bigger than a cavern. "Two years is a long time to wait for justice, but we need to be patient."

A blue sedan pulled into the driveway. Susan straightened and grabbed Kerry's hand. "Do you think Teresa's inside the car?"

A tall, leggy blond slipped out of the driver's seat. When the woman pulled open the rear door her sister sucked in a large breath, and then grimaced. The lady stood, holding a package in her arms—not a child. Susan closed her eyes, and a tear trickled down her face.

"I'm really sorry, Susan, but we don't know Teresa's not inside the house."

She sniffled. "Maybe." She turned to Kerry. "Do you think your knight in shining armor can really help?"

"I bet he'll try."

* * *

WHEN KERRY ENTERED into the cabin's driveway, Hunter's truck sat parked in front. Damn. He was going to be pissed she'd left without telling him.

Too bad. Susan had needed her. If she'd called Hunter and told him her plan to scout out Brad's house for her sister's daughter, he would have told her to stay put. Then where would Susan have been? As it was, her sister had been so upset, she'd said little on the way back.

"Come on," Kerry said, as she pushed open the car door. "Let's see what Hunter can do."

Dread filled her just thinking about his reaction.

Susan eased out and looked around. "This is quite romantic. The trees add a lot of shade."

What an odd observation. The trees were the least of Kerry's worry and romance was not on her mind—absolutely not on her mind. Maybe this was Susan's way of avoiding her demons.

The front door burst open and Hunter stood in the doorway with his gun dangling by his side. Crap. Eyes narrowed and every muscle taut, Kerry steeled herself for a fight.

Hunter strode toward her and shoved the gun in his shoulder holster. "Where the hell have you been?" His voice boomed louder than a megaphone.

Before she could answer, he wrapped his arms around her and squeezed her tight. "You scared the crap out of me." His whisper was so close to her ear, his lips brushed her skin.

For a brief moment, Kerry let herself relax against his strong chest, inhaling his musky scent. God, did she need his hug or what.

Hunter leaned back and lifted Kerry's chin. Their lips nearly touched. Time stood still. All fear and anxiety drifted to the back of her mind, and she was convinced Hunter cared about *her* as a person, and didn't think of her as some client who was in trouble.

"Ahem," Susan said. "Hi, I'm Kerry's sister, Susan." She stuck her hand out.

As if they'd been caught necking by their parents, she and Hunter sprang apart. A slow heat drifted up her face. "Yes, this is my sister." Typical Susan—the queen of bad timing.

Hunter and Susan shook hands. "Let's move out of the heat." His gaze swung from the ground to Kerry. "And you, Dr. Herlihy, will tell me why you disobeyed an order."

"Disobeyed an *order*? I don't do *orders*. Suggestions, maybe, but only if I believe in them."

His comforting stance disappeared as he stomped back into the house. Kerry and Susan trailed behind. No need to rush to the firing squad.

"Seems like a nice guy," Susan whispered, as they walked along the slate path to the house. A hint of a smile crossed her lips. "And hot."

"He is—nice that is." She wasn't going to confess she found Hunter physically appealing. "And don't act so smug. You need him to help find your daughter."

At Teresa's reference, Susan's smile disappeared. "You're right. I do need his help."

When they entered the cabin, Hunter had already dragged a dining room chair into the living room. His shoulders remained rigid.

He swept a hand toward the sofa, keeping his gaze on Kerry. "Please sit."

She and Susan sat next to each other on the sofa. "Let me explain," Kerry began.

"Please do." While he wasn't yelling, the tension in his voice reminded her of her father when he became angry, which wasn't a good thing.

Susan placed a hand on Kerry's thigh. "It's my fault. I needed Kerry's help."

Kerry's sister told Hunter about how Brad had stolen their baby two years ago and how she'd spent most of the child's life trying to find him and her daughter. Now she had.

Hunter's brows pinched. "How did you locate him this time?"

Had he forgiven her for running out? Kerry could only hope.

"I hired a skip tracer a few months ago, but he came up empty-handed. Brad had disappeared. I was running out of money just as my ex made a mistake, one that caused a red flag on Tony Tesner's computer. You see, Brad's a good tennis player. Always has been. He had the misfortune of winning a tournament, and his name and hometown were plastered in several papers. Tony saw the win, found his address and called me."

"Okay," Hunter said, "but why did you need Kerry?"

"For support."

"Didn't Kerry tell you about the person stalking her?" Hunter shot back. Susan nodded. "How can you two be sure he didn't follow you here?"

A burning sensation stabbed Kerry in the belly. "I never thought about anyone following us." What had she done? Hunter had been so careful. Now, she'd screwed up. "I'm sorry."

Hunter stood. "We should probably move. I'll make a few phone calls, but I might not be able to find another home for a while. Susan, where are you staying?"

"I've moved into my grandfather's now that Kerry is here with you."

No one would mistake one for the other. "When you and Kerry are done bonding, I'll drive you back."

"Thank you."

Hunter's cell rang. He stepped toward the entranceway, keeping his back to them. "Markum...She give you anything? ...Did you ask her about the surgery?...Thanks."

He swiped off his phone.

"Who was that?" Kerry asked.

"Jeff Shapiro, the lead detective on the Nancy Donello-Sanchez case. Once I provided him with her name, he followed up. He wanted to let me know he'd spoken with Nancy's mom, but she offered little help."

"Nancy Donello-Sanchez?" The name didn't sound familiar.

"Sorry. The woman who was washed up in the Bay. You were right. She had used the River of Hope shelter on several occasions."

Kerry brightened. There might be a connection then. "Did he say who'd performed her plastic surgery?"

"When Shapiro contacted Nancy's mother, he didn't think to question her about it. He said it didn't seem relevant at the time."

"Did he have any idea who might have killed her?"

"Nope. I actually learned more about Nancy's life than he had. Going to the shelter led me to the woman's dead ex-husband and to her boyfriend."

"What's your next step?" Kerry asked.

"If there is a connection between her death and the four Jane Does, I need to ask Nancy's mom about the surgery." The lines around his eyes had etched deeper in the last week and dark smudges under his eyes had given his face a hallowed look.

"I want to come with you. I can help."

"No."

She had her answer ready. "If I'm with you, I won't be able to get in trouble."

He glanced from Kerry to Susan and back again. "It's probably against my better judgment, but you do have a point."

"I'm not trying to interfere in your job. I merely want to do mine."

"Only because I can't trust you to stay put, I'll take you along."

"Thank you." The air cleared about why she'd left, she broached another topic. "After we visit Nancy's mom, do you think you could help Susan extract some information out of Brad?"

Hunter dragged a hand through his hair. His eyes were bloodshot and his posture lacked his usual energy. Asking him to add more work to his hectic schedule gave her pause, but Susan needed his help.

"I'll give it a try, but on one condition."

"That being?"

"I don't want you with me. Brad might be dangerous."

This time, she wouldn't argue. He had harmed Susan, so there was no telling what he was like now. "I'll either stay locked up here or be at the lab."

Kerry glanced over at Susan and they exchanged relieved smiles.

"Thanks," Susan said.

Hunter's scowl deepened. Now what was that for?

* * *

ON THE DRIVE to Nancy Donello-Sanchez's mother's house, Hunter told Kerry about the medical examiner's van picking up Willie Wyble.

"I don't understand. No one at the ME's office would have anything to gain from burying bodies. We have to account for each one."

"I know. I have no explanation. I'm only telling you so you'll be ultra careful. Trust no one there."

"Hunter, you drive me to work and pick me up. I'll be safe." She crossed her arms. "Do you always believe what men of the street tell you? They most likely have a drinking problem and a bad memory."

He liked her *men of the street* phraseology.

"According to Phil, Tanner Nash wasn't making this up." No use discussing the pros or cons of the man's story without more facts. He'd ask Phil to look into the case further. "We're here." Several cars were parked outside. "Looks like Betty Donello's support group has arrived," Hunter said.

"Good. Everyone needs people around who care, especially in a time of need."

From her wistful tone, Kerry must be speaking from experience. For some reason, he wanted to know what drove her so hard to help others, what she dreamt about, where she saw herself in the years to come. Had her brother's disappearance been the only catalyst for her need to give comfort, or had something else traumatic happened to her? He refused to analyze why she pushed his curiosity button to the max.

A portly gentleman in his late thirties with wispy blond hair answered the front door. Hunter flashed his badge. "Hunter Markum, Hillsborough Country sheriff's department."

"I'm Nancy's brother, Colin. My mother's in the living room. Come in."

Nancy's mom was sitting on the sofa with her head in her hands, sobbing.

"Mom, the police are here about Nancy."

Betty Donello dabbed her eyes with a red handkerchief and looked up, her white hair drooped around her chin. A cane lay across the sofa, and a Bible rested on a chair across from her. An older woman sitting next to Betty Donello had an arm draped around the mom's shoulder. A second lady sat across from her.

The taller of the two stood and helped the short, frail lady grab hold of her walker. The tall one looked over at Hunter, and then turned back to Nancy's mom.

"Betty, we'll wait in the kitchen."

Once her friends disappeared, Betty Donello straightened her hair and shirt. "I want whoever did this to die. How can I help?" She sniffled and blew her nose. "Nancy's horrible death came as such a shock. She was such a lovely girl and a wonderful daughter."

If she'd been so wonderful, how had she ended up in a shelter and not with her mom? Nancy had been missing for two months. Didn't her daughter's disappearance make her think something might have happened to her before now? "I'm guessing you didn't see your daughter often?"

"Not as much as I'd have liked. Nancy was busy working. She didn't have much time for me." Betty dabbed her eyes. "To be fair, I was at my sister's in California since the end of May. She'd been ill." The mom tapped her chest. "Heart."

"My sympathies." Questioning a grieving family member had to win the what-I-hate-most-about-the-job award. "From the autopsy, we found Nancy had had some plastic surgery performed. Can you tell us about it?"

Anguish and guilt skipped across her face. "After her husband hurt her, I finally convinced Nancy to leave him. She stayed here until she met Ron Whipley. Then she moved in with him. I didn't like how she rushed into a new relationship, but she was thirty-three. I couldn't stop her."

Kerry touched Hunter's hand and his pulse sped up.

"I'm Dr. Herlihy. I noticed Nancy had a scar behind her ear that appeared to be recent. Do you know what the surgery was for?"

Betty Donello pointed to the sofa and love seat. "Where are my manners? Please sit."

He and Kerry sat next to each other, moving the Bible off to the side. "The surgery?" Hunter said.

"Oh, yes. Poor Nancy. She'd been in a bad fight with Ron over her long hours at work. He hit her pretty bad, then cut her with a knife near the side of her face—nearly killed her too. She came here, blood dripping from ear to chin."

Hunter leaned forward and scribbled notes in his pad. "When was this?"

"Right before I went to see my sister."

That would make her injury about the time of her death. "Did she go to the ER?"

"Yes, they patched her up, but the scar was bad. I suggested she see if that wonderful Dr. Dalton wouldn't mind working on her face. He'd done her surgery after that bastard Rick—that's her ex-husband—broke her nose."

Kerry straightened, her hands bunched at her side.

"And did he agree to help?" he asked.

"Yes. He was amazing. I could hardly tell she'd been hurt."

"Do you think Ron had anything to do with her death?" Hunter made a note to arrest the bastard for assault. It didn't matter if Nancy was now dead. She deserved to have someone pay.

Betty cried again and dabbed her nose with a tissue. "I don't know what to think. Nancy insisted it was her fault that Ron cut her. She went back to the bastard."

Hunter's heart sank. Why did women continue to expose themselves to these monsters? "Did his temper improve?"

"I don't know. I left for California. Nancy called me a few times, but she wouldn't discuss Ron."

Basically, the mom hadn't had contact with the daughter in the last two months, so she wasn't much help—other than providing the name of the good doctor. He placed his card on the coffee table. "Let me know if you think of anything else."

CHAPTER TWENTY-TWO

EVER SINCE LIZ CULBERTSON of Channel 8 news had called Hunter and told him to watch the five o'clock news, Kerry hadn't been able to concentrate on her clay model. The strips kept slipping.

At a few minutes to five, she paced the cabin's small living room wondering what was so important on the news.

"Sit, Kerry. Please. You're making *me* nervous."

Hunter turned up the volume when the news anchor threw to Liz Culbertson out in the field. Kerry stood in front of the TV, her arms crossed over her chest.

About fifty people stood behind Norwood and his wife, some with lit candles, others with posters that read, "Find Janet's killer."

"Good evening. I'm Liz Culbertson, and I'm speaking to Chris Norwood and his wife Sharon. Two years ago their daughter disappeared. Recently the police found her remains along with the remains of three other women."

Hunter leaned forward. "They're in front of the sheriff's station. Shit."

"Can all those people protest in front like that?"

"It's the right-of-way."

"What does Mr. Norwood hope to accomplish by going public?"

Before Hunter could answer, Norwood spoke. "My daughter, Janet, was cruelly murdered. My wife and I want answers. Janet would have been thirty-one today. I'm offering a fifty-thousand dollar reward for information leading to the arrest of the killer."

Norwood continued, but Kerry's mind spun with questions after the big announcement of a reward.

"Thank you, Mr. Norwood. This is Liz Culbertson, Channel 8 News." A picture of Janet appeared, along with a full screen graphic indicating how to get a hold of the family. The web address scrolled along the bottom.

Hunter flicked off the TV.

Kerry finally sat, leaned against the sofa and tried to grasp what had happened. "This publicity should be good for us, right? We might get someone calling about our other victims."

"Maybe. Unfortunately, every time there's a news report, our guy goes crazy." His body tensed. "We'll need to take extra precautions."

Great. He better not suggest she move into a holding cell at the sheriff's department for safekeeping. Knowing Hunter, she wouldn't put it past him.

* * *

THE NEXT MORNING when Hunter drove them to the sheriff's department instead of to Kerry's lab, she thought her worst nightmare had come true. Thankfully, instead of taking her to a cell, he directed her to the room where the two of them had first met to discuss the case.

His hand rested on the knob of the closed door. "The meeting won't take long. The homicide team needs to go over the details of the recent murders, and I thought it might help clarify things for you."

Never before had he included her in the details. Something was up. "You just don't want to leave me alone at the cabin, do you?" It didn't matter she hadn't received any threatening phone call after the news broadcast aired. Then again, she wasn't staying at her grandfather's.

He met her gaze. "You caught me. Once I've personally spoken to

John, I'll feel better about dropping you off at your work. I'll ask him to check in on you every hour."

"You can't keep me hostage." She leaned closer to him. "If I get fired because I skipped out on work, I'm holding you personally responsible."

Hunter had the nerve to smile. "Don't worry, I'll take care of any issues that come up."

The man definitely had a white knight complex. "You better."

Hunter opened the door. Four people sat around the large oval table. Hunter pulled out a chair for her and introduced her to the group. She'd met Phil at the gravesite. He sat next to a striking black woman, Gina something, in a low cut top and too much makeup. Hunter's boss, Jack Andries, sat next to Jeff Shapiro, the man who'd called Hunter at the cabin.

Jack Andries flipped open his folder and took a sip of his drink. "Phil, tell us what you've have on the Willie Wyble case."

"Haven't a clue who might have killed him. A bum, who shared an overpass with Willie, told me that a medical examiner's van picked up Willie a couple of times, supposedly to drive him to some graveyard. I plan on stopping at the morgue and question everyone who drives a van."

Kerry shook her head. When Hunter had mentioned this absurd possibility, she'd gone through the staff members who worked at the morgue. No one there would drive an indigent anywhere—especially in a marked van, even if the act wasn't illegal.

"Excuse me. I work there. If some technician asked a homeless man to do something for them, do you think he'd tell you?"

"Not at first, but most people don't lie well," Andries said.

Whatever. She wished him luck. He was definitely looking in the wrong grave.

The cops would have more luck if *she* asked John Ahern what he knew about this Willie person. He might come up with a list of possible drivers who the police could then question. John had mentioned he contracted out the drivers sometimes when things became too busy.

Phil leaned forward on his elbows. "I think Willie was trying to tell us the name of his killer when he died."

Jack Andries' eyes widened. "That so?"

"After he was shot once in the head, he managed to get off the tractor and into the woods. He was clawing some letters in the dirt when he bled out."

Gina's lips pulled tight. "I disagree. I've been thinking about what I said. I don't think he'd been able to climb off the tractor with a bullet to the head, crawl ten feet, and then write letters." She pulled up her top an inch. "Maybe I imagined the scratches on the ground were actual letters because I wanted them to be."

"Don't discount your first impression." Her uncle's jaw slackened and his gaze looked upward. "Wait 'till you've been around a few years. There was this one case where a victim was shot three time in the head and wasn't aware she was seriously injured until paramedics brought her to the hospital. She was coherent enough to give a detailed description of the shooters. Amazing how the brain works."

She straightened and smiled. "Cool."

Hunter tapped his fingers on the table, a nervous habit Kerry wished he'd drop.

"Which letters?" The tension and intensity in Hunter's voice scared her.

"It's only conjecture, mind you," Phil said, "but we believe he was drawing a 'D' or possibly an 'O' followed by an 'A'. A CSU tech said the third letter had a vertical line in it, but didn't want to take a guess what it might be."

Phil shoved the folder to the middle of the table, and Hunter slid the picture toward him.

Kerry leaned over to look and inhaled a whiff of Hunter who still smelled fresh from his morning shower. She nudged him. "Could the name Willie was trying to write be, Dalton?"

"Oh, shit."

"What is it?" Hunter's boss asked.

Hunter gave them the rundown on the fact three of the four Jane Doe's had contact with Dr. Paul Dalton. "As a matter of fact, Shapiro's case is also connected. Nancy Donello-Sanchez had plastic surgery. Guess who the doctor was?"

"Dalton," Andries answered.

"Yup."

"Get a warrant and search his records."

"I'm on it. In the meantime, I'll tail him to see if it leads us anywhere."

"Be careful. We don't want to tip him off."

Gina squeezed Phil's arm. "We could do a sting operation."

Phil tilted his head toward her. "Forget it. All these women were abused. You wouldn't fool anybody."

Andries Adam's apple bobbed. "Gina. Don't even think about doing something stupid like that."

"Whatever."

The group sat in silence for a few minutes, some taking notes, others reading a copy of Phil's report.

Kerry tapped Hunter's shoulder. "If Dalton stole head #3, and you find it at his place, that would incriminate him, right?"

"Of being a thief, but not of murder. I can't get a search warrant for the skull without tangible evidence he stole it."

"Damn." There had to be something she could do. "It seems as though you have to almost catch him in the act of killing someone before you can arrest him."

"Sometimes that's true."

* * *

DR. DALTON CLOSED the blinds at the River of Hope shelter clinic. The upscale instruments and supplies at the downtown office were superior, but the regular clientele would have been offended if the women from here showed up downtown.

For a charitable operation, Evelyn Cortland had done a good job providing necessary supplies.

"Can you fix me up good as new?" Chanel Carlitta asked.

She'd been such a beautiful woman. Once. The first time she'd had work done on her face was after a near fatal car wreck. Her husband had been drinking and ran off the road. Bastard walked away from the scene with hardly a scratch.

Long after the accident, Chanel learned her husband had been trying to kill her when he'd driven into a pole. The doctor had warned Chanel to leave him. Like so many others, she hadn't listened.

Dalton leaned over her and checked out her injuries, and Chanel squirmed in her seat. Her cheek was badly swollen and a large, poorly healed cut rimmed her eye. The gash above her forehead appeared to be the most serious injury.

"What happened, Chanel? It pains me to see your beautiful face messed up again."

Her lower lip trembled. "It was Gabe."

The husband, shit.

Dalton pulled up a chair and leaned close, looking at her new scars as anger boiled inside. "Tell me what he did."

Her eyes widened. "Does it matter?"

"Yes, it matters. I thought you promised you wouldn't go back to him, but I see you have. How far along are you?"

"Eighteen weeks." A tear streamed down her cheek. "I tried to leave him once, but that was before I knew I was carrying his child. I don't have a good job or much money saved. I had to stay. When I told Gabe I was pregnant, he was nice for a while. He promised he would be good."

"See? All men tell you what you want to hear."

She sniffled and nodded.

"Tell me what he did. I need to understand the extent of your injuries." Bullshit. *I need to see if Gabe was as vile as my dad.*

"We had a party."

The doctor would listen to every word of her pathetic story. She seemed to need urging. "Go on."

Chanel licked her lips. "I thought everything was going real good, but I guess I didn't clean up enough for Gabe's standards. Once the guests left, he started in on me. Yelling, punching, pushing. Next thing I knew, he'd cut me." She choked out a sob. "Am I going to lose the baby?"

For a moment, the doctor could feel the punches, hear the yelling, feel the knife slice through the skin.

"Doctor?"

"Yes? Oh, sorry. I don't know about the child, but I imagine the baby is fine if the beating happened when? A few weeks ago."

"Yes."

"Then don't worry. Your face I can restore. You'll hardly see any marks. Trust me."

When she grabbed Dalton's gloved hand, the doctor wanted to rip it out of her clasp and strangle her right there, but he needed to control himself.

A knock on his door startled Dalton. Evelyn Courtland walked in, and behind her was Detective Markum. Christ Almighty. Dalton's stomach soured for a moment before confidence kicked in. *They'll never catch me.*

"Chanel, if you'll excuse us. I think it would be best if we wait until after the baby is born before I fix your scars. I don't work on pregnant women. Promise me you'll see a family doctor to check out the health of your unborn child."

Her lips turned downward. The bitch better not cry. "Okay. Thank you, Doctor."

When she left, Dalton faced the detective. "What can I do for you?"

"What can you tell me about Nancy Donello-Sanchez?"

Nancy? *Be cool.* The detective can't know what happened. He was fishing. "Evelyn can tell you more than I can. She worked with Nancy for years, right, Evelyn?" *If my stupid nephew fucked up this job, I'll personally strangle him.*

Evelyn's face pinched. She was sour personified.

"The detective wants to know her from your perspective. After all, you understand these women better than anyone."

Flatterer. "I'll try. Nancy first came to me about, oh I don't know, two years ago? Her husband, now her ex-husband, had savagely beaten her, and my heart ached for her. You know I do this work," the doctor waved around the office, "pro bono?"

"Yes, Evelyn told me. The community is in your debt."

Patronizing asshole. *Don't let him get under your skin.* "Nancy had massive facial contusions, a broken jaw, and I believe a broken collarbone." The detective wrote down every damned word.

"After you repaired the damage, did you see her again?"

Clever man. "Yes. Maybe four months ago. I can't tell you the exact date. I'd have to consult my calendar back at the office."

"And why did Nancy come to you this last visit?"

"What is this all about?" Dalton succeeded in sounding both put out and concerned.

"Nancy Donello-Sanchez is dead. She was shot once in the head."

"Oh my God." Dalton slid onto the seat. "I'm so sorry. What can I do?"

"I'm here to see if you'd know of anyone who might have wanted to harm her?"

Take your time. Think. "Nancy seemed to attract abusive men. Her latest boyfriend—I can't recall his name—was no exception."

"Ron Whipley."

"You've spoken with him?" Dalton placed both palms flat on the desk to show no fear.

"Yes, but we don't think he had anything to do with her death."

"Oh? Why come to me then?"

They locked gazes, but Dalton didn't flinch.

"May we have a copy of Nancy's records?"

"Sure. Stop by my office. I'll have Mary Ellen pull them for you."

"Thank you. You might hear from me again."

"Any time, Detective."

The detective was halfway out the door, when he swiveled around. "I forgot to ask. Do you know a Willie Wyble?"

Shit. Dalton took in a deep breath and rapidly tapped a finger on the desk. "Wyble. I don't believe so. I mostly deal with women."

"Where were you Thursday night?"

The night Willie died. "At the symphony. Why?"

"We found Willie Wyble dead Friday morning."

"Are you accusing me of something?"

"No. Just asking." The detective rubbed his temple. "What size shoe do you wear?"

"What?"

The detective repeated the question.

"A 9C, why?"

"We found some footprints near a crime scene. Just playing Cinderella. Good day."

Cinderella? The cop was a whack job. But a smart whack job. He was someone who needed watching.

CHAPTER TWENTY-THREE

CHANEL'S BODY spasmed as her unborn child jerked, forcing her to grab the kitchen counter to steady herself. Bile rose up her throat. At four and a half months, she should be over the queasiness, or so her friends had claimed. These same friends had drilled into her she shouldn't take any medication during pregnancy, but her stomach hurt. Bad.

If only her momma were still alive, she could have told her what to do. And Gabe? He should have been home by now. Then he could have driven her to the hospital.

Crap. Why hadn't he come home for dinner? Or called. Stupid man. He was probably gambling or out boffing some slut he'd picked up on Kennedy Avenue. If Chanel wasn't carrying his child, she'd consider leaving her old man.

Another pain stabbed her gut, causing tears to drip down her cheek. If she didn't get help now, her baby was sure to make an unwanted entrance. She couldn't wait for her no-good husband to get back.

An ache made her back arch. This wasn't good. Chanel grabbed her purse, slipped into her car, and headed toward the Emergency Room.

If she'd called an ambulance, Gabe would have hit her for sure. They couldn't afford no fancy care, he'd said.

Her momma had claimed her aches and pains came from nerves. It was always nerves, but maybe her momma was right this time. When Chanel found out she'd have to wait another six months before getting her scars fixed, she'd cried the whole way home. Scars she never should have gotten in the first place. If she hadn't made Gabe so mad that one time when he was drunk, he wouldn't have beaten her to a pulp.

Chanel's stomach soured. Damn hormones.

Her car clipped a cinder block someone had tossed on the side of the road, and her heart jetted into overdrive. *Pay attention, girl*. With her focus back on the road, she wove her way through the trailer park. Lights blazing, Mildred was on her front porch knitting something—probably another doggie vest. The old woman waved, but Chanel could only manage a nod.

She pulled out of the park onto the near empty thoroughfare and pushed the accelerator hard. Another wave of nausea blasted her, but she kept her full attention on the street. As she rounded the first curve, headlights flashed in her rearview mirror.

She looked up. It was too dark to see the make of the car. "What the hell could he want?" she mumbled. She was going over the speed limit as it was. Could that be Gabe behind her? She slowed a bit.

The lights flashed again. The unidentified car pulled real close behind her and honked. She accelerated. "What are you doing, mister? I don't have time to stop and chat." Her heart sped up. "Crazy bastard," she muttered. Oh shit. Maybe it was the police. She slowed again.

The car following her pulled along her left side—in the oncoming lane. It didn't look like no police car. Was the man insane? She looked ahead. Thank you, Lord, no car was coming toward them.

She gripped the wheel hard, taking the next turn too fast, her tire running over the grass berm. She jerked back to the pavement and blew out a long breath. On the straightaway, she peeked to her left. He was still there. All she could see was someone waving her over. She slowed.

"For God's sake."

Oh, crap. Was gas leaking out of her tank or something? Was she about to blow up? Gabe said once they had some money, she should have her car looked at. Three years was too long to go without a service call.

A strobe light flashed in his dash. Damn. It was the police in an unmarked car. She didn't need no ticket. Her pulse raced, and the baby acted up again. Chanel slowed and pulled off to the side but left the engine running. She reached for her cell phone to call Gabe, but she couldn't find it in the bottom of her messy purse.

The man got out of his car and shined a flashlight in her eyes. She squinted.

"Roll down your window, please."

Something deep inside told her not to do what he asked. Her hand stalled on the handle.

He slapped his palm on the window. "Open up."

Definitely not Gabe. She couldn't see the man's face, but he was wearing a suit and tie, like a detective might wear. She needed to get this over with and on her way. The police were safe.

She locked her door and rolled down her window part way. "What is it, Officer?"

All she saw was a gun pointed toward her belly. A large, black gun, and her eyes widened as her heart did a flip inside her chest. She sucked in a large breath waiting for him to hurt her. A scream bubbled up just as blast ripped through her. Her mind stopped working, as pain ricocheted in her abdomen and raced down her legs.

Chanel grabbed her stomach, but the blood bubbled up through her fingers. "Noooo!" Sweet Jesus, he'd shot her.

"Cunt."

That voice. She knew that voice. Her heartbeat raced. Who was he? The pain stopped. She was going to die without ever holding her child in her arms. "Why?" she sobbed.

He pressed the cold muzzle against her head. A click sounded, and stars splintered across her vision before fading to black.

* * *

KERRY HAD SPENT yesterday afternoon photographing, measuring, and cataloguing #4's dry, clean bones. This morning she'd begun to arrange them in anatomical position. Not only were a few missing, she had some little bones left over. It reminded her of when she'd helped a friend assemble a bike for her daughter's birthday. The bike seemed to work fine, despite all the left over screws.

Kerry was staring at the body, trying to figure out what she'd done wrong, when John Ahern walked in.

"Any luck?"

She didn't look up. "Not yet. I feel like all the King's horsemen and all the King's men couldn't put this together again."

John chuckled. "Coming from a forensic anthropologist, that's scary."

Kerry stepped over to the sink, removed her gloves and washed her hands. I need to think for a moment."

"Always a good idea."

She was about to ask him about the medical examiner's van that might have picked up Willie Wyble, when she noticed where she'd left the small bones—between the woman's legs. "Oh my God."

"What?"

"Give me a sec." Small bones, the size of lima beans huddled together in no pattern. Most were pitted and soft from decay. "It's a fetus. I can't believe I didn't connect the dots earlier."

"Could it be because you just began the process?"

"That or because most of the fetus's bones are either missing or had turned to dirt. None of the bones are even connected, so I didn't realize what I was seeing."

Sickened by her find, she raced around to locate the correct instruments to gauge the baby's age. Kerry measured the length of the only metacarpal she could identify. "Hand me the growth chart on the counter over there, please."

Kerry studied the chart. "The fetus is between three and four months in development." She tried hard not to let this new fact bother her, but it did. This baby was the same age as hers when she'd miscarried.

Don't cry, don't cry.

"So Jane Doe #4 was pregnant," he stated.

"Yes."

"That makes two of them."

"Two?" Her heart pounded.

"I received the tox screen back from Janet Kopetski. She had high levels of progesterone and estrogen in her tissues."

"Shit." Kerry bit her lip. "Sorry."

"Do you think we're looking at a killer who only kills pregnant women?"

"I hope not." Her hands trembled.

"I need to check on something."

John spun and left her room. She immediately grabbed her phone and dialed Hunter's number.

"Kerry, what's wrong?"

She almost smiled at his overprotective behavior, but the ramifications of what she was about to ask sickened her. "I'm fine." She told him about the two pregnancies. "Do you think you can find out if Tameka Dorsey was pregnant?"

"I'll try. By the way, I have something I'd like to do after work. Is there any possibility your sister could drive you to the cabin? Assuming you keep a close watch in your rear view mirror."

"I can do that. Don't worry about me. We'll be extra careful. Is it about the case?"

"I want to speak with Tameka's fiancé, but that's not what will hold me up. It's the second anniversary of Melissa's mom's death today. I'd like to spend some time with her."

Kerry had trouble swallowing. She noted he didn't say the second anniversary of his wife's death. "I'm so sorry, Hunter."

"Yeah. It's tough on her."

And on him too, she bet.

* * *

"So what did you say that hunky detective was doing tonight?" Susan passed Kerry the package of cooked chicken strips from the cabin's refrigerator.

Susan wasn't nosy as a kid, but apparently she'd changed. "I didn't say, but he's working on the case." Susan didn't need to know the details, and she didn't need to know his wife had died only two years ago.

"You like him, don't you?"

Don't go there. "Why the third degree? He's my bodyguard. That's all."

"Do you trust him?"

Kerry didn't want to be having this discussion, couldn't have this discussion. The pain scratched at her brain and raced down to her belly. Her emotions were twisted, and she no idea what she was feeling. "Trust has nothing to do with anything."

"You know what I think?" Susan had a wicked look in her eye.

Kerry arranged the chicken on the tortillas, sprinkled a handful of leaf spinach on top, and then doused the roll-up with Parmesan cheese. To hell with watching her weight. "No. What do you think?" She was tempted to tell her sister to mind her own business, but Susan was too stubborn to listen.

"I think Hunter is worming his way into your heart. I heard how you talked to him over the phone."

Kerry's fingers froze. "You are so off base. Hunter loves his work and loves his daughter, but there is no room in his life for a girlfriend, if that's what you're hinting at."

"I merely stated—"

"Besides, I don't think I could handle being with a cop. He's always gone. He could be injured at any time. Nannie always complained about Grandpa's long hours, if you recall."

"Yes I do, but me thinks you protest too much."

"Hand me the salad dressing. I'm hungry."

Before Kerry could carry her meal to the dining room, someone knocked on the front door.

Susan's eyes bugged out. "Do you think it's the killer?"

Kerry refrained from rolling her eyes. "A killer wouldn't knock. I bet it's Hunter. He probably forgot his house key."

Kerry acted cool, but inside, fear clawed its way up her spine. Now where did Hunter keep his gun?

Duh. He had it with him.

"Lock yourself in the bathroom," Kerry whispered to her sister.

"Hell no. You said it was probably Hunter. I'm not leaving you alone in case it's not."

Now her sister wants to be there for her? "Just go. And here, take my phone."

"Why?"

"If you hear me scream, call 9-1-1."

Despite Susan's stubbornness, she did what Kerry asked. Once the bathroom door closed, Kerry went to the front door. No peephole. Shit. "Who's there?"

"Phil. Hunter's partner." Even though his voice came out muffled, it sounded like him.

She prayed it really was Phil. She threw back the latch and opened the door. Her shoulders sagged. "Hi." Her hand flew to her chest to calm her beating heart. "Has something happened to Hunter?"

Phil laughed. "No. May I come in? The bugs are eating me alive out here." He stepped into the foyer. "What took you so long to answer?"

"Just making sure you weren't the boogie man."

"Me?" Phil's eyes sparkled.

"Yes. Wait a sec. I'll be right back." She knocked on the bathroom door. "It's okay. You can come out."

Once Kerry introduced Phil to her sister, she offered him a beer. He deserved a drink for driving all the way out to this place. She needed a drink too. Susan declined.

"Not to be rude," Kerry said, "but why are you here?"

"Hunter was worried about you."

She always suspected her bodyguard cared but hearing confirmation from a cohort sent a warm, gooshy rush through her. "I'm safe as long as I stay in the cabin."

Susan grabbed Kerry's arm and shook it. "Ooooh. The detective likes my sis-ter."

"Susan. Stop it." God. "Phil, please sit." Kerry needed to regroup. "As you can see, we're perfectly fine." Could this get any more embarrassing?

"I had to come. Hunter would have chewed out my ass if I hadn't checked up you two. Besides, he wanted me to tell you he found out that Tameka Dorsey was pregnant—something like a few weeks along."

Her heart broke. "Damn." Another baby dead. "Why couldn't Hunter have called to tell me?"

"He wanted me to make sure you were safe."

"Oh."

Phil gulped down half the bottle. "I think some good can come out of this. We now have a motive."

"What? The killer believes in zero population growth?" She couldn't keep the sarcasm from her tone.

"Maybe, maybe not."

Kerry made a mental list. Jane Does #1, #2, #4, plus Nancy Donello-Sanchez were all pregnant. Kerry had found no evidence that #3 was pregnant, but if she were only a few weeks along, there wouldn't have been any evidence of a fetus.

Kerry's cell rang, and her heart nearly stopped. "Excuse me."

She retrieved her phone, checked the caller ID, and answered. "John?"

"Kerry, I'm sorry to disturb you. I know you only do bones, but we found another woman tonight. She was about four months pregnant. I thought you might want to take a look at her."

How much more could she handle? "You think there's a connection to my case?"

"You'll have to tell me."

Her mind raced. "Ah, yeah, sure." She jotted down the directions. "I'll be right there." Kerry hung up.

Before she had a chance to explain her circumstance to Phil, his phone rang.

"Sorry." He answered it. "Where?... Just a sec." He glanced up at Kerry. "Where are you going?"

She told him.

He returned his attention to his caller. "I'll be right there. Tell the medical examiner I'll be bringing Dr. Herlihy with me." He disconnected. "Looks like we will be spending some time together."

Susan stood. "That means I get to lose *another* game of Scrabble to Grandpa."

"I'm sorry, Susan. Duty calls."

"No problem."

Kerry wanted to lay a hand on Susan's shoulder to say all was forgiven, but she didn't feel comfortable with her emotions yet. "I'll remind Hunter about helping with Brad."

Susan's lip trembled. "That would be great." Susan leaned over and hugged Kerry.

"Let me pack up your chicken dinner." Kerry pulled away. "I don't want you to starve." Kerry's upbeat tone came out fake even to her ears.

* * *

POLICE LIGHTS SWIRLED on the side of the road as a stream of cars slowed. Damn rubberneckers. They didn't need any more accidents on the road.

Now that Phil and she were at the crime scene, Kerry almost wished she hadn't eaten dinner. Bones. She liked bones. Not decaying flesh. The female's brain matter had oozed out of her skull, and coagulated blood had pooled on the victim's distended abdomen. She hoped both the baby and mother had died quickly. Kerry covered her nose with one hand and wiggled her fingers with the other. "Mask." The rancid odor made her gag. Some anthropologist she was.

"Here," one of the technicians said.

Flies buzzed the body as the crime scene unit processed the scene. She still didn't understand why John Ahern had asked her to come.

"Kerry, tell me what you see."

She peered into the half-rolled down passenger side window and swatted away the flies. The woman had toppled over onto the seat. "The contusions and bruising on her face look a few weeks old. Unless she was strangled, she died from either the gunshot wound to her head or bled out from her abdomen."

"My money's on the head wound. You see any evidence of plastic surgery?"

Kerry hadn't wanted to check, but she knew she had to. With gloved hands, she reached through the window and touched the woman's face. "Same as the ambient temp. What was her time of death?"

"Rigor's come and gone. I'd say she's been dead about twenty-four hours."

She checked for sutures around the hairline and behind the ears. "Nothing here, but she could have had surgery on her arms or legs. An X-ray would confirm."

"I can do that."

She pointed to the scars around the female's eye. The ones on her forehead had a pinkish cast to them. "These scars look to be a few months old from the amount of scar tissue, but these ones nearer the scalp are fresh. Someone beat this woman about the face not long before she died." Her stomach did a somersault. This woman had been abused, pregnant, and possibly in need of plastic surgery.

Dear God. What had happened here?

She stepped away from the vehicle, in part to get away from the flies, and in part to distance herself from the grief that surrounded this woman. Kerry swallowed to find her voice. "Who found her?"

This woman had bled to death in her car, and it had taken hours before anyone bothered to stop and check why a car with blood spattered windows sat abandoned on the side of the road.

John nodded toward a kid, no more than fourteen, standing next to his bike.

"Did he see anyone leave the scene?" she asked.

"No."

Phil stepped next to her. "Any identification on our vic?"

Again John shook his head. "Just the clothes on her body. No purse."

A petite woman, whose nametag read, Sanders, strode up to Phil. "We ran her tags. Car belonged to a Gabe Carlitta. I'm guessing that's her husband."

"Did you notify him?"

"I called but was unable to reach him. Dispatch said the husband called the station to report his wife missing around midnight last night."

Kerry couldn't believe someone hadn't found her sooner. "No one went looking for her?"

"The department's hands were tied. They had to wait until she was gone at least forty-eight hours before investigating."

The poor husband. He would be so distraught when he learned of their deaths, unless he was the one who killed her. She turned back to John. "Do you think there's a connection to my case?"

"At first, no, but considering she was pregnant, perhaps."

Kerry forced herself to remain calm. To kill a woman was bad enough, but to kill a pregnant woman was lower than scum.

A young male officer came over and held out a small device to Phil. "We found this under the back bumper."

Phil lifted the piece of metal from the officer's hand. "A tracking device." He handed it back to the man. "Process it."

"Will do."

Someone tapped Kerry on the shoulder. She jumped. From the spicy scent, it was Hunter. She turned around and smiled. "Hi. How did you find me?" Having him at the scene lifted much of the tension.

"Phil called and told me." He turned to John Ahern. "You need Kerry much longer?"

"She can help me with the autopsy tomorrow. Take her home."

She grabbed her boss's arm. "Can you tell by looking if the caliber of the bullet that killed the victim was the same as the one in Nancy Donello-Sanchez?" *Please say yes.*

"I won't know until after I open this one up, and the crime lab makes the comparison." He placed a hand on her shoulder. "I'd sleep with one eye open if I were you."

Before his comment sunk in, Hunter wrapped a possessive arm around her waist. She couldn't tear her gaze away from the car and blood streaked window.

"You shouldn't look at the body too long. It'll give you nightmares," he said.

"And bones don't?"

"Caught me. I wanted to get you away from here. It's not safe. Our killer could be hiding in those trees." He leaned a head toward a line of trees about one hundred feet ahead on the right.

Kerry snuggled closer to Hunter, her protector. She squinted into the wooden area, but couldn't see anything.

For the first time in a long time, she was glad she wasn't pregnant.

CHAPTER TWENTY-FOUR

"You've barely said a word since we left the scene," Kerry said. "Were you thinking about the crime? Or your wife?" The anniversary of Hunter's wife's death must be an agonizing time for him. She hadn't planned to broach the topic, but she believed if he could discuss his grief, he might start to heal.

"Amy? Yes and no."

Now what did that mean? She wasn't one to pry, but the frown on his face needed smoothing. "You want to talk about it?"

"There's nothing to talk about." Clipped response that held a lot of hurt.

Liar, liar. Or was he in denial? Hunter was a mass of knots that needed a healing touch, but she wasn't sure it was her touch he wanted or needed.

Hunter pulled to a stop in front of the cabin, shut off the engine, and jumped out. She raced after him.

"How did your wife die?" she blurted out.

There. She'd asked the burning, and yes rude, question. She couldn't help herself. Understanding what made him tick would help her know the man better and how to deal with him. They were, after all, a team.

Stop it, Kerry. Don't lie. You want to know what drives him, what turns his heart to mush, what makes him risk his life for people he doesn't know. You want to know him.

Hunter always acted as though he carried the weight of the world on his shoulders, but no one should believe they were responsible for everyone—even the mighty Hunter Markum.

The protector ducked into the kitchen and snatched a bottle of water from the fridge. "You want something?" He used his elbow to motion to the contents inside.

"Yes, an answer." She sucked in an audible breath. "I'm sorry. Look, if you don't want to talk, I understand."

When he turned to face her, his remarkably blue eyes transformed to dark gray. He let out a breath. "Amy was driving and talking on her cell—to me. She never implied she was in a car." He stabbed a hand through his hair. "I should have recognized the background noise, but the office can get real loud. I would have made her hang up if I'd known where she was. It was so stupid."

"What was?"

"The argument. She wanted me to watch Melissa that night but I had a case I was working on. We fought. We should have talked face to face. It's my fault she died."

"What happened?"

"She was hit by a train."

Kerry sucked in a breath. "Wasn't there a barricade?"

"No. It was out by Odessa, where it is rather rural."

"Which was way you probably didn't hear any cars on the road, especially if she had her windows rolled up."

"Maybe." His shoulders slumped.

"A lot of people make calls when they drive." She tried never to do both.

"I bet if she hadn't been focused on explaining her side of the disagreement, she would have seen the train coming." His jaw clenched. "I heard the train's brakes screech and Amy's screams. The sound of metal collapsing will be etched in my brain for life."

"Oh, Hunter, I'm so sorry." What could one say to such trauma? Kerry wanted to hug him, to give him whatever strength she had, but

Hunter stepped past her and strode into the living room, his boots smacking against the wooden floor.

"There's nothing for you to be sorry about," he called back. His voice was thick with emotion. "Amy's gone. I've moved on."

She didn't believe he'd remained unaffected by her death—especially every time he looked at his daughter, who probably looked a lot like his wife. Mr. I-want-to-protect-everyone must have felt powerless when his wife, the mother of his child, had died.

Her heart tore at his loss. Out of the blue, her mom's smiling face flashed before her, yanking her heartstrings. Death sucked.

For both their sakes, she decided to let the conversation drop. As much as wanted to get inside his head, now wasn't the time. Vulnerable men always drew her into dangerous waters. She had a job to do and didn't need Hunter messing with her mind.

Kerry followed him into the living room. "Is there something else bothering you?" She wanted to give him a chance to change the subject.

He dropped onto the sofa and nearly polished off the rest of the bottle. "Yeah. I recognized the woman in the car."

Kerry's knees almost buckled, so she slipped into the chair next to the sofa. "You knew her?"

"I saw her for the first time yesterday at Dr. Dalton's office. I think her name was Chanel, like Chanel No. 5, the perfume my mom used to wear." He dragged one hand down his cheek. "The bastard's guilty, I know it."

"Who?"

"Dr. Dalton." He finished his water.

"Then why are we sitting here? We need to go after him." Her pulse soared.

He reached over and clasped her hand for a moment, most likely to keep her from rushing out the door, and his warmth shot to her heart. Leaning against the sofa back, he released her hand, his gaze jumping from her to the floor. She was so tempted to drag his strong fingers back to hers.

Hunter blew out a breath. "I have no proof he's guilty of anything." His jaw clenched. "Don't worry, I'll question him when I know more."

Damn. "Don't you see? Chanel's death fits the pattern of the other women."

"Because she was pregnant and abused?" His voice came out gruff as sandpaper. "The MO is different. If he killed Chanel, why didn't he bury her?" He grabbed the edge of the sofa cushion and squeezed the life out of it.

When Hunter looked up, she guessed his question wasn't rhetorical.

"Different circumstances called for different methods?" Not an enlightening thought. *Think*. "Maybe someone came along the road right after he killed her, and not wanting to be near the scene, he split, taking his chances no one would connect him to the murder."

"What about our Bay woman, Nancy Donello-Sanchez? That murder was premeditated. He would have had time to bury her. Christ, he tied a cement block around her waist and dumped her in the water. The docks were in plain view of the cruise repair center. That took balls."

Kerry prayed there was only one person involved. The thought of two sickos churned her stomach. "Premeditation doesn't mean fool-proof. Maybe the killer only wanted the person dead and didn't realize her gases would cause the body to rise." Her mind spun with possibilities.

"If the killer was a doctor, he'd know that."

Damn. "With Chanel, once he'd shot her, perhaps he figured removing the body might leave some trace evidence behind as well as on his clothes." She snapped her fingers. "Or maybe he used different techniques so the police would be fooled into believing there were different killers." Kerry sorted through her racing ideas. "If the crime lab can prove the bullet that killed Nancy Donello-Sanchez came from the same gun that killed Chanel Carlitta, we'd be close to connecting all of their deaths."

"Good luck. I'm still convinced we're dealing with different killers." As if something had bitten his butt, he jumped up and made a small circle around the living room. "This killing has to stop. I have to do something."

"You're not the only detective on the squad, you know." His solo attitude wasn't healthy. It could get him killed.

Her belly soured. Hunter dying would be a terrible loss not only to Melissa, and to Jen, but to her too. The tension vibrating around him nearly choked her.

"Why don't you call Dr. Dalton and ask where he was last night?" she asked.

He snorted. "You think he'd answer once he saw the caller ID?"

"He would if he has nothing to hide. Didn't you say he gave you his cell number?"

"Yes. I have it in my notebook, which I left in my truck."

"Then get it. You won't know until you try."

He shrugged. "Be right back." He jogged toward the door, his step lighter than she'd seen in some time.

The moment Hunter disappeared outside, the coziness in the cabin evaporated. She strained to hear the truck door open and close, but only silence bounced back.

She waited. For an insane second, she pictured someone subduing Hunter. Her fists clenched. That was stupid. No one knew where they were--unless someone had followed her when she and Susan came here the other day. Damn. She should have been more careful.

His truck door slammed and she closed her eyes, thankful for the small blessing.

Hunter sauntered in, skimming through the pages of his notebook. "Got it."

She let her breath out slowly.

Feet wide apart, his hand gripped the phone so hard his knuckles whitened. He punched in seven numbers. A quick flash of surprise crossed his face a moment later.

"Dr. Dalton?... Detective Hunter Markum..." He gave Kerry a quick flick of his brow. "I have a quick question for you. Can you tell me where you were last evening from about six to nine?"

With his back turned to her, Hunter dropped his head back, as though we were gazing at the ceiling. With each second that passed, a little piece of her died. She was sure the man was making up some alibi. Hunter straightened. "Sorry to have bothered you."

Hunter clacked the phone closed and turned around. Defeat raced across his face. "Shit."

"What did he say?"

"You won't believe this. The guy was at an award's banquet with the Mayor!"

"You believe him?"

Hunter stomped over to the sofa and dropped like a stone sinking to the bottom of a lake. "I do, because it's too easy to verify his story." He punched the sofa seat. "You know what pisses me off?"

"What?"

"It was as if the smug bastard was expecting my call."

* * *

DALTON FLIPPED on the kitchen light, poured a scotch, and then pressed number four on speed dial.

After a good ten rings, the good-for-nothing nephew answered. "Hello?"

Stay calm. "Tell me why you..." Dalton staggered from a sharp chest pain. "Why did you leave Chanel Carlitta on the side of the fucking road. The police called me about her death."

"What's the problem? You had an alibi, didn't you? It's what you wanted."

After three long breaths and the pain subsided. "I didn't expect them to figure anything out this fast. Your incompetence is unacceptable. My alibi is solid, but Detective Markum isn't ready to exonerate me on all the other cases."

"Just chill. The cops are too dumb to piece together anything. Look, I gotta go."

"Wait. I have another job for you." Dalton tensed, knowing a fight was inevitable.

"No. I told you I was finished with killing. It's too dangerous. Shit, I didn't even have time to dispose of Carlitta's body."

Breathe deep. Push aside the hatred. "If you refuse to do what I ask, I'll use the proof I have against you. Don't think I won't tell the police how you killed your father."

"If you turn me in, don't think I won't tell the world your little secret."

"Don't even go there. Listen to me. We're a team." Dalton knew how to play to the jerk's hatred of the family unit. "You detested the abuse as much I did."

"True, but—"

"We're in this together, right?" Dalton's teeth ground hard against each other.

"I guess so."

Asshole. "Listen good. My plan involves Kerry Herlihy."

The weasel hesitated. "If I help you, you gotta promise this will be the last time."

Sniveling bastard. "Sure. The last time." *Before you die.*

* * *

HUNTER GUZZLED his second cup of coffee while he arranged his folders on his desk, trying to find a commonality among all the killings. He yawned. Two cups weren't going to do it. He needed a few more. He'd spent a sleepless night thinking about Amy, about the poor dead woman, Chanel, and thinking about Kerry. Mostly, he thought about Kerry. Every time there was a hint of danger surrounding her, an intense anguish clawed at his gut. He wanted to wrap her in his arms and keep her there until the killer was caught, but that wasn't going to happen unless he put his ass in gear.

He had work to do, and she had work to do. If he did ever get to hold her, he might not be able to let go. Kerry was all kindness, all-caring, and way too trusting—of everyone but him. He couldn't figure out why she pulled away every time he got close, though perhaps the old adage of the pot calling the kettle black, was true in this case. Regardless, he wanted to learn who, besides her family, had hurt her.

Phil knocked on Hunter's desk. "Wake up."

Hunter lifted his head. "I'm awake." He yawned and sat up in his chair. "Just thinking with my eyes closed. Whatcha got?" He slugged down more coffee. Crap. The brew was old and bitter. The aroma of hot java from Phil's cup made him want to want a refill of the good stuff.

"I called the Mayor's office like you asked. I hate being put on hold. By the time someone answered, I was rerouted—"

Hunter lost his patience. Phil was so long-winded, he could have been a Congressman. "What did you find?"

Phil slipped a hip on the edge of his desk. "Dalton was where he said he was. It was an awards dinner to, get this, award *him* for his community service."

"Shit. Then who killed Chanel Carlitta?"

"Ah, the big question."

Hunter squeezed his eyes shut, trying to block out the horror of the woman's face. He pushed back his chair, and it sent out a loud groan. "I'm going to check something out."

"What?"

"It's personal. Kerry needs me to run something down."

He figured as long as he wasn't in charge of the Chanel Carlitta case, he could afford to spend an hour with Susan's boyfriend. The quick in and out might earn him some bonus points with the sisters. Problem was, he wasn't exactly sure what he was supposed to ask the guy.

He needed to stop by the M.E.'s office anyway to see if Kerry could be more specific about Susan's issues. He convinced himself he wasn't stopping by simply to see her.

Traffic going north was a bitch for some reason, making him edgier than he'd been all morning. Fortunately, the woman at the Medical Examiner's front desk was the usual gal and waved him on back, but not before she tossed him a smile that bordered on flirtation. Her offer didn't interest him.

He knocked on Kerry's lab, but no one answered. Just as Hunter turned to leave, John Ahern came down the hall.

"She concentrates real hard sometimes," John said as he punched in the code to Kerry's space. "Since she's not dealing with any killer pathogens, she ought to prop open the door."

Hunter pulled open the heavy steel door and entered. Sure enough,

Kerry was bent over the metal gurney, mumbling to herself. No wonder she hadn't heard his knock.

He refused to address the lightness in his chest as he studied her—tall, limber, and sexy as hell. Not to mention intelligent, soft-hearted, and yes, challenging. The sense of cheer and hope rushing through his veins was like water going over a dam—hard and fast.

"Hello," he said, as softly as possible, trying not to scare her.

She whirled around, slapped a hand on her heart, and sank onto the chair next to where she was working. "Hey."

"I didn't mean to startle you."

"I was deep in thought. It's okay." She ripped off her gloves and tossed them in a bin marked for disposal. "How did you—"

"John let me in."

"Oh."

Tears wet her cheeks. "What's wrong?"

Hunter squatted in front of her and took her ice cold hands in his. He rubbed them, willing warmth into her fingers, waiting for her to pull away, but she didn't. Now he knew she was upset. Kerry didn't take comfort willingly.

"It's Baby Doe. I always get like this when I have to work on a child."

He understood. Depression zapped him when a child died, but Kerry wasn't the type to let her emotions get the best of her, or so he'd thought. "Tell me." Hunter sensed there was more to the story.

"Tell you what? I don't know what happened to Baby Doe."

"I'm not talking about the child. I want to know why you're crying."

"I..." She stopped and sealed her lips closed.

With his thumb, Hunter reached up and brushed a tear from her cheek. Her lips parted and a sob bubbled out.

After she composed herself, she sniffled. "It's a long story."

Hunter pulled over another chair and sat on the edge of the seat, elbows on knees, his hands dangling between his legs. "I have time."

His pulse raced, waiting for the shared moment. Kerry dried her cheeks and then took a deep breath, as though stalling for time.

Perhaps she couldn't decide whether or not to share her inner soul with a man who held back his fears and emotions as often as she did.

"When I, ah, lived in Ohio, I dated a man who wasn't who I thought he was. Excuse me." Kerry reached over, grabbed a tissue and blew her nose. "Peyton, that was his name, was wonderful, or so I'd believed. I thought we were going to be married. When I became pregnant, he went crazy. You see, he was already married, only I didn't know it."

Rage roiled inside him. Hunter wanted to fly up to Ohio and punch the shit out of this guy for hurting her. The word *baby* then sunk in and a yearning nearly felled him. "You were pregnant? What happened to the child?"

She stared at her twisted hands. "I miscarried. I was so devastated —still am."

Hunter placed a hand on her knee. "Is that why you came down here? To get away from him?"

"In part. I also received a good job offer at Brahman University, one I couldn't afford to turn down. Grandpa had already survived cancer and when he suffered a stroke, I had to come."

A caregiver to the max.

"I'm sorry about what happened to you. I can see why you're skit-tish around men." Boy, could he.

"I am?" She waved a hand as if to erase her comment.

He opened his mouth to say something when she cut him off.

"You didn't come here to find out about my history."

"True." From the cool, composed tone, the story telling was over. "I stopped by to ask you something about Susan's boyfriend. What do you want me to find out from him?"

CHAPTER TWENTY-FIVE

KERRY WASN'T sure how she'd managed to convince Hunter to let her tag along when he interviewed Susan's ex-boyfriend. Hunter had been so over-the-top protective every time she suggested she help with any kind of investigation. Hell, he complained when he had to leave her alone at work. It must be because of the ramblings of the homeless man who claimed he saw a medical examiner's van pick up Willie Wyble.

Apprehension bit her at meeting this Brad person. Hunter first had driven by Brad's home to see if perhaps Teresa might be playing outside. Unfortunately, she wasn't, nor was anyone home. If the snoopy, but helpful, neighbor hadn't come out and told them where Susan's ex worked, they'd be back to where they started.

Hunter pulled into the parking lot of an all-glass building where Brad worked. "We're here."

"Upscale place."

Finding where he worked had been easier than getting in to see him. Only people with security clearance could enter the contract manufacturing plant. Go figure.

Once Hunter flashed his badge, the secretary turned pale, nodded and then brought them into the work place. She didn't see what required the security.

With a ramrod back, the receptionist led them to Brad's cubicle— one among at least one hundred.

"Brad?" the receptionist said, in a soft tone. "There are some people here to see you."

Brad stood and the receptionist tossed them a wan smile before scuttling back to her desk in front.

Susan's ex was not what Kerry had expected. Instead of this evil troll she'd imagined, the guy was nearly as tall as Hunter. Despite the maroon Polo being a size or two too big on him, his belly managed to protrude. Brad's face was pleasant enough, but he wasn't handsome like Hunter. One eye socket sat lower on his cheek than the other, but that was something only she'd notice.

Brad didn't blink when Hunter showed his credentials, which implied he might not have anything to hide?

"What can I do for you, officers?" He sounded smooth, educated and in control.

Hunter didn't correct his misconception about Kerry's identity or give away who she was, thank goodness. Since Brad didn't recognize her, it was obvious Susan had never shown him her picture.

"Mr. Stafford," Hunter began. "Ms. Susan Nottingham came to us claiming you and she had a child together."

Stafford froze, his gaze flicking to his left. The clacking of the computer keyboard and the nearby phone conversations dimmed. His shoulders relaxed, and he wiped invisible moisture off his brow. "Wow, that name came out of no where. She was pregnant when we broke up, but I haven't heard from her in over two years."

"That's not what Susan claims," Hunter said.

Brad ran a finger around his buttoned collared shirt. "Can we, ah, go someplace more private? There's a conference room at the end of the hall." He glanced around at the many pairs of eyes staring back.

"Sure."

The officemates returned their chairs to the recesses of their cubicles. Brad moved toward the end of the hall looking like he was on a death march. He swiped a badge to open the door, and the activity behind them returned to normal.

She and Hunter entered. The place had a high-end designer look, all tan and black leather chairs, large mahogany table and wall art of computer components. Interesting.

"Please sit."

He maneuvered around the table and sat opposite them. The aroma of warm coffee lingered in the air. What she wouldn't give for a cup right now. Her throat was bone dry—no pun intended.

"So what's this all about? Is Susan pressing charges or something?" His lower lip trembled. "She said she didn't want help with child support, and I believed her."

"Nothing like that. Ms. Nottingham is interested in laying claim to her child. She says you kidnapped the baby, and then disappeared back to Ohio."

Kerry held her breath. The bastard better own up to what he'd done with Teresa or she wasn't sure what she'd do to him.

He leaned forward and then slapped the desk. "I never left Florida. As you can see I'm here." He grinned and opened his arms wide.

"What can you tell me about your daughter?" Hunter said.

"Bonnie?"

Kerry touched Hunter's arm. "You have two daughters?"

"No."

"What are you trying to pull? Tell me about Teresa," Kerry demanded.

Brad's half-smile melted into a frown as his gaze shot to the ceiling. "Fuck. We have a problem. Or should I say, I have a problem?" Slack jawed, he shook his head.

She'd had enough of this guy. "What kind of problem?" She didn't bother to keep the frost from her voice.

"You see... Bonnie is...um, dead." His gaze clung to the ceiling tiles.

"Bonnie? I'm talking about Teresa." Teresa couldn't be dead.

He cleared his throat. "Susan named her Teresa. I changed her name to Bonnie."

Sirens sounded in Kerry's head and traveled down to her stomach as vomit rolled up to her mouth, forcing her to swallow hard. "She's dead?" Blood pounded in her ears.

"Yes."

Kerry didn't want to believe him. Something wasn't right. "Why did you change her name? Was it so your child's mother couldn't find her, or because you didn't want anyone finding out what you'd done to her?" It didn't matter she had no proof Brad had harmed the child, abusers often didn't stop at adults."

Hunter grabbed her hand and squeezed. His comfort meant the world to her, but nothing could contain the black, evil thoughts that swirled inside her.

"It wasn't like that."

Hunter leaned forward. "Tell us what happened." His tone came out cold and forceful, but not nearly as angry as she would have sounded had she been able to speak.

Brad stabbed a hand through his neatly groomed hair. "We were living in Ohio when Susan gave birth. In the hospital, I asked Susan to marry me, but she said no."

If Brad didn't bring up the abuse, she sure as hell would. "Go on," she spit out, not knowing how she formed the words through her grief.

"About three months after the baby was born, Susan and I had this fight about my job taking up too much time." He pressed his lips together so hard they turned white. "She complained she had to spend all her time nursing the baby and taking care of our child. She said I wasn't pulling my weight." He clasped a hand over his mouth, and then dragged his fingers to his chin. "I'm not proud of the way I handled things. I slapped her." His gaze shot downward.

Kerry sucked in a breath. These were all lies. As if some monster took hold of her mind, Kerry leapt from her chair. Before she could reach across the table to get at Brad, Hunter grabbed her around the waist and pulled her back down.

"I'll handle this, Kerry. Continue, Mr. Stafford."

Her foot tapped out a beat and her hands knotted at her sides. She bit the inside of her cheek until blood tinged her mouth.

"I wanted Susan to understand how much I helped around the house, so I stayed away for as long as I could, hoping she'd call and say she forgave me. Only she never did." He stretched his hands out to her. "When I couldn't take it anymore, I went back to the house to beg her forgiveness, but Susan and the baby had moved—disappeared without a trace." His cheeks sagged. "I couldn't blame them. But dammit, the baby was mine too. I wanted visitation rights, wanted to be part of my child's life, only I couldn't find them."

"My sister told me you followed her to Florida and *kidnapped* the baby."

Brad's eyes widened. "You're... you're, Kerry?" He leaned his head back against his chair, defeat written on his face.

Hunter's jaw clenched.

"Yes. Now tell my how my niece died."

Brad looked around the room as if some spirit from above would whisk him away. No such luck for him.

"I haven't been able to sleep much since she passed. The baby was my life. The guilt of what I'd done has eaten away at me. My work has suffered big time. I've lost weight." As if to prove his point, he stood and pulled out the waist of his pants, exposing a good two inches. He then dropped into his seat. Brad squeezed his eyes shut for a moment and held up two hands, palms facing outward. "I admit I took our child. I wanted to share custody, but Susan wouldn't hear of it. I begged her to return to Ohio with me, to marry me, but she refused. So I stayed here, hoping she'd change her mind."

"It's no wonder she wanted nothing to do with you. Susan was smart enough to stay away from an abusive man."

Brad glared at her. "It wasn't like that. You wouldn't understand. I loved Susan. I loved our baby." He swiped a hand over his eyes. "I admit I got drunk a few times. That was when she said she wanted to leave me. The baby was three months and four days old. I hit Susan— once. It was not my finest moment."

Liar. "Why would you steal a child away from her mother? That's sick." Spittle flew from her mouth.

"Mr. Stafford," Hunter said, before Brad could answer. "Do you have a copy of the death certificate?"

Kerry narrowed her eyes at Hunter. What was he trying to do?

Hunter's face remained even. Wait. Did he think Brad was lying about Teresa's death?

"I don't have one." Brad tugged on his already opened collar.

"And why is that?"

"I gave my daughter everything. She was my life. I showered her with toys. When I came into feed her one morning, she was dead." Brad's face contorted in pain as a stream of tears streaked down his cheeks.

Something inside Kerry snapped. She wanted to hate this man, but she couldn't. Perhaps he was telling the truth.

Kerry touched Hunter's arm and tried to show him she'd calmed down. He blinked slowly once, and then Kerry turned back to Brad. "Why didn't you call Susan to let her know Teresa had died? She had every right."

"Her number was out of service. I swear to you."

Damn. Susan changed phones all the time, fearing Brad would find her. "Did you at least alert the authorities?"

"And be arrested for kidnapping? I couldn't go to jail. It would kill me. Calling them wouldn't have brought Bonn-I mean Teresa back to life."

He dropped his hands into his head and wept, as giant sobs wracked his body. When he finally looked up, his stained cheeks and red-rimmed eyes confirmed he wasn't acting.

Hunter took out his notepad. "Where did you bury the body?"

Brad described the isolated area near Braham University. Hunter shot a glance to Kerry, and her heart sank to her stomach. It's where they'd found Baby Doe. She shut her eyes for a moment to gather her composure.

"We found a small body in that vicinity clad in a jacket. Did you bury Teresa in clothes?" Kerry said.

"God, yes. What do take me for? A monster?"

Yes. "What color was her jacket?"

"Pink, I think. Yes, pink with green trim. I also buried her with a teddy bear. I wanted my daughter to have a friend when she went to heaven."

A giant sob lodged in her throat. Hunter covered her hand with his.

Poor Susan. She wasn't sure how she was going to tell her sister that her years of hiding and searching were over. Closure wasn't all it was cracked up to be. Crushing Susan's hope of ever finding her child alive would send her into a spiraling pit of depression.

"Mr. Stafford, did Susan have a restraining order against you?" Hunter asked.

"A restraining order? No. She disappeared without filing one." His Adam's apple bobbed hard. "Why?"

"Because if that's the case, you didn't kidnap your child."

He looked confused. "But—"

"A father has a right to see his own child, unless Susan had a court order to stop you."

"You mean if I'd called the authorities when Bonnie died, I'd be okay?"

"That's right. By not reporting her death, however, you will go the prison."

Brad's face crumbled. Betrayal snapped at her. Susan should have mentioned she hadn't taken any legal action against the man. Then again, why hadn't she thought to ask her sister?

CHAPTER TWENTY-SIX

AFTER HUNTER DROPPED Kerry off at work, he escorted Brad Stafford to the sheriff's department. She had insisted on returning to the lab to identify Jane Doe #4. Her lips had quivered, and her voice had been thick with emotion. It tore his heart up real bad. Hunter wasn't good with women, but he knew people. Arguing with her wouldn't have earned him any bonus points.

As much as he wanted to comfort Kerry, and tell her everything would work out in the end, but shit, why lie? Her relationship with Susan would never be the same.

His heart ached knowing the anguish and turmoil Kerry's sister was in for. A pain that cut so deep, the wound might never heal—like his continuing ache over Amy.

Amy.

His wife's usual fresh face had been less distinct, and less real of late. Kerry's smiling image had crowded his dreams, not Amy's. Caring, bright, passionate Kerry. Though he was guilt ridden to admit it, Kerry was more of a mate than Amy had ever been. Kerry listened to his theories, and even saw through any illogical conclusions he might draw. Amy's life was all about her climb in the banking world. Even Melissa came second, he third.

Kerry understood why he had to search for the criminal, whereas Amy wanted him home to take care of the lawn and the house.

Kerry understood death and what it did to the soul—like he did.

"Detective? Are we getting out?" Brad said.

Drowning in his thoughts had made him forget Brad Stafford in the back seat. "Sure."

Hunter slid from the car and opened the back door and led the man into custody. As he turned back toward the desk area, Brad called to him. Hunter turned. The man's eyes looked hollow. "Do you want me to give you a DNA sample? If you find my daughter, you'll see I didn't harm her. She died of SIDS, I promise."

Maybe the guy did have a heart after all, or else he didn't want to face a murder charge too. "The sergeant will take care of you." Kerry believed Baby Doe was Teresa, but it wouldn't hurt to have Brad's DNA in the system.

Hunter headed back to his cluttered desk. He'd pulled out his chair when his cell rang.

Phil. "What's up?"

"Ahern just called. The bullet that killed Chanel Carlitta didn't come from the same gun that killed Nancy Donnello-Sanchez."

"Damn."

"But there is good news."

"Tell me." He wanted to strangle his partner right now.

"Here's the interesting part. I ran the ballistics on the bullet that killed Willie Wyble."

"And?"

"Same caliber as Chanel's."

"You shitting me?" The results might throw Kerry's theory down the drain.

"Nope. We won't know if it came from the same gun until after the lab finishes processing it."

"That's an interesting twist. Thanks." He hung up.

What did Chanel and Willie Wyble have in common? Kerry had been so sure Nancy Donello-Sanchez was a victim of the serial killer. She'd been abused, pregnant, and had plastic surgery. But Willie Wyble? He didn't have any of those characteristics. Shit. They must have been looking down the wrong barrel—or else they were faced with two different killers.

His phone trilled again and he snatched it off its cradle. "Yeah?"

"Detective Markum?" The woman's voice wobbled, sounding old, frail, and scared.

"Yes?"

"I'm Helen Szemansky. I've been afraid to call, but when I saw you and that pretty woman on TV the other night, you both looked so kind and nice I thought what harm could come from checking."

"Excuse me?"

"The bust of the missing woman your woman friend showed?"

"Yes?"

"I think the woman might be my granddaughter. Bea, that's my daughter, didn't want me to call."

"I'm glad you did."

She coughed several times. "Sorry."

"Would you like to come in and take another look?" He thought her breath hitched. Poor woman. "Up close?" Perhaps it'd give her closure and them a positive identification.

"I'm afraid I can't walk, and it's too much for me to get my daughter to take me. She hasn't been the same since Deidre left us."

His mind raced. "I could come to your place, if that would be easier." Her sigh of relief made him smile. "I have a good quality photograph of the model."

"That would be wonderful. And bring that nice woman with you."

* * *

THE TIME HAD COME to face Susan. Conflict tore Kerry up. Denying the father the right to see his daughter was wrong—unless Susan believed he'd harm the baby. Kerry was determined to find out what really happened in Ohio—and Florida.

Regardless of the outcome, she would finish the facial reconstruction of Teresa, if only to give her niece the respect she deserved. Having found no evidence of any stress fractions or damage to the bones, the autopsy had concluded the baby could have died of SIDS as

Brad claimed. For that, she was grateful. For now, Brad seemed to be telling the truth.

She checked her watch. Hunter had called and said he was on his way to pick her up. ETA about fifteen minutes. She cleaned up her area, and then trashed the paper gown and booties. As she headed out to the front, Steven burst through the door, a serious look on his face. He stopped, his eyes widening.

"Hey," he said. "You still here?" He wiped his palms on his lab coat.

Quarter to six wasn't exactly overtime material. "I'm about the leave. Cutting the clay strips for my new reconstruction took longer than expected." Total babble. Until she spoke to her sister, Kerry wouldn't discuss the identity of Teresa. "And you?"

"Thought I'd clean out the vans while Dr. A's not here. I can't clean while he's ordering me around." Steven smiled, his teeth perfectly white and straightened.

Money. He must have been raised on the stuff. She wondered why she never noticed before. "I'm sure Dr. A will be pleased."

"I hope so. But I'm doing it for selfish reasons. Last time I rode in the white van, I thought I'd puke, and I have a cast iron stomach when it comes to smells."

She agreed the seats in that vehicle smelled like vomit and death. "Sounds like fun. I wasn't aware Dr. A had left."

Hunter was not going to be pleased Dr. Ahern cut out of his babysitting gig early.

"He took off about an hour ago, saying he was coming down with a cold."

Good reason. "Well, goodnight."

"Kerry?"

"Yes?"

He shook his head. "Nothing." Steven smiled again and moved past her down the hall.

Yikes. Maybe the young man had a crush on her, though she hoped not. He wasn't her type. Hunter's face appeared in her mind and her pulse quickened.

* * *

"ARE YOU OKAY?" Hunter asked the moment Kerry slipped into the car.

It might be hot and humid outside, but the heat couldn't be the only cause for her blotchy face.

"Just a lot on my mind." She faced the side window.

"Have you figured out what you're going to say to Susan?" Hunter pulled into traffic.

"Not yet."

"What's wrong?"

"I was thinking about Steven."

"John Ahern's assistant?" He'd only run into the kid a few times, but he seemed nice enough.

"I can't put my finger on it. He kind of creeps me out."

Hunter stopped at a light and turned toward her. "What did he do?"

"Nothing, really. He smiled at me."

"Oh, okay." Hunter laughed. "I think with so much going on, you're understandably seeing something that's not there." He reached over and squeezed her hand wishing he could do more to bring her comfort.

She half smiled. "That must be it. Thanks."

He tapped the steering wheel. "Good news."

"What?"

"I received a call from a Mrs. Szemansky about Jane Doe #4. She thinks the woman may be her granddaughter."

Kerry grabbed his shoulder and her heat seared his skin. Her smile moved him, sending a rush of desire straight to his groin. Though the dark circles under Kerry's eyes worried him, her renewed energy gave him a jolt. A car behind them honked.

Green light meant go. He took off.

"That's great. Did this Mrs. Szemansky give you any details as to why she thought the model might be her granddaughter?"

Before he could answer, a car sped past his cruiser, going at least twenty-five miles over the speed limit. Idiot. While he didn't stop folks for speeding anymore, he was tempted to put his siren on and tail the guy.

"No. Talking seemed to be an effort for her, so I cut the conversation short. We'll know soon enough. We're on our way there now."

"That's wonderful news."

He kept his eyes peeled for the Bearss Avenue exit. Fifteen minutes later he turned off the interstate. After a few turns, he found the woman's street, near where a prostitute had been brutally slain last week. White paper mixed with brown leaves blew and floated along the side of the road.

Kerry waved the scrap of paper he'd written the directions on. "That's it." She pointed to a small, pale yellow house.

Hunter pulled to a stop in front of the mailbox. The grass needed some cutting and the house could use a fresh coat of paint, but the blooming flowers showed someone cared. They slipped out, and he locked the car doors. No use tempting fate, especially around here.

The humidity had taken a small holiday and a cool breeze blew enough to relieve the intense heat. Hunter pressed a hand to her back and led Kerry to the front door. She stiffened but didn't move out of his reach, a sure sign she was thawing toward him.

A woman in her late sixties answered his knock. The condition of the house was a palace compared to the landscape of the woman's face. Only because she was standing did he know she was alive.

"Mrs. Szemansky?"

"No. That's my mother. I'm Bea Flower." Her voice came out hoarse, like she smoked three packs a day.

He introduced himself and Kerry. "May we come in?"

"Sorry. I don't know where my manners are." Shoulders slumped, she showed them in. "Please sit."

A sweater and a shirt were tossed on the back of the sofa, and two full ashtrays along with a half-full plate of something unrecognizable sat on a side table.

Two kids ran past an elderly woman in a wheelchair, one waving a plastic sword and the other fending off the attack with plastic nunchucks. The old lady smiled a toothless grin. From all the eye rolling and pursed lips, the older girl, who was in her early teens, was doing her best to pretend she was enjoying herself. The younger sister, dressed in a Tae Kwon Do outfit, was screeching and laughing. Both were mirror images of each other.

An unexpected stirring shot through him at the thought of Melissa having another child to play with.

Hunter refocused as he took in the living room. Books and toys littered the room, and a small television that flickered displaying some cartoons had the sound muted. The furniture had mismatched flowered covers tossed over them, and small figurines were stuffed to the max on the bookcase. He sneezed. The dust quotient was out of control.

"Molly and Danielle, go play in the den," Mrs. Flower yelled. She coughed, and then pulled out a pack of Marlboros.

She lit one, and the acrid tang slid down his throat and made him choke. Damn allergies.

Bea Flower took a deep drag as though it would be her last breath.

Kerry's face fell, for she too must have sensed this woman was at the end of her proverbial rope.

"Mrs. Szemansky and Mrs. Flower, I've brought a photo of the reconstruction." Hunter handed the picture to Mrs. Flower.

Bea's hand clawed at her shirt and her face paled. She dropped the photo on her mother's lap. "It could be my daughter, Deidre. Her eyes were set close together like this woman's and they both had high cheekbones and a small chin."

Both waited for the elderly woman to agree or disagree. "The nose isn't quite right, and Deidre never wore her hair that way." The elderly woman glanced up. Pain dragged her mouth as she covered the photo with her palm.

"I guessed at the hairstyle," Kerry said. "Same with the ears, nose and lip thickness."

Mrs. Szemansky nodded. "Then maybe it is her, but I can't be positive."

The older lady flipped the photo face down on her lap, and Hunter took it back from her.

"Can you tell me what happened to Deidre?" Hunter didn't address either of them in particular.

The smell of popcorn floated in from the kitchen. The kids giggled, as if they knew they should wait for dinner.

"Deidre and Trent were married fifteen years ago," Bea Flower began. "Everything was going real good until about two years ago." She turned back toward the kitchen. "Deidre was supposed to be at work. She had two jobs, you know, trying to support the family. She did some accounting work for an elderly gentleman. When took sick one day, she came home early."

Bea took another drag and seemed to savor the taste, the smell, and the high. "She, ah, caught Trent pawing Molly—she's Deidre's eldest. Molly was only twelve at the time."

Kerry drew in an audible breath and squeezed the arms of the chair. "That's despicable." A small bubble flew from her mouth, and she swiped her lips.

He wanted to take Kerry away and comfort her, but she'd protest and insist they finish the interview.

"What happened?" Hunter kept his voice low, but his heart pounded in his chest at the injustice.

"They were at their house, mind you, so I only heard this second hand. Deidre went after him with a kitchen knife. That's when things got real ugly. She cut him on the arm. He then grabbed the knife from her and sliced up her face. Deidre was able to reach the phone and call 9-1-1. Trent got scared and split."

Hunter scribbled a note to himself to look up the call. "Were charges filed?"

"Yes. The bastard's in jail, thank God. Doesn't help Molly though. He already ruined her. She's only now enjoying herself again."

So much for the husband killing the wife. "Mrs. Flower, if the woman we have in the morgue is your daughter, did you know she was pregnant?"

Bea's hand flew to her mouth and her brows arched. She choked out a response. "No." Her body crumpled onto the chair next to them, her breaths rapid.

"Was she dating anyone?" With her hubby already in jail, Deidre would have been with someone at least two to three months before her death.

It took a moment before she answered. "Yes. Chris. Chris Auger. He showed no interest in the kids, so Deidre thought he was safe. Too bad he wasn't nice to my daughter."

"Was she injured again?"

Her bottom lip protruded over her top lip. "Yes, but Deidre claimed she'd been in a car accident. Her injury occurred right before she disappeared. She said the airbag exploded and smashed her face up pretty bad. Broke the bone above her eye, but I never believed her."

"Did you think Chris abused her?"

"Yes. I didn't have the heart to ask the kids about it. I didn't want to scare them."

"Can you give me Chris' address?" He'd definitely check out the guy.

"Sure." She reached into the coffee table drawer and withdrew a notebook. "Here it is."

Hunter copied it down.

"Did she have surgery to repair the eye socket?" Kerry asked.

Hunter was glad Kerry had popped back to the realm of the living.

Bea sniffled. "Yes. She went to a plastic surgeon." A hint of a smile lifted one corner of her lips. "And then she sent the bill to Chris. Apparently, when he saw the amount for the procedure, he went ballistic. Deidre called me that night, crying, saying she had to leave him. She was worried about the children. I told her I'd watch the kids while she figured out what to do." Her lips trembled. "That was the last time I heard from her."

Hunter had to ask as Kerry looked lost in thought again. "Do you recall the name of this surgeon?"

"Yes. I'll never forget. She was so excited he made room for her in his busy schedule. It was Dr. Dalton. He works over on 56th Street."

Anger stabbed at him. Proof. Somehow he'd get the proof the bastard killed those women. "Thank you."

Hunter stood and Kerry reached out a hand to stop him. "Mrs. Flower, do you have a hairbrush of Deidre's?" She explained the DNA process.

"Everything of hers is boxed up in the garage. I suppose I can look through her things."

"We'd appreciate it."

Hunter grabbed Kerry's hand. It was cold and lifeless. Something other than losing her baby had thrown her for a loop while talking to Mrs. Flower, and he was determined to find out what had shaken her to the core.

CHAPTER TWENTY-SEVEN

KERRY SUGGESTED Domino's Pizza for a dinner to-go. She sure as hell didn't feel like cooking. Hunter agreed and picked up a large Pepperoni pizza along with a couple of Cokes.

As they headed home, she couldn't pry her mind off of poor Molly. How could a father touch his own daughter? It was beyond detestable.

Her mind skipped back in time. Dad and Susan—together. That was worse than a snake slithering into your crotch while your hands and legs were tied.

Move on, Kerry before you break down and cry. She swiped a tissue across her nose but refused to let the tears fall.

Hunter jerked the cruiser to a stop in front of their remote cabin but left the engine running and the air conditioner going full blast. Pinpricks of light filtered across the pond from the neighbors.

He faced her. "You haven't said much since we left Bea Flower's place. Is something wrong?"

Now it was Hunter's turn to question her silence? "Her story is sad, that's all." She tried to brush it off, hoping he'd drop the topic. Her own ache cut too deep.

He rubbed her arm. "There's something more, isn't there? Her story hit home."

His tender tone flipped a switch inside her brain. Dare she tell him about the abuse, how unloved she'd felt her whole life? Light from the three-quarter moon mingled with the illumination from the front porch lamp and streamed inside the cab. His blue eyes pooled with sympathy.

Tell him. Tell him.

"Yes, there's more." There. She'd said it, though she had no idea how he'd take her confession. She felt like she'd jumped off a cliff into the warm water below. Were there ragged rocks under the surface, or soft sand?

Hunter took her hand. This time she didn't pull away.

"Tell me."

Kerry inhaled. "My father abused my sister." She waited for a negative reaction but none came. His hands clasped hers more firmly, urging her on. "It wasn't until this visit that I learned Susan had protected me from my own father, the man I thought I could trust. All these years, I believed she'd left me to go play with her friends. I thought Susan was like my mom who frequently deserted us to audition for some play, but I had been so wrong about my sister." Kerry pulled one hand from his grasp and wiped her eyes. "I've lost so many years of knowing her. Susan suffered a lot more than I ever did."

Then the dam broke. Tears gushed from her eyes and down her face. Sobs racked her body. Hunter drew her close and caressed her back with a tender hand, helping to calm her. Kerry struggled to push back the guilt, the betrayal, and the lost time. She sniffed.

"You were young, right?"

"Yes, but I should have f-f-found out about what my dad was doing to Susan. I was so angry when my sister didn't come to our mother's funeral, I never stopped to think she may have had a good reason." Kerry used the hem of her shirt to wipe the tears from her cheeks. "I didn't know she was in hiding from her abusive boyfriend either." The guilt nearly made her burst into tears again, the vulnerability still raw. "Once my parents died, I balled up all my insecurities and fears and placed them on her."

Hunter looked upward for a moment, and then lowered his chin.

He stroked her cheek. "I can understand why you reacted the way you did."

She believed him. For the first time in her life, someone understood who she was and how the events in her life had shaped her as a person. "Thank you."

"It's not your fault you jumped to that conclusion," Hunter said. "Abuse is insidious. It causes all kinds of hurt. You did what you had to do and so did Susan. You protected yourself by building a wall around your heart."

She sucked in a sob. Could the man really see into her soul?

He leaned back against the seat and closed his eyes. "As long as we're sharing our deepest, darkest secrets, you might as well hear mine."

She swallowed, her pulse speeding. "Is it about your wife?"

"No, my sister, Denise." He gazed at the ceiling. "Man, she was amazing. She had the brains of the family." He let out a low chuckle. "Ivy League education, followed by Harvard law. She even became a prosecuting attorney at a prestigious, downtown law firm. She was unstoppable when it came to going after the bad guys. Denise was my hero." His tone came out wistful.

"What happened to her?" Kerry's heart nearly split from the pain pouring off him.

He cupped his hands behind his head. "Someone broke into her house one night and bludgeoned her to death. He then dumped her body in an orange grove not far from here." His lips curled. "Left her there to rot. It was months before a migrant worker found her body."

Kerry gasped and grabbed his arm. "I'm so sorry. Was Denise older?"

"Yeah, by ten years. I was a senior in college when the police found her. That's when I decided to go back to school and go for another degree, this time in law enforcement."

Her heart nearly broke at the trauma he'd suffered. "What had you majored in the first time?"

"Math, can you believe it?"

"From the way you analyze every situation, yes I can."

"I'm happy I moved into law enforcement though."

For that she was glad. "Did they find her killer?"

He scrubbed a hand down his face. "No. All that was left of my sister was her bones. It took them quite a while to even identify her."

The image of the four women skated across her mind. "Oh, Hunter. Seeing those women in the graves must have been so difficult for you."

The pieces to the puzzle slipped into place. Hunter's passion and his loner attitude probably stemmed in part from Denise's death. Toss in a wife who he believed died because of his carelessness, and she could see why he acted so protective toward her.

"Yes. I kept thinking one of them could have been Denise." He looked over at her. "I think we should go inside."

"Sure."

Hunter grabbed the pizza, cut the engine, and jetted out of the seat to come around to her side. He pulled open the door, and she swung her legs out. He cradled his arm around her waist and helped her stand. Their gazes caught. Naked. Vulnerable. Trusting.

Trust? Did she trust him? Her heart screamed, yes. She'd shared her innermost fears and he'd shared his. Both understood each other's pain.

Hunter set the box on the car roof and then reached behind her to close the passenger door. He guided her back against the cruiser, never taking his gaze off her. His lips parted and her heart stopped. The grief that had speared and shredded her composure raced to the far recesses of her mind. Hunter was hurting, just like she was. They were one.

The wind whistled through the trees. Pine scented the air. She inhaled to enjoy the moment and to forget the past. His hands cupped her chin and raised her face a notch. Kerry sealed her mind from the hurt, from the pain, from the despair, and allowed only Hunter to enter her soul...her heart.

The second his lips met hers, her body melted against him. It was as if she'd finally given herself permission to let go and explore. Her fingers molded over his sculpted chest. The censure in her mind gave a final gasp, and she dared to move her itchy fingers lower. She pulled his shirt from his pants as her tongue dipped into his mouth that tasted of cinnamon, spicy, and everything nice.

After a few tugs and a couple of popped buttons, his shirt drifted downward and pooled around their feet. Hunter undid her blouse and bra and dropped them. She leaned back to catch her breath, to look at his marvelous body that was rippled and tough and amazingly sexy.

He flicked a thumb over her hard nipple. "I think we should go inside. It's too hot out here—and too buggy." His voice turned raspy.

"Yes." The inside of a volcano would be cooler, though she was sure it wasn't the air temperature heating her core.

The gentle breeze kissed her nipples as she wrapped her arms around his neck and backpedaled into the house. No way was she going to let him go. Not now, not ever.

Over his shoulder, Kerry caught sight of Hunter's blue shirt and her white lacy bra strewn on the ground.

xxxHunter kissed her all the way into the house. He picked her up and crossed the bedroom threshold. They tumbled onto his bed with the cool, crumpled sheets that smelled like him—all man and musky.

When he nipped her breast with his teeth, a torrent of lust slammed her so hard she couldn't breathe. She loved the way he kissed and couldn't wait to explore the hard planes and contours of his body and face. He was all muscle, sinew, and raw power. Kerry's heart wanted to go slow, but her body wanted warp speed. God, she felt like a nervous virgin.

Hunter pulled off her shoes and pants with ease, and then cupped her hot sex. She sucked in a breath. Not letting him have the upper hand, she grabbed his crotch. Oh my God. His erection peeked above his low cut jeans, straining to get out.

Her eyes widened. Hunter laughed. "Don't worry. I won't hurt you."

Her mind froze for a moment. How could she go from zero to sixty in five seconds? Was she rushing into something she shouldn't?

Shut up and enjoy.

Her conscience was right. Hunter was everything she wanted in a man—and best of all she trusted him.

"You okay?" He ran his callused palms over her sensitive nipple. "You left me for a moment."

She grinned, and then giggled. Actually giggled, something she hadn't done in years. "Yes, but I'm back."

Before she had another thought, she shut down all thoughts, and then unbuttoned Hunter's low-slung pants and struggled to get him out of his clothes.

"Here. Let me help you with those."

Quicker than she could blink, Hunter ditched his shoes and pants and was on top of her—stark naked. Wow. She ran a finger down a thick scar on his shoulder. She located another one near his rib cage and a third low on his hip.

"Police work is tough," she said.

He chuckled but said nothing, as his eyes glazed over with lust. It had to be lust because he couldn't have true feelings for her, could he?

When Hunter plunged a thick finger into her swollen, wet opening, all questions flew from her mind. She relaxed and let go, enjoying herself.

Hunter was gentle and rough, fast, yet slow. He made her come alive again even as her hands and mouth worked feverishly over his body.

The air conditioner clicked on, cooling the slick sweat on her skin. They became twisted in the sheets, laughed, unrolled, and kissed some more.

Intense need whipped her into a frenzy. She wanted all of Hunter—his passion and his body, but most of all his heart.

With his knee, Hunter parted her thighs and plunged into her with one slick move. She gasped and Hunter stilled.

He cupped her cheek. "Did I hurt you?"

"No." She grabbed his hips and began pumping her legs. Blood pounded in her ears, helping to erase her past. Hunter must have understood her need for more, for he too matched her rhythm.

"What you do to me is beyond words," he said.

His admission sent her soaring. When she tried to answer, all that came out was a groan.

With his eyes closed, he moaned, kissed, and touched her everywhere. Oh, God. Stars exploded behind her lids, and she climaxed hard. A second later, Hunter came.

Once they caught their breath, he kissed her hard once more, and then rolled on his back taking her with him.

The sweet smell of sex perfumed the air.

Like a limp doll, she placed her face on his heaving chest, his hairs tickling her face. She'd never been happier.

Her cell rang, but Kerry didn't move, didn't care.

"You going to answer that?" he asked.

"Can't. You killed me with passion."

He laughed. "I hear ya."

Together they basked in the wonder of their lovemaking. The sharp trill of the phone stopped. "It was probably Susan, and I can't talk to her yet."

Hunter kissed her, and his musky scent sent her into the thrill zone once more. "You want me to come with you when you speak with her?"

"Would you?" Her pulse beat hard.

"I might be able to give not only moral support but some background information."

"I'd love that. This will earn you mega bonus points." She ran a hand down his rough face, the hairs prickling her hand.

He smiled and her heart began to heal. "Do you know what we forgot?"

"What?"

"We left the pizza outside on top of the car."

She giggled. "My mind was on other things."

"Me too." Hunter sat up. "I don't want the animals to get it. Be right back. We can chow and then maybe have a repeat performance."

"Now you're talking."

* * *

THE SUN MIGHT BE SHINING and the air warm, but there was nothing good about this morning. Susan's car sat in Grandpa's drive. Kerry dreaded telling her sister her child was dead, but with Hunter by her side, she'd find the strength.

Kerry and Hunter entered the house through the back door. The smell of omelets and burnt bacon lingered in the air, but the kitchen was empty. "Grandpa?"

Susan came from the living room into the kitchen wrapped in a pale gray fleece robe and no makeup. Kerry couldn't imagine wearing something so hot in the summer.

"Hey. You two come for breakfast?"

"No, we ate earlier." Not really. They'd had coffee and juice, but Hunter's kisses had fed her all morning.

Buster pranced around the corner, looking cool and calm—and quiet for a change. He sniffed Hunter, bounced over to Kerry and sat, his tongue hanging out. She dropped to her knees and rubbed his head, and then his belly. Buster barked once in appreciation.

"Come join me," Susan said. "Sit and stay a while. Grandpa is picking up more juice at Publix."

Kerry's sister looked tired, but her spirit seemed upbeat. That was about to change.

Kerry dragged the kitchen chair next to Susan and took her Susan's hand.

Terror and hope splashed across Susan's face. "What's wrong? Is it Brad? Did you find Teresa?"

Hunter scooted his chair closer to the table and the legs ground against the wooden floor. "We arrested Brad. You won't have to worry about him hurting you anymore."

Susan volleyed her gaze between them. "Arrested him? Why?"

"Susan. I don't know how to tell you this, but—"

"But what?" Susan squeezed Kerry's hand.

"Teresa is dead." The three simple words stole her breath away.

Susan shook her head. "No. That's not possible. She was a healthy baby. Did Brad hurt her?"

"She died of SIDS, Susan. It could have happened even if she'd stayed with you."

Through tears and hugs, Kerry told her what she knew about sudden infant death syndrome, and Hunter filled in the rest—about the illegal burial, about the lies.

Kerry speared Hunter with a glance. He masked his emotions, but the ache behind his eyes caused his lids to sag.

She loved him. As surely as she knew she had to identify her women, she knew Hunter was meant for her.

"Poor Brad," Susan said.

Kerry sat back. "Poor Brad? Don't feel sorry for him, Susan. He hurt you, just like Dad did."

"Brad wasn't that bad. I think I overreacted," Susan said, as she cast her gaze downward.

Any glow of happiness she'd felt a moment ago, evaporated. "You told me he abused you." Kerry tamped down her anger.

Susan bit her lip. "Emotionally, not physically—except once, when he was drunk. But I provoked him. I was mad because he'd leave me alone to take care of Teresa all the time. He said he had to work late, but I didn't believe him at the time."

"You thought he was having an affair?" That would be the only reason to get on his case.

"Yes. After I moved to Florida, I learned he really was at work." Susan's face turned ashy gray. "I think I want to lie down. All of this is so hard to understand."

"Do you want me to stay?" Kerry couldn't remain mad at Susan. Her sister had been through so much.

"No. I'll call you later. Okay?" Her voice came out small and pathetic.

"'K."

Kerry leaned over and hugged Susan, all past issues forgotten. Her sister dropped her head on Kerry's shoulder and cried. When all the tears had been shed by both, Kerry and Hunter left.

They were half way to the cabin, when Kerry realized Hunter hadn't mentioned anything about his plan to capture the man who'd murdered so many women. "So what are we going to do about Dr. Dalton?"

He flicked a glance over at her as he pulled to a stop at a light. "I want the bastard as much as anyone, but we don't arrest people without evidence."

"Evidence is highly overrated." Her bones told her Dalton did it. "Will you talk to him at least?"

"And ask him what?"

I guess questioning him about the five murders is not a good idea, but can't you put a twenty-four hour tail on him to see if he's stalking the women?"

"I did tail him for a few days, but the guy was clean. The department won't authorize any more time, and I don't want to leave you alone to follow him after hours. So, we'll have to find another way to get him."

"The bastard will slip up."

"Let's hope."

* * *

KERRY'S JOB at the M.E.'s office was drawing to a close. They'd identified three of the four victims found in the mass gravesite, and a fellow anthropologist at Brahman was helping to make a two-dimensional model of the female's head that had been stolen. Given her overreactive mental state, she wasn't ready to face John about the theft of the skull. The possibility of prison scared the shit out of her, and she refused to lose her license to practice anthropology because she was trying to do her job. She'd find the skull if it was the last act of her free life.

Kerry studied #3's bones, hoping to find something to tie the victim to Dr. Dalton. She slapped the cold table at the lack of evidence.

The eerie silence in the building prevented her from concentrating. No squeaking gurneys to distract her, no racing footsteps, no buzzing of excited voices zipping down the hall.

Kerry even missed Sheri, the receptionist who she'd seen flirt with Hunter a time or two. The girl had obviously taken an early weekend.

Her only break came when Steven had wandered in and seemed to be in a chatty mood. Since Dr. A was in his office slammed with paperwork, Steven must have nothing better to do than bother her.

He nodded to #3. "So, who do you think did her in?"

Poor choice of words in her opinion. "My job is to find out her identity, who loved this woman, who's missing her, not who killed her."

"You're right. Sorry." He hopped up on the counter. "You and your detective have any guesses who might have done this terrible thing?"

His sincerity made her regret her sharp tone. "He has his theories."

"Like what? Maybe I can help."

He'd seen his share of death, so maybe he could help. "All of the women were pregnant."

He scrunched up his face. "That's sick. Did you see if they had the same OB/GYN?"

"No, but that's a good thought."

He smiled and leaned forward. "What else?"

"All the woman had been associated with a local shelter."

"Is there someone in the shelter who would want to harm the women?"

"Not that we're aware of." She wasn't sure if she should spill all the beans about the investigation, but Stephen might have some good ideas given he was in med school. "There's one other thing they have in common."

"What?"

"They all had plastic surgery before they died."

His lips puckered. "That's a big coincidence. Don't you find it odd that women from the shelter could afford plastic surgery?"

"If they've been abused, the shelter has doctors who do Pro Bono work."

He slid off the counter. "And you think one of those doctors would fix up the women, then kill them?" He laughed. "That's a crazy idea."

A rush of anger surfaced. "It's not crazy when we found out the same man was the surgeon for all the women."

"What's his name?"

"Dr. Paul Dalton."

Steven's face paled. "I've heard of that guy. He's a legend. No way would he hurt anyone." He was practically shouting.

"Maybe, but as I said, it's only a theory."

Steven's stiff shoulders relaxed. "Gotta go. Let me know if anything else turns up."

With that, he slipped out. Kerry finished cleaning up and started her paperwork. She was about to call Hunter and tell him she was ready to call it a day when her autopsy door swung open and smashed against the back wall. Steven's hands gripped the doorframe, his face gaunt.

"What's wrong?" She tensed.

"You gotta come. Dr. A just called. The police uncovered another mass burial pit. They need you."

Her mind shattered into pieces. "I thought he was in his office doing paperwork."

"So did I, but he got the call and left, apparently."

"I need a second to gather my tools."

She'd unpacked her bag to clean the brushes and tools. The items lay strewn on the black countertop. Kerry scooped them up tools. "Can you hand me that brown satchel over there?"

Between her work and Steven's help, they managed to collect her gear in under five minutes. Kerry and Steven ran down the empty corridor, the sounds of their feet slapping against the linoleum floor. Dr. Ahern would have shovels in his medical examiner's van.

By the time they made it to the parking lot, Kerry was out of breath. The high humidity sucked the rest of the air from her lungs. At least the black clouds scudding above blocked out the intense heat of the sun.

"Let me help with your gear." He opened the trunk of his car.

"Why are we taking your car?" she said.

He shut the lid, jumped in the driver's seat and started the engine. He rolled down the window and waved her to get in. "Dr. A took his usual van. The one I often use is locked, and I couldn't find the keys. Maybe Dr. A took the keys with him. He was in a rush. Come on, get in."

As if on autopilot, Kerry obeyed. They headed toward the interstate, hitting all the green lights. Kerry wasn't ready for more tragedy. Shards of pain shredded her belly. "Did they find skeletal remains?" Or would she have to look at bodies blown to smithereens.

"Kind of. Whoever did this burned the bodies before burying them. Identification is going to be a real bitch."

"Oh, God." Images of charred bones, the stench of burnt flesh raced through her mind. While no crime scene was pleasant, this one would be particularly bad.

They rode in silence as Steven headed north on the I-275. Near Busch Boulevard, a torrent of rain blasted them, making the roads slick, and the traffic slowed to a crawl. Several cars had pulled off to the side, but Steven drove through the storm.

They passed Bearss Avenue where #4's mother lived. The next exit was twelve miles away. "Where is this site?"

"Off 54." He sounded excited, almost as though this were some grand adventure.

"Do you help at crime scenes often?" Maybe this is what seemed to rev his engine.

"Not until now. Dr. A. said because of the holiday, we're short staffed. He asked me to help."

Kerry was pleased for him. She understood how much becoming a doctor meant to him. Though digging in the rain would not be fun. Some Fourth of July.

Hunter. Damn. Given it was five already, she probably would be working late into evening. Kerry wanted to let him know he didn't need to pick her up until quite late. She twisted around to the back seat to get her purse. Darn it. Steven must have dumped all her stuff in the trunk.

"Do you have a cell? I need to call Hunter."

"Sorry. Mine's dead."

Steven took the State Road 54 exit and headed east past a several new condo developments that sat on the east side of the road. The rain abruptly halted as quickly as it had begun.

He turned north on Bruce B. Downs. The developed land disappeared and the road narrowed to two lanes.

"Whoever buried these people didn't want anyone to find this site, did they?" She kept her tone upbeat, attempting to squash the sick feeling in her gut.

Steven made a sharp right turn down an unpaved road. Kerry looked for the sheriff's cruisers, the M.E.'s van, or any sign the CSU team had arrived. Nothing. Off to the right, amidst a forest of shade trees sat a Port–O-Potty and about a five hundred square foot slice of cleared land. Only an abandoned tractor graced the property. Thoughts of the digger man, Willie, entered her mind. Gina had been convinced Willie was somehow tied to the killings. Now, he too was dead.

Steven pulled off the dirt road and parked under the trees. Kerry unlocked her door and jumped out, needing air, needing her freedom. Steven popped the trunk.

She looked around. "Where is everyone?" she said. "I thought Dr. A was already at the site?"

Steven didn't answer. He pulled something from the trunk. She leaned over to grab her purse, when Steven's hand clamped down on her wrist. "I don't think you'll need that."

She turned. His eyes had a wild fury in them, and his mouth was twisted into a sneer. "What's going on? I need to call Hunter."

"There are no bodies here, Kerry—at least not yet."

Before she could respond, Steven stabbed a needle into her arm.

CHAPTER TWENTY-EIGHT

KERRY'S EYES immediately lost focus and her legs gave way seconds after the hot liquid scorched through her veins. Her rear hit the muddy ground, and a cruel, insidious laugh invaded her mind. Her eyes rolled back into her head as she banged against something hard and sharp.

When she awoke, she was sitting in some kind of portable potty. The heat and the stench of feces overwhelmed her, though the foul odor was the least of her problems. Her mouth was taped shut and her wrists were tightly bound behind her back with duct tape. Kerry looked down. Sweet Jesus. The bastard had stripped her bare.

Shit. Shit. Double shit.

Blood sped through her veins at warp speed. The four females at the gravesite had been naked too. The finality of that act hit her hard. There was no burning between her legs, so he hadn't raped her—yet—but no telling what his future plans entailed. Steven had acted interested in her as a woman. Now it seems his flirty looks were all lies. Could he kill her in cold blood?

Damn him.

To make matters worse, Steven had put her right ankle behind her left and wrapped them together, making walking impossible even if she'd been able to escape. And her head pounded like a bitch.

Breathing hard through her nose, she tried to assess the situation. As John Ahern always said, "Tell me what you see."

Kerry attempted to keep the bile from rising up from her gut as fear short-circuited her ability to think. She had to get out of here, wherever here was.

Soft light eked its way through the semi-translucent plastic sides, but the illumination didn't bring much comfort. Gray light snuck in between the cracks where the door hinged on the confining tomb. Two rolls of toilet paper were lumped on a shelf next to her.

Why the hell had Steven kidnapped her? Surely he wasn't responsible for all the mass gravesite deaths.

Kerry closed her eyes to concentrate on the sounds around her. She wanted to find something to help identify what was going on. The tree limbs banged together, but no breeze dared to sneak into her neat little closet. If she could manage to stand, she might be able to turn around and push open the door.

Then what? She couldn't walk. Kerry slumped back down on her perch. *Kind* Steven had left the seat up. Guessed he didn't want her soiling her cozy home.

Wait.

The sound of a tractor roared to life. Tractors dug things.

Dear God. Was Steven digging a grave? Kerry's heart nearly jumped out of her skin. Sweat trickled between her breasts and crotch, and tears slid down her cheeks. Her nose clogged. Not being able to breath was the last thing she needed. With her hands behind her back, she was unable to remove the tape from her mouth.

There had to be something she could do. The urinal on the side wall had a ragged edge. She leaned over and dragged her face across the sharp edge. Ouch. In the process of trying to free the tape, she scraped some of the skin off her face. One end lifted. Progress.

She repeated the process. Before she'd got the entire piece off, the door flew open, and panic clawed her insides.

"I see you've awakened from your nap."

The rumbling engine was silent. Damn it. When had he stopped digging?

She refused to answer him. She wanted to cover her breasts, but her hands were tied behind her back.

"You have any last requests?" He had the balls to smile as he ripped off the tape from her mouth.

Last requests? Like he'd grant them? She gasped for air, and then swallowed hard. Her gaze ran the length of him, assessing the situation. Even with her legs tied together, she could kick him, but what good would it do? She'd never get away.

Kerry tilted her head, refusing to let him see her beg. "Tell me why? Why this? I thought we were friends. What did I do to you?"

"To me? Nothing."

"Then why…" The word, *kill*, stuck in her throat, "take me?"

"It's a long story." He held up a needle and squirted out a few drops.

Her thoughts jumbled as her blood pressure soared. She had to stop him. Had to convince him killing her would serve no purpose. "I've got time."

He laughed. "Not much."

Kerry squared her shoulders. "Give me one reason why I have to die."

"So I don't."

"That makes no sense." She kept her voice low and non-threatening.

"You want to know why? I'll tell you why. My *uncle*, the one and only Paul Dalton, is blackmailing me."

"Your uncle?"

"Yeah. It was only a matter of time before you figured it out. My last name is Dalton."

"I never paid attention."

"I know."

She shifted in the seat. "Why is he blackmailing you?"

"I killed my father, and he knows it." He laughed, only this time his voice was filled with self-loathing.

She sucked in a breath. Steven was a murderer. "How old were you when you…"

"Killed him? Eighteen."

Of legal age. Her insides turned to liquid. He couldn't let her go after confessing. *Think*. "My father abused my sister. I know she wanted to kill the bastard, and she would have too if he hadn't died of a heart attack first." A lie, but she was desperate to connect with him, convince him he didn't have to kill her.

"I wish mine had died by some flesh eating disease." Steven's lip curled. "God, but I hated him. My dad wouldn't leave me alone. Ever. Like his dad before him, he had to take out his hatred of life on me." Steven spat on the ground.

She bet his dad didn't rape him like her father had done to Susan. "How did he hurt you?" She leaned forward, acting as horrified as she could.

"He'd beat me whenever he got drunk, even tied me up, and locked me in a closet when he didn't want to deal with me."

Despite her fear, sympathy tugged at her. Steven basically was doing to her what his father had done to him. "I'm so sorry. Surely, the law would take your circumstances into consideration. You could claim self-defense." *Please let him see reason.*

He laughed again, his eyes wild. "Won't wash." He snarled. "Besides, I killed two other women—on *Uncle* Paul's request. I'm not buying your little sympathy ploy." He leaned inside the tomb and stabbed her with the needle again before she had a chance to react.

"And if I don't kill you now, he'll kill me. Goodbye, Kerry."

All hope vanished of seeing Hunter again. She wanted to cry out for what would never be, but her eyes rolled back into her head.

* * *

HUNTER GLANCED at his watch for the fifth time and tapped his desk with his yellow pencil. Kerry should have phoned by now to pick her up. She'd told him she wouldn't have a full day of work. Damn it. He'd left several messages on her cell, but she hadn't returned his calls.

Phil rushed over to him with a smile on his face. "We got him." He slapped a folder on Hunter's desk.

"Got who?"

"Dalton."

Hunter straightened, adrenaline spearing his heart. "Tell me." Two phones on nearby desks rang and an unruly prostitute made a racket fifteen feet from his desk.

"We received the lab results back from the shovel Gina and I found at the cemetery."

"You think it might relate to the shovel mark in the dirt Kerry found?"

"Yes. Her mark showed a bent edge, as did ours, so I had the lab process it. Not only are Willie Wyble's prints on the handle, but Dalton's are too."

"Holy shit. Dalton's prints must be on file then."

"Yup. He works at the shelter, which means he's a county employee."

"You know his prints alone don't put him at the scene of the crime. They just mean he touched the shovel." There was always a catch. "Though how or why Dalton would be using a shovel located at the cemetery is anyone's guess."

Phil leaned on the edge of Hunter's desk. Hunter always left the right corner bare for him. Chairs weren't Phil's thing.

"True, but coupled with the fact the belt loop we found near one of the gravesites matches the missing belt loop on Willie's jeans, I'm thinking we got Dalton."

"You might have Willie Wyble at the scene but not Dalton. The evidence is purely circumstantial on the good doctor, but it might get us a warrant to seize his records just on the fingerprints alone."

"I'm hoping."

"Let me know the moment you hear."

"You got it." Phil shot a look at his watch. "Aren't you late picking up Kerry?"

"She has to call me. I tried to contact her earlier, to check up on her, but she's not answering her phone." He ripped the phone off the handle. "I'm calling Ahern to see what's holding her up."

John answered on the fifth ring. "Ahern."

"It's Hunter. I'm worried about Kerry. She hasn't answered her phone in the last hour. Have you been checking on her?"

"Sorry. I had to leave work early. I've been—" John sneezed. "Been home with a cold. Let me call my assistant and see if he can hunt her down. Call you right back."

Phil grabbed Hunter's coffee mug, took a swig, and skewed up his face. "What's in this shit?"

"Cold coffee."

"It needs sugar." Hunter put the cup down and stood. "Or a microwave. I'm going downtown and see what's keeping her."

"I guess our search for Dalton's records will have to wait. It's a holiday. No one will be around."

"Bummer."

"I've got to head that way myself. I was thinking, why don't we three grab a bite to eat? Kerry will want to celebrate, I bet, once she learns we're going to nail the killer."

It might be nice to have a real date with her, even if Phil had to tag along. "Where's Gina?"

"At her mom's. It's Lucinda's birthday today."

Lucinda? He knew her mom's first name? It must be serious. "Then sure, if Kerry is up for having dinner with two old homicide detectives." Hunter could use a little R&R. As he finished packing his gear, his cell rang. "Yeah."

"It's John. Dalton isn't answering either. I don't know what to tell you."

Hunter's heart nearly stopped as he halted in his tracks. "Did you say, Dalton?"

"Yes." John's tone came out leery.

"Any relation to the plastic surgeon, Paul Dalton?" *Please say no.*

"As a matter of fact, Paul Dalton is Steven's uncle. Why?"

"Shit."

He told Phil about the identity of Steven Dalton, forcing his voice to stay calm as the two of them took off toward his car. "John, I'm going to let Phil fill you in."

He slid into the driver's seat. Phil jumped in and slammed the door closed.

When Phil finished detailing what they knew about Dalton and his connection to the murdered women, Hunter grabbed the phone back from him. "Can you meet us at the office? I want to make sure I can get in the building."

"No problem." John sneezed again.

Hunter turned on the siren and raced through I-275 traffic. Fortunately, the traffic in his direction wasn't a problem.

When they arrived in front of the Medical Examiner's office, John Ahern was waiting for them, pacing back and forth with a handful of facial tissue pressed to his nose. Hunter and Phil dashed out of the car.

"I just got here myself," John said. "I haven't checked to see if she's here."

Hunter searched for worry or panic lining Kerry's boss's face, but found none. Good.

Once John opened the door, Hunter pushed past him and raced down the hall. The echo of his feet against the tile matched the blood pulsing in his head. Two more pairs of feet matched the cadence right behind him.

Hunter pounded on the door, but received no answer. John stopped next to him and pressed the code. Lights out, the scent of human decay filled the room. His chest constricted. He flipped on the overhead bank of lights. "Kerry?"

He didn't really expect an answer but he'd prayed she'd fallen asleep in her chair. He searched for her big brown satchel that held her gear, but it was gone. Perhaps she was out in the field where she couldn't get cell phone service.

"I'll check a few other places," John Ahern said.

"What do you think?" Phil asked, standing behind him.

"I don't know what to think. There has to be a logical explanation, like she didn't recharge her batteries or something."

John panted as he entered. "I just looked in the other rooms. She's not there. Nor is Steven. I didn't see his car in the lot when I drove up." A hint of anxiety laced his tone. Crap.

Hunter tunneled his fingers through his hair and forced his mind to think where she might have gone. "Would she have been called out on a case?"

"Not without me being notified."

"Then Steven took her. I know it."

"Now don't jump to conclusions," John said. "Steven's a fine young man."

Hunter whipped around to Phil. "I don't know if we should try to find Paul Dalton or go after Steven."

"Have you tried calling her house?"

"Yes. She wasn't there or with her sister."

John sneezed again. "How can I help?"

"You ever tail anyone before?"

"Once. My daughter when I suspected she was doing something I didn't approve of. She never caught me."

"Fine."

"If you think Paul Dalton is such a creep, give me his address. I'll drive by and see what I can find out. He doesn't know what I look like," John said.

"Thanks. I appreciate your support." Time was of essence.

John grabbed the door handle and stopped. "You know, Steven talked about building a home in North Tampa. You could check out his property if you really suspect him."

"Do you have the address?" Hunter said, pacing the room.

"Not the one in North Tampa, but I do for his Seminole Heights home."

"Good. We'll check there first." His gut twisted. Was his imagination going wild? "Give me another sec."

He raced over to Kerry's computer and logged onto the Hillsborough County Property Appraiser's site. A minute later the printer spit out the information he needed.

Dread ripped at him like a dull edged knife. Kerry might be with Paul Dalton and not with Steven.

Uncertainty clawed at his belly.

Phil grabbed his arm. "You coming?"

"Yeah." Hunter growled, flicked off the room light and raced out of the cold lab.

John headed towards Paul Dalton's office, and Hunter and Phil to Steven Dalton's Tampa home. He handed Phil the directions as he leapt into his cruiser.

Ten minutes later they arrived at Steven's house. He pounded on the door. No answer. Shit.

"Let's go around and look in the window," Hunter said.

He had to climb over a bush to see inside. It was dark and apparently quite empty.

"Now what?" Phil asked.

"We try his north Tampa place."

"Just because Steven is related to Paul Dalton doesn't mean he's dirty."

"I know, but we may have two killers on our hands. We know Paul Dalton couldn't have killed Chanel since he was with the Mayor, but these murders all scream Dr. Dalton—pregnant, abused, and scarred. Someone had to help him, help set up an alibi."

He raced back to the car with Phil right behind.

"Doesn't mean Steven did the deed," Phil said.

Phil barely got in the passenger's seat when Hunter took off. He jetted out of the parking lot and headed toward I-275—toward Steven Dalton's property.

Phil's phone rang. "Tedesco."

Hunter glanced over at his partner whose lips were pressed together.

Phil thanked the person on the other end. "You are not going to believe what the lab turned up on Chanel Carlitto's driver side window."

"What?"

"A handprint."

"Whose?"

"Guess."

If both hands weren't on the wheel, he'd have strangled his partner. "Phil."

"Steven Dalton's."

"Motherfucker. The bastard is guilty."

"Your gut telling you Steven Dalton has Kerry?"

"Yeah. The worst part is that she trusts him. He's driven her to crime scenes before. It would be easy for him to get her in the car. Fuck."

An avalanche of emotions flooded his system. Anger, frustration, guilt and some other factor he couldn't name—fear perhaps that he'd lose the woman he'd come to...love? Yes, he loved Kerry. She inspired him. And as corny as it sounded, she made him whole. Her passion matched his like no one else's ever had.

"We still need proof," Phil said.

Hunter knew what his partner was doing. Trying to calm him down, but this time it wouldn't work. Not where Kerry was involved.

His cell rang. With one eye on the road, he pulled his cell from his pocket and glanced at the display. It was his boss. Shit.

"Markum."

"It's Jack. You won't believe this. You know that new guy we hired to work cold cases?"

Hunter didn't have time for this, nor did he remember the rookie's name. "Sure."

"Guy's amazing. He unearthed some evidence regarding Denise's death."

The cars in front of him seemed to stand still, and his hands went numb right along with his mind. "Denise?"

"Can you imagine? With ten years of improved technology, the rookie decided to rerun some tests. He found flecks of blood on Denise's pants that aren't a match to her."

Kerry, Denise. His mind froze. "Do you have a person of interest?"

"We have a name, or rather a witness. Seems some vagrant saw the murder."

A shot of adrenaline brought his body back to the living. "Why didn't he come forward before?" My God. All those years of waiting, wondering would have been erased. His fingers gripped the wheel as his foot pressed harder on the accelerator.

"Name's Chester Gomez. Says he'll only talk to you. He's in Tampa General Hospital. Dying. You need to come now. The doctor said the guy may not make it through the night."

More than anything Hunter wanted to know who'd killed his sister, but Kerry needed him more. "I can't."

"You shitting me? The case may go cold forever if you don't talk to this guy. Do I have to order you? I'm outside his room, but he won't say a word other than your name."

"Kerry needs me. The bastard took her." Denise was dead. Soon Kerry might be if he didn't reach her in time. "Here's Phil. He'll fill you in."

"Hun—"

Hunter handed the phone to Phil as he raced up I-275 to State Road 54. They had the man who knew Denise's killer. If he died before Hunter got to him, his family may never have closure, but that couldn't be helped. Kerry needed him. Now.

After a short conversation where Phil asked for backup to help save Kerry, he dropped the cell on the seat beside him but didn't toss out any accusations. Phil had every right to ask why Hunter didn't try to find out who'd killed Denise. Hunter's admiration for the man took a few leaps upward, especially since Phil's older brother had been engaged to Denise.

As his siren whirred and shrieked, no one moved aside. Either every car was blasting the stereo, the drivers were on the phone, or they were daydreaming idiots.

After he weaved through one clump of cars after another, Hunter finally reached State Road 54. The moment he exited, he cut the siren. No use announcing his arrival.

He'd been on Bruce B. Downs Boulevard no more than ten minutes, when Phil jabbed a finger at a dirt road. "Turn right."

"Shit man. Give me a little warning next time," he said as he slammed on the brakes and fishtailed up the road, dust billowing behind them. He slowed. "So what's our plan?" Hunter wasn't able to formulate much in his state of mind. "Do we drive in and confront the bastard, or sneak in?"

"I say we go in to see if he's there then decide."

Having a semi plan, and backup on the way, Hunter's pulse calmed. He steeled his mind against what was at stake and pretended this rescue mission was for someone else's woman.

"He's sure to see us coming for a mile." Hunter eased off the gas pedal, as his gaze searched for a car, a truck, or some kind of vehicle.

"I think I saw something red peek behind the branches."

"Where?" Hunter had lost his sharp senses.

"There. Behind those trees."

Less than two hundred feet to go, Hunter pulled off to the side, engine idling. "I say we go in by foot."

Phil grabbed his arm. "No. Dalton doesn't know us. Let's just pretend we heard there was a squatter on the property."

"I'm not so sure he won't recognize me. I've been to Kerry's lab several times."

"We have to chance it."

Hunter eased back onto the road and drove straight to the recently cleared land, taking the bumps slow. A blue Port-O-Potty sat off to the right. A young man with a shovel in hand stepped out of the forest, matching the description John Ahern had given him. The man waved and smiled. Okay that was not what Hunter expected from a killer.

Once he made sure his weapon was secure, Hunter cut the engine and eased out of the driver's seat. Phil knew to stay by the cruiser until the right moment. Their routine was solid.

"Hello," Hunter called. He flashed his badge. As he approached, he let his gaze flick over the property for Kerry. When he saw no sign of her, doubt slammed into him. Was he way off base?

A dark cloud pulled a drape over the sun and a low rumble of thunder echoed in the sky. A quick breeze brought relief against the blinding glare and the oppressive heat.

Hunter needed to bring in Steven Dalton for questioning. He'd like to see him explain away his fingerprints on Chanel Carlitta's window, but he wanted to ask a few questions first.

"What can I do for you, Officer?" Polite and charming with a hint of confidence.

"I'm looking for Steven Dalton."

"You found him." The man's wide-legged stance, along with his arms slightly edged away from his body, contradicted his overly friendly tone.

"I'd like to ask you some questions about Chanel Carlitta."

Hunter watched the spray of emotions skate across his features that consisted of surprise, guilt, and arrogance—in that order.

"I don't know anyone by that name."

Hunter expected the denial. He could have handcuffed him right then, but he wanted answers about Kerry. "So what are you digging?" His tone came out congenial—or so he hoped.

At first, Steven didn't seem to understand the question. Then he looked down at his hand. "Oh, this. I'm doing some... soil testing. I bought this property recently and wanted to see if I could put in a pond. I needed to send the contractor some samples from around the property."

Hunter didn't believe him. More thunder rumbled and Steven looked up. Splatters of rain hit Hunter on the nose, but he ignored the potential thunderstorm and inched toward his prey.

He didn't detect any bulges in Dalton's blue jeans where he might hide a weapon. His tight T-shirt confirmed the man was unarmed. "I'd like you to put the shovel down."

Steven hesitated, and then tossed the garden utensil on the ground. "What's this about?

Out of the corner of his eye, Hunter spotted a brush half-hidden behind a rock—a brush with a red handle. Just like the one Kerry owned.

CHAPTER TWENTY-NINE

HUNTER TENSED at the sight of Kerry's tool. The brush implied Steven had kidnapped her, but hunter refused to admit Steven might have already harmed her.

Phil had ducked into the side woods as Hunter expected him to. Thankfully, Steven's gaze didn't leave Hunter's face. Forcing his body to relax, Hunter moved toward him slow and easy. He sure as hell didn't want to spook Dalton.

Sweat ran down Hunter's back and forehead, despite the sun's disappearance. A salty drop stung his eye, but he didn't wipe it away, not wanting his adversary see how his nerves were eating away at him.

A Nike swoosh symbol emblazoned the side of Steven's sneakers. Christ. They looked close to a size ten, the same size as those near Kerry's grandfather's place. Had he broken into Tom's house and stolen the skull? If he were the killer, it would make sense he'd want to screw with Kerry's ability to identify the victim.

Hunter stopped and shoved his left hand in his pocket, keeping his gun hand loose by his side. "I have another question for you. I was hoping you'd know where I can find Kerry Herlihy."

Steven's gaze didn't falter. Damn. "Haven't seen her."

Again, his answer came as no surprise. He certainly wouldn't admit to harming her.

A tractor, Dalton's empty car, and an old Port-O-Potty were the only manmade items around. Where could she be? Could Steven have hidden her in the trunk of his car? Was she tied up on the floor of the back seat? Or had he killed her? His hand shook and his legs weakened at the thought.

Right on cue, Phil slipped out from the woods behind Dalton, his gun raised. Hunter's muscles instinctively flexed. Lightning lit up the sky, and five seconds later a loud clap of thunder shook the ground. Dalton didn't flinch and Phil didn't shoot.

Hunter shuffled his feet on the dirt path and kicked a stone into the leafy underbrush in an attempt to cover Phil's movement as his partner snaked closer.

Time to go for the kill. "Mr. Dalton, we found your hand print on Chanel Carlitto's car window. Can you explain how it got there?"

A twig cracked behind Steven. Shit. Dalton spun around. In one fluid motion, Steven pulled a 45-caliber pistol from the back of his jeans, drew and fired at Phil.

"Noooo." Hunter wrenched his Glock from his holster, pulled back the slide and nailed Steven in the back. Both Phil and Steven dropped to the ground just as the rain came down in earnest, as if to punctuate the grand finale.

Adrenaline kicked into high gear as panic threatened to freeze Hunter's muscles. He leaped toward Steven, kicked Dalton's gun away from his hand, and then sprinted to Phil.

A large red splotch between Phil's shoulder and heart oozed blood. Writhing on the ground, Phil moaned. His face paled. His partner was going into volume shock.

"Hold on, buddy."

"It hurts... like a ...bitch."

Hunter winced at the effort it took for Phil to say those few words.

At least he was alert. That was a good sign. Hunter shielded his phone from the rain and called 9-1-1. He gave the dispatcher Phil's respiration rate and other vitals he could guess without any equipment. "I need my hands free to stop the blood," he told the woman on the line. He knew she'd ask him to remain on the line until help arrived, but he had to give Phil assistance.

Hunter stashed the cell in his pants pocket, ripped off his own shirt, and told Phil to hold the wadded material over the wound to stem the bleeding. "I'll be right back."

Hunter raced to the car, snatched a blanket from the trunk, and zoomed back. He shoved the soft fleece under Phil's head, which rested in a one-inch deep puddle. "This should be more comfortable, buddy. The ambulance is on its way. Hold on."

Phil coughed, and blood dribbled out of his mouth. Fuck. Phil couldn't die. He might have been a pain in the ass some times, but he'd had Hunter's back more times than he could count.

Less than five minutes later, a van raced up the road. He glanced over his shoulder at the racing ambulance. God the EMTs were fast. Gotta love 'em. Hunter leaned over his partner to keep him comfortable and to give him support. A door opened and closed. Footsteps sounds behind him. He waited for the paramedic to drop down next to him.

Instead, the click of a gun sounded right behind Hunter's head, and his heart stopped.

"I hear you've been looking for me."

Paul Dalton.

Hunter's body shot to high alert. The doctor jammed the gun against Hunter's scalp. He froze, debating whether he should whip around and attempt to disarm his attacker. If Hunter and Dalton struggled, and the gun went off, Phil could be shot again.

Hunter glanced down at Phil's face. Eyes closed, his breaths were coming out in short bursts, and his complexion was waxy. Phil was losing blood fast. He didn't have long to live.

Hunter didn't turn around. "Howdy, Doc."

"Stand up. Slowly." Paul Dalton could have frozen fire with his command.

Hunter held up his hands and stood, not wanting to piss off the doc.

"Drop the gun, Detective."

Hunter lifted his weapon from his holster and lobbed his Glock five feet from him. He turned around in slow motion and prayed backup would arrive soon.

Dalton came dressed in his green scrubs, which by now were rain soaked. He must have been in quite a hurry. His nephew probably called him after taking Kerry—if he had Kerry. Or had the doctor killed her already?

Kerry. Hunter's soul burned.

"You killed my nephew." Paul Dalton spat in Hunter's face, but Hunter didn't react.

"He shot my partner," Hunter tossed back.

Keeping his tone even had been the hardest thing he'd ever had to do. He wanted to beat the shit out of Paul Dalton, but if he too was shot, who would search for Kerry? For her he had to stay cool.

"Doesn't matter now. They're both going to die."

He wanted Dalton to focus his attention away from Phil. "Take a look. I think Steven's still clinging to life."

Dalton's eyes narrowed as he backed up. A quick flash of hope crossed his face, surprising Hunter that the man was capable of caring.

"What are you doing up here?" Hunter asked the good doctor.

"None of your business." Hunter hadn't expected him to say he was here to harm Kerry.

"Mind if I tend to my partner? Killing a cop will shorten a person's freedom. If Steven lives, it would be in his best interest if Phil does too."

Dalton seemed to mull over the situation. He sidled over to Hunter's gun, picked it up and chucked it far into the woods. "Go ahead, but don't make any sudden moves."

God, the man sounded like he was a scriptwriter for a bad B movie.

As Hunter knelt next to Phil, he angled his body to keep an eye on both the uncle and the nephew. The doctor leaned over Stephen and felt for a pulse. His back stiffened.

"Is he alive?" Hunter wanted Steven to live, to pay for what he'd done.

"Barely."

Hunter swiped the rain from his eyes, wondering where Dr. Ahern was. After all, his sole job was to follow the doctor.

Sirens sounded in the distant. Gotcha! Hunter wondered what Dalton would do when the cavalry arrived.

He didn't have to wait long.

Dalton jumped up. "Sorry, Detective." He aimed his gun at Hunter. "I see you already called for backup. I can't afford to have any witnesses. You've been a thorn in my side for way too long."

Out of nowhere, John Ahern sprang from behind Dalton's auto and wrapped an arm around the man's neck. Dalton's gun fired, the bullet missing Hunter by inches.

Ahern and Dalton struggled. While the forensic pathologist was no Bruce Lee, and the man's arthritis put him out of commission more days than not, surprise was on his side. Hunter flew toward him, and wrenched the weapon from the doctor's hand.

"John, it's okay. I got him," Hunter said. "Get the cuffs from my cruiser."

Hunter spun Dalton around and slammed his face against the Mercedes. Ahern backed away, his breaths coming fast. A diesel engine vehicle roared up the road.

"I hope you'll enjoy prison," Hunter said.

"Fuck you. You have nothing on me."

* * *

ONCE THE AMBULANCE transported Steven Dalton and Phil to the hospital, and backup had carted Dalton off to jail, Hunter slumped against his car. The rain had disappeared as fast as it had arrived.

"You find any signs of Kerry?" John asked.

His gut soured. "No, just her satchel in the trunk of Steve Dalton's car. If Paul Dalton came racing up here, Steven must have called and said he had her. Let's spread out."

John headed for the Port-O-Potty and ripped back the door. "She's not here."

"Kerry has to be somewhere."

"I'll check the other side of the drive."

Hunter studied the area for clues. The shovel meant Steven had been digging. Only where?

A strong claw twisted Hunter's gut as he headed into the woods. He halted the moment he spotted a large rectangular plot of fresh dirt packed down. Oh shit. He doubted the guy was taking soil samples. That job belonged to the EPA.

His mind reeled back to when he'd first met Kerry. The mass gravesite they'd worked on looked like this one, and panic clouded his brain.

"Ker-ry," he yelled and dove to the ground, furiously pawing the dirt.

Tears stung his face as he scooped handfuls of mud and tossed them aside. She can't be under there. She can't be dead. The bastard couldn't have killed her. Not Kerry.

Please God, don't let her be dead.

A second pair of hands joined his. "Jesus Christ. You think the bastard buried her?"

"I don't know." Hunter fought for air as blackness pushed its way around his heart.

The two worked in madman tandem. John was bent over the mound like an egret digging for worms as he helped claw away the dirt.

"She's in here. I can feel it. We have to get her out. We have to dig." Hunter swallowed his tears. "Faster." Stones and twigs cut his fingers. His muscles burned and his fingers bled as he scraped the dirt from the earth. He touched something. "Wait." He brushed back more dirt. I hit wood." His body froze.

John moved next to him, shoulder to shoulder, and together they pushed aside the earth. Hunter nearly suffocated from lack of air.

"It's a coffin, all right," John announced.

Kerry's coffin?

"Keep digging," Hunter commanded. "I'll get a crowbar."

Faster than he'd ever moved, Hunter did the hundred-yard dash to the cruiser in under twelve seconds, or so it seemed. He wrenched the crow bar from the cruiser's trunk and flew back to John. He dropped to his knees and winced when his kneecap cracked on a rock. Hunter pried up the top.

And lifted the lid.

CHAPTER THIRTY

Empty

.

The goddamn coffin was empty. Air whooshed out of Hunter's lungs as he collapsed back. "If she's not here, then where the fuck is she?" His voice cracked, and he didn't bother swiping away the tears that cut a ridge down his cheek.

John grabbed Hunter's arm in a tight grip. "She has to be here. We have to keep looking."

Without either giving directions, the two of them raced into the woods at a forty-five degree angle. Less than a minute later, John called out. "Over here. There's another grave."

Hunter crashed through the underbrush to reach John. Tree limbs scraped his arms and bare chest. Bugs flew at him and a spider web lodged in his mouth, that he didn't even bother to spit out.

When he saw the fresh dirt level with the ground, he knew all hope was lost. Another grave, another coffin. But this time, he knew the coffin wouldn't be empty. Or would it?

What had possessed Steven to dig two holes? Digging was a bitch. Was this a joke? Or merely a game to drive him insane?

Steven had left a second shovel against a nearby tree. Hunter snagged it and tore through the dirt, while John churned at the mound with his hands.

A strong breeze whipped through the trees and blew the topsoil, almost as though God were trying to help in a small way.

"Kerry. We're here, sweetheart. Hold on," he yelled.

In case she could hear him, he wanted to assure her help was on the way. He refused to believe she was dead, though his mind screamed he was in denial.

John's breaths turned shorter—too short, in fact. Hunter feared the older man wouldn't be able to hold out much longer. "Come on, come on," Hunter urged, pushing himself just as hard.

"Oh, shit. Kerry's has some hand shovels in her satchel," John said with a hint of excitement.

"Wait. Bring the other shovel Dalton dropped near the car."

"Yes." The big man lumbered away, each step seeming to take more effort.

Hunter threw himself into uncovering the grave. Kerry couldn't be dead, she just couldn't be.

"I love you, Kerry," he sobbed. Sweat poured down his face and over his back.

John returned with two hand shovels as well as the one Dalton had discarded. They must have looked like rabid dogs searching for a bone. Hunter was the first to hit wood.

"I'm there."

He tossed down the shovel, grabbed the crowbar and cracked open the small end of the coffin, wanting to get air inside.

"We're going to get you out, Kerry. I promise." He continued to babble as he smashed through the casket. Bare feet glistened in the light. "Oh God. She's in there." His heart stopped. The cop in him knew she was dead, but his soul refused to give up hope.

Blood pounded in his ears as he cracked open the top. With one fell swoop, he lifted the lid and tossed it away. It bounced and crashed on the ground.

Kerry lay in the casket.

Naked.

Eyes closed.

Skin gray.

Duct tape clung to her mouth, hands, and feet. Dear God what had the man done? A primordial scream nearly bubbled out.

John leaned over the casket and dragged his two fingers over her throat. "There's no bloating. She might be alive."

Hunter held his breath, willing away all his possessions if only she'd be alive.

"There's a real weak pulse," John said. The relief in his voice pumped up Hunter.

"Call 9-1-1 again," Hunter shouted as he straddled the grave and gathered her in his arms. Nothing gave him a higher high than holding her once more. Her warm body seared his skin. He planted kisses on her cold cheeks. "Kerry, can you hear me? Wake up, sweetheart."

Hunter stepped away from the grave, knelt, and wrapped her in his arms, thankful this maniac had used a coffin instead of burying her in the cold earth. Someone had drilled holes in the side of the wooden casket. Why? To give her air? Or to let the worms eat at her faster?

It didn't matter now. Hunter unpeeled the tape that covered her mouth, trying not to rip her skin. Removing the tape off her wrists would require him to set her down, and he wasn't ready to let her go yet.

John stood, the phone pressed against his ear. He covered the mouthpiece. "I have scissors in a kit in my car," John said. Hunter didn't care if the man was going to Mars.

"Hey. Grab the blanket I used to prop up Phil's head." The damp air could give her a bad chill. Not only that, he didn't want Kerry to wake up and find herself naked.

Kerry's face slowly turned pink, and joy raced through him. He stroked her face, her arms, and her hair, reveling in the silkiness.

When John returned, he handed Hunter the rather wet blanket. At least it would cover her. John wiggled a small pair of scissors. "May I?"

All Hunter could do was nod. His throat dry, he couldn't take his gaze off her as John cut away her bindings. Poor Kerry. He couldn't imagine the horror and fear she'd experienced at the hands of Steven Dalton.

With much tenderness, Hunter kissed her lips. Her eyelids fluttered, but they didn't open. Her breathing was rough and her skin clammy. *Dear God, please make her whole.*

John Ahern stepped back and dropped to his knees. A low groan escaped his lips. His hand clutched his arm.

"John? You alright?"

The ME's eyes widened as sweat popped out on his forehead. His breaths came faster and faster.

"John?"

Without a word, John Ahern sank on the ground and passed out.

* * *

HUNTER SAT by Kerry's hospital bed, never leaving her side, looking for any sign she'd awaken soon. An oxygen tube poked out of her nose, and the constant pulse of the air from the tube was slowly driving him crazy.

Why wouldn't she open her pretty leafy green eyes and smile at him? One smile. That's all he asked.

"Mr. Markham?"

Hunter swiveled around. A tall doctor in green scrubs approached, his face devoid of tension. "Yes?"

"I have an update on Dr. Ahern."

Hunter straightened. "How is he?"

"He suffered a heart attack, but we're monitoring him. He's lucky you were there to call for help."

His friend was alive, thank God. "Thank you. When can I see him?"

"We're doing more tests. When we're done, I'll let you know."

Relieved John had survived, Hunter returned his attention to Kerry. She hadn't moved or fluttered her eyelids since her arrival. He'd asked her doctor about possible brain damage, but all the man would say was it was a wait-and-see game. People buried alive usually had serious after effects. No matter what happened to her, Hunter would remain with her—for better or for worse.

He was determined to stay until she awoke, until he heard her voice one more time. Too bad the adrenaline rush of finding her had depleted his resources. He craved sleep and food, but he wanted to be the first person Kerry saw when she came to.

The hospital room door creaked open and Gina tiptoed in. "How is she?" Her mouth was pulled into a thin line.

"The same. The doctors are running a tox screen on her. They figured she must have been drugged or she wouldn't have been able to stay alive so long."

"The killer gave her a drug to slow her heart down? Why would he do that?"

"The only person who knows that answer is, I believe, dead. I'm guessing he wanted her to die a slow death." He couldn't think of the horror any more. "How's Phil?" Like he'd seen Kerry do many times, he crossed his fingers. It worked for her, why not him?

She shook her head and pulled up the other chair in the room next to him. The cramped room grew smaller. The red eyes and red nose told him it was bad. "Is he...?" Hunter couldn't say the word.

"Dead? No. He's alive. Barely. He came through surgery, but the bullet hit his spinal cord."

Hunter's heart cracked. "Shit. What's the damage?"

"The doctors told me he'll be in a wheelchair for the rest of his life." A giant sob erupted. He hadn't realized she'd cared so much.

Hunter dropped his hands in his head. "This will kill Phil, you know." He looked up but couldn't talk about the tragedy. The news would take time to absorb. "How are *you* holding up?"

She shrugged. "I always knew police work was dangerous, but now I'm not so sure I want to be an officer anymore. Phil needs me."

Her statement surprised him. "You going to be his nurse or something?"

"Maybe." Her eyes shimmered with tears. Man had he misjudged her.

Gina's uncle, and Hunter's boss, stormed in. "How's Dr. Herlihy?" His breath was ragged. He clasped Gina's shoulder but kept his gaze on the beautiful woman in the bed.

"Still sedated." Or at least he hoped that's what was happening.

Jack Andries' jaw clenched. "Steven Dalton didn't make it."

"I know. I wanted him to pay for what he did to Phil, to Kerry, and to whoever else he hurt."

"You'll have to settle for the uncle."

Disgust filled him. "All we have on him is attempted murder. I want to nail the bastard for at least the first four murders. I know the SOB is guilty."

"We're searching his place as we speak." He squeezed Gina's shoulder. "Phil's asking for you."

Her face lit up. "How's he—"

"Awake, but don't expect much."

"I know, but I was hoping with time, he'd have some feeling in his legs." Gina lowered her chin, pushed up on the chair arms and said goodbye.

Jack's eyes narrowed for a moment before he shifted his focus to the floor. "Your sister's informant died last night."

If possible, the weight on Hunter's shoulders grew heavier. "I'm sorry—"

"Don't be. You did the right thing. Kerry's alive. That's what matters."

Hunter nodded, thankful Jack Andries left off the other half of the thought. Denise wouldn't have come back to life even if he'd gone to the vagrant's deathbed. "I wonder why he only wanted to talk to me?"

"He wouldn't say."

Jack stood. "Let me know when Kerry wakes."

"Sure." If she wakes. A giant claw scratched at his heart. Hunter wanted to break down, but he dug deep to keep strong.

* * *

SUN STREAMED in through the hospital blinds, waking him. Hunter sat up with a start, and his back protested from sleeping in a chair all night. Someone must have built a sand trap inside his mouth.

Hunter grabbed Kerry's hand and when he rubbed his thumb over her palm, a wave of emotion slammed into him. Kerry meant more to him than he ever could have imagined.

"I love you," he whispered.

He waited for his words to sink in, waited for her to respond to his declamation, but her chest rose and fell in an even manner, and her face remained devoid of color.

His stomach grumbled. It wouldn't do her any good if he couldn't concentrate. He needed food and coffee. Or rather coffee then food.

He stood and stretched out the kinks before checking in with the nurses' station. He asked them to keep an eye on Kerry while he went to the cafeteria.

The place wouldn't win any culinary awards, but the hot java, hamburger and fries did wake him up—even at eight in the morning.

On his way back to the room, he popped his head in Phil's room. The thought his good friend would never be able to do his job again sickened him. He tried to plaster on a cheery face.

Phil's eyes opened. "Hey." His voice came out weak.

"Hey yourself."

Gina and Jack stood. "We're going to grab something to eat," Jack said. "Visit with Phil a while."

Hunter appreciated the time alone with his partner. But what could he say to someone whose life had been shattered?

"Rehab's going to be a bitch, but you'll be back on the force in no time." That sounded lame, and he knew it the moment the words slipped from his lips.

Phil shook his head. "No, I'm finished." The dejection in his voice nearly felled Hunter.

"We'll find something to keep you busy."

He shook his head. "Gina said you found Kerry. Is she going to be okay?"

Hunter understood the change of subject for what it was. Denial. "Yeah." No way would he let on that she was still in a coma. Phil had taken a bullet for her.

"At least my injury wasn't for nothing."

"Hey, man, you saved her life. If Dalton hadn't shot you, I wouldn't have gotten the drop on him, and Kerry would be dead."

"I heard the bastard kicked the bucket." Phil attempted a smile, but Hunter saw his partner was fighting for his life.

"Yeah, you got him good."

They talked about nothing until Gina and Jack returned. Hunter was chomping at the bit to return to Kerry. "I'm down the hall, buddy. Yell if you need me."

They clasped hands, and Hunter raced out of the room before he broke down. Vibrant Phil would be no more.

As he entered Kerry's room, a female doctor with hips wider than the bed, bent over Kerry, her body blocking his view. Hunter bulled his way in. "Any change?"

"See for yourself."

The tanker-sized woman moved, and Hunter nearly dove toward the bed. She was awake.

Kerry looked up at him. "Hi."

His broad smile made his cheeks hurt. "Hey." Hunter pulled up a chair and clasped her cool hand. "How do you feel?"

"Feel? My head's pounding, I'm starving, and I'm cold, but other than that, I'm great."

The look on her face made him burst out laughing. She smiled. No doubt about it, he'd found the woman for him.

* * *

KERRY finally convinced Grandpa and Susan she felt well enough to go into work after doing nothing but rest for eight days. Her job at the M.E.'s office was over, but she wanted to come clean to John Ahern about bringing home #3's skull. She knocked on John's autopsy door, and then pushed it open. The cold blasted her. The man must have Eskimo blood.

A Negroid male lay on the gurney. John had made a barn door cut in the corpse's chest and was pulling the heart out when she cleared her throat.

John looked up and smiled. "Give me a sec." He dropped the organ on the scale, made a note on his hand recorder, and then pulled down his mask and removed his gloves. "So, you're getting ready to leave us?"

"Yes. Other than one woman's identity, the case is solved."

"We'll miss you."

"Same here." Hunter had told her about John's heart attack. "Why aren't you home resting?"

"Like you?"

"I didn't have a heart attack."

"Is being buried alive better for the body than what happened to me?"

Clearly, she wouldn't win any argument with him. She twisted her fingers together. "I have a confession to make. One that might cause me to lose my license." Not to mention prison time.

He shook his head. "Kerry, there's nothing you could have done that's that bad. Tell me what's on your mind."

"I was so pressed for time that I brought home #3 skull to do a clay reconstruction and... someone stole it."

John walked over to her and took her hands. "Don't worry. Hunter told me all about the theft."

Anger grabbed her. "He had no right to tell you." So what if he chose cop rules over his relationship with her?

"Hold on. He called this morning to tell me they recovered the skull at Steven Dalton's place. She's safe and sound in police lock up."

The relief caught in her throat was replaced with annoyance. Why hadn't Hunter had the courtesy to tell her himself? "That's wonderful." She knew she sounded less than enthusiastic.

"I think he plans on going on the news with the skull. Maybe we'll get our ID yet."

"Not yet, he can't. I only glued on the tissue depths markers. I need to put the clay on the face. I guess that will be my job for the next week." Not to mention preparing for her classes.

"Well, good luck." Her mentor gave her a quick hug.

"Thanks."

Kerry turned away before the tears came. She wasn't so much upset because she was leaving this office, because she could visit, but losing Hunter... He hadn't trusted her enough to share his find. He knew she worried about going to jail, so why hadn't he called?

Sure, he'd phoned once or twice this past week and asked how she was feeling, but now the threat of the killer was gone, he'd practically disappeared. She thought they'd had something special. What a fool she'd been.

She punched in the code for her lab door, left it ajar to air out the place, and dragged herself over to her chair. The sterile room looked as lifeless as her soul.

The bright lights hurt her eyes. She'd miss this place, but not the trauma. Teaching, at least, would be a safer job than trying to find the victim's identity.

Safer, yes, but also more boring.

And lonelier without Hunter.

God, why did everyone abandon her?

Her shoulders slumped as the lab door eased open. She looked up.

"Hunter?" Her heart beat so fast she thought it might burst.

He was dressed in black slacks, a fitted white shirt open at the throat and loafers. Loafers? Hunter wasn't the loafer type. But man, did he look hot.

"In the flesh." His smile melted her heart. She pushed everything bad aside.

He swung his right hand around as he came near. In his grasp were twelve blood red roses. He held them out to her.

"For me? I thought −"

"I know. I'm sorry. I've been busy thinking."

Before she could say anything, he lifted her up from the chair and kissed her. Wow. Her lips sizzled from his touch and his musky cologne nearly sent her over the edge with desire.

"Hunter."

He grinned. "Save that thought. Gather your things." His voice held a mystery.

"What's going on?"

"You'll see."

The depression that had taken over her was suddenly gone. In a flash, she picked up her brown satchel with her now clean tools along with her purse.

Outside, the heat hadn't relented, but at the moment, Kerry didn't care if the temp shot up to a hundred and ten. Being with Hunter was all she cared about.

He escorted her across the street and stored her gear in his trunk.

"I don't want to leave my car in the lot," she said.

"Not to worry. Susan picked it up an hour ago."

"Susan?"

Hunter held open her door. "Your sister. She even packed a bag for you."

"A bag?" Why did she keep repeating everything he said? Kerry slid onto the passenger seat not comprehending what was happening. Hunter jumped in and jabbed the key in the ignition.

Kerry wanted to clear the air between them. "Dr. A told me you found #3's skull. Why didn't you tell me?"

"I wanted to surprise you."

"Surprise me?"

He pulled out of the parking lot and headed toward the Interstate. "You'll just have to trust me."

Trust. There was that word again.

CHAPTER THIRTY-ONE

AFTER A WONDERFUL LUNCH at a restaurant overlooking the Gulf of Mexico, Hunter headed further south toward Siesta Key. Windswept trees and colorful plants, abloom with pinks, oranges and yellows surrounded the homes that faced the Gulf.

Natural, beautiful, serene.

"Where are we going?" Kerry asked for the umpteenth time. She hadn't been able to contain her excitement ever since he'd picked her up. No one had ever surprised her like this before.

"As I said, it's a surprise, but I will give you one piece of good news to help tide you over."

She wanted to smash him. "Tell me."

"When we searched Paul Dalton's house and office, we found mementoes from the women he'd killed."

"Mementoes? Like what?"

"Mostly jewelry. Something to remind him of the women he *saved* or so he claimed. I've been spending every waking moment meeting with the victim's relatives and friends, trying to confirm the jewelry belonged to the deceased. Believe me, it wasn't easy."

"Wait a minute. Paul Dalton admitted to killing those women?"

"*Saving* those women, you mean? Yes."

That made no sense. "How did killing them save them?"

Hunter pulled to a stop at a light and turned to her. "He said he and his older brother had been abused as children. Seems his father had an untimely death. Paul Dalton was never sentenced, but the locals are still convinced he killed his dad."

"Steven Dalton told me how his father, Paul's brother, would beat him when his dad got drunk. He also admitted to killing his dad. Their stories sound the same."

"Abuse runs in families."

"In a way, I don't blame either of them for killing their abuser." The look on Hunter's face made her hold up her hands. "I know that's illegal, but I can see why he'd be pushed to murder. Abuse can destroy all sense of morality."

"I see you two bonded before he buried you."

"Not so much bonding—more like bondage." God, what a nightmare that had been.

The light changed and Hunter drove on. Kerry pushed aside the Dalton family saga. Instead, she marveled at the clean row of upscale shops and sidewalks lined with palm trees.

Hunter pulled into a pink and green one-story motel. Small cabins dotted the shore. "I thought you could use a little R&R after your experience."

"That sounds wonderful, but I wanted to work on skull #3. She's not finished and I wanted to get her in front of the camera as soon as possible."

"That's part of the surprise. Once we had proof that a serial killer murdered the women in the field, Jack Andries was willing to foot the bill for someone to finish the recreation. In fact, he found your old instructor from the FACES lab for the job."

"Kimberly?"

Hunter nodded.

"That's wonderful. Now I know we'll find #3's identity."

Kerry was able to relax for the first time in months. Once Hunter checked them in, he carried their bags into the tiny efficiency. Clean, with a seaside motif, it was a perfect for a romantic getaway.

"Change into something cool." Hunter opened his suitcase and pulled out a pair of blue swim trunks. "I want to walk on the beach with you by my side."

Excitement rippled through her. "That sounds divine."

As she turned, Hunter's cell rang. "Hi, Jack."

Now what did his boss want? If Hunter had to leave on another case, she'd scream.

"No fucking way. You sure?" Hunter faced her, his brows raised to the sky. Then came a chuckle. "I never would have guessed." A smile lit Hunter's face.

She mouthed the word, what, but Hunter held up a finger.

"Sure, I'll tell her." He disconnected. "You will not believe this."

"What?"

"Paul Dalton is a woman."

The wind through the palm trees, along with kids screeching on the beach must have made her misunderstand. "Did you say Dr. Paul Dalton, our resident killer, is a woman?"

"Yup. Carla Pendowski, who's a computer wizard at the department, researched Paul Dalton's background once they saw he was missing his man parts when they checked him into jail."

Man parts? "It's called a penis. You can say it."

"Yeah, well, anyway. Paul, or rather Paula, was raped as a child. She married at age eighteen to get away from dear old dad and was severely beaten by her new husband. As a result, she needed plastic surgery to repair the damage. Once under the knife, she decided to have facial reconstruction to look like a man, complete with a new brow ridge and a more masculine jaw."

"That's amazing. What about gender reassignment surgery?"

"She didn't have that done. Only a hysterectomy and lots of testosterone shots."

"It makes so much sense now. She didn't want other women to suffer like she had. My God, why didn't she get help?"

"We'll never know. She hanged herself this morning."

Kerry gasped. "Part of me feels sorry for her too."

"Don't. She/he was a vicious vigilante." Hunter pummeled his fist in his palm. "I should have seen the signs. Dalton was small for a man and had the nicest hands. I figured that's why he became a surgeon." Hunter held up his large, meaty palms. "I could never hold a knife with any precision with these paws."

Kerry wanted him to hold something else. "I say we put Dr. Paula Dalton to rest and move on with our own operation."

Hunter dragged her to him and peered into her eyes, into her soul. "Sounds like a plan."

She wanted to strip him naked and spend the entire day in bed with him, but the thought of walking on the beach, smelling the salt air won. She'd have her feast later.

After they changed, they stepped through the open sliding glass doors on to a small, cement patio. Hunter unhooked the metal gate and voila, the beach. Her bare feet sunk into the warm, fine-grain sand, and the wind whipped through her hair. Kerry closed her eyes, tilted her head to the sun, opened her arms, and inhaled the wonderful salt air.

She relaxed and turned to Hunter. "I couldn't be in a better place right now. Thank you."

His grin puckered his cheeks. "Come on. I have a proposition for you."

No way would he propose. Their courtship had been too quick. She expected a wall of fear to restrain her, but instead joy spread through her.

Hunter got a glint in his eye. "Race you to the water?"

"You're on." Sprinting as fast as she could, she fell farther and farther behind the speed demon. Naturally, he won.

He grabbed her around the waist and spun her around. "We'll have to get you in training."

"Riiight."

Hunter's face turned serious as he gazed out to sea. Kids ran behind them, and then ducked into the water, sending sea spray their way.

"I've been worried about Phil," he said.

Whoa. Not what she thought he was going to say. "So am I."

"This past week I've been doing a lot of thinking, about him, about us."

She liked the *us* part. "What about?"

"If Phil doesn't think his life has value, it'll kill him. So he and I came up with a plan—and you're part of it."

"Me?" He sounded edgy for some reason.

"Phil wants to work, but he'll be too frustrated behind his old desk. As chance would have it, Braham University called a few weeks ago and spoke with our boss. They said some philanthropist, whose wife and daughter had died recently, wanted to donate a state-of-the art forensic facility on campus. They need someone with a police background to run it. So Phil plans to interview for the job once he gets out of the hospital."

She smiled. "That sounds perfect for him. But you said I'm part of this. How?"

"Whoever gets the top job will be in charge of hiring the best of the best. And you fit the bill. You can still teach, but Phil and I figured with your talent in 3-D modeling you'd make the perfect candidate for the forensic anthropology position. Given the nature of the lab, we figure there'll be many skeletons in people's closets that will need identifying."

"I love the idea. When I'm not teaching, I could help identify the victims; something you know is dear to my heart."

"And I would be there to protect you." Hunter pulled her a few feet into the swirling water and the cool foam lapped at their ankles.

She reached up and kissed him briefly. "Tell me more. Would we be working directly for the sheriff's department, or what?"

Hunter headed north along the beach, still holding her hand. "No. You'd be paid extra by this lab. The new owner understands if any faculty members are hired, they shouldn't announce their moonlighting activities to Braham University."

"So we'd be working in secret?"

"Kind of looks that way. The kinks haven't been worked out yet."

Her mind raced with possibilities. "Would anyone other than law enforcement be able to access the lab?"

"Most definitely. Any private citizen who wants the lab to work on a paternity case, cold case or whatever, could hire the lab—for a hefty fee, I might add."

"This sounds too good to be true. A state-of-the-art lab. We wouldn't have to wait months and months for DNA testing."

"You got it."

"Well, count me in." Anything to keep Hunter in her life.

Hunter did a one-eighty and headed back to the hotel. "Come on. I have something better in mind than talking shop."

* * *

THE HOTEL ROOM brought relief from the sun, sand, and crowds. The moment they stepped into the cool room, Hunter pulled her to him and kissed her hard. Kerry still couldn't get used to Hunter being such a free spirit. He'd always been so in control.

He patted her on the butt. "I say we don't waste water. Let's shower together."

He didn't have to ask her twice. He led her by the hand into the bathroom. The joy and excitement of being with him made her laugh.

"What's so funny?" he said, as he stripped naked.

His erection stood at attention. The sparkle in his eye told her he was glad he pleased her.

"Nothing." She ran her nail down his chest and twirled the tip along the head of his cock. "I'm just..." How could she explain this newfound glee? "Happy."

He grabbed her hand. "I think we better shower first before your happiness carries you away."

"Spoilsport."

He ran the water to heat it. Kerry stood there enjoying him move, the soft light bouncing off his muscular body.

"Are you going to undress or what, Ms. Happy?" She didn't move. "Here, let me help."

As he helped her pull down her bathing suit, she laughed. Hunter stopped the strip job and nuzzled her neck. "Hey, don't get sidelined." God, when was the last time she'd flirted with a man? Probably never.

"Not a chance." In a flash, she was naked, her sandy clothes tossed carelessly near the door.

When steam spewed from the shower, they stepped into the stall and closed the glass door. The four-foot by four-foot shower barely fit both of them, but she wasn't complaining.

Her back to the water, she dropped her head and wet her hair, enjoying the pounding heat on her scalp. As she poured a palmful of shampoo onto her head, Hunter grabbed the soap and lathered first her shoulders, and then her hips.

She giggled. "That tickles."

He looked crestfallen. "You'll have to sacrifice for cleanliness." He conveniently stopped his soapy hands on her breasts and scrubbed them thoroughly.

Between the lavender soap, the lemon shampoo, and the delicious sensations coursing through her was almost too much to handle. Having more important things to do than worry about the knots in her hair, she quickly rinsed.

Hunter ducked the soap between her legs, and Kerry perked up. She grabbed the bar from him before he excited her too much and ran the slippery soap first over his well-formed chest, and then over his rippled abs. "I think these may be your best feature."

He tossed her a look of mocked horror. "And not this handsome face?"

She kissed him. "The face will do. Turn around."

After she lathered his back, he returned the favor. When their fingers wrinkled, they rinsed, touched, and kissed. As her tongue danced inside his mouth, his fingers worked magic on her sensitive G-spot.

Her elbow smacked into the wall. "Ouch."

"Maybe we should try something a little safer."

"Like?"

"You'll see. I want more room to explore you properly." Hunter reached around her and turned off the water. "This time, I want to go slow."

"I like slow." Okay the truth. "I like fast too."

"You are easy."

"Only for you."

After they stepped out of the shower, they grabbed towels and dried each other off. "I can't wait any longer," he said.

Hunter wrapped an arm around her waist and led her into the bedroom and onto the bed. He crawled on top of her, supporting himself on his elbows.

He brushed aside a wet strand of hair. "You are an amazing woman, Kerry Herlihy."

"Ditto, Detective Markum."

He rolled off her and stroked her face. "When you were in that grave, I thought I'd lost you."

She'd been about to interrupt when he cast his gaze downward and his chin trembled.

"I offered all my possessions to God if you'd be alright. Did you know that?" he asked.

She opened her mouth to speak, but nothing came out.

Hunter placed two fingers on her lips. "I never thought I'd find someone who understands me the way you do. I can be a jerk or treat you like a princess, and you still are wonderful to me." He brushed his mouth across her lips before leaning back again. "What I'm trying to say, and doing a bad job of it, is that I love you."

She'd waited a lifetime to hear those three words. "I love you too."

She wanted to hold him—forever.

Without saying a word, he slid down between her legs and ran his fingers along the inside of her thighs. His tongue flicked her sensitive spot, causing her to nearly climax.

Kerry dragged her hands through his soft air then ran her fingers over his muscular shoulders. When Hunter continued his assault, she climaxed more times than she had in her entire life. She explored his face and then his broad shoulders, angry she didn't have ten hands to touch all of him at once.

"I can't wait any longer, Kerry."

Hunter crawled on top of her and eased into her. She wrapped her legs around his waist, and he let her set the pace. Her rhythm sped up and her breaths turned ragged. Someone moaned, but she couldn't tell if the sound came from her or Hunter. Lost in her own world, the blood pounded in her ears and she let loose all her anxieties and all her anger toward those who'd wronged her. She loved Hunter with her whole being.

Clawing his back, Kerry pumped her hips until he ejaculated, just as she reached another mind-blowing climax.

"Oh my God, Hunter, that was amazing." Kerry closed her eyes to catch her breath.

He smiled. "Well, if you get pregnant, I hope you're ready to name our son after my father."

"Our son?"

"Okay, if it's a girl, you can name her after your mother."

"What are we talking about here?"

He looked at her like she was a dimwit. "I guess I suck at proposals, but if in a few months, you're still able to stand me, I figure a nice little wedding ceremony in oh, Hawaii, would be nice."

She couldn't believe her ears. "You want to marry me?"

He laughed and hugged her. "Absolutely. I don't want to spend another day without you. Been there, done that, and I didn't like it one bit."

Hunter's phone trilled. "Damn it." He didn't move.

"Aren't you going to answer it? It could be important."

He sucked her hard nipple. "If you insist." Hunter rolled over and picked up his cell off the nightstand. "Markum."

He turned his back to her and spoke in hushed tones. She wasn't sure she liked being out of the loop. After all, they were partners. Hunter dropped the phone on the nightstand and rolled over.

"You won't believe who that was." He stopped for a moment. "I can't believe I just did that. I sound like Phil. Let me rephrase that. Besides being able to spend the next gazillion years of your life with me, what would make you very happy?"

She took a moment to think. "Finding the identity of our last Jane Doe."

"Well, your wish is granted. That was most likely #3's mother. She's positive the model is that of her daughter."

Kerry threw her arms around Hunter and hugged him again. "That's the best news I could have gotten."

"I thought the best news would be if you got pregnant."

"That too."

He ran a calloused palm over her sensitive nipple. "Then I say we spend the next few years trying to achieve that goal."

* * *

EXCERPT FROM BURIED SECRETS

DON'T FORGET to sign up for my newsletter to receive three free books, as well as up-to-date information on my stories. If you prefer to only receive notices regarding my releases, follow me on BookBub.

I hoped you enjoyed Kerry and Hunter's story. Next up is <u>Buried Secrets</u>. Here is the first chapter.

* * *

THE SMART MOON had blanketed itself between two big, fluffy clouds, probably to keep warm. Jenna Holliday tugged close her police issue jacket wishing she could do the same. "Damn." Florida wasn't supposed to be this cold in December.

From outside the closed cemetery's gate, she peered in at the faintly lit mausoleum that housed her mom's remains. "Hey, Mom. I just finished the late shift, which was why I didn't make it in time for your birthday. I'm sorry." Jenna leaned her forehead against the wrought iron bars, gripping them tight. "I know it's late, but I wanted to talk to you. No, I *needed* to talk to you. I missed passing the exam to make detective by five freaking points. Can you believe that?" She huffed out a breath. "Dad will be ballistic when he finds out. Not that I care." She slapped her palm against the cold metal, the guilt of what she'd done so many years ago welling inside.

Let it go. You were only twelve. You had to tell Mom you saw Dad with another woman.

Keeping her gaze focused on her mother's crypt a few hundred feet up the path, she stepped back from the fence and waved goodbye. She coughed into the sleeve of her jacket as she glanced around, hoping no one caught her talking to the dead. All clear. The lot was empty.

A loud crash came from the other side of the mausoleum that sounded like rocks breaking. Jenna spun back to the cemetery. A flashlight traced an arc across the lawn. What the hell was going on? Whatever it was, it wasn't good.

Not thinking about her safety, she hopped onto the hood of her car and scaled the six-foot high cemetery gate, landing onto the paved walkway. *Ouch.* Her sore knee screamed.

Move. Halfway up the concrete path, more rocks exploded. Was that granite breaking? Ohmigod. They better not be touching Mom's grave—or anyone's grave for that matter. Her fingers shot to the gun on her hip.

Someone cursed. From his high-pitched voice, it sounded like a kid. She darted down the middle aisle of the mausoleum, trying to make as little sound as possible despite her breaths coming out hard and fast. She plastered her back against the far wall before making her move. The biting wind whooped and howled down the corridor.

"Let's get out of here. We already got five heads." The kid sounded scared.

"No, dumb ass. We don't get paid until we have seven."

They were stealing *skulls?* Not with her around they wouldn't. She checked around the corner. Two teens, one blond and scrawny, the other beefy and dark, hovered over a coffin that was halfway out of the bottom vault with the lid partly off. The granite faceplate lay in pieces on the ground. Dear God. Half the coffins in the bottom row were out and exposed. The smaller kid had what looked like a king-sized pillowcase slung over his shoulder. She could take both of them if she had to.

Jenna stepped into the open, her finger on her holstered gun.

"Police. Put the sack down and get on your knees—both of you. Hands behind your head." She counted the coffins. Her mother's grave was sixth from the end. Dear God. They'd broken into Mom's vault. Her stomach tumbled, but she kept her hand steady.

Before they did as she'd asked, something hard came down on the back of her head. Her knees buckled, sending her to the concrete. Her cheek planted on the ground, and a tsunami-sized ache raced down her body. When she tried to pop to her feet, her attacker delivered a sharp kick to her hip.

"Bitch." The voice was deep, ugly, mature, and quite unforgettable.

He moved back, and her police training kicked in. Jenna pushed aside the pain and scrambled to her feet. Everything hurt, but she raised her gun, nonetheless. Her damned arms wobbled. The hooded man, dressed all in black, raced away, zigzagging right, then left.

"Police. Stop." Her vision blurred long enough for him to disappear. She turned around to apprehend the kinds. Damn. They were gone too. *Go after the guy.*

On her second step, vomit rolled into her mouth and her legs gave way, dropping her to the ground. Crap. Police procedures raced through her mind. *Suck it up and stop them.* She stood, crouched low, and checked right, then left.

Shit. Other than the sound of the wind whipping through the trees, there were no footsteps, no voices, nothing. How had they vanished? Fuck. She'd screwed up—again.

Think. There were at least three perpetrators. Checking the surrounding area without a flashlight and being in a weakened state would be super stupid. No. She needed to call this one in, but damn, she'd have to admit she'd failed to stop the jerks.

A sharp pain stabbed the back of her head, and she touched her scalp. Gooey blood coated her hair around a wide laceration. She said a few words even her sheriff department father would have been appalled to hear.

She swiped her cell and called the precinct. "Hey, Tanner. I need backup." She gave him the rundown about the kids, the coffin, and the skulls, including the fact one of them belonged to her mother. "I would have stopped them if some dude hadn't attacked me."

"You okay?"

"Yeah, but he hit me hard in the back of the head." Bad move. She shouldn't have told him she'd been injured. Now the whole precinct would hear about her fiasco. After working hard for five years on the force to earn the men's respect, she let some creep get the drop on her and ruin everything.

"What are you doing at a cemetery, Holliday? Didn't you just get off work?" Old Tanner Trundell kept track of everyone and everything at the precinct.

No way he'd understand why she needed to visit her mom in the dead of night. "I was driving by when I saw something and stopped." That was close to the truth.

"We'll send a unit and an ambulance."

"I'm good. I don't need an ambulance." Could this get any worse?

"You're getting one anyway."

Kill me now. After she disconnected, she made her way to the end of the aisle and dropped to her knees in front of where her mom was laid to rest. A gust of cold wind crawled up her shirt and she zippered up her jacket. Tears burned the back of her lids. The coffin sat open, the head missing. Stolen. Her throat clogged and a metallic taste leaked into her mouth. Mom's blue Sunday dress was still neatly pressed, her leathery fingers clasped over her belly. Jenna reached out and placed a palm over where her mom's heart would be. She glanced skyward, knowing her mother's soul was with God, and that she wasn't really *missing*, but the theft dredged up the pain of mom's suicide again.

A slow boil ran from her stomach to her throat, and she pounded the walkway. "I'll get back what you stole, you bastards." She said it loud enough for them to hear, wherever they were.

She wanted to put back the carelessly tossed covers to give the dead respect, but this was a crime scene. Jenna stood and did a quick scan of the cemetery grounds. Were the boys and their leader watching her from behind some tree, and laughing about how they managed to get away? If they came back, she'd be ready.

Fists clenched, she paced in front of the coffins, trying to figure out how the man was able to sneak up on her. She should have checked the scene and taken her time instead of rushing in to save the day. She'd been stupid. Maybe she didn't deserve to be a detective.

Not true. Her father had raised her to be a cop. She knew the ins and outs better than anyone. So how had she screwed up so bad? Rotten karma, she guessed.

"Hey, Jenna?" That was fast. It was her boss, Captain Lucas.

"Over here."

Four men and two women rounded the corner. One was Lucas and the second was Larry Bernard, a veteran officer. The next two were CSU techs she didn't know, and the last was her father. She gritted her teeth and marched over to the captain, trying to ignore the intense pounding in her head. "Why is my father here?"

"I invited him."

"You had no right," she whispered. Everyone knew she'd joined the Tampa Police Department and not the sheriff's department to get away from the probing eyes of the man who basically had caused her mother's death.

"You were hurt," Captain Lucas said. "I thought he'd want to know. Besides, he's one of us."

Dad stood off to the side ramrod straight, not even attempting to console her. Typical. He was dressed in his sheriff department garb despite the fact it was one in the morning. He must never sleep. Other than his gray beard stubble, he looked like he'd come from work. Hell, maybe he had.

Her father nodded to her, and then stepped over to Mom's grave. He lowered his head and his shoulders drooped. Jenna never remembered seeing him anything less than the tall, straight, always-in-control dad.

She might as well get this over with and walked over to him. "Hey."

Her father faced her. The overhead light reflected off what she thought was a tear. She was about to touch his arm but decided against it. No way would she let her heart melt toward him.

He looked up. "You okay?"

Now he asks? "Never better." *Don't show any weakness* had always been his motto.

Three camera flashes went off in succession, indicating the CSU techs were documenting the scene. The captain sidled up to her. "What happened exactly?"

What could she say? She let someone get the drop on her as two kids were stealing the skulls from the graves. Jenna explained the best she could.

"If we catch them, they'll be up for assaulting an officer too."

She didn't care. All she wanted was her mother's skull returned. "I want this case."

"No. It's too personal. Besides, Bernard here has been working another grave robbery case for the last few months."

She remembered hearing about that one. "Did the thieves only take the skulls?" Maybe they weren't related.

Bernard stepped forward. "Actually, six coffins in four different cemeteries were dug up, but they stole the whole body."

"Any leads?" Jenna pulled her coat tighter. It was colder than a concrete slab in winter.

"We've zeroed in a particular occult store in Ybor City, called *Botanica*. Rumor has it a high priestess is using human bones to put evil spells on people, but we don't have enough evidence to get a warrant to search the place."

She glanced one more time at her mother's grave, along with the other ransacked vaults and turned to the captain. "I want to go undercover there."

Her father drew his gaze away from Mom's coffin. "The man who hit you might work there and recognize you."

Who made him head of TPD all of a sudden? "This isn't your decision. Look, I need to do this. For Mom." *If I hadn't told her your little secret, she wouldn't have taken her life. I owe her.*

He turned away and headed to the end of the row of vaults.

Lucas nodded at her father. "I think your dad's right. You could be recognized. Besides, it's dangerous."

"I'm willing to take the risk."

Captain Lucas stared hard at her. "I will admit you'd be perfect for the undercover job. You're young, kind of hip, waiflike, and look no more than twelve."

Kind of hip? She'd been battling the you-look-no-more-than-twelve comment her whole life—all twenty-nine years of it. "I want this."

He took a big inhale and his eyes turned soft, almost as if he was regretting the words he was about to say. "I'll give you one month to bring me hard evidence. Not a day more. I'll have to reassign Phelps though."

Her partner, Greg Phelps, who she loved like a father, was due to retire in six months anyway. She had to get used to life without him soon enough. "I'll tell him if you want."

* * *

JENNA'S barely twenty-year old customer curled her lip. The girl sported a kissing snakes tattoo that peeked from under the strap of a skimpy tank top, and she had more body piercings than Swiss cheese had holes. Jenna mentally shook her head as she scanned the to-be-purchased items. Dear God, who had the money to throw away on this crap? Careful not to expose her disgust, Jenna rang up the African mask, eye of newt powder, and paper-thin snakeskin.

"That'll be fifty-seven dollars and thirty-two cents, please."

Just looking at the girl's tattoo made Jenna's fake skull on her forearm itch like hell, but she didn't dare scratch it. Too much was at stake.

The girl tossed down her VISA card. "Here ya go." She turned to her girlfriend and began gossiping about the cute guys they'd met at the bar down the street. Considering the friend's purple hair and orange eyebrows, Jenna could only imagine their definition of cute.

She flashed back to last week to when her dad had come into the store to lecture her on proper police procedures when doing under-cover work. First came the pursed lips, followed by the intense body scan, making it clear he didn't approve of her studded collar and pomaded hair. He acted as if she should have been wearing a plaid skirt and ponytails. In retrospect, she wished she'd dyed her blonde hair green or pink just to piss him off some more.

Jenna handed Miss Kissing Snakes a bone-shaped pen to sign her receipt and checked the clock again. Only twenty minutes until closing. Yay. On the down side, she only had a week left of her undercover job. And she still had no evidence of foul play.

Jenna leaned on her elbows. "Can I ask you guys something?"

They eyed each other. Kissing snakes nodded. "Sure."

"My boyfriend has been stalking me, and the police won't do shit." Jenna narrowed her eyes. "I really want to find someone to put an evil spell on him. Do you have any ideas who I can ask? I got money."

"Why not ask your boss? She did one for me about six months back."

Jenna's shoulders relaxed. "Really? I've been afraid to ask her. I thought she might get mad. How much did she charge?"

Kissing snakes shrugged. "She only charged me seven fifty since I'm such a good customer."

"Seven dollars and fifty cents? I can handle that." Acting dumb took work.

The girl rolled her eyes while orange eyebrows giggled. "Seven hundred and fifty *dollars*." She tugged on her eyebrow ring. "If that's too rich for your blood, I know of someone else, but he's not as reliable."

Marna was considered reliable? Jenna widened her eyes real big. "Wow. That's way outta my league. I'll get back with you." Seven hundred and fifty dollars for some priestess to stir a pot of junk and wave a hand over it? This world was messed up.

As soon as the two girls split, the owner of the store, Marna Willows, waddled out, her long crinkle shirt dragging on the floor. She didn't look like a high priestess to her. She was way too frumpy. A priestess should be tall, lithe, and very beautiful.

"Jenna, I need a favor." Her thick black brows creased on her too pale face.

"What's wrong? Is it the baby?" Marna's very pregnant sister, Shelby, had another month of her term left. The sister had worked at the store the first week, but then went home to wait out her time.

"Her midwife is out of town, and Shelby's in a panic. She's gone into labor and needs me to look after the kids, and that deadbeat husband of hers won't lift a finger. Do you mind putting the money in the safe and closing the store?" Before Jenna had a chance to answer,

Marna unhooked two keys from her broom keychain. "This one's for the front door." She placed it in the palm of Jenna's hand. "And this gets you into my office. Be sure to lock the door before you go."

"Don't worry about a thing." Inwardly she celebrated.

She made a production of straightening the mess on the counter as Marna rushed out. Jenna itched to check out the back and look around. Her boss spent hours in her one-room hideout doing who-knew-what. Twice in the last three weeks, Jenna had gone to speak with her only to find the door locked. Even Jenna's knocks had failed to rouse a response. She could only conclude Marna was either into meditation or doing some kind of spell and didn't want to be disturbed.

Since her boss wasn't here to oversee her actions, Jenna turned off the eerie background music designed to enhance the gothic element of the place and extinguished the incense that irritated her sinuses. Not wanting anything to look out of order to an outsider, she waited until exactly ten to lock up.

"I'm going to put you back together, Mom. Don't you worry. I'll find those thieves."

With money in hand, she headed to the inner sanctum. Marna's office sat wide open even though her boss had given her the keys. Interesting.

As she'd done for the past week, she flipped on the computer and entered the money into *QuickBooks*, happy not to have her boss breathing down her neck for a change. When she finished, she searched My Documents for something incriminating. After fifteen minutes, she shut down the machine. Cleaner than a picked bone. Damn. If her boss were into something sinister, she didn't keep a log of it here. Jenna leaned back in the chair and shoved her hands through her stiff hair. Her chances of finding her mother's skull was slipping through her fingers with each tick of the clock.

The captain made it clear Jenna needed proof someone was doing spells in this building using *human* remains before he could even ask for a warrant. She shivered just picturing her mom's head being doused with bodily fluids and other foreign substances.

"Don't dawdle."

As she placed the money into the safe next to the closet, she got a whiff of something foul, like an animal had died. She could only hope the stench was human. After a quick glance over her shoulder to make sure Marna hadn't materialized out of thin air, Jenna tugged hard on the closet handle next to the safe. It creaked open and a moldy stench blew out.

She'd expected to see a pile of stacked boxes, but instead found a dark hallway, lined with crumbling brick, that led to another ancient-looking door. Determined to find out what secrets the old building held, Jenna headed down the unknown path, pushing down the knowledge she had no right to be there. The scarred, pine floorboards creaked under every step. She tugged on a ratty gray string hanging from the ceiling, and a dim bulb lit the long, narrow corridor.

This could be stupid. "Who am I? Buffy the Vampire Slayer?"

She hurried to the end of the walkway and tested the knob. Locked. Crap. The need to find out what was behind door number two overtook all rational thought. She raced back to the office and ripped open Marna's desk drawer, regretting never having learned to pick a lock. The key to the door had to be someplace. After a three-minute search, she found a ring of keys in the fourth drawer that looked like they came straight from Home Depot. She didn't give a flip what they looked like as long as one of them let her get inside.

Rushing back down the hall, Jenna focused on the worn door. The first two keys failed to work, but the third one did the trick. She noted the time on her cell phone. She couldn't afford to waste time investigating in case Shelby's scare turned out to be a false alarm, and Marna came back to check on her new employee. Always one to cover her bases, Jenna ran back and slipped the keys into the fourth drawer.

Hurry. For her mom's sake, she had to push ahead. Two hard pulls later the door groaned open.

"Oh. My. God." Dead fish rotting in the hot sun would smell better. She covered her nose.

Determined to find answers, she crept inside. The light switch was mounted next to the door, not that it did much good. The bulb couldn't have been more than fifteen watts. Eerie, spooky shadows danced on the wall as she stepped inside. Her stomach in knots, her eyes widened at the brownish red streaks covering a cracked wall. It could be blood. That looked like warrant material to her. She whipped out her cell phone and snapped some photos. The flash washed out the markings, but it was the best she could do under the circumstances.

One red image consisted of an arrow through a two-foot diameter circle. A second one resembled a cross that had half fallen over. Could have been an X, but the horizontal bar had fancy pointed ends. A few of the other symbols looked like some kind of Pagan secret code, but none resembled the usual pentagram used in witchcraft. Even though she'd spent much of her recent days studying different Pagan religions, she had no clue what these slash marks symbolized. If she had to guess, she'd say they were closer to the black magic cult associated with Santeria rather than the more benign Wicca.

A whisper sounded behind the side wall, and she stilled. If she believed in ghosts, she would have sworn her mother was trying to tell her something. The reasonable side concluded the noise probably came from a bunch of kids outside. She half jogged over to the far side of the room where the stench grew stronger and images of dead bodies came to mind.

A loud bang behind her made her jump. She whipped around and slammed a hand to her chest. "Stupid thing." A wooden altar lay on the ground. Her swingy skirt must have knocked it over.

Get out of here. Now.

"One more minute." *Please God, let me find something to help my mom.*

Against the opposite wall sat another altar covered in dark stains. More blood, she bet. Her pulse raced. She'd find these thieving kids and take back what belonged to the families if it was the last thing she did. While she didn't have a CSU kit to test for blood, she could scrape the wall with her fingernails and hope the small flakes would be enough for the test. She stepped closer and reached out a hand.

"What are you doing here?" said a voice behind her. The blood drained to her belly. That voice. Low, dark, evil—and totally unforgettable.

She whipped around and froze.

THE END

ABOUT THE AUTHOR

Love it HOT and STEAMY? Sign up for my newsletter and receive MONTANA DESIRE for FREE. Click here

OR Are you a fan of quirky PARANORMAL COZY MYSTERIES? Sign up for this newsletter. Click Here

Not only do I love to read, write, and dream, I'm an extrovert. I enjoy being around people and am always trying to understand what makes them tick. Not only must my romance books have a happily ever after, I need characters I can relate to. My men are wonderful, dynamic, smart, strong, and the best lovers in the world (of course).

My Paranormal Cozy Mysteries are where I let my imagination run wild with witches and a talking pink iguana who believes he's a real sleuth.

I believe I am the luckiest woman. I do what I love and I have a wonderful, supportive husband, who happens to be hot!

Fun facts about me

(1) I'm a math nerd who loves spreadsheets. Give me numbers and I'll find a pattern.
     (2) I live on a Costa Rica beach!
     (3) I also like to exercise. Yes, I know I'm odd.

I love hearing from readers either on FB or via email (hint, hint).

Social Media Sites

Website: www.velladay.com
    FB: www.facebook.com/vella.day.90
    Twitter: velladay4
    Gmail: velladayauthor@gmail.com

ALSO BY VELLA DAY

A WITCH'S COVE MYSTERY (Paranormal Cozy Mystery)

PINK Is The New Black (book 1)

A PINK Potion Gone Wrong (book 2)

The Mystery of the PINK Aura (book 3)

Box Set (books 1-3)

Sleuthing In The PINK (book 4)

Not in The PINK (book 5)

Gone in the PINK of an Eye (book 6)

Box Set (books 4-6)

The PINK Pumpkin Party (book 7)

Mistletoe with a PINK Bow (book 8)

The Magical PINK Pendant (book 9)

The Poisoned PINK Punch (book 10)

PINK Smoke and Mirrors (book 11)

Broomsticks and PINK Gumdrops (book 12)

Knotted Up In PINK Yarn (book 13)

Ghosts and PINK Candles (book 14)

Pilfering The PINK Pearls (book 15)

The Case of The Stolen PINK Tombstone (book 16)

The PINK Christmas Cookie Caper (book 17)

PINK Moon Rising (book 18)

A VOODOO & VAMPIRE MYSTERY (a spinoff of A Witch's Cove Mystery)

Call Me Ghostly(Book 1)

Better Late Than Staked (Book 2)

Ghosts Just Want To Have Fun (Book 3)

SILVER LAKE SERIES (3 OF THEM)

(1). <u>**HIDDEN REALMS OF SILVER LAKE**</u> (Paranormal Romance)

Awakened By Flames (book 1)

Seduced By Flames (book 2)

Kissed By Flames (book 3)

Destiny In Flames (book 4)

Box Set (books 1-4)

Passionate Flames (book 5)

Ignited By Flames (book 6)

Touched By Flames (book 7)

Box Set (books 5-7)

Bound By Flames (book 8)

Fueled By Flames (book 9)

Scorched By Flames (book 10)

(2). <u>**FOUR SISTERS OF FATE: HIDDEN REALMS OF SILVER LAKE**</u> (Paranormal Romance)

Poppy (book 1)

Primrose (book 2)

Acacia (book 3)

Magnolia (book 4)

Box Set (books 1-4)

Jace (book 5)

Tanner (book 6)

(3). <u>**WERES AND WITCHES OF SILVER LAKE**</u> (Paranormal Romance)

A Magical Shift (book 1)

Catching Her Bear (book 2)

Surge of Magic (book 3)

The Bear's Forbidden Wolf (book 4)

Her Reluctant Bear (book 5)

Freeing His Tiger (book 6)

Protecting His Wolf (book 7)

Waking His Bear (book 8)

Melting Her Wolf's Heart (book 9)

Her Wolf's Guarded Heart (book 10)

His Rogue Bear (book 11)

Box Set (books 1-4)

Box Set (books 5-8)

Reawakening Their Bears (book 12)

OTHER PARANORMAL SERIES

PACK WARS (Paranormal Romance)

Training Their Mate (book 1)

Claiming Their Mate (book 2)

Rescuing Their Virgin Mate (book 3)

Box Set (books 1-3)

Loving Their Vixen Mate (book 4)

Fighting For Their Mate (book 5)

Enticing Their Mate (book 6)

Box Set (books 1-4)

Complete Box Set (books 1-6)

HIDDEN HILLS SHIFTERS (Paranormal Romance)

An Unexpected Diversion (book 1)

Bare Instincts (book 2)

Shifting Destinies (book 3)

Embracing Fate (book 4)

Promises Unbroken (book 5)

Bare 'N Dirty (book 6)

Hidden Hills Shifters Complete Box Set (books 1-6)

CONTEMPORARY SERIES

MONTANA PROMISES (Full length contemporary Romance)

Promises of Mercy (book 1)

Foundations For Three (book 2)

Montana Fire (book 3)

Montana Promises Box Set (books 1-3)

Hart To Hart (Book 4)

Burning Seduction (Book 5)

Montana Promises Complete Box Set (books 1-5)

ROCK HARD, MONTANA (contemporary romance novellas)

Montana Desire (book 1)

Awakening Passions (book 2)

PLEDGED TO PROTECT (contemporary romantic suspense)

From Panic To Passion (book 1)

From Danger To Desire (book 2)

From Terror To Temptation (book 3)

Pledged To Protect Box Set (books 1-3)

BURIED SERIES (contemporary romantic suspense)

Buried Alive (book 1)

Buried Secrets (book 2)

Buried Deep (book 3)

The Buried Series Complete Box Set (books 1-3)

A NASH MYSTERY (Contemporary Romance)

Sidearms and Silk(book 1)

Black Ops and Lingerie(book 2)

A Nash Mystery Box Set (books 1-2)

STARTER SETS (Romance)

Contemporary

Paranormal

www.ingramcontent.com/pod-product-compliance
Lightning Source LLC
Chambersburg PA
CBHW021311250626
47155CB00002B/486